SNOWFLAKES (
COVE

LUCY COLEMAN lives in the Forest of Dean in the
UK with her lovely husband and Bengal cat, Ziggy.
Her novels have been short-listed in the UK's Festival
of Romance and the eFestival of Words Book Awards.
Lucy won the 2013 UK Festival of Romance:
Innovation in Romantic Fiction award.

SNOWFLAKES OVER HOLLY COVE

Lucy Coleman

First published in the UK in 2018 by Aria,
an imprint of Head of Zeus Ltd

9 7 5 3 1 2 4 6 8

A catalogue record for this book is available from
the British Library.

ISBN: 9781035903504

Aria, an imprint of Head of Zeus
First Floor East
5–8 Hardwick Street
London
EC1R 4RG

Also by Lucy Coleman

The French Adventure

About *Snowflakes Over Holly Cove*

As the snowflakes start to fall, Holly Cove welcomes a new tenant to the beautiful old cottage on the beach…

For lifestyle magazine journalist Tia Armstrong, relationships, as well as Christmas, have lost all their magic. Yet Tia is up against a Christmas deadline for her latest article Love is, actually, all around…

So Tia heads to Holly Cove where the restorative sea air, and rugged stranger Nic, slowly but surely start mending her broken heart.

Tia didn't expect a white Christmas, and she certainly never dared dream that all her Christmas wishes might just come true…

Set in Caswell Bay on the stunningly rugged Gower Coast, the cottage nestles amid the limestone cliffs and the woodlands; the emotions run as turbulently as the wind-swept sea.

As cosy as a marshmallow-topped mug of cocoa, fall in love with a heart-warming festive story from the bestselling author of *The French Adventure.*

To Mark and Jim
Thank you for bringing sunshine into my life
every single day, even when the rain is
hammering down outside.
Love you always and forever. x

Prologue

Mum and I link arms, faces turned upwards towards the heavens. Our eyes scan the dense and strangely opaque grey sky, as a flurry of large snowflakes rain down upon us. Like a feather pillow which has burst its seams, we are bombarded by a cascade of soft, white clusters of icy crystals. Having to constantly blink away the fluffy white particles as they hit our eyelashes, we hug each other and begin laughing, totally enthralled.

With cheeks starting to glisten as the ice melts on contact, already the heavier flakes begin to settle on our hair and thick winter coats. As carefree as children, we survey the scene in awe. The street outside our boutique hotel is being turned into a winter wonderland in front of our eyes.

The combination of a heavily-laden sky and the soft carpet beneath our feet muffles every little sound; even our footsteps no longer echo as we head off in search of the bright lights. I know that this is a memory that will be etched on our minds forever, as Mum squeezes my arm and turns to smile at me. I feel like Santa dispensing a little Christmas magic, as what I see reflected in her eyes is a moment of almost child-like happiness and joy. And to me that is priceless.

As we turn the corner, ahead of us is a cacophony of sounds softened by the backdrop that is almost a mini blizzard now – a snow globe brought to life. The traffic has slowed, but horns still toot and sirens still screech; a city that never sleeps cannot be stopped.

With last-minute shoppers and people now eager to make their way home, the sidewalks are so busy that the pitching snow is quickly trampled underfoot. Being swept along with the crowd, as if we are New Yorkers and not merely visitors, it's easy to soak up the ambience.

Suddenly, a guy wearing a Santa outfit appears in front of us ringing a small hand bell and holding up a bucket, part-filled with coins. He's an older man and his beard and moustache appear to be real. I'm guessing the flowing white hair is a wig, as it's as white as the snowflakes that continue to fall. It looks like some of that padding around the middle might not actually be padding, though. He's even wearing half-moon glasses, perched low on his nose. Everything about him embodies the Santa images I remember from my childhood.

'Ho! Ho! Ho! Merry Christmas, ladies. Do you have a few coins to spare to make my bucket a little fuller? Help the homeless at Christmas.'

Mum turns her head to look at me, a bemused smile on her face. We immediately dive into our handbags to pull out a handful of coins each, that clatter as we throw them into the bucket.

'Merry Christmas and I hope it's a truly wonderful one for you both.'

'Thank you, Santa, and good luck filling that bucket.'

His eyes crinkle up when he smiles back at us and for some reason he reaches out to place his gloved hand on Mum's shoulder.

'The season's blessings upon you, my dear. Enjoy this special holiday.'

With that he moves on past us, leaving Mum and me to stare after him as he continues to greet people and accept donations. Even when Mum and I link arms and begin moving forward again, the tinkling sound of that little bell seems to float on the air.

'It's like another world,' Mum exclaims, totally captivated and more than a little overwhelmed by the skyline that towers above us.

'So good, they named it twice – the city *and* the state!'

Ahead of us a Starbucks offers a chance to warm ourselves up a little and we hurry inside. There's a table for two in the window and I settle Mum down before I head off to order our coffees.

In the background the sounds of *Rockin' Around the Christmas Tree* add to the lively and festive atmosphere. Most of the people who are seated have a pile of carrier bags stuffed beneath their seats and there's a real buzz in the air as the holiday season is about to begin.

'Eggnog Latte or Chestnut Praline Latte?'

Mum looks up at me, raising her eyebrows and giving a shrug of her shoulders. 'Surprise me!'

'Eggnog Latte, then. Why not?'

When it's cool enough for her to take that first sip, a little smile creeps over her face.

'This reminds me of my father. He always made eggnog at Christmas. It was his only contribution, as my mother even carved the turkey.' She laughs to herself, transported back to a special moment goodness knows how many years ago.

'I'm not even sure how it's made,' I admit. I'm pretty sure it's a drink I've never tried.

'The secret is in the nutmeg, he always said. It's milk, cream, a little cinnamon and vanilla mixed with eggs, sugar and bourbon. It was a luxury in those days. Even the smell of it conjures up Christmas, to me.'

It's wonderful to sit here and hear her talking about Christmases from her own childhood. 'This is truly magical, Tia, thank you so very much. My wonderful, darling daughter, what would I do without you in my life? Spending time with you is gift enough, so today I'm doubly blessed.'

I vowed then, that in future we'll celebrate every Christmas Eve in style at a very special destination. I can't think of a better way to repay her for all those wonderful Christmas memories from my childhood. Losing my father, and then a family row distancing my brother from us, has blighted far too many Christmases already.

Our first trip had to be New York; home of the iconic yellow taxi cab, Central Park and the Statue of Liberty. And, of course, the setting for one of the greatest Christmas movies of all time: *Miracle on 34th Street*. But who knows where we'll be this time next year? My only wish is that the snowflakes will begin to fall, as that's the little bit of magic that makes Christmas special, no matter what age you are.

1

Christmas Past

Tiredness from a long, foot-wearying but exciting day sees Mum sinking into a deep sleep almost as soon as her head touches the soft, one-thousand thread count Egyptian cotton pillowcase.

In the semi-light, I glance across at her bed on the far side of the room and wish I could see her face, but her back is towards me. I wonder if today was too much for her, and whether tomorrow we should be a little less ambitious in our plans. I forget that time marches on and with it come the aches and pains she says are only natural at her age. Not wishing to spoil the festive mood I push aside my worries and indulgently allow my thoughts to wander.

So, what was the best Christmas you can remember, Tia? I ask myself. Gazing up at the ceiling, I find myself smiling as images flash across my mind. Like little vignettes, curiously colourless for some reason, as if each is merely a shadow. But the emotions I feel as I become a voyeur of my own memories are powerful. Tears begin to form in the corners of my eyes and I have to suck in a deep breath, for fear of letting out a howling sob. Dad and Will's faces appear and my chest constricts with anguish for what has been lost.

As I concentrate on sorting a random collection of clips into some semblance of order, I begin to realise that the best Christmas was actually the one shortly after Dad had been made redundant. The company he worked for had closed their doors overnight; it was a family concern going back three generations and the news came as a bitter blow to everyone. I didn't really understand what was happening at the time, only that money was suddenly very tight. Every interview he attended in the days leading up to Christmas was dispiriting. He would come home with a deep frown on his face and I clearly remember him talking about which of his ex-colleagues were at the same interview. But Mum and Dad counted their blessings; they had some savings and Mum knew how to make a pound stretch.

'Waste not, want not as my mother used to say,' was her favourite little quote in those days.

But our Christmases had never been about over–indulgence, partly because Mum's parents weren't well-off and her upbringing had made her appreciate the small things in life. The things which really matter because it helps to raise your spirits and spread the joy. So, our holiday celebrations were all about family and friends we welcomed into our house to join in the singing and general merriment. Mum cooked everything herself from scratch and we ate well but the focus was on feeding many, not overly indulging a few. The presents were never extravagant, with my brother and I each receiving one special present and then sharing several smaller things with which we could both play. Mainly books and board games which could be passed on once we'd tired of them.

But the year of Dad's redundancy Mum gathered us all around the kitchen table, poured out a cup of tea and placed a slice of Victoria sandwich cake in front of each of us.

'This year I think it would nice if we made the gifts we give to each other. What do you think?'

I was nine at the time and thought I was very grown up; the Santa thing was no longer a part of my vocabulary but looking back now I missed the impact that rite of passage had on Mum. She had kept that little bit of Christmas magic going as long as she could and Will later told me she'd warned him not to spoil it for me. Ironic then that the year it was over for me was also the year of great upheaval and uncertainty for our future. Her head must have been in a spin and her heart heavy, but she didn't show it.

Anyway, Dad had nodded, his own head too full of anxiety about his latest interview and the long wait over the Christmas holidays to find out whether he'd been successful. Whether *his luck was in*, as he referred to it.

Will and I had raised our eyebrows and exchanged a glance. I don't think either of us were thinking about ourselves, but what on earth could we possibly make to give as gifts? Usually we saved our pocket money and Mum would take us into town a week or so before the big day. It was fun hunting around for something small but meaningful we could wrap up and lay beneath the tree.

'Bet I can make something better than you can,' Will had chided me and the challenge was on.

Mum made us each a personal hamper. Simple baskets purchased from the Saturday market but filled with our favourite homemade biscuits and sweets. Mine had marzipan fruits, shortbread biscuits with lemon zest and fudge.

Dad utilised his love of working with wood and I had a box in which to store my treasures. He'd carved apple blossoms into the lid and it's still one of my most treasured possessions. Mum received a blanket box and Will an ornate shelf to display some of his sports trophies.

Will invented his own board game and I have to say it was pretty good. Based on the old snakes and ladders concept, he'd brought it up to date by using a space setting with black holes and jet packs. Well, at the time we all thought it was rather good and it passed many a happy hour over the holiday.

Me? I knitted everyone a scarf with over-sized knitting needles the thickness of cotton reels. The results were like something out of Dr Who's wardrobe but in terms of reaction and the amount of laughter generated, my presents won that day. Mind you, I can't ever recall seeing any of them wearing the fruits of my labour. Just this one memory alone is enough, though, to put a smile back on my face and remind me that even the hard times were good. I just didn't have enough life experience to appreciate that fact.

Mum had somehow rescued what could have been a rather dismal Christmas just by being a source of constant inspiration and positivity for us all. She made sure our home was filled with love and laughter; her family always came first.

It was early in the new year that Dad was offered the position and we all breathed a sigh of relief. However, it was tinged with sadness because so many of the families around us were still counting the pennies. Men desperate to work were going from one interview to the next on a rollercoaster ride of rejection after rejection. We constantly had school friends to tea as Mum and Dad kept a close eye on the kids in the neighbourhood. A little hot food was appreciated and we learnt a lot about sharing in times of need from the example our parents set us.

Maybe I'll dig those old needles out of my treasure box and surprise Mum next Christmas with a new scarf. We can then sit and laugh about old times because it's true what they say, laughter is good for the soul.

Four months, three weeks and four days later...

2

Life Goes On

'Welcome back, Tia, you've been missed. Glad to see you looking so well.'

Clarissa Cooper doesn't do sympathy, or empathy. My gut instincts tell me that's probably going to be the full extent of my back-to-work interview. Even the chief editor can't ignore HR's policy for staff returning to work after being out on compassionate leave.

In fairness, *Love a Happy Ending* lifestyle magazine is a little empire. With its print sales, website and app, it runs like a well-oiled machine. Since Clarissa took over two years ago, sales have steadily climbed and no one could ask for a better mentor.

I suck in a deep breath as quietly as I can, thinking that if I keep my mind focused on getting through this meeting, then I'm less likely to embarrass myself and dissolve into tears.

'I have an exciting project lined up and the whole team agree that you are the right person to tackle it.

How do you feel about three articles, each one looking at two very different types of relationship? They are due to run in the November, December and January issues and will look at what makes the relationships work.

'We've already picked the couples from varying backgrounds and age groups. Our readers will be keen to know how they keep the love alive. How does love change as the years go by? What sort of gifts do they give each other at Christmas? I want pages oozing with sentimental festive cheer. And the January one should slant towards New Year resolutions and shared goals for the coming year. It's going to be our biggest headline this winter and we're all very excited about it. We're going to run this in tandem with a series of competitions sponsored by Green Fern Spa Centres and we will be giving away one hundred vouchers for free *his and hers* pamper sessions.'

I was right. Her employer obligations have been fulfilled; box ticked, now back to the business in hand, which isn't simply hitting those sales targets, but knocking them for six.

My stomach sinks into my boots. Clarissa Cooper's steely-grey eyes sweep over me, appraising my reaction rather like a fine-tuned minesweeper in action. If I hesitate now she'll know I'm not ready to come back yet, and warning bells will start sounding in her head. I can't risk being side-lined for some younger, smarter version of me, because Mum would be horrified to see me throwing away all those years of hard graft.

'Great. I love the idea – sounds exciting.'

My mother died four weeks ago today and it's my first day back. Interviewing loved-up couples gushing over their wonderful relationships is about as surreal to me at this moment as the fact that I can't pick up the phone and talk to Mum. Still, not bad, Tia, you managed to sound enthused. That's quite an achievement, especially since you have just waved goodbye to thirty and obviously have no idea at all how to keep a long-term relationship alive. I ease my shoulders back and down, forcing my body not to sag and I seem to have convinced Clarissa I'm up to the task.

'Well done, you. The sign of a true professional is someone who can roll with the punches and remain standing afterwards. I thought, given the circumstances, a little stay away from the madness of London might aid your concentration. The details are in here.'

I can't trust myself to utter another word, so I plaster on the widest smile I can muster and grab the folder she thrusts in my direction. Already her attention is elsewhere and she doesn't even look up as I turn and run.

Clearly, Clarissa has never lost a close loved one. Come to think of it, does Clarissa actually *have* any close loved ones? All she ever talks about is work, but although she doesn't wear a wedding ring I suppose that it's not inconceivable she has a partner. Or is it? It's hard to think of a sentence in which the words *Clarissa and emotion* would sit well together. For cool, read icy. For efficient, read microchip processor. It's an incredible skill, obviously, but there has to be something more, something that touches the soul. The only people she appears to make time for are from the publishing world too, because it's all about being seen with the right people and making contacts. She does spend quite a lot of time accompanying Oliver Sinclair to drinks parties, but then he is her boss and I suppose she is a little different around him. But whether that's a softer side creeping in, or the result of her well-practised social skills, who can tell?

I'm being a little unkind and I know it. What did I expect? The world goes on and whether I like it or not I have to earn a salary to pay the bills. Despite the fact that, at the moment, every morning it's a struggle to drag myself out of bed and face the new day ahead. Life will never be the same again and now, as someone very kindly pointed out to me at the funeral, I'm an orphan. I remember recoiling, wondering how on earth anyone could ever think that was an appropriate thing to mention. The word was like a bullet through my heart, but I had to agree it was true. My father died many years ago, but for some stupidly naive reason, I thought Mum would go on forever.

The one inevitable thing in life is death. And I've just been reminded of that. What made it even harder is that I didn't have a chance to say goodbye. She died in her sleep; a heart-attack they said and a peaceful way to go. But even after seeing her coffin disappear behind those curtains, I still can't take it in. OK, so I'm grieving and it's pretty obvious I'm having trouble moving on from the denial and isolation phase. Maybe that's because I'm not sure I can handle the anger phase.

It's as if I'm living in a bad dream and when I wake up everything will be back to normal. Time to face up to reality, Tia, this is no dream and you have to snap out of it. Your career-hungry peers are snapping at your heels and shadowing Clarissa is a privilege you must never take for granted. That hunger to continue climbing the ladder and be the one sitting in the editor's chair will return. When it does you need to be prepared to do battle again and fight off your opponents, sorry – colleagues. Allow yourself this one assignment to ease yourself back in and prove you can come out triumphant. Don't just do a good job, do a brilliant job and make everyone realise you're more than ready for the next step.

Jeez, am I really giving myself a pep talk here? Or am I scared that none of it means anything to me anymore? That's nonsense, I tell myself. And Clarissa's one of the best, so you are lucky to be able to chase the dream. Stop moaning, Tia, it's not your style and get on with it.

Jumping on the Tube I spot a seat and virtually dive across the space with gritted teeth and firm determination. I look up and smile apologetically at the two guys who narrowly missed getting there ahead of me. Both spin on their heels trying hard not to show even a hint of a scowl, but in all honesty, I don't care. Life isn't fair, I've discovered, and it's time for me to toughen up.

I fold back the cover of the folder and begin rifling through the papers. I barely glance at the information sheets giving the backgrounds of the couples I will be interviewing via Skype. Ah, here it is – a six-week rental agreement for Beach View Cottage, Holly Cove, near Caswell Bay. The map indicates that it's situated in a part of South Wales known as the Gower coast, an area I've never visited before. Suddenly I find myself wondering if the rumours that Clarissa doesn't actually have a heart are exaggerated. When it comes to the mention of business expenses her eyes usually narrow and her hands stiffen, as if preparing for battle. And she questions everything, every single little thing.

As I look at the photo of a rather charming cottage, which appears to be sitting on the edge of an area of dense woodland, it's suddenly all rather appealing. Initially, my reaction had been that I'd simply stay at home in my very comfortable, loft-style apartment and who would know?

As I glance around the packed carriage while my brain processes the pros and cons, the Tube train speeds towards the outskirts of London. It's spring and yet I spend all my time surrounded by a landscape of buildings and advertising boards. Only the rare glimpse of anything that is even a vague reminder that nature is waking up, brightens my working day. Wouldn't it be nice to breathe in that sea air and get away from the bustle of the city?

My heart tells me that it's rather like running away from the harsh realities of life, but my head is firm. *Just do it, Tia.* I know there's a catch and the fact that Clarissa is taking her time to reveal all is a little worrying. But I find myself imagining those long beach walks; the tranquillity is enticing. Maybe it's not such a weird idea after all, and fate has decided I deserve a break – in more ways than one.

Yeah, well, maybe if I wasn't a journalist I might be tempted to believe that. I know I'm not being banished, as such, but I also know that it's highly unlikely Clarissa is sending me away simply for the good of my health. Maybe this is a test and I have to prove to her that I haven't lost my edge and even the worst of life's trials can't keep me down for long. The photo is so enticing and I swear I can already smell that bracing sea breeze. Holly Cove here I come, but how on earth I'm going to throw myself into mince pie and mistletoe mood, I have no idea.

3

A Change is as Good as a Rest

'Is it far from the station?'

I hand the taxi driver a piece of paper bearing the address of the cottage, then yank open the door to begin throwing in my bags. Clearly, he feels I'm a capable woman who isn't in need of any assistance whatsoever, and I don't know whether to be flattered, or mildly annoyed. For all he knows I'm a tourist, a visitor to the area and, besides, this is my first encounter with one of the locals. At the very least, not offering to help me isn't very welcoming but it's also rather rude. As I push in the last bag and clamber inside, he turns his head my way.

'It's about seven miles. Do you need any help?'

Using the back of my hand, I brush the beads of sweat off my forehead as I collapse back into the seat.

'No, I'm fine thank you. I'm stronger than I look.'

He nods, unaware I was being sarcastic. Admittedly, I'm five-foot-six-inches, with an athletic build but, by the look of it, he could probably lift all my luggage using just one of his, no doubt extremely hairy, muscular arms. He has no excuse whatsoever for being so ungentlemanly, though.

In truth, I don't play the "I need help" card because I'm a natural *doer*. I can't sit back and let people take over. I suppose that working in such a competitive environment compounded that and, coupled with my obvious inability to find a man I won't tire of in less than a week, I'm used to fending for myself. But at the moment, I'm running on empty and feeling drained. If there was anyone I could reach out to I probably would, but my inner circle of one is no longer. Everyone else is merely a distant relative – which now, sadly, includes my uptight brother and his family – a work colleague, or a casual acquaintance. I don't let people get close. Maybe that's why Clarissa employed me. I hate to admit that there are moments when I fear I'm becoming a younger version of her. Am I still single because I'm happily married to my work, or because fate has already decided that it's going to be the only constant in my life?

'You like peace and quiet, then?'

The taxi driver's voice breaks my chain of thought. What?

'I work in London, so quiet is appealing.'

'Well, no shortage of that in Holly Cove.'

His tone reflects a mix of irony and humour.

'It's secluded, then?'

He laughs, which comes out more like a snort. Did he just check me out in the rear-view mirror?

'You could say that.'

Glancing out of the window, it's clear that Caswell Bay isn't quite the large seaside town I'd envisaged. It looks very sedate, with a couple of cafes and kiosks around a small promenade adjoining the beach. But the scene beyond is breathtakingly beautiful.

'Population of two hundred and eighty-nine according to the last census,' he informs me with what sounds like a sense of pride. 'Most of the people who work around here are locals born and bred. Then we have the seasonal visitors and the monied folk. Those who can afford to have more than one home and can write a cheque for a million-pound property without blinking an eye. Born in London, were you?'

He's very inquisitive considering his rather unfriendly attitude.

My mind jumps back in time to the little village where Mum was born. It was home until I was twelve, when the company Dad worked for relocated to London. A huge upheaval at the time, it actually turned out to be an exciting adventure. I wonder now what Mum felt, having to leave behind her friends and family; turning her back on the place where she was born.

'No, but it's home now.'

'Well, no one will be bothering you out here.'

That seems to amuse him in some rather bizarre way.

We descend a steep hill and the scenery changes quite dramatically as we pass through a heavily-wooded area. Here and there I catch tantalising glimpses of a succession of rather grand houses, set way back from the road as the land rises up and disappears from view. As the car slows to take a left turn I see a stark white signpost bearing just the one name, *Holly Cove*. Less than five minutes later we pull up alongside a very charming property that is every bit as picturesque as the photo. However, my eyes are immediately drawn towards the view, which stretches out in front of me. The cottage nestles, quite literally, alongside an outcrop of rock on the edge of a small, sandy cove.

'It was originally a holiday cottage built for the owner of a coal mine in the valleys,' the driver informs me. 'That's thirteen pounds, Miss.' He makes no attempt to exit the cab and I thrust fifteen pounds at him through the grille.

'Can I have a receipt, please?'

Swinging open the door I literally shove the mound of bags out onto the ground and straighten up to approach the driver's window.

'Very generous of you, thanks,' he mutters, before I have time to object to the lack of change. I grab the piece of paper from his hand and immediately the engine kicks into life.

'Enjoy your stay, Miss.'

I'm left standing, open-mouthed and feeling more than a little annoyed, as the last thing he deserved was a tip.

As I look around it's obvious there is nothing here; nothing at all except an achingly beautiful cottage. The stout holly and pine trees feel like they are stationed in the garden; on guard like towering sentinels. As I walk back up the lane a little to peer in through the fence at the rear of the property, there's only a tiny strip of grass and a few small shrubs poking up like sticks in the ground. Beyond that it's mainly holly, pine and fir trees and because the land rises quite steeply, the forest seems to go on forever. But somewhere in between is the road we travelled along and now I can fully appreciate the views those million-pound houses must enjoy.

Towards the front of the cottage there is a picket fence that was once painted white. The salt-laden wind and rain have peeled away most of the paint giving it a worn, shabby chic look that isn't entirely unattractive. It's a large area that has been sympathetically landscaped. It dips away, meeting the beach where there's a swathe of shingle. At the far end of the beach there are two substantial-looking wooden huts, sitting almost side by side. Admittedly they do add to the overall ambience of the otherwise deserted cove, but the overwhelming thought is that this isn't just peaceful, it's completely isolated.

Come on, Tia, I encourage myself, grabbing as many bags as I can and making my way along the worn flagstone path to the front door. This is just an assignment with perks. I suspect Clarissa has calculated the cost of installing me here will be well worth it. I'm far less likely to dwell on recent events if I'm away from my home environment, where everything is a reminder of my loss.

However, when I finally manage to open the front door and step inside I wasn't expecting such a large, open-plan space. I turn around to face the window on my left and stare straight ahead. The view is totally unobstructed showing the sea below a pale blue-ribboned sky, the waves virtually twinkle as if they have been showered with silver glitter.

'With a view like that it's going to be very hard to focus on work!'

The sound of my own voice is rather startling, but I can't drag my eyes away from the perfect vista which is truly mesmerising. Framed, either side, by dipping boughs from an assortment of wispy young holly and pine trees which line the gentle drop down to the cove; an artist could not have painted better. Well, it might be isolated, but it's a little slice of heaven and I deserve it.

'Time to unpack,' I throw out the words just to break the silence. Seriously, even in the wee hours at home there is always that distant hum of intermittent traffic; albeit made worse by the fact that it's mostly lorries, loud motorbikes and the occasional ambulance thundering by outside my window. But here, inside the thick walls of a stone cottage, the silence feels heavy, so much so that it almost hurts my ears.

I reach out to open the window and after a hefty shove manage to swing it wide open. As I take a deep breath, letting the cool breeze waft over my face, my nose is filled with the sharp tang of the sea. There's a soft swish from the waves washing up on the shore. An overlying cacophony of intermittent birdsong is heartening to hear. Noise I can cope with, silence – well, that might require a little adjustment, I suspect.

The sitting room is spacious as the wall in the original hallway has been taken out. However, it doesn't feel odd stepping straight into such a large room, as it adds to the charm. The stripped pine floorboards have a whitewash finish and colourful chenille rugs in hues of plum and lavender warm the room. Generously-proportioned sofas sporting silver-grey linen covers show that the owner went for comfort as well as style, so it works very well. All the walls are natural stone, painted white, which makes the space feel light and airy.

I assume that it isn't crammed full of belongings because it's a rental, but there's enough here to make it feel lived-in. A large collection of books lines the wall to the left-hand side of a door leading through into the rest of the cottage. A pair of French doors in the centre of the back wall lead out onto the rear garden and the wilderness beyond. Obviously, it was once a stone wall with a window and you could argue that there's little point in having doors to such a tiny outside area. But, rather cleverly, the additional light is another reason why this cottage has a contemporary feel – whoever did the work here loved this place. A lot of money and attention to detail has been lavished upon it, and it shows.

Pushing open the internal door, I'm surprised to find myself standing in an even bigger, open-plan space. This kitchen/dining room is on a par with those you see in country home magazines. The units are pale grey Shaker style, with oak worktops and the matching dressers display an array of beautiful, old blue and white china.

There are three windows in total, two at the front of the room facing the sea and one to the rear. A door in the centre of the back wall opens into a surprisingly spacious and pristine bathroom; it's obvious that the extension takes up the bulk of the garden. The remaining space forms the small patio area to the rear of the sitting room.

The dining table is old pine. The dents and dings reflect a lifetime of wear and tear and an assortment of white-painted, shabby chic chairs complement it perfectly. To my right is another door and swinging it open I find a narrow staircase that is rather dark, even the white walls unable to combat the shadows. I flick the light switch on the wall and recessed twinkly lights immediately brighten the space.

Climbing the stairs, it feels cosy, in a warm wrapping-itself-around-you-like-a-hug, way. I've never experienced such an immediate and overwhelming sense of well-being in a house before. I stop to admire some of the photographs displayed on the side walls. They are all photos of the sea, taken at different times of the day and night, ranging from a perfectly calm sea in the height of summer, to the raging white fury whipped up by a winter storm. They look like professional photographs, rather than just snaps. Whoever owns this cottage is very lucky indeed and if it was mine I'd be loath to rent it out at any time of the year.

Upstairs, all three bedrooms lead off from the single landing, which runs the entire length of this one-room deep, rectangular cottage. Two of the rooms are a really good size, each accommodating a double bed, a small seating area and built-in wardrobes. The third bedroom is smaller and is home to a stylish day bed and an office area with some expensive-looking computer equipment. Pure white walls and pale blue and white striped bedding lend an air of simplicity to the upstairs rooms. Each room benefits from a slightly different angle looking out across the cove, but the view still dominates everything. I decide to settle myself into the bedroom above the dining area below, which is the middle one of the three.

In some ways, it feels too loved to be a holiday let. Everything here is of very good quality, although simple and minimalist in its presentation. In fact, even the bookshelves downstairs have been carefully, and lovingly, arranged. Both old and new books lined up side by side, according to height. But they are not simply books that have been bought to fill a couple of hours of relaxation time, or a random selection left behind by previous visitors. They appear to be a personal collection including biographies, reference volumes, a wide range of fiction, and coffee table books by famous photographers. I struggle to understand how anyone could leave their prize possessions here, knowing strangers will be passing through.

Instinctively, my feet head towards the window again and I stare out to sea. A small fishing boat is bobbing about on the waves, which are rather choppy considering it's such a beautifully sunny day. When I open the window, the light breeze is refreshing. I try to imagine how awesome it would be looking out on a stormy winter's day, when the rain is lashing down and the turbulent sea generates a frenzy of white foam to crest the steely-grey waves.

Idly, I wonder whether it's a commercial boat, or merely a passion which has the added advantage of delivering wonderfully fresh fish to the table. As far as I can tell there's only one person on board, so I guess it's unlikely to be a commercial fisherman.

Oh, how I wish I lived here – experiencing a simple life surrounded by nature. But how do people earn a living wage round here? There can't be many who can afford to snap up a property and walk away from their busy lives. Maybe this cottage is someone's retirement dream and renting it out is merely a way of keeping the property ticking over in readiness for a change of lifestyle. It must be awful to own a unique property like this and never have the time to enjoy it. The dream of being able to get away from it all spoilt when you end up having to rent it out until that can happen. I wonder if the property is sad when it stands, cold and empty, unloved between visits from a stream of strangers.

'Hello?'

A voice filters into my daydream and reluctantly I start to wend my way back down the staircase.

'Just coming.'

I wonder who it can be. Maybe the landlord has come to check me out. After all, he or she is entrusting their beautiful cottage to a stranger for a whole six weeks. They aren't to know that I have already fallen in love with Beach View Cottage and it couldn't be in safer hands.

Walking into the kitchen I peer through the open sitting room door and see the shadow of a figure pacing back and forth. As soon as I enter the room a rather jolly looking lady turns, smiles and steps towards me, holding out her hand.

'I'm Olwen, Olwen Morgan and I'm your housekeeper.'

Housekeeper?

I step forward and we shake. 'Nice to meet you, Olwen. I'm Tia Armstrong.'

'I've been hired to clean through, change the beds and do the shopping. They've booked me for an hour, three times a week. If there is anything at all you need, please don't hesitate to ask.'

'Oh, that's a surprise. I didn't realise a cleaning service was included. I can now understand why it's so beautifully presented.'

'I wish I could take the credit for that, but it's down to the owner. No, I live in the village and I run a small cleaning business. A London firm contacted me and said you were going to be busy while you were here. They wanted someone to make sure you had everything you needed.'

Clarissa has arranged all of this for me?

'Well, um, I'm not sure I'm actually going to need anyone to help out. I mean, there is only me and I'm not a messy person.'

Olwen laughs, her tone reflecting the warmth of that wonderful Welsh accent. Her mop of tight, curly hair bounces around her ears like a hat, as her multiple chins wobble just the teensiest bit.

'Oh, I won't make a nuisance of myself, I promise. I'll just keep everything ticking over – shopping, washing and ironing – whatever will help to make your stay as pleasant as possible. It sounds like the company you work for want you to have some thinking time with no distractions, so you might as well take advantage of that. You must be a good friend of Nic's.'

I look at her in surprise.

'I don't know him at all, actually. This was all arranged for me.'

She does a double-take, her eyebrows shooting up into her curls.

'Really? You are one lucky lady, that's for sure. My other half, Rhys, runs a holiday lettings business in this area and he's always trying to talk Nic into renting out this place. A few of the local residents move out for the lucrative spring and summer months, just into cheaper accommodation in the village, or one of the local farm houses. It's a nice boost to their income, as employment opportunities here are rather limited.'

Her words are a revelation and I'm rather surprised she's being so candid with me.

'I was thinking it's a shame this was a rental cottage, as it's so beautifully done, but I had no idea.'

'Well, maybe he's decided that renting out the cottage to supplement his income is a good move. A lot of people around here have several jobs. I also do the mid-morning playground duty at the local school. You see the same faces popping up all the time, you'll get used to us!'

She laughs and I can't help but smile, as her friendliness has certainly relaxed me.

'Well, now I know it's his home I can only hope he really is happy to allow me to enjoy it for a while,' I remark.

'Oh, if Nic isn't happy with you, he'll let you know. Sometimes we all have to do things we wouldn't normally do, in order to pay the bills. That's the price of getting away from city life.'

She sounds very matter-of-fact and I have to stop myself from asking whether my landlord is a born and bred local, but it would be unfair of me to question her.

'Well, he has no worries with me. I'll love Beach View Cottage as if it's my own while I'm here. And yes, I think my boss wants me to focus on work and forget about my troubles.'

Olwen glances at me, a frown creasing her forehead but she quickly returns to smiley-mode.

'Well, welcome to the Gower coast and Holly Cove. Here's my card if you need anything urgently, but aside from that I'll see you the day after tomorrow. I've stocked up the cupboards and the fridge-freezer, so you have plenty to keep you going.'

I nod my appreciation and follow her to the door. As I do, I notice that the boat which was previously bobbing about on the waves is now heading inland towards the cove. What I'd love to do is to take a walk along the sandy shoreline, but I make myself turn back to begin unpacking.

Day one at Beach View Cottage and already I feel like it's home.

4

Settling In

I have no idea why it makes such a difference to me that Beach View Cottage isn't just a holiday rental that is merely a temporary home to a stream of visitors. But for some reason it does. There is a sense of homeliness here that is welcoming and comforting, as if the cottage is filled with positive karma.

As the light begins to fade and I walk around turning on side lamps, I reflect upon the fact that there is little here I would change if this was my home. Not that I'm ever likely to be able to afford the sheer luxury of a holiday home. Even as an investment. Living in London is so expensive, and the only thing that can even be loosely described as 'generously proportioned' concerning my apartment is the mortgage.

Once the suitcases are empty and my clothes are hanging neatly in the beautifully distressed oak armoire, I need to find somewhere to set up my desk. The office upstairs still has files and paperwork laid out on the desk top in front of the computer. I feel it would be an imposition to clear it off and use that space. I also notice there is no TV here and that's totally unexpected. I don't think I know anyone who doesn't have one, so does that mean he took it with him? Now if I had decided to rent out my apartment then, obviously, I would have taken my IT equipment with me, but not the TV. Upon further investigation, I finally discover a Wi–Fi modem tucked away in the kitchen. It's connected to a power source, but not turned on. I flick the switch hesitantly, but within a couple of minutes the whole row of lights are lit, and a sense of relief settles over me. There's a sticker on the top with the password and I grab my iPad to get connected, mentally ticking off another item on my *settling in* list.

There's a programme I used to watch on TV called *Through the Keyhole*. As the presenter walked around a celebrity's home, talking about the contents, a panel of three people had to guess the person's identity. The clues were subtle but allowed you to build up a picture in your mind of the sort of person who would live there. By the end of the episode it was always fairly easy to guess the celebrity's identity.

I finish laying the table and settle down to a cup of coffee and cheese on toast. I'm going to have to find a recipe for Welsh rarebit while I'm here as I've heard it's amazing and the mixture is actually poured over the bread. The well-stocked fridge seems to have everything in there and the Welsh cheese does taste that little bit better, in my opinion. I find myself musing over whose house this is and conjure up a picture of the man Olwen referred to as Nic. I assume that's short for Nicholas, which is quite a traditional name. As my eyes scan the kitchen, I notice that there aren't really any distinctly feminine touches. I realise that what I thought of as minimalist, was probably the orderliness of a man who likes to keep things simple. And yet he has a vision and a sense of style that complements the cottage. And he's an avid reader – everything from crime to humour. I'm guessing he took early retirement, maybe after a failed relationship, or loss of a partner. That thought makes me gulp, as a sense of sadness suddenly rises within me and I have to push it back down. How must it feel to reach a time in your life when you stop striving to make things happen and decide to walk away? A tinge of sadness creeps over me, knowing that I've temporarily displaced him, but I focus on the fact that the influx of cash might have relieved a few worries.

My iPad kicks into life and it's Clarissa, Skypeing. I quickly brush any crumbs from around my mouth and click the accept button.

'We have a problem.'

Really? It's seven o'clock on a Saturday evening. Clarissa's expression is always the same, probably because of the amount of Botox she's had and I'm not being bitchy here. It's a fact. There is never a huge smile, or a desolate frown, just an almost unbelievably perfect, wrinkle–free complexion that belies her age.

'Oh, sorry to hear that.' *And good evening to you, too, Clarissa.*

'We are one couple down and I need you to find a replacement. Make them interesting; our readers want to be inspired. Is there anything you need?'

The question is thrown in as an afterthought and I'm half tempted to ask Clarissa how she discovered this place. I open my mouth to begin, but immediately think better of it. Clarissa merely barks orders; she's unlikely to know any of the tedious detail, as it's always someone else turning her commands into reality.

'No, I'm good, thank you. I'm sure I'll come across someone who is interested in earning a little extra cash in return for their personal story. I, um, haven't really met anyone except the housekeeper yet.'

One eyebrow lifts, but it's hardly perceptible.

'Really? Well, when you find the right person phone their details through to accounts and we'll send out the standard letter with the small print.'

Clarissa doesn't like loose ends.

'Of course.' My reply doesn't really register and I can see Clarissa's mind is already elsewhere. 'I'll be in touch once the interviews have begun.'

She nods and her image disappears, leaving me staring back at myself. I had no idea I looked quite so tired and pale. The frown on my face seems to exaggerate those fine lines in a particularly unflattering way. I probably look at least twice as old as Clarissa, despite the fact that it's the other way around. But almost a whole day has passed without a morbid thought and that's an achievement for me.

I know I should clear the dishes away and then start work. I have a schedule of interviews to plan and a lot of background information to read. But it's Saturday evening and although I'm well aware I've just had a month off work, I need to ground myself. This is my temporary home for a while. It's important that I adjust to my new surroundings and make myself comfortable, so I can settle down to work. Besides, I'm curious about the owner now and perusing his library of books in more detail might throw up a few extra clues about him.

*

I awake feeling refreshed and having had what seems to have been a dreamless sleep. I'm actually excited at the prospect of exploring Holly Cove and the immediate vicinity. Besides, I have to find a suitable candidate to interview and I need to start meeting people, in order to achieve that. So, a quick coffee and toast and finally I can feel the tingle of the salty breeze on my face.

It's a gentle incline down towards the beach itself. The wind has driven the sand in between small tumps of dried grasses, but it's still quite firm underfoot. There's a crunch as I navigate a swathe of dried leaves, mostly holly I note, which would be very unforgiving on my feet if I wasn't wearing sturdy shoes. Another few strides and the texture changes completely. Walking out in front of the sheer cliff face to my left, I look back at the cottage. It's perfectly positioned to take maximum advantage of the view. Surprisingly, though, there's a signpost saying *Private Beach*, at the point where the partially-gravelled lane gives way to the area of sandy soil. Within a few yards I'm walking on soft, dry sand and my leg muscles have to work harder as my feet sink lower with each step I take. There's no one to be seen, but I'm sure it would have been made clear to me if the beach was out of bounds.

I stand and look along the length of the sandy shoreline of Holly Cove. The beach itself is in the shape of a horseshoe. To my left, it extends maybe two hundred yards and to my right no more than fifty yards. Bordered by sheer, limestone cliffs, a flat ledge projects forward from the base before disappearing beneath the soft sand. As the light breeze whips my hair around my face I dig into my pocket for a hair band. Facing into the wind, I quickly grab and twist the strands, then fasten it in a ponytail.

Turning my attention to the horizon in front of me, I watch the little white foamy crests as the water ebbs and flows quite vigorously. The breeze is constant and a little bracing at times. It's a bright, spring day, but whenever one of a succession of big, fluffy white clouds obscures the sun there is a slight chill to the air. I fasten my jacket and begin walking in the direction of what looks like two beach huts, which are set back against the rocky cliff to my left.

The sand is so soft underfoot that it's already making my calf muscles ache, so I meander across the beach towards the firmer sand, where large swathes of sea shells and seaweed have been strewn by the tide. As I get closer, I see that they aren't simply beach huts, but are much larger wooden structures which appear to be dwellings. Rather like wooden chalets, spaced about twenty feet apart. The gap between them has a flat roof and as I stroll by I notice there's a boat nestling behind locked, metal gates. It appears to be a workshop of some kind.

Both cabins are of exactly the same size and construction, with an offset door and a panoramic window facing the sea. Sitting on a large, extended concrete base they are raised off the ground by more than a yard, with a set of wooden steps leading up to each door. Rather surprisingly, there are six solar panels on each roof. With a metal flue projecting upwards from the rear of each cabin, I assume the heating is generated by a wood-burner. If these belong to the cottage, I wonder whether the owner is staying here. However, there's no one around and I walk on, wanting to investigate the shoreline and see if there is another bay beyond this one.

When I reach the end of the beach I start to clamber over the low, rocky outcrop. Little rock pools are home to an assortment of tiny crabs, limpets and even the odd starfish. With one hand seeking out handholds on the surrounding cliff wall, I go as far as I dare towards the water line, before accepting that there is no way to see around the projecting headland. It's easy to see why this is a private beach, quite simply because it's cut off. Admittedly, the tide is low as it's clear from the line of shell and seaweed deposits that at high tide it advances much further up the beach. But nowhere near the wooden huts. Reluctantly, I turn back, as the salty droplets carried by the wind begin to turn from a light spray into an almost rain-like assault. I hear a low mumble, barely audible over the sound of the water crashing and lapping against the rocks. As I steady myself ready to turn around, someone grabs my arm. I turn in surprise, but gratefully take the other hand that is extended out to me. It occurs to me that, unaided, there was a real danger I could slip and tumble into the sea. Suddenly, adrenalin is pumping around my body and my heart beat begins to race.

It takes a while to retrace my steps back across the irregular, rocky surface and myriad of rock pools, even with the help of a sturdy arm to guide me. It isn't until I have two feet firmly back on dry land that I can acknowledge my helper and my heart rate begins to slow.

'Thank you. I think that my curiosity got the better of me there and that was quite a silly thing to do.' My trainers are soaking wet and a chill begins to claw its way up my legs.

My rescuer is an older man, probably in his sixties, with short-cropped silver hair and a matching full beard. His skin is weather-beaten and tanned by an outdoor life and exposure to the elements, but the effect is softened by the gentle, greyish-blue eyes smiling back at me.

'I was a bit worried, to be honest. It's easy to slip and you wouldn't be the first. But the beach falls away quite sharply just beyond the rocks and it's quite deceiving. The current is strong and even a fairly good swimmer would struggle.'

I nod, feeling much calmer now my pulse is no longer racing and pounding in my head. 'Thank you, I'm really very grateful you saw me and came to my rescue. I hope I wasn't trespassing—'

'No, I saw you yesterday, looking out of the cottage window when I was fishing. You have as much right to be here as I do.'

The man doesn't say anything else; we exchange pleasant smiles and, in tandem, turn to begin heading back up the beach. I feel I ought to engage him in conversation out of politeness, as it's clear he isn't going to say anything more.

'Are you a local?' I notice there's a hint of a Welsh lilt to his voice but it's not as pronounced as Olwen's accent had been.

He turns his head, his eyes scanning my face for a few seconds before he responds.

'You could say that. I live in the cabins over there.' He nods in the direction of the two wooden structures that look much more like holiday chalets from this angle.

The wind is starting to whistle around my ears. The sky is no longer blue, but an oppressive shade of pale grey that makes it hard to distinguish where the sea ends and it begins.

'There's a storm coming,' he warns.

We stop in front of the gate to the cottage and I hesitate for a moment, because he seems to be lingering, as if he's waiting to be invited inside.

'Can I offer you a hot drink, or something, for saving me from my own folly? It's the least I can do.'

He smiles, those soft, gentle eyes at odds with his well-worn and rather stern demeanour.

'I'm not really a people-person, Miss. But thank you for the thought.'

He turns and trudges back across the sand, his heavy boots leaving a clear trail of footprints behind him. It's rather comforting knowing there is someone close, even if I have no idea exactly who he is, or why he lives here on the beach.

5

Back in My Stride

Well, the adrenalin boost isn't wasted and after a strong, hot coffee I sit down at the dining table and set up my office. The Wi–Fi seems to work well on both my laptop and the iPad, so it doesn't take long to begin pulling things into shape. Six weeks seems to be a reasonable amount of time for the assignment. While the subject is how people from varying backgrounds keep the love alive, it's really three standalone articles; each one will be contrasting rather than comparing two very different lifestyle choices. And now, of course, I'm one case-study short.

If I broadly assign one week to each article, then I know that the time is going to fly by and it's not as generous a timescale as it might seem at first glance. But there's still this little niggle in the back of my mind about the motivation behind Clarissa's thoughtfulness. It's so totally out of character for her, even though I will admit I don't think I could have coped with this without the change of scene. Here, at least, it's peaceful and there aren't any reminders of what I've left behind. It's as if my worries have been set to one side for a short while and I'm able to take time out to focus exclusively on the task in hand.

Of course, Clarissa said that everyone thought I was perfect for this project, but does that mean everyone else turned it down? Maybe that's why she decided to present me with a *fait accompli*, as the French would say – a done deal. She knew that it would be virtually impossible for me to refuse when she already had the arrangements put in place.

I sigh and reach for my phone. As much as I don't want to speak to my brother, I suppose I'd better tell him where I am in case he needs my input. We're joint executors of Mum's will, although it's unlikely he'll seek to involve me in any way at all. He thrust two pieces of paper under my nose, asked me to sign and since then he's dealt with everything.

'Will, it's Tia.'

He clears his throat and there's an angry, almost dismissive, edge to the sound. 'I left a couple of messages on your answerphone.'

I grit my teeth, realising he's cross with me because I haven't been in touch, but then he could have tried my mobile too.

'Sorry. I'm back at work and I have a new assignment, so I'm staying on the Gower coast for the next month or

56

so. I'm just checking in to see if there's anything you need me to do.'

'It's all in hand. It's not a quick process.'

I won't know that if you don't tell me what's going on.

'If you need to contact me, use the mobile number as there's no landline here. Is everyone all right at that end?'

I don't want to annoy him by asking directly about my sister-in-law Sally, or my niece, six-year-old Bella. Before Mum's death, we hadn't spoken for nearly four years. It all began when Mum started getting close to an old family friend called Edward. Ed had been Dad's best man at their wedding and their friendship went way back to their school days. Dad was only in his forties when he passed away, quite suddenly, from a massive heart attack. Ed and his wife were there to help Mum through the worst. Then, about seven years ago, Ed's wife died of cancer. He was a lost soul for a while and it was only natural that Mum was there for him.

But as they grew closer together, it seemed to anger Will and the tension began to build. One day he turned on Mum, implying that Ed was using her. I stepped in and, after an explosive rant, Will walked out of Mum's house and never set foot over the doorstep again. Until the day she died. When he responded to my call I had no idea what his reaction would be. As we waited for the ambulance to arrive to take her body away, he thanked the doctor in attendance and asked all the right questions, but there was no sign of emotion. I was kneeling at her side, holding her hand and I remember looking up at him.

'Do you want some time alone with Mum to say goodbye?' I'd asked him through my tears.

'It's too late for that,' he'd replied, coldly. And I knew that I would find it very hard to forgive him for his harshly-spoken words.

*

Having sent a draft interview schedule off to Clarissa's PA, Hayley, to set up as quickly as she can, I start gathering background information on the interviewees. Each person has filled out a general questionnaire but I want to dig a bit deeper before I start having those one–to–one sessions. If people realised how much information is readily available about them online if you simply type in their name, I'm sure many would be appalled. Most of the participants are on several social media platforms and I begin taking notes and generally gleaning whatever information I can.

Suddenly my phone pings and I'm delighted to see it's Hayley.

Hiya, how's it going? I'll start getting those appointments set up first thing tomorrow.

I know full well that she will have a million other things to do on a Monday morning, so I appreciate the fact I'm jumping the queue.

> Did I ever mention you are a star? And have the patience of a saint!

That will make her laugh. She holds the record for being Clarissa's longest-serving PA and, in fact, the only one who made it past six months in the job. It's now a little over a year and counting.

> Once or twice. I was going to phone you, but I wasn't sure if you were busy.

I stop texting and call her. She answers immediately and it's nice to hear a familiar voice.

'I can't believe you are checking your work emails on a Sunday afternoon! Haven't you anything better to do? Or has he exhausted you already?'

Hayley snorts, bursting out in that trademark high-pitched laugh of hers. She's in the loved-up phase with her latest boyfriend and they spend every moment they aren't working, together. I take much delight in joking with her about it, but it's lovely to see. It helps restore my faith in the belief that it is possible to find *the one*.

'Jack had to go into work. An emergency, apparently. I'm home alone and feeling abandoned.'

Now it's my turn to laugh. 'Poor you, so desperate you turn to work. If it's any consolation at all, I've only crossed paths with one person today, even though he might have actually saved my life.'

There's a sharp intake of breath and I regale her with the tale of the little episode I had on the beach this morning.

'Hey, you have to be careful, Tia. I need you to come back here in one piece. I'm already counting the days until your little beach holiday is over. I mean, I need someone to whom I can vent occasionally. You know you're the only person here I can trust.'

I, too, miss our little chats.

'It's only six weeks, and two days of that have already flown by. I'll be back at my desk before you know it. Dare I ask who has taken up residence in my absence?'

There's a moment or two of hesitation before Hayley responds.

'Finlay.'

As usual, I find myself grinding my teeth at the very mention of his name. Finlay Robertson-Smythe is a fast-track trainee who joined us a little over a year ago. He's ambitious with a capital A and keen to prove himself to Clarissa. Which is fine, but I've discovered that he's also not above playing a few devious tricks to get what he wants. At least two fairly prestigious features ended up on his desk when he gained Clarissa's ear and sowed a few seeds of doubt. I hasten to add they weren't assignments that were coming my way, but now he has his feet firmly planted beneath my desk and he'll be savouring that. I wonder if he's trying to undermine me whenever he has the chance, as that seems to be his style. After being out for a whole month and now away for an additional six weeks—

'Don't go worrying about it. He's nowhere near as good as you are and you know it. Clarissa knows it, too.'

Hayley is a great supporter and we always have each other's backs, but this doesn't look good. And, somehow, it doesn't feel right.

'Was it Clarissa who suggested Beach View Cottage?'

I wonder if that was one of Finlay's little ideas.

'Yes, it seemed to be.' Hayley sounds quite confident about that, so maybe I'm being a little paranoid here. 'Clarissa and I were alone when she gave me the instructions to set everything up for you. She said it was a place she'd visited many years ago and that she remembered a cottage tucked away on a small private beach next to Caswell Bay. She was pretty sure it was called Holly Cove, but suggested I call the local tourist information office as it didn't appear on the map. I rang them and they gave me the number of a holiday letting agency. It took a couple of phone calls to track down the owner, as the cottage itself wasn't listed. He took a day or two to think it over, then I received the go-ahead. OK, I admit I was totally taken by surprise. I mean, Clarissa talking about a memory not connected with work, for starters. And then the fact that—'

Hayley grinds to a halt, not sure how to broach the subject.

'Don't worry; it's not something I can avoid talking about. I'm actually very grateful to Clarissa, as I will admit my head has been all over the place. I used to talk to Mum every day as soon as I arrived home from work. At least being here it's a different routine yet again, so it's easier to focus on what I have to do. By the time this assignment is over I'll be ready to do battle in the office again. So, tell Finlay not to get too comfortable in my chair.'

'I will. And it's good to know you're doing OK. I mean, I'm here if you need to chat about anything at all. Hearing all about the goings-on of a little seaside resort would brighten my day.'

'I think it's a little too sedate for there to be *goings-on*, as you put it. But the views are breathtaking and the private beach is perfect.'

'And you already have a protector, you say?' Her voice lifts with innuendo.

'He's probably in his sixties and as I don't know anything at all about fishing it's unlikely we have anything in common.'

'Well, keep me posted if you meet anyone, you know, *interesting*.'

I find myself chuckling, thinking *if only*.

'I will. Sleep well and we'll speak later this week.'

As the line disconnects, I try my best to put Finlay out of my mind. What's the worst that can happen? He worms his way into Clarissa's good books and when I get back I'm demoted from the A-team, into the B-team? We affectionately refer to them as the Achievers and the Better Next Time teams. I've only fallen out of grace with Clarissa once and that was over a difference of opinion. What should have been a straightforward interview, unwittingly threw up some rather unpalatable facts about an A-list celebrity. Clarissa took a few quotes she found in my notes and, without consulting me, made some changes to the article. It turned nasty and the magazine was threatened with a lawsuit, so Clarissa had to publish an apology in the next edition. But I was left feeling mortified and looking as if I was guilty of wantonly divulging information that was never meant for publication. Sales that month hit an all-time high, which quickly overshadowed any negativity in Clarissa's eyes. I *took one* for the magazine and as there was no financial penalty, Clarissa's gamble paid off.

'I'll sort Finlay out if he starts getting up to his old tricks again,' I announce out loud, as I stretch my tired arm muscles and think about making dinner.

Is talking to oneself a sign of madness, or the sign of a woman not used to being on her own for long periods of time? Guess I'm about to find out.

6

We're All Very Different

I'm up at six, throw on my jogging bottoms and a hoodie, and go for a run on the beach. With only another ten days until the end of May, today it really does feel that summer is literally around the corner. There's hardly any breeze at all coming off the sea and with a clear blue sky reflecting down upon the water, it looks calm and inviting. I run in a loop, straight down towards the water's edge and then in parallel to the sea, along the wet sand. As the rocky cliff looms up in front of me I curve away, my route taking me back up to the area that is softer underfoot, which slows me down. There's no sign of my fisherman, but then he could still be asleep.

. As I approach the cottage once more, I decide I might as well test my stamina and I start the uphill climb. It doesn't take long before my calf muscles are screaming. I slow to a walk, but I'm determined to make it up to the road, content in the knowledge that walking back down at least gravity will be on my side.

Either side of the lane are swathes of tall trees. The woodland is quite dense in places as I climb higher. There's an almost constant sound of raucous calls and flapping wings as birds swoop in and out amongst the branches overhead. Something moves at ground level just a few feet away from me but it's only a rabbit. He's gone in a flash, disappearing into a bank of bronze bracken and gorse, amongst which the new growth is fighting its way through.

I'd forgotten the sounds of nature in all its glory. And I hadn't realised how attuned I'd become to the sounds of traffic and people in the thronging metropolis that is London. Up here, among the trees, the air you breathe in has a rich sweetness to it, in sharp contrast to the intense and slightly bitter, saltiness of the sea air at beach level. What puts the *fresh* into fresh air is the lack of pollution from bumper-to-bumper, idling car engines. But there's also an earthiness that pervades my nose in waves and reminds me of mushrooms before they are washed. I smile to myself.

And that one thought is enough to trigger a flashback. I remember a camping holiday in Devon: it was the year after Dad died and our first holiday without him. As kids, Will and I didn't realise how big a deal it must have been for Mum, but we had a great time and one afternoon, in particular, she took us mushrooming. We traipsed through a wood, very similar to this one; Will often trailing behind as he insisted on dragging a big stick behind him. The pointed end left a thin, but visible trail, on the ground. He said we could retrace our route and I realise now that maybe he carried a sense of responsibility, as the eldest child, to step into Dad's shoes. I remember feeling irritated and constantly turning to call out for Will to hurry up, but Mum was very patient with him. Eventually she put her hand on my shoulder and looked down into my eyes.

'He's fine, lovely, let him be. Boys love a little adventure and Will is looking out for us.'

Her face is there, in front of me, every feature so clear that I could reach out and touch her and then it's gone. She's gone. My stomach constricts and I brush a stray tear away from the corner of my eye.

'Stay strong, Tia. Stay strong.'

The main road lies straight ahead and I decide it's time to turn around and head back for breakfast. Checking my mobile, I see there's no signal here, and there probably wouldn't be in the cottage if it weren't for the signal booster. I begin thinking about the owner of Beach View Cottage again. I wonder whether the isolation of this spot ever bothers him, or whether it's what attracted him here in the first place. To me it feels like I'm hiding myself away and I'm not sure that's something I could ever feel totally comfortable about. I decide that when Olwen pays me a visit today, I'm going to try to find out a little more about this mystery man.

*

Feeling more energised than I've been in a long while, I work as I munch on hot buttered toast and marmalade. Setting up individual files ready for the interviews and filing away the information I already have makes me feel I've made a real start.

Shortly after ten o'clock, Hayley texts to say that one of the couples will be jetting off to Spain tomorrow, but they are free today if I wanted to catch them before they go. It's a lot to do in one day, as I want to interview them together as a couple and individually. But if it works for them, then I'm up for it.

> That's great, thanks Hayley. I'll need an hour to get organised, so tell them to expect a call at eleven a.m. Can u text me their Skype ID? I have to go and make myself presentable. Guess I really am back at work now. Oh, and happy Monday!

I rush around the cottage manically, sorting out something more appropriate to wear and then blow drying my hair, which is still damp from the shower. A little make-up and I start to feel more like the old, professional me.

Tidying the paperwork on the kitchen table, I check the camera angle of the laptop so that my image sits within the frame. With the dresser displaying the vintage blue and white crockery as a backdrop, it's a very calming scene and perfect for what I want to achieve.

Then I spend ten minutes going through their file once more. Veronica and Liam are professional people, have been married for eight years and have no children so far, by choice it confirms. From middle class backgrounds, they seem to have achieved what looks on paper to be an enviable work/life balance.

It's time to set up the digital voice recorder next and then pull out my interview sheets, where I've listed some questions to help the interviews flow. I find that some people need to be led, while others will simply talk non-stop. I have no preference either way, as long as there aren't awkward silences that don't give me any information at all.

Finally, I can sit back in my chair and re-align everything on the table top in front of me as I check I have everything I need. Nerves begin to kick in as the clock edges around to the hour. Come on, Tia, you've done this hundreds of times before and once the first interview is out of the way you'll be on a roll.

The couple staring back at me are sitting close together on what looks like a sofa in a very stylish room. Everything in the shot behind them looks shiny and sleek.

'Hello Veronica and Liam, lovely to meet you both. I'm Tia Armstrong. Thank you so much for taking part in our winter feature, we're all very excited about it at this end. You guys just look so perfect together.'

Oops, that last comment sort of slipped out without any thought, but they do look like the perfect couple. Judging by the angle of their arms I think they are holding hands, but that's out of shot.

They smile back at me and then turn to face each other, sporting big grins.

'I guess he'll do,' Veronica laughs and turns back to face me. 'Sorry about the rush, but we're flying out tomorrow and will be gone for five weeks.'

'No problem at all, I'm grateful you guys are prepared to put the packing on hold. It should take about an hour for the joint interview, then probably no more than twenty to thirty minutes for the individual sessions. We can take a break at any time to suit you both. Maybe do the joint interview first and then stop for lunch, if that's OK with you both? Where are you going?'

Liam's voice is low and very smooth. I see from the information on file that he's a doctor. 'Kuala Lumpur first, then Ho Chi Minh City, and then on to Da Nang and Hanoi. We're in your hands, Tia, but that sounds good to me. What do you think, darling?'

Veronica nods in agreement. She's a paediatrician and I wonder whether being around children all the time is the reason starting a family doesn't seem to be a part of their forward plan. Seeing the day-to-day reality of parenting might be a reminder of how life changes once you have kids and, in their case, it would be a radical change. But that's outside the brief, even though it was information they included in the questionnaire and I need to keep focused.

'Is it OK if I use a voice recorder, as well as making notes as we talk? It helps when I'm writing up the article.'

Both nod in agreement and their body language doesn't give any impression of nervousness at all.

'Has our photographer booked an appointment with you to take a few shots?'

'He came last Saturday, actually. We haven't seen the photos which will be used in the actual article, but we were very happy with what he showed us.'

I'm annoyed with myself that I didn't ask Hayley to keep me informed of the photographer's itinerary.

'Did he ask you to pose for any Christmas-inspired shots?'

I hold my breath, hoping there was at least one shot with maybe a little tinsel or a bauble in sight.

'No. Why, is that a problem?'

It's my fault for not being ahead of the game.

'It's just that I'd like to get a feel for the way you guys celebrate Christmas.'

Liam immediately jumps in.

'No problem. I'll send you a link to our private YouTube account. You are very welcome to take screen shots from that, if it helps. Last year we spent Christmas in a log cabin in Luosto, an idyllic resort in the middle of Lapland. It was an amazing experience.'

Of course they were in Lapland. Why am I not at all surprised?

'Did you see the Aurora Borealis?'

'We did. And it was mind-blowing. We managed to get some footage and that's in the video, too.' Suddenly my life begins to feel very ordinary and mundane, by comparison. And as for the video, well, I can imagine that they don't have one bad angle between them. I find myself fiddling with my hair and hoping it doesn't look quite as flyaway as it did in the mirror.

The hour flies by and when we end the call to break for lunch, I find myself sitting here staring around and feeling very alone. The contrast to my own life couldn't be more complete: a couple who believe in living life to the full on every conceivable level. It's not jealousy that rears up inside of me, it's more akin to longing. OK, so their dream isn't quite the same as mine, but to have found that person. The one. And to have your life sorted so you can afford the lifestyle you want and that work/life balance falling quite nicely into place. I groan and sag a little in my chair.

As I'm preparing a quick sandwich there's a knock on the door and it's Olwen.

'Come on through, I've just put the kettle on.'

When she follows me into the kitchen she hesitates as her eyes take in my temporary office on the kitchen table.

'Oh, I don't mean to disturb you, Tia, really. I wondered if it was convenient to clean through today?'

'It's fine, honestly. As I said, I don't make much mess. What I'd really like is a little company. Do you have time to stop for a sandwich?'

Olwen looks a little surprised. 'I'm being paid to pop in every other day for an hour. I don't want to take advantage—'

I smile, reassuringly. 'I won't tell, if you don't. Slip off your coat and take a seat. Ignore that end of the table. I have about fifty minutes before I have to begin interviewing again, but you'd be doing me a favour as it's nice to have a little company.'

Olwen removes her coat and pulls out a chair. 'To be honest I'm glad to sit down. Mondays are my worst day of the week as I go from one cleaning job to another. In between I fit in the morning playground duty, which is always a juggling act. It's non-stop.'

As I carry two plates across to the table Olwen smiles, a little embarrassed.

'It's a long time since anyone waited on me.'

We both laugh. I carry the mugs across and take a seat opposite her.

'You seem to really enjoy your job and they obviously think highly of you. What do you do, exactly?'

'I'm a feature writer for a magazine. The interviews are for a special winter spread about how couples keep the love in their relationships alive.'

Olwen swallows a mouthful of ham sandwich and raises her eyebrows.

'Goodness. It makes it sound like hard work. I always receive flowers for Valentine's Day and my birthday, and I thought I was lucky after all these years. I'll have to buy the magazine and I can wave it in front of Rhys on the odd occasion we're in bed together and actually awake. After twenty-three years together, it's all about getting through each day, to be honest.'

I almost choke on my sandwich as I start laughing.

'Do you have children, Olwen?'

She nods. 'Three. One at uni, one at college and the youngest one is still at school, she's only twelve.'

No wonder Olwen and her husband don't have much time for themselves.

'I doubt you are missing out on very much. You must be doing something right as you're still together.'

Olwen's plate is already half-empty and she picks up the mug of coffee in front of her.

'I wouldn't be without him, flaws and all. That man still has some annoying habits, but I figure the good outweighs the bad. Now, me, it goes without saying that I have to be perfect to put up with him.'

The wicked grin on her face tells me Rhys thinks she's a handful, but underlying that is a real sense of contentment with her lot. Obviously, it's difficult juggling her various jobs and family life; anyone would find that tiring, but it's clear Olwen doesn't resent the pressure she's under. Like most working mums she simply longs for the luxury of having a little time to sit and catch her breath occasionally.

I remember that what I really wanted to ask her was about Nic, but that will have to wait for another day.

'It takes all sorts to make a world and it would be very boring if we were all the same. Besides, we don't always end up where we thought we'd be and I guess that's down to fate. I hoped I'd find my Mr Right and be juggling family and career by now. Instead I live in fear of turning into a mini version of my boss and that would be a tragedy.'

'Oh, so being here is a perk of the job, is it?'

Swallowing a mouthful of coffee, I look directly at Olwen.

'I'm here because my mother died nearly five weeks ago and I've been off on compassionate leave. I had a bit of an... episode actually, but no one knows that. I couldn't cope with the news when it happened and the doctor ended up prescribing me a sedative. I had an allergic reaction to it and, well, let's say that I wasn't in a good way.'

Olwen reaches out and places her hand on my arm.

'Sorry to hear that, Tia. The grieving process is a long one and it's a bumpy ride, that's for sure. We never get over losing the people who touch our lives in a meaningful way, but I believe their love is always around us.'

By the look in her eyes I can see that loss has touched her, too.

I glance at the clock and regretfully it's about time I made a move. Olwen notices, and rises from her seat.

'Thanks for the little chat, Olwen. I needed that.'

'Any time. I'll see you the day after tomorrow but if you need anything in the meantime just give me a call. Lovely sandwich by the way – it hit the spot!'

7

Powering Through the Disappointment

I don't know whether my mind begins to dwell on recent events after chatting to Olwen, or following the interview with Veronica and Liam. The harsh contrast between the life of the *perfect* couple and my own, non–existent, love life is a bit of a slap in the face if I'm being honest.

What isn't helping is that the moment I close my eyes at night my head is full of old memories. Mostly Christmas re-runs, which is probably to be expected given the slant of the articles I'm working on. But it hurts because my feelings are still so raw and I dread waking up in the morning for fear I'll remember the details of some pretty intense dreams. On several occasions I've literally woken myself up as I sob in my sleep.

The worst was re-living the memory of the first Christmas after I started school. Most of my friends wanted the latest doll who could drink water from a bottle and shed tears. I wanted a desk just like my teacher's. And I was pretty specific about what had to be in the desk. At the top of the list was a register just like the one Miss Merchant ticked every day as she called out our names.

'I can't possibly be a real teacher without a proper register. Santa will bring me one, won't he, Mum?'

Looking back, I'm sure I gave her an impossible task. I mean, where on earth did you go to buy a real school register? Most of the other items in my letter to Santa were pretty standards things you could easily pick up in any stationery store but I kept on and on about the register.

Now for Christmas morning we only had one rule and that was that we stayed in our beds until six a.m. However, this Christmas my excitement was tinged with the fear of disappointment. What if Santa brought me something else, or the desk was there but it was empty? I tossed and turned until the early hours of the morning and I swear my eyes never closed once. Eventually I crept downstairs, too afraid to venture into the sitting room I simply sat on a step halfway down the stairs. I figured that if I saw him then I could ask the question and if he had forgotten then I was sure he'd fly back to the North Pole so as not to disappoint me.

It was probably an hour or two later that Mum found me shivering in just my cotton nightie, my eyes glued to the semi-open door.

'What on earth are you doing sitting here in the dark? And you're so cold, darling.'

She had immediately slipped off her dressing gown and wrapped it around me, hugging me close to her and rocking gently.

'I don't want Santa to forget my register, Mum. But he hasn't been yet. He will come, won't he?' I pleaded, searching for reassurance.

I remember gazing up into her eyes, my own filling with tears. Her own eyes brightened as she gave me a watery smile in return.

'Let's take a look, shall we?'

I remember sucking in a deep breath.

'But it's not six o'clock yet because the alarm hasn't gone off.'

She'd buried her head into my hair and then pulled away, planting a kiss on top of my head.

'I won't tell anyone if you don't. Come on.'

Mum pulled me to my feet, adjusting the fabric wrapped around me so I wouldn't trip and hand in hand we'd descended the stairs. As we approached the sitting room door I'd turned to look at her and she'd nodded at me to push open the door.

Even in the semi-gloom I could see the presents around the tree and to one side a wooden desk and a little blue chair, similar to the one I had at school. My hands had flown up to my face.

'Shall we have a peek inside?'

Mum led me by the hand and stood, now shivering slightly as the chill in the air took hold. I stood with my hand hovering over the hinged lid, painted in a bold blue colour to match the plastic chair. I wanted to fling it open but I was scared. Scared that my dream would fall apart because I'd thought of nothing else since I'd written my letter to Santa. I had often dreamt of sitting on that chair with a pen in my hand calling out the names of my imaginary class.

Even though Mum was rubbing her arms to keep the chill at bay I hesitated and the seconds passed. Then slowly, very slowly my fingers hooked around the edge of the lid and I lifted it high in the air, half-afraid to look inside.

And there it was and that was all I needed to know. Mum led me back to bed, tucking me in and planting a kiss on my forehead.

'He didn't forget, Mum,' I half-whispered, fighting to keep my eyes open.

'Santa knows what a good girl you are, Tia. Now get some sleep so you aren't too tired to set up your school in the morning. After all, you have a class of dolls and teddies who are counting on you to teach them everything you know, my precious little one.'

Her voice had faded as sleep finally claimed me. And in my dream, it was as if I could feel her looking over me and I was that small child once more. But the gut-wrenching sadness I felt on awakening has left me in dread of the next memory that will be triggered.

Ironically, the interviews are going well, though, and there is plenty to engage the readers and give them food for thought. The only little blip is when I do the one-to-one with Veronica. She makes a reference to children at one point and I sense that the decision not to start a family is a sensitive topic. As it is totally outside the brief and none of my business, it isn't something we cover when it is Liam's turn. However, when people chatter away quite happily it's often what they don't say that stands out like a little red flag. Liam never once mentions children, in any context. For him, keeping the romance alive is about the wonderful experiences he and Veronica share together on their many travels. I have the distinct impression that his forward plans extend way into the future. Could there be trouble brewing in paradise, I wonder.

Anyway, it's time to watch the YouTube video of Veronica and Liam's trip to Lapland last Christmas. I sit back in my chair with a cup of coffee and a bar of chocolate within easy reach. My goodness, they certainly like their video footage, that's for sure. Liam has quite a gallery going on here. I click on the one entitled *It's Christmassssss*.

The opening shot shows heavy snow and in the distance is a log cabin surrounded by tall pine trees. As the camera moves closer to pick up the detail, there's a light on a small post next to the cabin and a warm glow shines out from the windows either side of the door.

Suddenly Liam jumps into view, arms outstretched, wearing black snow gear, including the goggles.

'Welcome to our Christmas adventure. Come on in; the fire is lit.'

Whoever is doing the filming follows Liam as the door to the log cabin is thrown open and we step inside. The cabin is a good size and the screen immediately zooms in onto the log fire flickering away nicely in the open fireplace. In the next shot, Liam and Veronica are sitting on the rug in front of the fire, raising up their mugs in a toast.

'To a wonderful Christmas full of lots more hot chocolate with marshmallows, sleigh rides and the hunt for the Aurora Borealis.'

There's laughter and a hubbub of general chatter in the background. As the video continues two other couples appear at various times and if there was ever an advert to entice you into booking a snow holiday, this is it.

There are shots of huskies lying in the snow, presumably before and after a run, and in between a few moments of film of a sleigh ride. But in other shots Veronica can be seen cuddling a very young, husky pup with a snowy white coat. The look on her face is one of pure delight.

I can only imagine how wonderful it must be to experience Christmas in a place that is a veritable winter wonderland. The video contains shots of reindeer, snowshoeing, cross country skiing, snowmobiling and ice skating. There's even a drinks party in the sauna at one point.

But when the camera zooms in on the Aurora Borealis, that's something else entirely. Liam gives a commentary all the way through several minutes of footage. It's after one a.m. and they're out on the snowmobiles for the third night in a row to chase the elusive northern lights. It seems they've been watching a faint green glow that is low down on the horizon, for quite a while. The point at which filming recommences the heavens are full of stars, in front of which curtains of green light, infused with almost a purple hue giving it a 3D effect, dance in the sky. It's one of the weirdest, but most awe-inspiring things I've ever seen.

I take a couple of test screen shots and I'm sure it's going to be possible to grab a few of these for the article.

Having drained my coffee that chocolate bar is calling to me. I sit back once more, savouring the sugar rush and close my eyes. Suddenly I'm in that log cabin and I'm looking out of the window at the deep drifts of stark white snow. Sleigh bells start to tinkle, but for some reason they sound more like cow bells. But hey, this is my daydream and I'll probably never experience either first-hand, so I go with the flow. I'm wearing a jumper covered in a blue and white snowflake design and grey, fluffy earmuffs, despite the roaring log fire. Suddenly I hear the opening lines of Chris Rea's *Driving Home for Christmas* and it conjures up memories of the winter experiences of my childhood. Several Christmases had involved a sprinkling of snow and one in particular I remember with great clarity.

Nose pressed against the window pane, I'd waited patiently for Dad to arrive home after his last working day before the holidays. Mum had promised we could take out the sledge I'd virtually forgotten existed, as it had been tucked out of sight behind the old shed for several years. It wasn't quite on a par with a Lapland experience but to a small child it was incredibly exciting and magical.

My eyes flick open. OK, I'm sold. I now have the content I need and this article is going to really jump off the page as the sort of lifestyle many people can only dream of – Clarissa is going to be delighted with it.

It takes most of the afternoon to analyse the information and make a bullet list of the salient points I want to include in the article. By that time my back is beginning to feel a little stiff and I'm in need of some fresh air.

I tidy everything away into the folders and five minutes later I'm heading down towards the beach.

There's a slight nip in the air as the sun sinks lower in the sky, although it's probably at least a couple of hours until it slips below the horizon. I turn up the collar on my jacket and dig my hands into my pockets, as I saunter along just above the waterline on the beach. The thoughts churning in my head are summed up in one word: disappointment. This isn't just about losing Mum, I realise. It's about feeling that I've wandered onto the wrong path in life and looking ahead it seems to stretch out endlessly, without any options at all for getting back on track.

I'm not naive and this isn't about wanting to be one half of *the perfect couple*, really it isn't; or letting loose the green-eyed monster, because wanting what someone else has isn't a solution – it's a complete and utter waste of time. But what really worries me is that I don't know what I want, anyway.

'Are you hungry?'

A distant voice seems to come out of nowhere and I realise that the fisherman guy has been watching me, but for how long exactly, I have no idea. I was so deep in thought I've been oblivious to his presence. I turn to walk closer to him; he seems to be preparing a brazier, layering small chunks of wood into the metal basket in front of the workshop.

'I had a good catch today and you are welcome to join me if you like fish.' He nods in the direction of a small bucket next to his seat.

'There's another chair just inside the workshop. Help yourself.'

I figure what harm can it do and, besides, if I head back the thoughts in my head are going to keep nagging away and without any distractions they'll run unchecked.

'Thanks.'

The chair is one of the old-style deckchairs you don't often see these days. It's a bit fiddly to erect, but comfortable once I lower myself into it.

I watch him from the other side of the brazier, as the smoke begins to drift down the beach and tiny red embers start to glow.

'I'm Tia, Tia Armstrong.'

'Max Hartington.'

That's all he says. I lapse into silence as I watch him laying out the fish on a large stone to begin preparing them for the fire. He takes off the heads first, then trims the fins, and starts to clean them up. He has a bottle of water next to him and when he's done he washes each one individually; then spreads them out on a tray. I'm not really sure what they are, but anything freshly caught is bound to taste good.

He finishes off with a drizzle of olive oil and a little salt and pepper, placing the tray on his temporary stone table.

'The fire's not quite ready yet, it needs to burn down a little or the fish will cook too quickly.'

Without saying anything else he disappears back inside one of the wooden cabins and returns with a wicker basket. When he places the basket on the sand next to his chair, there's a little chink.

'I have a bottle of good wine I've been saving; it was a present in return for some mackerel. Do you drink alcohol?'

I nod, as Max pours a hefty slug into two whiskey glasses and hands one of them to me.

'Well, this is lovely and a real treat.'

It's a little awkward, but I feel a toast is appropriate. I raise my glass and Max duly raises his. 'You rescued me yesterday morning and now you are cooking me supper, so I think that calls for a heartfelt thank you, Max.'

And now he's saving me from a miserable evening of depressing thoughts.

He nods, takes a large gulp of wine and sits back in his chair to watch the brazier.

The silence is actually rather relaxing, as it dawns upon me that Max is used to his own company and isn't expecting me to make idle conversation. Sitting here, instead of my mind dwelling on things I don't want to think about, I can simply enjoy the surreal uniqueness of our setting. This deserted sandy cove, flanked by the limestone cliffs, feels like a secret place to hide away from the world at large.

As the light begins to dim, Max fetches three lamps from his workshop and sets them down in a semi-circle. The soft glow against the fading light and the gentle lapping of the water on the beach is calming to the soul.

This is a little piece of heaven and something so unexpected, that I feel privileged to be here.

With the tall flames now reduced to little flickers here and there, Max places a metal grid over the top of the brazier and lifts the tray of fish on top. As the tray heats the air is filled with a tantalising smell that makes my stomach rumble. After a few minutes, he pulls two small clusters of tomatoes on the vine from the basket and adds them to the tray. The oil starts to sizzle beneath them and the sweetness as they cook adds another note to the orchestra of flavours assaulting my nose. This man knows how to cook, that's for sure.

Within minutes Max hands me a melamine picnic plate the size of a platter and a metal fork.

'The bones shouldn't be a problem, as the flesh will just fall away.'

There is a large, flat fish and several smaller ones, a chunk of unbuttered baguette and a cluster of tomatoes. The smell is amazing.

I wait until Max has prepared his own platter and we begin eating in silence. Well, I say silence but I can't stop myself from making appreciative 'mmm' noises as I eat. It's embarrassing but it's involuntary. I don't think fish has ever tasted this good to me, before.

'Turbot and brill,' Max throws the words out, breaking the silence.

'I'm not sure I've eaten either before, but Max, this is amazing. You could be a chef.'

He grunts.

'I could be a lot of things, Tia. I have been a lot of things but I've not always been proud of myself. The simple life is where I'm at now and it suits me.'

I look up, surprised at his honesty and feeling that he isn't expecting a response. We continue to eat in silence until we're done and my stomach is feeling very happy.

Max stacks the platters onto the tray and ferries them back inside the cabin. Before lowering himself into his seat, he pours out a little more wine.

'You're very kind,' I reflect.

He looks directly at me, as if surprised by my comment.

'Sometimes folk need a bit of company. And that includes me. I'm out of practice, is the truth of the matter.'

He knows nothing at all about me and yet he senses something isn't right. Maybe he connects on some level with the turmoil that is still within me.

'It's a crazy world, isn't it, Max? We find ourselves in situations we never anticipated and it can all become a little overwhelming at times. I like the peace and the solitude here: it's cathartic.'

We lapse back into silence for a good five minutes before Max starts speaking.

'If you ask me, the whole world has become too darned materialistic. Money doesn't necessarily bring happiness. I know that only too well.'

I'm not sure how to acknowledge that and when it becomes obvious that he's going to continue, I sit back, content to see where this goes.

'When you have everything you think you want and wake up one morning realising it's all window dressing and that inside you're very unhappy, well, it opens your eyes.'

I nod and he raises his glass, the soft light from the lamps sending little glistening shards of rainbow light, bouncing off the crystal-clear liquid inside.

I give him a resigned smile and raise my glass back at him.

'I'm not sure I could have understood that a year ago, but at this moment in time I know exactly where you are coming from.'

He nods, sadly, as if he's sorry for me and whatever situation I find myself in. For some inexplicable reason, that touches my heart.

'Losing someone you love is life-changing. Realising you don't actually have a life is shocking.'

That weathered forehead with a lifetime of deep-set frown lines etched upon it, acknowledges my anguish.

'Are you running away, or recharging your batteries?'

'Both, I think. I'm usually office-based, but as long as I have a phone and the internet I have everything I need. I'm easing myself back in after a period away and London would be a bit much to face at the moment.'

'Ah. Wise lady. Get yourself back onto an even keel and you'll be ready to re-enter the war zone.'

I laugh and he smiles.

'War zone? Was it that bad?'

He purses his lips, a hint of playfulness reflected on his face.

'You really want to hear the sorry tale of a man who ends up living in a cabin on the beach?'

'Try me.'

In the twilight, I can see there's a twinkle in his eye.

'Well, here's the short version. Met someone, fell in love, ignored the warning signs and got married. What followed wasn't hearts and flowers, let's say. Messy divorce, family disowned me and eventually I took sanctuary in the only place I could connect with.'

I study his face and there's no sign of anger, or sadness; merely a wicked sparkle in those eyes of his.

'And yet you're happy?'

'Happiest I've ever been. I don't judge other people and there's no one here, now, to judge me.'

There's a story here with hidden depths, but Max isn't an interviewee.

'Well, there are many who would envy your state of happiness, that's for sure.'

Max tips his head back and emits a raucous laugh, which seems to echo around the cove, but makes no comment. Maybe that's something for another night.

'Am I trespassing when I wander down here? I assumed the private beach belonged to the cottage.'

I watch his reaction closely, but he seems chilled.

'It did, once upon a time. I feel "ownership" is a rather misleading term. I'm a custodian of the land for my lifetime only, so who am I to stop anyone enjoying what nature has to offer? Besides, it's rare to see anyone strolling along Holly Cove beach, whatever the season.'

And yet I sort of feel he was half-prepared to share his meal tonight, maybe even hoping I'd take an early evening stroll.

'Is today a special occasion?' It's a stab in the dark, but this man is so hard to read.

He pauses momentarily, then nods.

'It's my sixty-fifth birthday today. Best party I ever had.'

He winks at me and I begin laughing, acknowledging that sometimes things really do happen for a reason. I guess tonight it threw together two people from very different walks of life, but who both happened to be in need of a little company.

8

Stir Crazy

I sleep so soundly that I wish I'd set the alarm, as I don't wake up until just after eight a.m. this morning. Going to bed on a full stomach and with all the fresh air, I can barely recall my head hitting the pillow.

As soon as I finish washing up the breakfast dishes, I settle myself down to work. Hayley hasn't been in touch to confirm any more interview slots, so I have uninterrupted time to concentrate on fleshing out the first article.

By lunch time I run out of steam, or maybe that's the ability to continually enthuse about a couple who are high achievers and have the enviable quality of making it all seem so easy. Their ability to hold down lucrative careers, travel the world and have almost constant fun together, without making a wrong decision, seems too good to be true. Unless either one of them comes to feel, at some stage in the future, that something is missing. They will reach a time, no doubt, when they have to slow down and what then? Will a more normal, day to day existence be too mundane to keep their relationship alive and spontaneous?

I find myself thinking about Max. Disowned by his family, he said. That's harsh and yet he's happy enough – or seems to be.

I decide to forego a walk on the beach, not wanting Max to feel I'm always going to be turning up on his doorstep now I know it's his domain. But without a vehicle I feel disadvantaged here. Then I remember the receipt for the taxi and I go in search of it. On the reverse side is a mobile number and the words '24-hour Taxi Service – no trip too small.'

'Hi, I wondered if it was possible to book a taxi for about an hour's time.'

I'm pretty sure it's the same guy who dropped me off before.

'Yeah, I can do that. Beach View?'

'Um, yes.' That's a little unnerving.

'It's the accent. Where are you going?'

'Well, I don't know the area, but on the map there's a place referred to as Mumbles. I want to look around the shops for an hour and then perhaps you could pick me up at some convenient point and bring me back?'

'See you in an hour, then.'

*

93

It turns out that Mumbles is less than a couple of miles away and only a ten-minute drive. Five pounds covers the fare and a small tip. We don't make any small talk and it's a relief, as I want to concentrate on the scenery and try to get my bearings.

An hour isn't enough to do Mumbles village justice, as it's larger than it looked when I Googled it. A lovely mix of coffee shops, high-end fashion, arts and crafts shops, and the usual takeaways and restaurants, is a delightful surprise.

When I arrive back at the car park, I see the taxi is already waiting. The engine is ticking over and even from a distance I can hear the radio blaring out some music with an ominously thudding beat. The driver catches sight of me in his rear-view mirror and the noise disappears as I open the rear passenger door.

'Do you do tours?'

He spins in his seat. 'What sort of tours?'

This guy isn't exactly easy to talk to, that's for sure.

'The route between Caswell Bay and Langland Bay looks like it has amazing views. Is it possible to take a detour and go back that way?'

He shrugs his shoulders. 'Whatever you like.'

As he pulls away I settle back, looking forward to a leisurely drive along the scenic route. Except that I don't even catch a glimpse of the sea until we are literally back at Caswell Bay. As we drive past the small promenade, then take the next turning on the left down to Beach View Cottage, I'm feeling cheated.

'Is that it?'

The taxi pulls up alongside the cottage and he kills the engine. We've been in the car for about fifteen minutes, tops.

'Yep. The scenic route has to be done on foot. It's a walk along the limestone cliffs. That will be eight pounds fifty.'

Really? I mean, he couldn't have explained to me that the road goes inland through housing estates, rather than hugging the coast?

'Keep the change.'

'Thanks, here's your receipt.'

I try not to snatch it out of his hand, although I'm sorely tempted to do so, as I feel annoyed and a little silly. Maybe I should have zoomed in on the map and traced the road. But he could just as easily have enlightened me.

'How would I get to Caswell Bay if I was on foot?'

'There is a path through the woods, but I wouldn't recommend it for someone who doesn't know the area.'

Helpful. Not. Oh, well.

He's staring at me. What have I said, now?

'I'm about to clock-off as the dog needs his walk. I could be back here with him in fifteen minutes and you're welcome to tag along.'

Oh, maybe I was a little too quick to judge him, after all. I'm a customer going from A to B and I can't expect him to act as a tour guide; so this is a kind gesture.

'Thanks. I gather there's a café at the Langland Bay end, so the coffee and cake will be on me.'

'No problem. See you shortly.'

*

I scan my emails and check my phone, but there's nothing there that can't wait. I still seem to be out of the loop a bit, and that suits me at the moment. I don't feel I have to respond instantly, or that anyone expects me to do so.

A quick brush of my hair and I tie it back, as no doubt there will be quite a breeze on the cliff tops. I change my jeans, dig out my walking boots and pull on a medium weight sweatshirt over my teeshirt. Grabbing a lightweight jacket on my way out, as I'm locking the front door the taxi is already back. The driver opens the rear door and a reddish-brown and black ball of fur dashes out of the car and disappears into some low shrubs.

'Sid, come back here, you daft mutt!'

Great, I know the dog's name but I have no idea about his owner's name.

'What breed is he?' With his little pointed ears and short tail, he definitely isn't a mongrel but I can't place the breed. He looks a bit like an Airedale.

'I believe he's a Welsh terrier. I'm not sure he likes me too much, to be honest. And he needs a lot of walking.'

Did he steal him, I wonder? I guess not, because Sid comes haring back, wagging his little tail. He seems happy enough to wait while his collar is attached to a retractable dog lead. I give him a gentle rub on his back, noticing that the soft, fluffy top coat has an inner, more wiry layer beneath it. He's a lovely dog and obviously demands a lot of attention.

'He's not yours, then?'

It's awkward talking to someone when you don't know their name, or anything about them and you are just about to enter the woods together. But Sid is straining on his leash, impatient to run on ahead and I speed up to tuck in behind them.

'No, he belongs to a friend.' The guy half turns his head as he speaks so that his voice carries over his shoulder.

After a minute or two, Sid settles down and his pace begins to even out.

'Try to create a little slack on the lead; it will make him less anxious and less inclined to pull.' We had a short-haired terrier when I was a child, Miffy we called her. She was always overexcited at walk time, but usually settled down pretty quickly.

He adjusts the leash to allow Sid to dictate the length and once he realises he's not being held back, he slows to a trot and his interest turns to scanning the area for wildlife.

'Great tip, thanks. I'm repaying a big favour, so aside from doing some odd jobs around the farm, I'm also the newly-designated dog walker.'

It's the first thing he's said so far that makes him sound reasonably pleasant. As we're now totally surrounded by quite dense woodland, at least I don't feel quite so uncomfortable in his company. We pass a sign that says *private property*.

'This isn't exactly a path, is it?' I ask, curious as it's very apparent there is no well-worn track to guide us forward and the sign indicates we're trespassing.

'No. It's a short-cut through to Caswell Bay, which is the other side of this cove. Only the residents of Beach View Cottage would be likely to walk through here. Holly Cove is private and there's nowhere to park, except for alongside the cottage. Strangers to the area would never be tempted to stop and investigate. Besides, it's not named on the map, but if you look closely you will see it is there. If it wasn't for the way the headland juts out here to cut it off, it would adjoin the beach at Caswell.'

It doesn't take long before we're descending quite a steep bit of track and as soon as we are clear of the woods, we have a spectacular view looking out over Caswell Bay.

Sheltered beneath limestone cliffs and with holly and pine-clad slopes, the large swathe of sandy beach is picturesque. Visible on our left, I recognise the small promenade and the cluster of huts and kiosks you see when driving along Caswell Bay Road. What you don't see from that viewpoint are the giant fingers of rock that extend out onto the beach in several places. One particular stretch seems to almost divide the beach into separate coves. At high tide, it would make access between the two impossible.

'Now that's what I call a view,' I say, just a little breathlessly.

Sid is straining on his leash again. I carefully follow on behind them until our feet are finally resting on the sandy beach.

'Do we need to worry about the tide? I mean, our path won't be cut off, will it?'

'No, it's low tide now and high tide isn't until after eight tonight. So, this is your first time here?'

We walk in step quite comfortably, now, side by side. Sid is happy to trot along a few paces in front. His head darts back and forth as seagulls swoop and land on the muddy flats before us. There are quite a lot of people milling about, but because the expanse is so vast it still looks empty.

'I'm Tia, by the way.'

He turns his head to look at me. 'I know. I'm Nic.'

Well, that kills the conversation for a while and I'm glad when we reach the end of the beach and begin the long climb up to the cliff path. My head is buzzing with questions. If Max owns Holly Cove, did he sell the cottage to Nic? How long has Nic lived there? And why on earth didn't Nic say something on the day he picked me up from the station?

The climb isn't arduous, but you do find yourself puffing and panting a bit. Certainly, of the straggle of walkers heading in both directions, most are walking in silence and in single file. Here and there are benches for people to stop and catch their breath, or simply enjoy the view.

Right up on the top of the headland the ground is covered with low-growing gorse and bracken. Rabbits skitter through every now and again, their little white tails bobbing up between the wind-blown shrubs.

Nic shortens the leash and nods in the direction of a seat looking out to sea, a few feet away from the cliff edge. The wind is battering my ears, but it's blowing against us and it's a bit of a fight to push forward. We sit and he pulls a shallow container filled with water from his pocket, taking off the lid and placing it on the floor next to the bench. Sid's tail wags as he starts to lap it up. This man can't be all that bad to be so considerate.

'That's Caswell to the right and to the left is Langland Bay. It's always windy here because you catch it from two directions. It's something, though, isn't it?'

My eyes squint a little, as the sun is bouncing off the white crests of the waves and sending out blindingly sharp glints of light. It must be magnificent in winter, although dangerous if the wind is in the wrong direction, or after heavy rainfall when the grass was slippery. I can't even begin to imagine how far the cliff drops down to meet the sea beneath our feet. If someone strayed too close to the edge, would it be possible to survive a fall like that, I wonder.

As soon as Sid has finished, we move on. The path dips and climbs as it winds its way around to the next bay. From some of the lower spots you can see the water up close, as little inlets where the rock has worn and fallen away over time have eroded the cliff inland. In those places the drop is probably only twenty, or thirty, feet. Then you find yourself climbing again and the sea is way below you, the sheer cliff face dropping steeply away, out of sight. But for the most part the path is a very safe distance away from the edge. Although it looks a long way, it only takes about forty-five minutes before a place called the Langland's Brasserie appears, rather welcomingly, in view.

The last part of the trek is a comfortable slope and before we know it, we're walking across the terrace and collapse, with a sigh of relief, into the bistro chairs.

'They do a great afternoon tea; fresh scones, cake and Earl Grey.'

Hint taken and when the waiter appears I place an order for two. Sitting back in my chair I keep my eyes straight ahead, desperately trying to appear as if I'm concentrating on taking in the surroundings. This bay is much smaller and the Brasserie sits lower within it. It's also rather conveniently sheltered by the land that rises up behind it. It's quite busy and we were lucky to find a table.

'Most popular time of the day,' Nic offers. 'People tend to set off for a walk either after lunch, or mid-afternoon and then head back. The seafood is good here and it's worth booking a table and doing dinner.'

I'm not sure how to handle this now he's lost his reserved, rather frosty attitude. I sneak a glance at him while he's leant over giving Sid a pat.

He's tall, six-foot-one maybe, with short dark hair and pale blue eyes. I mean, he's a good-looking guy and I'm guessing he's probably late twenties, early thirties. He's the sort of guy you wouldn't expect to be living on his own.

'OK. I know this is kind of awkward and I do owe you an apology,' he admits.

He catches me staring at him and it's too late to pretend that wasn't precisely what I was doing.

'I think that maybe we started off on the wrong foot, that's all, so no apology needed. It's taking me a while to get used to my new environment and it's quite an adjustment. I'm... um... a little sensitive, at the moment.'

Oh no, why did I say that? Too much information, Tia. Keep it simple.

'Same here,' he laughs. 'I'm not sure farm life suits me, if I'm honest, so major adjustment for me, too. And, no offence meant, Sid, but dog walking isn't my favourite pursuit, either.'

He pats Sid affectionately, or maybe, a little apologetically. He doesn't have animals of his own, then, but I already knew that as the cottage is way too pristine.

'I feel bad, knowing I've thrown you out of your beautiful cottage. It's a lot to give up for six weeks and I really appreciate it.'

I mean what I say, I know it's a transaction but it's still a hardship by the sound of it.

'Well, that's generous of you. But I need the money as the roof needs some attention before next winter and the central heating boiler won't creak along for much longer.'

'Ah, I see.'

The waiter returns with a large tray and what looks like way too much food for two people to eat. Nic pours the tea, while I arrange the various plates on the table and dispense with the tray.

'Looks delicious,' I remark and see that Nic has already piled a spoonful of strawberry jam onto his

103

scone. He begins ladling on some clotted cream.

'Thanks for the treat.' With that he lifts it to his mouth and takes a huge bite. Sid looks equally happy as he takes the small piece of dry scone from Nic's other hand which he has slipped, rather discreetly, under the table.

'My pleasure and thank you for allowing me to tag along.'

9

I Have a Plan

When I arrive back late afternoon I'm half-tempted to saunter down to the beach, to see if Max is around. But all this healthy fresh air and exercise is energising and the files on the table are calling out to me. I blitz my inbox and then concentrate on writing up the first draft of Veronica and Liam's story.

A long email from Hayley confirms that she's done well setting up the Skype meetings, although she expressed her apologies for the fact that they weren't as evenly spaced as I would have preferred. I won't have time to finish what I'm working on before I'm due to call the second couple, but that's the way it goes.

By late evening I've taken it as far as I can, although it will need a lot of polishing before I can even think of letting Clarissa take a glance at it. But it's enough to put me in a frame of mind for a cup of hot chocolate with marshmallows, by way of a reward. I change into my PJs and while I'm waiting for the kettle to boil I pull up one of my music compilations on the laptop. With strains of John Newman and Northern soul in the background, I take myself off to the sitting room.

Curling up on the sofa I notice I have a couple of missed calls and a text. Both Hayley and my brother rang earlier this afternoon and when I open the text it's from Hayley.

> Tried phoning you. Checking U R OK. Found any interesting strangers on the beach? Text me when you pick this up.

Harrumph. Well, Max is interesting but I'm not into older guys. Strangers on a beach, indeed.

> I'm fine. Focusing on work. No interesting strangers to report. Hope this isn't interrupting your fav programme, if it is serves u right for being curious. Speak tomorrow and stop worrying.

It's too late to call Will now, so that will have to keep until tomorrow. At least he remembered to phone on the mobile, so I guess he was listening to me when we spoke the other day.

It's strange, but when I first arrived here it did cross my mind that it might feel a little eerie at night, but that's not the case at all. But it is rather nice knowing that my neighbour, Max, is almost on the doorstep.

And what a surprise Nic has turned out to be. He's a bit strange, sort of blowing hot and cold. Long, awkward silences stretched between us, to which he seemed to be oblivious. Then when he did say something, he appeared to be quite comfortable talking to me. There's a story there, lurking behind those pale blue eyes. I think it might be the story of a broken heart and love lost. I know that isn't quite the slant Clarissa intended, but maybe it's just what's needed to put things into perspective. And Nic did say he needed funds to do work on the cottage. Perhaps I'll invite him around for a drink and a chat one evening, and ask whether he'd be interested in being interviewed for the feature.

But first, I need to find out a little more. Hopefully, when Olwen calls in tomorrow I can grab the opportunity to ask her a few harmless little questions about him.

As I grab my empty mug and walk towards the door, my eyes flick over the floor-to-ceiling bookshelves to the left-hand side of the doorway. Meticulously arranged in height order, with the larger books at the bottom, I notice that one book at eye-level seems to have been pushed above the row of books and lies horizontally just below the shelf above. It's too small a gap to ease it out and it almost looks hidden. I have to pull out two of the books beneath it in order to get my hand in. It's *The Notebook by Nicholas Sparks*. I know the story, having read it several years ago and needing almost a whole box of tissues to get me through it. A story of tenderness and love, it is both heart-warming and heartbreaking.

Tucking it under my arm, I turn off the light and, after washing out my mug I make my way upstairs. Why would Nic have this book amongst his collection? He doesn't strike me as the sort of man who reads love stories and it's unlike anything else he has on his bookshelves.

I clean my teeth and climb into bed. As I reach across to turn out the bedside light I stop and, picking up the book, ease open the cover. It wasn't a gift as there's no inscription but I can see by the creases in the spine it's been well read, probably more than once. Someone loved this book and it meant something to them. I leaf through, wondering if perhaps there is a bookmark, or anything that might give some sort of clue. People often use old tickets, or whatever happens to be at hand, but nothing drops from the pages. And then I see it, written in pencil on the very last page, the blank page they insert before the back cover. It's faint, but legible:

I know you are crying, you always do. I'm here to hold your hand and wipe away your tears. Always.

I wonder who wrote that poignant note? Has this been passed on from person to person, maybe ending up here in Nic's collection more by chance, than selection? Or did it belong to someone who shared this cottage with Nic, but who doesn't live here anymore?

Whatever it's about, the words are rather haunting and, clearly, whoever wrote the message was well aware of the impact of this story on the reader. Well, maybe

Olwen will know if a woman has ever lived here with Nic in the past. If it's a sensitive topic then maybe my proposal won't go down well – money, or no money. The last thing I want to do is offend him in any way, so I'd better tread carefully.

I stifle a yawn and know it's time to snuggle down and let sleep overtake my busy thoughts. Sometimes I really wish I didn't have this inquisitive nature, but then I suppose that's what attracted me to journalism, in the first place.

*

I awaken once again feeling refreshed and full of energy. A quick run along the beach and back is exhilarating, as this morning the nip in the air is enough to make the salty spray sting a little. And the breeze coming off the water makes the waves choppy and angry looking. As I run past the cabins there's no sign of Max, but there's a little curl of smoke rising up from the metal chimney in the second cabin, before it's whisked away and quickly dissipates.

I begin editing the draft article on Veronica and Liam, as I seem to have made them sound a little stiff. There was a lot of positive body language going on in their joint interview. Maybe I've focused a little too much on the materialistic side and the exciting life they lead because of that. It's easy to forget that the thread that holds it all together is the love they have for each other. I guess the words I read inscribed in that book last night struck a chord with me and I look at what I've written with a fresh set of eyes.

Shortly after nine I decide to call the office. I want to run my idea past Clarissa and I really need to reassure Hayley that I'm doing OK; her text yesterday left me feeling a little guilty for not having been in touch.

'Hi girl, how are you doing?'

'Well, it's good to hear your voice and I'm fine. Clarissa and Finlay had a falling out, yesterday. He was in early this morning and he hasn't moved from his desk. Sorry, I mean, your desk.'

Ah, the reality begins to bite.

'Poor Finlay. Was it very public?'

'In the middle of the general office, no less. You could hear a pin drop, as everyone froze. It wasn't very pleasant when she tore into him. But in all honesty, he deserved it as he took it upon himself to change the layout of one of the features without checking with her, first.'

I hear myself draw in a sharp breath between my teeth, as I imagine her reaction. No one questions Clarissa's editorial decisions. The magazine is her baby and her life. And she's good at what she does. It's a tough industry and it spawns tough individuals, people who have a lot of self-belief and can also make things happen. These days it's a fight for survival and under

Clarissa's leadership we've not only survived, but incredibly we've continued to increase our market share. Perhaps my job is safer than I think.

'He'll learn and that's a mistake he probably won't make again. By the way, I might have found a suitable candidate to replace the couple who dropped out. Could you send me the paperwork with the fee details so I know what the maximum is that I can offer him?'

'Him? Shouldn't it be *them*?'

'Well, I have an idea but I need to run it past Clarissa first.'

'And is this an interesting *him*?'

I can't stop myself from letting out a little chuckle.

'Not in that way. He's a bit of a loner and I think there might be a broken heart hidden from view.'

'Ah, shame. But at least you are meeting the locals. I did wonder if it was going to be a little too isolated for you.'

'In an ironic twist, Clarissa was right. If she was worried the little depression I'd sunk into would affect my work, then putting me in a totally new and surreal environment gives me plenty to occupy my mind. I have to admire the woman, despite my reservations. She knows how to get the best out of her employees. And while I remember, can you make sure the photographer emails me before he visits any of the interviewees, so I can specify a few particular shots I need him to get?

Otherwise this very Christmassy feature will end up with no glitter at all.'

'Will do; sorry, I should have known that. It's not easy thinking of Christmas at this time of the year. Anyway, I'm glad this idea of Clarissa's was the right thing to do, even though her motive wasn't purely about what's best for you. She's just finished her call, I'll put you through. Good luck.'

While I'm waiting, my ears are subjected to the jangly sounds of something I don't recognise, but is probably in the charts. It makes me feel old and out of touch not being able to name the artist. I realise that in the last few years I've cut virtually everything out of my life if it didn't involve work. When was the last time I dated, even? Sadly, I'd have to give that a lot of thought—

'Tia, good to hear from you. How is the Gower Coast?'

She's in a good mood and at least that bodes well.

'It's great, just the tonic I needed. I've begun interviewing and am working on the first article.'

'Any ideas yet for the replacement couple?'

As usual, straight to the point.

'I'm looking at options.'

'Already? You have settled in quickly and hit the ground running, by the sound of it. I will admit I'm missing you here, but when you get back I need you to be one hundred per cent fit.'

Stable, is the word she chose not to use.

112

'I was kicking around the idea of coming at it from a slightly different angle to wrap up the feature. Judging by the first couple, I think you'll be delighted as they are literally the perfect *grab life and run with it* type. The sort of thing many people dream of achieving. With the interviews lined up there's a fair spread of age and social status, so we're pretty much covered for the widest audience possible. How about turning it around for that last one and looking at love lost, as well? The impact it has on the way someone approaches the dawning of a new year?'

There's a moment or two of silence as Clarissa mulls over the idea. Her brain will be evaluating the pros and cons like a microchip processes information.

'I like it. If you can make it work, we'll go with it. But I'll reserve my judgement until I've seen the finished article.'

'That's a deal; I appreciate your trust, Clarissa, thank you.'

10

Reeling Him In

Checking the schedule Hayley sent me, I have the first of the next round of interviews this afternoon. I'm talking to the guy first, as his partner isn't available until Friday. I pull their file up and begin trawling through, making notes as I go.

A couple of hours pass before my back begins to ache and I have to stretch my legs. I wander into the sitting room and glance out of the window, but the beach is deserted, as usual. In fact, if I saw anyone I didn't recognise, I'd probably be concerned. I spot something moving out of the corner of my eye and I see Olwen's car pulling up adjacent to the cottage. I wave, walk over to unlock the door and go back into the kitchen to pop the kettle on.

'Morning. Thought I'd come a little early and give the place a quick clean. Just a dust and a mop through. I won't disturb your work, I promise and I'll be as quiet as I can.'

I'm not even sure it needs doing, but Olwen has a job and I don't want her to feel I don't appreciate her time.

'Great, thanks. Do you have a key, in case I'm not here at any time?'

She manoeuvres a small trolley on wheels, laden with cleaning materials, into the corner of the kitchen. Slipping off her coat, she takes a seat at the table and I place a mug of coffee in front of her.

'Yes, Nic had one cut for me. He was surprised when I approached him, but pleased, I think. At that point, he wasn't sure what sort of tenant you'd be. He's more relaxed now you're here.'

'You've spoken to him?'

'Oh, I see him all the time. Besides driving a taxi, he's also a reporter for the local paper. He's into photography, as well and I think he sells some of his photos. Quite an interesting man, all round.'

I take my mug and join Olwen at the table. This is just the opportunity I'd been hoping for and I'm going to grab it while I can.

'Nic kindly let me accompany him and Sid on their walk to Langland Bay, the other day. It was a nice little trek.'

Olwen smiles, knowingly.

'Lots of long silences, I suspect. He's a man who enjoys his own company and his own thoughts.'

The look she casts my way is meaningful.

'To be honest, I'm surprised he doesn't have a partner in tow. The demographic for the area show that the females outnumber the males.'

Olwen nods, impressed. 'I suspected as much. We do have a lot of single ladies, but quite a few are in the wrong age group for Nic. They wish they weren't, of course.'

She beams at me and I agree, he is very easy on the eye.

'Has he always lived here on his own? There never was a woman to add those little feminine touches?'

For the first time, Olwen looks a little uncomfortable.

'Oh, sorry. That's just my enquiring mind. He's a very nice guy and I couldn't stop myself from wondering what his story is; he seems the type of person who needs a challenge and his life here is a little, well, basic.'

I'm trying not to imply anything that might possibly offend Olwen, but Nic is capable of more than being a taxi driver and writing for a small local paper.

'When he bought the cottage, about three years ago, he wasn't in a good place. He didn't mix at first and no one really knew anything much about him. He's a good man, though, and other people's troubles don't go by him unnoticed. There are a few elderly people close by he calls in on regularly to check they're OK. There aren't many strangers who settle in as quickly as Nic has and that takes effort.'

'But Max owned the cottage before Nic arrived?'

A frown travels across Olwen's brow and I get the impression that she's choosing her words carefully.

'Yes, but no one was even aware it was on the market and it was a complete surprise when Nic moved in. Max began building the wooden cabins a few years prior. He'd started coming here quite regularly to fish, mainly at weekends. Having been in the Navy, I suppose his love of the sea will always be with him. I think the cottage had been in Max's family for years, though, although it was hardly ever used. Well, except for a few years back when a young woman stayed here for maybe six months. I think she was convalescing but no one ever saw her out and about, and locals don't trespass on private land. That's a big no-no here. In general, the family kept themselves to themselves and it was a Friday night to Sunday afternoon thing. It was a waste of a lovely property, really.

'Gradually, the place began to look very sad indeed from the outside. I think inside was a lot worse, though. Nic has worked tirelessly, doing most of the renovation himself. I guess when Max decided to retire early and his beach home was ready, it was a great solution. A cottage in disrepair requires a lot of time and effort to bring it back to life. Max seems happy enough with his situation now and Nic likes to keep busy.'

She shrugs her shoulders as it isn't easy to understand the lifestyle Max has chosen, particularly when he could have been working on the cottage instead and have every home comfort. You can see the sea and the beach from every window. Living in a cabin is akin to living in a caravan, I should imagine.

'He doesn't work, then?'

'No. He fishes and he has quite a large allotment up behind the farm. He isn't totally self–sufficient, of course, but he does a little exchange here and there. It's more a lifestyle choice, I think. Someone who can afford a new Range Rover doesn't have to count the pennies.'

My eyebrows shoot up in surprise.

'I didn't think he had transport.'

'You haven't noticed it parked up on the top road, in the lay-by just before the farm?'

'I assumed that was owned by someone in the big houses set back from the road. I notice there's only a dirt track leading up to one of them.'

'No, Max bought it last year, brand new. Before that he had the old model. Like I said, I don't think money is an issue, but I know that I'd rather be surrounded by bricks and mortar, with a real roof over my head, than in a wooden structure. Right, time I did my job. It'll take about an hour and then I'll leave you in peace.'

I make myself a second coffee and return to my files. Darren and Paige are in their mid-twenties, having met at university. Paige is six months pregnant with their first child and they are due to be married in two weeks' time. For some reason, I find this scenario more engaging than the first couple's situation. It's not new love, exactly, but it has the promise of excitement, I suppose. Lots of firsts taking place and so much to look forward to, I find it inspiring.

Olwen is true to her word and I hardly notice her working away, but after she leaves the place has a sparkle to it. I know I can look forward to slipping between those freshly laundered sheets tonight.

*

What a great day. The interview with Darren was filled with optimism and energy. They have a big mortgage on a house they will outgrow probably sooner, rather than later, but Darren has just been promoted to his first managerial position. I don't think he uttered one sentence that didn't include reference to Paige and I can't wait to interview her on Friday.

As I shut down the laptop for the day, I'm rather pleased to see that it's only four o'clock. After the little chat with Olwen I have more questions than answers about Nic, going around and around inside my head.

It's still dry outside but the trees confirm the wind hasn't abated, so I wrap up and head off for a walk up to the farm. I figure it's a legitimate excuse to check out the farm shop and maybe buy a few items. By now Nic will no doubt have finished his shift and, hopefully, be back from walking Sid.

I'm living proof that the more exercise you take, the easier it becomes and today the walk up to the road is pleasant. I manage an even pace without having to stop once to catch my breath. The farm is only a short walk along the main road and it's not a very busy one so it's easy to cross.

However, I walk on a bit further to the lay-by to check out Max's vehicle. In gleaming metallic black, it's a large beast. It is a puzzle, as it's at odds with the simple life Max seems to have embraced. He could easily ride around in a tidy little pickup that cost a tenth of this status symbol. I notice there's a towbar on the back, but a vehicle this heavy would sink into the sand, as there's no concrete jetty at the cove. I've never looked closely at his boat, but maybe that too is a costly indulgence and not a charming little old fishing vessel. The workshop is probably twenty-foot wide, and together with the trailer it sits on, it does seem to take up virtually the whole length. If, as I suspect, the boat is of a good spec, then together with the Range Rover that could equate to almost a hundred thousand pounds. Is Max a smuggler?

OK, slow down that mind of yours, lady. That's one step too far. Anyway, you're on a mission today and it has nothing at all to do with Max.

When I enter the farm shop it's empty. There's a long meat counter, a dozen chest freezers with everything from fruit and vegetables to homemade cheesecake, all bearing the same logo and brand.

An older man appears from a doorway behind the counter.

'How can I help?'

Everything is very pristine and as I survey the rows of beef, pork and poultry, I feel the urge to cook.

'Do you have fillet steaks? And a chicken, medium size is fine.'

'I have a nice piece of fillet in the fridge out back, how thick do you like your steaks cut?'

'Oh, quite generous. Enough for two people, thanks so much.'

While I'm waiting, I pull out a baked New York-style cheesecake from the dessert section and go in search of a bag of frozen mixed fruit. If my plan works I need the meal to be simple, as I want to concentrate on the conversation.

On my way back to the counter I pick up a jar of olives, a crusty baguette and a bag of potatoes.

The guy returns with a white plastic carrier bag. 'Two steaks and one chicken. I'll grab another bag for your other items.'

As I'm waiting, the shop door opens and Nic steps inside.

'Hey, Tia, this is a surprise.'

His mouth curls up in a little smile.

'It's about time I cooked a real meal, instead of going for the simpler options. I'm taking the evening off and I'm in the mood for steak.'

'Sounds good and you've come to the right place.'

The guy is back and after I swipe my credit card and take the receipt, Nic sidles over and picks up the two bags, escorting me outside.

'Look, these are rather cumbersome for that walk back, so why don't I pop them down to you in a bit? I'll put the meat in the fridge in the meantime, as I need to change first. Sid's walk was muddier than usual as we headed over to the lake and he kept jumping up on me.'

I did wonder why Nic looked a little mud-splattered and I try my best to look sympathetic, rather than mildly amused.

'I'll tell you what, why don't you join me for dinner? The steaks are quick to cook, anyway. So there's no rush; it won't take long to get dinner ready once you arrive. Oh, do they sell wine or beer, here? I'm not sure that was on Olwen's shopping list.'

'Leave the wine to me and great, thanks. I'll see you in about an hour, then?'

'Looking forward to it.'

My stomach is doing somersaults for some reason. What if I'm reading him all wrong and Nic isn't the sort to be interested in taking part in my project? I don't want to offend or upset him, now that I've seen another side to my temporary landlord.

Well, nothing ventured, nothing gained as they say. I guess I'm about to find out.

11

Still Waters Run Deep

The moment I open the door I can see he's made an effort. As I stand aside to let him enter, I'm surprised by his choice of aftershave. It's one I recognise: L'Eau Bleue by Issey Miyake and it immediately conjures up the face of a former boyfriend. That was a whole three months of my life totally wasted on someone who turned out to be less than reliable, let's say. And that's letting him off rather lightly.

I flash Nic a pleasant smile as I shut the door and he follows me out to the kitchen.

'Is this weird, being invited to dinner in your own house?'

He laughs. A soft, warm sound. 'You could say that. Unexpected, but hey, I never turn down the chance of a free meal. May I?'

After placing the shopping bags on the floor, he slips off his jacket and instinctively opens the bathroom door to hang it on the hook. When he sees that I haven't taken my eyes off him, he makes a face, looking a little embarrassed.

'Sorry, force of habit. There's nowhere else for guests to hang their coats.'

'No problem, make yourself at home, please.' That makes him laugh once more, as he pulls out a bottle of red wine from one of the carrier bags.

'If you'd like to do the honours, I'm sure you know where to find the corkscrew.' Now I'm teasing him and I hope he doesn't think I'm flirting or anything. I'm really glad Olwen cleaned through today, as everything looks perfect and I want him to see that I'm taking good care of the place.

I've cleared away my temporary office and laid the table. Aside from two place settings, there's a dish of olives, two small dishes of extra virgin olive oil mixed with a little Balsamic vinegar and a roughly chopped baguette.

As I put the chicken in the fridge and start to peel the potatoes, Nic retrieves two wine glasses from the cupboard and pours out a little wine.

'Would a few candles be appropriate? It's missing a little something.'

He's right, of course, but I didn't think it was polite to go rooting around in someone else's cupboards, given the circumstances.

'That would be great, thank you.'

'Just saving on the electricity, really,' he remarks, shooting me a glance and I start laughing. I didn't realise he had such a sense of humour. The good thing is, it means he's feeling relaxed enough to joke around.

By the time the potatoes are ready and I've blanched the asparagus I found in the fridge, the steaks are done to perfection. Fillet steak needs to be seasoned well, browned and then finished off in the oven for just a few minutes.

'There you go.' I put the plate down in front of Nic with a bit of a flourish.

'Well, you seem to know how to cook a steak.'

He waits until I'm seated and we raise our glasses.

'Least I can do. One good turn deserves another. Happy Wednesday, we're halfway there.'

One eyebrow rises slightly and I guess that last remark was a typical one from a regular nine-to-five type of person. Nic's working week might not follow standard office hours. I've no idea if he works at weekends and doesn't enjoy that *Friday euphoria* feeling, either.

'Happy Wednesday.'

We eat in silence, which I think is probably a good sign. Nic devours his food very quickly and I wonder if I gave him a big enough portion. But he seems happy to sit back and begin tucking into the bread, olive oil and olives, while I finish.

'My kind of meal,' he says, dipping a chunk of bread into the oil.

I clear away and realise that the cheesecake and forest fruits will take a while to defrost. I should have thought of that. I tip out a bowlful of the fruits and put the cheesecake on a platter.

'Right, that will take about an hour to thaw out, so perhaps we should adjourn to the sitting room with our glasses?'

I grab the wine bottle and follow Nic through to the other room, waiting to see where he decides to sit. He takes the sofa facing the kitchen door and I settle on the adjacent one, after placing the wine bottle on the coffee table.

'Feel free to read whatever you like from my little collection,' he says, nodding in the direction of the bookshelves.

My stomach flips and I wonder if he's noticed that the copy of *The Notebook* is no longer in its hiding place. I decide to change the subject as quickly as I can.

'Thanks. It's very comfortable here. I bet you will be glad when I leave.'

He nods. 'The farm is OK though. They don't rent out rooms as such, but it's a sprawling farmhouse and they're good people. I'm enjoying helping out and Sid is gradually breaking me in.'

'Sid is such a lovely dog. And dogs are wonderful company if you are on your own.'

Smart move, Tia.

'Probably, but it's a responsibility, isn't it? I mean, a bit like having a person relying upon you. Once you've made the commitment you are no longer free.'

Ooh, that had a little sting to it, I think. We lapse into silence as I'm not quite sure how to respond to that and I decide to wait and see what happens. If I say nothing, will Nic start talking, or will this silence stretch out into an awkwardly long pause?

He takes a swallow of wine, replacing his glass on one of the coasters I set out on the coffee table. He fiddles with it, sliding it slightly to the right and then he looks up at me.

'So, what's your line of work?'

'I'm a feature writer. I'm working on an assignment that involves interviewing a cross-section of people about their relationships and their Christmas traditions. Life and style stuff.'

I can't mention that Olwen told me Nic's other job is a reporter, so I keep my answer simple. If he doesn't mention it, then I won't, either.

'Christmas already? Sounds interesting. How do you find the interviewees?'

My pulse quickens as I know that this is my one chance to get him interested.

'We work several months in advance and when everyone else is thinking *holidays*, I'm usually thinking *festive cheer*. When it comes to finding people to take part, we have researchers who do a lot of the leg work for this type of feature. Basically, they are given a spec and approach suitable candidates willing to be interviewed and featured for a fee. I have to write an article each month for the November, December and January issues. Each article will feature two very different couples.'

He nods, leaning forward to grab his glass and then sitting back to take a leisurely sip. I follow suit, watching for his reaction.

'What do they pay for that sort of thing?'

'It varies. If we are given access to the interviewee's home and they're up for photos, then that commands a premium. We're all about life and style, and our readers are curious about people from all walks of life. My boss would love this cottage.'

'Pity I'm not one of a couple, then.'

I feign surprise.

'Oh, I didn't know that.' It sounds convincing, although it's a little obvious. Plus, I've spoken to Olwen, but he's not to know that. He lapses back into silence.

'I think they're paying about a thousand pounds for each interview, with photos.'

His head jerks up and he seems surprised. It appears to have caught his interest.

'Really?' There's a lift in his voice and I can tell the money is a big temptation, even if it's not something he would normally consider doing.

'One of the couples had to drop out and I'm looking for a new candidate. I'm thinking about a different slant to help wrap up the January article. I want to tackle the fallout when a relationship falls apart and whether understanding the reasons behind it help the person to move on.'

'If it's not a couple, does that mean they only receive half the fee?'

I'm beginning to feel a little uncomfortable about trying to talk Nic into this by dangling figures in front of him. It feels a little dishonest, as I'm not sure he understands what's involved.

'No, the fee is per case study, if you like. It's not for everyone, as it's quite a thing to open up and give a candid interview, then see it in print. Why, are you interested?'

He twists the wine glass in his hand, deep in thought.

'Maybe. I can't think of any other way to get my hands on a quick influx of cash. No disrespect, but renting out the cottage isn't for me, I've discovered. So, my options are rather limited. Would I make a suitable candidate?'

This is going to become increasingly awkward from here on in, I think.

'Well, it rather depends on your back story. This isn't about your life, as a whole. The focus is showing readers how people keep the love alive in their relationships. We're covering people of all ages from mid-twenties through to mid-sixties. My idea for the final article is looking to the future as a new year is about to dawn. It will be from the viewpoint of a retired couple and a single person starting over again. How does long-lasting love stand the test of time and do they both look forward with the same goals in mind? Then contrast that with someone who is about to start over again. What I hope to highlight in my findings is that as time goes on, growing together has some sort of formula. And the way to prove that, I hope, is to find out from someone prepared to open up about why their relationship deteriorated to the point it fell apart. How will they avoid making the same mistakes as they begin moving forward?'

That wasn't easy to spell out, as at the moment it's more of a thought process than a plan of action. I know what I'd like to get out of it, but I won't know until I conduct the interviews whether I'm on the right track. What if it's not love that keeps some couples together into old age, but familiarity? That isn't exactly going to light up the page.

'Sadly, there's nothing at all unusual about my story. Two career-orientated people so caught up in grabbing what they think they want in life, that they don't appreciate what really matters. It's probably a little too mundane for your purposes, even if I could bring myself to share the sorry tale.'

He finishes his wine in one gulp and picks up the bottle, indicating for me to lower my glass.

'Actually, that's exactly what I need. The latest figures indicate that eighteen per cent of married or cohabiting couples are living in distressed relationships, where the likelihood of divorce or break-up is imminent. That's a staggering figure. It isn't so much about the very personal detail, but about the process of growing apart and then how that affects the person afterwards.'

'And you'd be doing the interviewing?'

I don't know if I'm happy now to even consider taking this forward, but clearly Nic is giving this some serious thought.

'Look, you need to think long and hard about this, as it has to be a considered decision. I don't have a hidden agenda and I'm sorry if I brought work into what was meant to be a pleasant evening meal.'

'That's OK. I was the one who started this conversation.'

To give Nic a little breathing space and also to dispel any awkwardness, I head back to the kitchen to see if the dessert is thawed enough to serve.

'I'll be a few minutes. Feel free to browse,' I toss the words over my shoulder, in an attempt to sound casual and, hopefully, upbeat.

Dessert is reasonable enough, without having to put in any effort, and it seems to hit the spot for Nic. He leaves around nine o'clock and I'm disappointed that there are still two burning questions which I couldn't ask. They have nothing to do with work and it's really none of my business, anyway. The first is how he came to buy the cottage from Max and the second is why he chooses to live here, in such an isolated place.

As I ready myself for bed, I reflect upon the fact that tonight couldn't have gone any better if I'd written it as a script. My phone pings, and I expect it to be Hayley, or my brother, whose call I forgot to return. It's a text, but it's from Nic. I guess he saved my number when I rang him to book a taxi into town.

> Sign me up. But don't send me the money until you have the information in case I find I can't deliver. I don't do counselling and it will be the first time I've told anyone the full story. Great fillet steak, by the way. Next time dinner is on me at the Langland's Brasserie.

<u>12</u>

And Then the Heavens Opened

Day six and as soon as I open my eyes I can tell from the grey light that the weather has changed, yet again. The lovely blue sky and the crisp morning air have given way to rolling grey clouds and lashing rain. Looking out there's no sign of Max, not that I expected to see him, as he couldn't take the boat out in this. The driving rain would also make for a miserable walk, even in waterproofs.

Once breakfast is cleared away I load up the washing machine and then set up the laptop, carefully laying out my files once again. The first job on the list is to text a reply to Nic and the second is to call my brother.

> Great. Consider yourself signed-up. I'm busy until the middle of next week but will be in touch. Thanks for bringing the wine last night.

I go to my missed calls list and redial Will's number. Sally answers.

'Hi Sally, it's Tia.'

'Oh, hi Tia. How are you?' Sally is always bright and cheerful. Maybe that's why she and Will work as a couple. My brother is miserable enough for them both and Sally is the person who makes it all bearable.

'Is Will around?'

Did I purposely call when I know he's more likely than not to be at work? Is there some psychological ducking and diving going on here that I'm afraid to acknowledge?

'No, he left an hour ago, I'm afraid. I think he was calling to give you an update. The charity van went in this week and collected what was left. The estate agent is due at the house tomorrow.'

She sounds a little subdued, acknowledging the fact that she understands it isn't easy to hear, but in a way, I'd rather hear it from her.

'Thank you. I am grateful, you know, that he's taking charge. I'm not sure I could face it.'

'Are you better, I mean *really* better?'

I cringe, hating the fact that anyone knows about my little incident and the meltdown.

'I'm back to normal... ish, but the grieving process takes a long time, doesn't it? But that's behind me now. I'm working on a project and I'm away from home for another five weeks.'

'That's probably a help. Will means well, Tia, but he struggles with the emotional bit.'

'Does he hate me, Sally?'

Her tone is one of shock. 'No, of course not. You just need to… let him help once in a while; it makes him feel good about himself. He wants to be the big brother you turn to when you need something, it's a role he's never had to fulfil. I know – what can't we women do for ourselves? I think it harks back to when your father died and, as young as he was, he became the man of the family. You're very self-sufficient and always have been. Allowing him to sort this out is likely to re-open the channels of communication between you both. Give Will his moment, Tia. That's all he needs.'

'I've never looked at it like that. Thanks. That's helpful to know.'

A moment passes and as I clear my throat to speak again, Sally jumps in.

'Well, it's good to hear your voice. Perhaps when you're back in London you can come and visit. I talk to Bella about you all the time.'

My heart skips a beat, wishing it were possible for me to have a relationship with them all. But we both know the first move has to come from Will. And so far, it hasn't.

'Soon, maybe. Will can always email me if I don't answer my phone. I have a lot of long interviews to do while I'm here and it's quite intensive. But if he needs to contact me urgently, tell him to text and I'll call him back the same day.'

'I will. Take care of yourself, Tia.'

As the line goes dead I know I can't face the turmoil that will begin to cloud my mind if I let it. Family stuff is inevitably going to lead me to think about Mum, and I can't do that now. It's too soon to be able to sit, go over old memories and end up with a smile on my face. I hope I will be able to do that at some point, but it's way too early for that at the moment.

Besides, it time to start work.

*

Aside from one short coffee break and a light lunch, I power through until just after six p.m. It feels good to be back in my stride and I've even roughed-out some questions to aim at Nic if we do, finally, manage to sit down together and talk.

I rustle up a quick omelette and then take the iPad into the sitting room, together with a glass of wine. Olwyn is a little star and I hoped there would be a bottle nestling away somewhere if I looked hard enough.

Before pulling the curtains I look out, but with the darkening grey sky and the light beginning to fade, there's nothing to be seen. Poor Max, I wonder what he finds to do on days like this and in the winter, when the bad weather lasts for days on end?

Out of nothing more than nosey curiosity, I open the iPad and type in his name. If Olwen is right, then I suspect there will be some mention of his name, somewhere. Even so, I'm very surprised when a long list of items appears on the screen in front of me. I open the first article and see it's from one of the larger newspapers:

Royal Navy lieutenant Maxwell "Max" Hartington is a senior training officer, providing accredited training to university students. He has been awarded the Queen's Voluntary Reserves medal in recognition for his service and dedication throughout his career.

Students are taught both leadership and seamanship skills, and as Royal Naval Cadets are given the rank of Midshipman. They are able to travel around European waters on dedicated patrol vessels, one of which was captained by Lt. Hartington for twelve years. Prior to that he formally left the service in 1999 and was asked to return as a training officer six months later. With a total of twenty years in the Regular Navy and twelve attached to the training unit, when interviewed Max said that he was completely surprised, but very proud to receive this award.

Well, that probably explains both why living so near to the sea isn't an issue and his lack of concern about his rather basic living arrangements. I wonder what he did after giving up his training role, as that seemed to mark the end of his career, which means he might even have lived in Beach View Cottage for a couple of years before selling it to Nic. I wonder what prompted the change in circumstances. It just doesn't add up, but then that's the way my mind has been trained to work. I can't stand loose ends, or mysteries. Both tend to niggle away in the back of my brain like unsolved equations.

Enough intrigue, my mind needs to switch off and I swipe the screen and click on the Netflix icon. I'm in the mood for a romantic comedy and what better than *The Holiday*, starring Jude Law? Maybe some equally romantic and soft-hearted guy will walk up the path to Beach View Cottage. Having taken a wrong turn, he parks, and then sees the glow from the light in the sitting room. He knocks on the door to ask for directions and one glance is enough—

OK – dream over, time to settle back and escape from reality for a while. Well, there's nothing else to do and I take a rather strange pleasure from being able to repeat some of the lines from the film, verbatim.

13

Raindrops Keep Falling on My Head

It doesn't stop. If this is spring, then goodness knows what winter is like. Strangely, I find myself repeatedly drawn to the window to marvel at the hostility of the sea. It's a top to bottom, wall-to-wall steely greyness, that is like a blanket and it's hard to see where the water ends and the sky begins.

After breakfast I have a tight timetable, as Paige's interview is booked in for ten and Olwen will probably show up sometime after eleven. I'm due to interview Darren and Paige together on Sunday at three, so I want to spend the afternoon pulling some notes together.

I text Hayley, just to let her know I think I have the final interview candidate sorted and that I'll be in touch over the weekend.

Once the interview begins I can see exactly why Darren and Paige are so well-suited. She's very bubbly, but isn't quite as practical as he is and they balance each other out.

'Darren is a sweetheart,' she tells me, her eyes sparkling. 'When the person you love would do anything to make you happy, well, it's so easy to give back, isn't it?'

'That's good to hear. When did you realise he was the one?'

She giggles, squirming around in her seat a little as she smooths her top down over her baby bump.

'At first sight. I grew tired of my previous boyfriends very quickly. They were either dull and boring, or thought too much of themselves. Some guys are so precious about their looks and their clothes. It's rather worrying when a guy takes more time to get ready than you do. Darren isn't like that, but he can dress up when the occasion warrants it. I've converted him to a few things. We do couples' spa facial evenings. At first, he wasn't sure about it, but now he'd even answer the door if the bell rang unexpectedly, mud pack or no mud pack.'

'So, tell me what plans you have for your first Christmas as a married couple.'

It's not even the end of May, but her eyes immediately light up and I can see that she's already given this some thought.

'Well, it's going to centre around the baby, really. The family have all agreed they will come to us to make it extra special. I'm sure that next year I'll be only too pleased not to be the one doing the hosting. But I will have plenty of help on hand, so it's all very exciting.'

It isn't just this interview that's triggered thoughts of Christmas then and Paige is already way ahead of the game.

'Is a family Christmas important to you both?' I wonder fleetingly what happens if one person is a *Christmasaholic* and their partner is more the *bah humbug* sort.

'Yes, most certainly. It isn't going to be easy to cram everyone in, but we'll manage somehow. I want the house to look like a winter wonderland. The theme is going to revolve around snowmen and reindeer. If you can hang on a moment, I can show you some of the things I've managed to find online.'

I nod, surprised that anyone is planning their decorations so far ahead of the event. She returns carrying a large box. I watch as she places it on the coffee table in front of her and eases off the lid.

'Don't you just love these twinkly lights?'

Paige holds up a string of little white snowmen sporting jolly smiles. She lays them on the sofa and the next item to appear is a white reindeer, covered in sparkly, pearl-white glitter. It glints a little as she turns it towards me so that I can get a better look.

Glitter. My worst nightmare. I refuse to buy anything with that awful stuff sprinkled over it. Now I'm sounding like a Christmas grouch and I'm not, but the sparkles stick to everything. If anyone sends me a card with it on, then it goes straight in the bin.

'Lovely. When the photographer calls can you have some of the decorations out on a table or something? If you have a plain tablecloth it might be a fun shot. Do you have anything specifically for the baby?'

She looks at me as if that's a silly question and disappears for a few moments. When she sits back down in front of the camera she waggles the arms of an enormous cuddly snowman, which literally spills out over her lap because of her baby bump.

'He's cute, isn't he? And I found this mobile for the cot.'

She moves the cuddly toy, placing him next to her and then reaches into a bag to gently lift out a rather pretty mobile. Hanging down from a plastic circular hoop are six strings. Each one has three snowflakes and at the bottom of each there is a felt snowman.

'It's obviously going to be a very exciting time. Has Christmas always been a big event for you?'

Paige settles back down, smoothing her hands down over her bump and wriggling around in her seat until she's in a comfortable position.

She shakes her head. 'No. My Grandma died on Christmas day, eight years ago. It hasn't been the same since and that's why this year I'm determined to make it extra special.'

A lump rises in my throat as I connect with the pain I can see so clearly reflected back in her expression. She takes a deep breath.

'It's time to make some new traditions, rather than dwelling on how Christmas used to be.'

It's all great stuff and I can't pretend I'm not a little envious of that level of excitement and anticipation. It sounds like it's going to be the best Christmas ever, for Paige and Darren. Personally, I'm dreading Christmas, but that's life I suppose. We have no choice but to work with the cards we're dealt. I guess watching The Holiday last night hasn't helped, either. Wouldn't it be great to stumble across someone's path and suddenly it all begins to kick off? Would I have dragged that mysterious stranger – who looked remarkably like Jude Law – over my doorstep and into my life.

Unusually for me, I have to keep my mind from wandering throughout the entire interview. I'm glad I have the recording as I'll have to run through it before I write up my notes, as I'm sure there are things I missed.

I hear a key in the door and, glancing at the clock, I see it's Olwen time.

'Hello,' her lilting voice filters through from the hallway.

'In the kitchen. I'm not interviewing.'

Olwen's smiley face appears, although she looks a little bedraggled, with water droplets running down her face. She's carrying her little trolley to avoid leaving wet tracks on the floor.

'You shouldn't have come out in this, Olwen. Seriously, there's nothing that can't wait.'

'I'd feel guilty not turning up and it's on my round. I'm doing lunchtime duty at the school today, so I can go straight from here. Do you mind if I dry my coat off a little on the radiator?'

I jump up. 'Of course, help yourself. I'll grab you a towel.'

I disappear into the bathroom as Olwen drapes her dripping coat over the kitchen radiator.

'Here you go. I didn't appreciate it was still so wet out there.'

'It hasn't stopped. Most of this is from the walk down the lane. I saw Max ahead of me and he's parked back a little from the cottage. He wouldn't park there, of course, if Nic was around. They don't get on. I'm not good at reversing, so I parked at the top.'

'To be honest I haven't seen him for a couple of days and I was a little worried.'

'He'd been shopping by the look of it. He also has a lady friend he visits from time to time. I'm not gossiping, it isn't a secret, but then I'm not sure what their relationship is, exactly. He doesn't say a lot.'

'It must be quite miserable for him being on his own in the cabin when the weather is bad.'

'Oh, you haven't been inside, then. It's not quite as basic as you might think. One houses a bathroom and bedroom. He recycles rain water and although he doesn't have plumbing, he has a composting toilet, no less.'

'Ah, I did wonder. What's in the other cabin?'

'It's a sitting room and kitchen. He prefers to cook outside whenever he can, but he has everything he needs so don't go feeling sorry for him.' Her tone is good-natured.

'I did wonder about the solar panels.'

'He never has power outages when the storms hit because there's a big unit in his workshop which stores up the power from those solar panels. And I bet his internet is way faster than the service you have in the cottage. He has his own external WiFi Antenna and some fancy gizmo that amplifies the signal. Very clever man is Max. Sound chap. I agree, though, there must be times when a little company would brighten his day.'

Is she dropping hints? I remember the chicken. I could pop it in the oven and brave my way down to the beach a bit later, to invite Max to dinner. It's about time I returned his hospitality. It won't taste half as good as his freshly-caught fish baked on an open fire, but it's free-range; besides, he might be glad of the company.

Olwen potters about changing towels and flashing through with the mop. I have my head down, working.

Before I know it, an hour has passed and she's putting on her coat.

'It's blowing over. At least I won't get wet walking back up to the car.'

I see her out and check the sky. It doesn't look exactly promising but she's right, the rain has stopped, so I grab some wellies and my thick coat. Pulling my hood tightly around my face I trudge along to Max's place.

The wooden steps are surprisingly solid, but then they are built off a very sturdy concrete base. I knock twice on the door. A couple of seconds pass and it swings open. Max stands there looking surprised.

'Hello. It's stopped raining I see. Step inside.' I gingerly step across the threshold and stand on a small mat on which Max's boots are neatly lined up.

'Wow, this wasn't quite what I expected. What a lovely space.' I wonder if it's rude to make that comment. It does tend to indicate I thought he lived in a shack. 'It's much larger than it looks from the outside.' I quickly correct myself, but he smiles knowingly.

'Do you have time to slip off your coat and have a cuppa?'

'No, I was just passing.'

He laughs at my awkwardness.

'Seriously, I came down to ask if you'd like to join me for dinner this evening at the cottage.'

Max looks surprised.

'Well, that's a kind offer.'

He's about to refuse, I can feel it, but I give him my best dazzling smile.

'That's very kind and of course I'd be delighted to join you. What time?'

'About seven. Hope you like roast chicken from the farm at the top?'

'The best,' he muses, as he follows me out the door. 'Glad to see you're well wrapped up. It's pretty fresh out here.'

Walking back, the wind is battering against me and I have to lean into it just to make headway. Spring? Call this spring? I mutter, looking up at the sky as I try to pick up the pace and hurry back to the toasty warmth of the cottage.

*

My hands warm up quite quickly once they are wrapped around a cup of hot chocolate. Then I'm head down again, on a mission to finish the task in hand. Finally, gathering together the scattering of notes I push them into the folder and start clearing the table. I want to pop the chicken into the oven by six o'clock, so I head straight up to the shower and change into some clean jeans and a jumper. I pull my hair up into a ponytail and head down to prepare dinner.

14

A Little Understanding Goes a Long Way

When Max arrives, he looks rather smart and on first sight I think my jaw drops a little.

'Come in. Let me take your jacket.'

He slips off his shoes and I think that's a rather thoughtful gesture. I do exactly the same thing, when visiting other people's homes because it's something I've always done. Then I remember that Max was the former owner of the cottage and this could be the first time he's been inside since the renovation work was carried out. Is this something he finds difficult, I wonder? I have no idea whether it's a place that holds a lot of memories for him, or whether he never had a real attachment to it.

'Um... chicken is cooking, roast potatoes are crisping nicely. I'll just pop your jacket on a hanger. I found a rather nice bottle of red wine in the cupboard, courtesy of Olwen. The glasses and bottle opener are on the coffee table if you don't mind taking charge?'

Max nods. The warmth in those greyish-blue eyes is genuine, but I can see he is affected by this room. It saddens me as I head towards the kitchen.

Maybe giving him a few moments alone is the right thing to do. Oh, Tia, what have you done?

I try to throw off my concerns, as I prepare the meal. I meant well and that's what counts. The laptop is playing a loop of classical musical, but the volume is low as I wasn't sure whether Max was a music sort of guy.

When I start to dish up he appears, a half-filled wine glass in each hand, which he sets down on the table. I reflect that there isn't anything at all about Max that isn't gentlemanly, or refined, despite his *old sea dog* demeanour.

'In my capacity as the honorary wine waiter, I took it upon myself to do the tasting. I can report on the fact that it's a fine and robust bottle of wine, with hints of cherry and notes of blackberry.'

I start laughing and as our eyes meet I know he's forgiven me my *faux pas*. Perhaps sometimes it helps to face the memories that haunt us, head-on and that's how we come to understand that trying to hold onto the past is pointless.

'I like what he's done with it.' Max turns, taking in the detail.

'It's pretty great, isn't it? But now I've seen the inside of your cabin I'm envious.'

Max winks at me. 'Not bad for an old fisherman, eh?'

I think I've figured him out. He deflects questions by presenting himself as this simple, older guy who has turned his back on the world. As if he never was a part of it and lacks the energy and enthusiasm to get involved. But having read that article, I know it's not the truth.

'Well, sixty-five isn't old for a start. And anyone who is clued-up enough to run their beachside home using solar panels, knows a thing or two about twenty-first century living. You're quite a surprise, Max, and I'm not falling for the old fisherman thing.'

His eyes widen in exaggerated surprise at being found out and he hangs his head to one side.

'Sorry. It's just so much easier saying little and expecting nothing from anyone.'

'Take a seat. You have my undivided attention this evening. You gave me the short version, now I want to hear the whole thing.'

He lets out an exasperated, if somewhat resigned, sigh. 'On one condition. You have a story of your own and I have a feeling there are many things you've chosen not to share with anyone, too. Is it a deal?'

I nod. 'You first.'

It's a leisurely meal and Max is happy to talk about his time in the Navy, not appreciating that I was already aware of his former career. He doesn't mention his medal, only shares a few of the stories from his time in service. Then he talks about his involvement with training the cadets. His love of the sea comes across so strongly in the way he talks about the skills a young man acquires during his training. Skills that encompass every aspect of their lives, it seems, and turns them from boys into men.

'The training makes the man, Tia. But the long periods of separation aren't good for personal relationships and it takes a toll.'

As I clear away the plates, I can hear the sadness in his voice, even though my back is towards him.

'Did you ever have any children?'

He glances across at me as I spin my head around.

'Two. But my son and I don't speak.'

It's clear he doesn't want to talk about that and I return to swilling off the plates.

'I have fruit sorbet, or cheese and biscuits. Which do you prefer?'

'I'm fine, thank you. Never had a sweet tooth and that was quite a meal. A home-cooked roast dinner is a rare treat for me these days. I'm a *throw it on the fire* type of man.'

'And delicious that is, too. So now you're on your own? And happy, or should I say, happier?'

'I wonder if divorce can ever be amicable. Mine most certainly wasn't. On paper, it must have looked like we were the couple who had it all. That included a big house near London and a holiday cottage down here with a private beach and woodland. Our son was following in his mother's footsteps and making a big name for himself in the City. But the truth was that none of us were happy.'

He stops abruptly and I don't think he's going to say anything more. I'm surprised, therefore, when he suddenly picks the conversation up again.

'I wasn't running away from the responsibility, I was trying to distance myself from the pain. Money and possessions, I came to appreciate, create mistrust and envy. They bring out the worst in people. I have money, more than I need. So, I gave a lot away and that was wrong, according to my ex-wife. I kept some as a nest egg and that was wrong too, apparently. I'm sure my ex-wife continues to be angry at everything I do and the lifestyle I have chosen will, no doubt, be an embarrassment to her. And that's why my family disowned me.'

I sit back down, facing Max across the table and trying to swallow the huge lump in my throat.

'But you survived,' I half-whisper.

'Yes. And it made me see that some people are judgemental and if you don't conform to their particular standards or ideas, then you become a threat of sorts. Some traits are so ingrained they are second nature and that applies to both sides of the argument. So, I choose to live on the beach and some people choose to see that as a failure that is an embarrassment. My wife is horrified and my son would prefer me to have what he would perceive to be a more acceptable lifestyle at my age. As for me, I'm perfectly happy where I am.'

He raises his glass in the air and the twinkle is back in his eyes. I raise mine and our glasses chink.

'Now, Tia, it's your turn.'

'I don't quite know where to begin and that's not a stalling tactic. I never intended to be a career woman, well, not to dedicate every waking hour of the day to my job... Shall we take this into the sitting room and make ourselves a little more comfortable?'

I pick up the wine bottle and Max follows me through. I top up his glass and pour a splash into my own, and then curl up on the sofa, facing him.

'Men have come and gone. I don't mean hundreds, but a few, and most were a couple of dates and move on. Maybe I get bored easily, I don't know, but I've never met anyone who could hold my interest. It seemed the more I found out about them, the less appealing they became. That sounds sad, doesn't it?'

'I would say truthful, rather than sad. I think you are being a little hard on yourself, though. You just haven't met the right person, yet.'

'Ah, a man who still believes in hope. Now that's comforting, as I thought you might be a little more jaded given the circumstances.'

The twinkle is back and I remember what Olwen said about Max's lady friend. Perhaps hope never dies. He doesn't respond, so I continue.

'OK. Wind forward and I hit thirty and it's all work, work, work. The only family member I had regular contact with was my mum, but I have a brother, a sister-in-law and a niece I haven't seen for over four years. Well, except at Mum's funeral.'

'That's hard. Death is a journey for both parties; those who pass over and those who are left behind.'

I sit back, staring at him.

'Do you know something, Max? You're the first person since Mum died to say something to me that is, actually, meaningful. People can't handle it, can they? And that includes me. The reason I'm here is that I went to pieces and the doctor gave me some pills. Then one night, instead of taking one, I took three. I keep telling myself I had an allergic reaction to them, but the truth is that I was scared. Alone, and scared. I popped a second pill, then a third and I washed them down with half a bottle of wine. My brother came to the house with some papers that needed my signature. He looked in through the sitting room window and saw me lying on the floor. He called an ambulance and it probably saved my life. And now that's another thing that stands between us; he accused me of being selfish.'

Max shakes his head and I can feel his empathy.

'The funny thing, though, was that I wasn't trying to kill myself, at all. I didn't want to die; I just didn't know how to cope with the pain of the loss, or the stark finality of death. I was very young when my father died, so I clung onto Mum. I suppose, with hindsight, my need actually helped her through it. But I never allowed myself to even contemplate life without her. She's the only person who ever really understood me, the bit in here that you never share.'

I touch my chest and lapse into silence. A sense of relief lifts my spirits and I'm amazed at how natural it feels opening up to Max. I'm proud of myself, as it's not an easy thing to admit and the fact that I've finally owned up to it makes me feel stronger, somehow. Before, I felt ashamed that I had been so careless and had risked my own life as if it were nothing.

'My boss accepted the story about the allergic reaction and I took a month off. When I was due to return to work, I didn't know if I could do it. You know – face everyone, knowing what I'd done. Having to listen to the well-meaning platitudes that people say, hoping I won't dissolve into tears in front of them. It was a surprise being sent here and I'm sure there's an ulterior motive behind it. Maybe I'm about to be demoted, who knows? I sink or swim, based upon the success of this project, I guess. I have five weeks left to deliver and prove myself. And that's the truth, the whole truth and nothing but the truth, as they say in court.'

Max is a real gentleman. Considering he's not a talker, he sensitively changes the subject and we talk about music, opera, books we'd take with us if we had to spend time on a desert island… and before we know it, it's past midnight.

As we part, Max leans in to give me a gentle hug and I pat his back.

'It helps, doesn't it?'

I nod and the look that passes between us is one of understanding.

'It's been cathartic and I thank you, Max. I never thought I'd hear myself say that out loud and now I have —'

'The sky didn't fall and the earth didn't open up and swallow you whole. Guess we have one quite important thing in common; we are survivors. Hang in there, Tia. Inner strength will never fail you and there are many who would envy you that quality.'

He pulls a torch from his pocket and as the latch on the gate at the bottom of the garden clicks shut, he turns and waves.

'You know where to find me if you need anything. Any time. Day, or night.' And with that he disappears into the darkness.

<u>15</u>

A Little Bit Country

I roll over with a start, my eyes registering the brightness around me even before I prise my eyelids open. The sun is streaming through the window and its daylight. Glancing at the clock I see it's eight-thirty and I have to squint to check I'm not misreading one of the digits. I really didn't intend sleeping this late because lazing around isn't going to help.

'OK, Tia. This is the first day of the rest of your life. So, what's the action plan?' My words echo around the room and my head is quick to conjure up a response.

I'm going to dress, walk up to the top road and catch a bus down to Caswell Bay. It takes less than an hour to grab a slice of toast and a coffee, have a quick shower, change and start the trek up the hill.

I jump on the first bus that comes along and the driver confirms that it runs every thirty minutes, but there's no service on Sundays. It's only a few stops and if it wasn't for the heavy rain yesterday, I would have been perfectly happy to attempt to find my way through the woods.

The bus stops across the road from the small promenade and it's quite busy, mostly families and a few older people milling around. Some are sitting on benches eating ice cream from one of the kiosks and the two cafés are doing good business. They are still serving breakfast and it's warm enough this morning for people to sit outside and enjoy the sunshine.

Pulling my sunglasses from my backpack, I head off towards the start of the coastal path.

As walkers pass on the trail I nod, smile and acknowledge their *good mornings*, but today is about clearing my head. I want to spend time thinking about Mum and remembering the good times and I want to think about the future. Am I really stressing over the fact that when I arrive back at work I might find Finlay has completely taken over my job? And if I am, do I care anymore?

Two-and-a-half-hours later I'm walking back down the hill towards Beach View Cottage and the answer, I've discovered, is *no*. Whatever happens, happens. As much as I love my job, it does mean that I am always the first person Clarissa turns to, as if I'm some understudy waiting in the wings. Of course, I want to be regarded as a consummate professional and good at what I do, but I don't want to end up being a clone of someone I often pity in many ways. I realise I walk and talk fast, which some people seem to find a tad intimidating, but that's a part of my character. My brain races ahead of me and once I latch onto an idea I'm off chasing it.

As I swing open the front door, still trying to get my head around that rather shocking revelation, there's a note lying on the door mat. It's from Olwen.

Tia, can you give me a call when you're back?
My number is on the pin board.
Olwen

Curious, I kick off my shoes, drop my backpack and coat in a heap and go in search of my phone. I really must stop forgetting to check it. It's so unlike me to distance myself from the outside world. There are a couple of missed calls and a couple of texts, which I ignore, while I dial Olwen's number.

'Hi, Olwen, it's Tia. Sorry I missed you, I did the coastal walk again and I've only just arrived back.'

'Glad to hear you're getting out and about, especially after that awful rain. There's a barn dance on tonight up at the farm and I wondered if you'd like to come along? We're going and taking our youngest, Rhona. It's five pounds a ticket and that includes a buffet and a glass of pear cider, which has been brewed on the farm. We always have a laugh and the music is live. What do you think?'

'Count me in. What time and what's the dress code?'

'We'll pick you up at seven-thirty and casual. It's a jeans sort of thing. It gets quite hot when you're dancing but you might need a jumper in between.'

'Great. See you tonight and thanks for thinking of me, Olwen. That's very kind of you.'

Well, that says a lot when another person I've only just met makes time for me. Maybe fate is trying to tell me something. I've lost my way and I've lost touch with the things in life that really matter. Now it's down to me to make some changes.

I tidy away the heap on the floor, grab my phone and sit down on the sofa. The first call I return is Will's.

'Hi, Will, really sorry I missed your call again. How are you?'

He hesitates. 'I'm... good, thank you. And you?'

'Great. I've just come back from a long coastal walk along part of the Gower Coast. I forgot to take my phone, again.'

'You sound well.'

'I'm doing better, really. The fresh air and exercise are revitalising. The assignment is going very well: I'm pleased so far. I'm off to a barn dance tonight.'

I can imagine the look on his face is probably one of total disbelief.

'How are Sally and Bella?'

'They're shopping for new school shoes. Bella lost another tooth yesterday, so she's still lisping. It's hard not to laugh and it sounds so cute.'

My brother, sharing stories about Bella and using words like *cute*? If I wasn't sitting down I think I'd fall over, in shock.

'I'd love to visit you all once I'm settled back in London. It's been too long. And I wanted to thank you for being there when I needed you most. I don't think I handled it very well, you know, it's hard not being in control. Anyway, how did it go with the estate agent?'

'He measured up and took photos. The house will go on the market sometime next week. It wasn't easy being there, if I'm honest.'

'I know. I wish I could have been there with you, to help you through it. But let's not dwell, Will. We can't change the past and we can't change what happened. Let's move on, as best we can. Is that OK with you?'

The pause that follows doesn't worry me too much, as I think he's taking a moment to compose himself.

'It's a great way to start, Tia. We need to be in each other's lives because that's the way it's meant to be. I lost my way for a while, there.'

*

By the time Olwen ushers us all through the doors, the dancing is in full-swing. Rhona and Rhys head for the dance floor and Olwen steers me in the direction of the bar area.

'The caller, the guy in the cool cowboy hat, is Mike. He owns the farm. He shouts out directions to the dancers and generally organises the band. He's from Manchester, but he's lived here for the last ten years. He speaks fast, so simply follow everyone else and don't worry if you turn the wrong way. People will point you in the right direction. They will also come up and ask you to dance, unless you have a plate of food in your hand, so you've been warned.'

We grab a drink and head down to a small table in the far corner, beyond which is a wall of hay bales.

'It really is a barn,' I shout. I doubt Olwen can hear me above the general noise.

'The real thing. Your first time?'

'In a barn and at a barn dance.'

'Tom, our postman, is heading in this direction so you'd best prepare yourself.'

I think my face might look a little panic-stricken. Tom says something I can't catch over the strains of the music, but Olwen gives me a gentle push.

'Her first time, Tom, show her the ropes.'

It's well over an hour before I manage to make my excuses and ease myself back onto a chair. Olwen is nowhere in sight.

It took me a while to get into it. Especially given that I had to strain my ears to hear what Mike was saying. The music is really loud and some of the actions didn't come naturally to me, as he directed the dancers. But Tom stayed with me the whole time and nursed me through a real assortment of dances. From the Virginia reel, to the Heel Toe Polka and I even danced to *Cotton Eye Joe*. I can't remember the last time I laughed so hard. The Square Dance had me totally confused as to which way to turn. The amount of times I bumped into people, often the same person more than once, made me laugh even harder. But it didn't matter because everyone was having such a good time.

I suddenly spot Nic in the crowd and he looks my way. I wave out and he comes across.

'Well, this is a surprise. I don't usually come to these things as I'm not much of a dancer. I thought I should at least show my face as I'm actually staying here at the moment.'

He takes the seat next to me and we sit watching the dancers weaving in and out. Mike directs them left and right, and round, and elbows left in a constant stream of words: which is fine if you know what you are doing and can react instantly to his commands. I seem to do everything a second or two after everyone else.

'It's a lot easier once you've been doing it for a while.' Nic leans in close so I can hear him.

'I'm a little relieved to hear that, as my brain doesn't seem able to communicate with my feet. Tom was showing me what to do and I simply followed everything he did. My feet are killing me now, though.' I grimace.

'You didn't walk here from the cottage, did you? Do you need a lift back after the buffet?'

'I came with Olwen, Rhys and Rhona.'

'Oh, good. I'll let her know I can pop you back. Are you hungry now, or do you want to give it a whirl again?'

It's obvious he's hoping that I'm not expecting him to extend his hand and lead me straight back onto the dance floor. In all honesty, I don't think my feet could take it, anyway.

'Food sounds good. Lead on.'

I grab my things and follow him into the crowd, then out through a side door and into a lean-to. There are bales of hay to sit on and probably the longest trestle table I've ever seen, straining under the weight of the food.

'Thank goodness for the walks around here, or I'll be going home a stone heavier,' I reflect, but it doesn't stop me reaching out for southern fried chicken wings and filled potato skins.

We move away from the table and settle ourselves down on a couple of hay bales. It's a bit prickly actually, but feels surprisingly sturdy.

'How's Sid?'

'He's coming around. We're establishing a sort of rapport, now. He doesn't strain on the leash as much and you were right, letting him feel he isn't too restricted when we start our walk really helps.'

I nod, trying to figure out how to tackle a chicken wing without getting it all over my face. In the end, I give up and just go for it.

Nic looks at me and wiggles a finger, indicating towards my left cheek. I give it a swipe with the napkin and nod gratefully. It's easier to eat in silence and I scan the room, but I don't see any faces I know. I don't think this will be Max's sort of thing and I haven't seen Olwen, or her family, for a while.

'I'll grab a couple of bottles of water, is there anything else you want?'

'No, I'm good, thanks.'

I watch as Nic disposes of the empty paper plates and disappears out to the bar. It's nowhere near as warm in here as it is in the main barn. I undo the jumper loosely tied around my waist and pull it over my head.

I love people-watching and what's nice about this evening is that it includes the whole community; from children of about ten, or eleven years old, up to some very sprightly looking senior citizens.

'Here you go. I saw Olwen and mentioned I'd drive you back. She said she'd see you on Monday, but give her a call if you need anything at all.'

'Thanks. It was quite a late one yesterday, so I am flagging a bit but I don't intend to leave until I've gotten you up dancing.'

He shakes his head and begins to roll his eyes. 'I should have guessed that was coming. Don't say I didn't

165

warn you when I mess it up. Guess we'd better get it over and done with, then.'

I finish my water and we head back inside, just in time to line up for what I think is another Virginia reel. As the music begins and I look across the gap at Nic, standing in line, he looks more confident than I'd expected. When Mike counts us down from five to one, we all walk towards the middle. Nic appears to know what he's doing and as the two lines begin stepping backwards, it's quite easy to keep time with the rhythm. We all take a couple of steps forward and Mike calls out "elbows". Each couple link arms and spin around in a circle. Then a few steps backwards and in we go again, changing arms this time and doing another spin in the opposite direction.

Our eyes are glued to each other as we step back in line once more. Then we surge forward to join hands, this time, and circle around. Letting go to step away from Nic, I suddenly feel as if we're all alone and the music and people around us seem to pale into the background. Eyes fixed, we meet once more in the middle, but this time we walk behind each other before returning to our starting position. A look of confusion is etched on Nic's face. It's clear we're having a moment, which has nothing at all to do with dancing. As the couple at the other end of the row link hands and gallop down the centre of the floor, the line begins to move down and suddenly it's our turn.

Nic grabs my hands and we skip to the right. Oblivious to the other dancers, we edge towards the end of the two lines of people watching us, as we gallop past. When it's time to let go and we face each other across the divide, my heart is pounding and inside my head I hear a loud and unmistakable, *Oh, no. This can't be happening. Not now.*

*

'I'll see you to the door. I usually turn the outside light on if I'm out for the evening.'

Nic guides me by the elbow as we negotiate the gate and start walking up the winding path to the door. It's almost pitch black and much later than I'd anticipated.

I fumble for the key, my nerves jangling and my mind a ball of confusion. What happened this evening? Nic waits patiently and eventually the key is in the lock and I hear the click as it turns. The door swings open and I take one step inside. My mouth goes very dry, so I don't say anything. In the darkness Nic takes one step forward and suddenly his face is up close, his eyes reflecting the same dilemma.

'I... um... need to kick off these shoes as my feet are killing me.' The words I manage to squeeze out don't flow very well and it sounds lame.

'Yeah. I don't think I've ever lasted that long on a dance floor before. It was fun. Unexpected, but fun.'

We're playing eye tennis and as I turn my head slightly to break the contact, Nic leans in to kiss my cheek. I don't think he was intending to kiss my mouth and it's a relief, because a little quiver passes through me and my legs begin to wobble.

'Sleep well,' he murmurs. He turns on his heels and is gone before I have time to think of something to say. I stand there with the door open wide, unable to move. The sound of the car engine kicking into life prompts me into action, and I lock up, kick off my shoes and make my way upstairs wondering what on earth was wrong with me tonight.

16

Is This Really How it Happens?

I'm up early, having spent a lot of the night slipping in and out of dreams that seemed to be driven by snippets of country music. I think at one point I was even dancing in my sleep. Nic's eyes seemed to be there at every turn, watching me, smiling at me and connecting with me.

Even lying back and closing my eyes, his face is still there, as if it's imprinted on the inside of my head. The music starts to fade and his hands reach out for mine. As our fingers touch he feels real, even though I know this is a daydream.

I vault out of bed and stand under the shower, letting the warmth of the water wash away my dream. There's only one way to calm a turbulent mind and that's to work.

Playing back Paige's interview, she said she knew Darren was the one when she first set eyes on him. And yet, leafing back through my notes from Veronica's interview, she said it wasn't until their third date she had this gut feeling that Liam was meant to be in her life. That has me scrabbling to check the guys' interviews.

Liam said that Veronica grew on him and suddenly dates weren't planned, they were taken for granted. That doesn't sound very romantic to me. Darren's response was very different. He said that he could read Paige's feelings, as he saw it in her eyes. He told me that relief flooded over him as it would have broken his heart if she hadn't felt it, too.

I'm a journalist, not an expert on love, because you need to experience it first-hand in order to understand it, I suppose. But the difference between these two couples was gnawing away at me, like a crossword clue you can't solve. I wonder what it was that I saw reflected back at me on Nic's face last night. I remember Darren's eloquent description when he talked about the moment he fell in love. You'd know if it was the *real thing*, wouldn't you? You couldn't mistake it for something else, like pure lust. Could you? And how do you recognise it in someone else?

I sit back in my chair, chewing the end of my pen. I'm not saying Darren and Paige are more in love than Liam and Veronica, but the younger couple seem to give out this innate sense of being on the same page with their relationship. Of course, the two lifestyles couldn't be more different. Maybe what I'm trying to do here isn't merely in the pursuit of clarity so I can do the article justice, but to understand *how* people fall in love. Am I looking for answers because ultimately I want what they already have? Or am I simply doing the job I'm being paid to do?

Suddenly a switch turns on in my head and I jump online, calling up Liam's YouTube page. Curiously, no new videos have been posted since the Lapland adventure. Cursoring down the long list of videos that in itself is unusual. Maybe it's a little early for him to be downloading the prequel to their current jaunt, although he's done that for most of their other exotic trips, but five months with nothing new?

I go back a year and click on a video of a trip to China. The opening couple of minutes is mostly panning around and I skip forward until I see Veronica's face fill the screen. She's beaming as she extols the delights of their stay at the Commune by the Great Wall. She explains that it lies at the foot of the fortifications and was named one of China's top ten new construction miracles by American Business Weekly in two-thousand-and-five. But it's not the words coming out of her mouth that catch my interest, it's the light in her eyes. Clearly she's looking at Liam and, yes, she's having a wonderful time but it isn't just the holiday that's enthusing her.

I stop the video and move down to the end of the list and after a little buffering I'm back in Lapland. That shining, almost flirtatious look has gone. Her smiles come from the way she sets her mouth and lifts her cheeks but her eyes don't smile *at* him anymore. It's as if there's some sort of disconnect. I click further along the progress bar at the bottom of the screen to catch the drinks party at the sauna. Sitting back in my chair to watch a scene that previously I hadn't really paid much attention to, it dawns on me now that I was blindly focusing on that Christmas feel-good factor.

The camera has been set up to run and this is probably only a portion of the original footage. With drinks flowing quite freely and people hopping in and out of the indoor hot tub to grab time in the steam room opposite, there's plenty to distract the eye. So, I concentrate on watching Liam and Veronica's movements. It's almost as if Liam is avoiding her at times. As she enters the hot tub, he eases himself out and heads off to reappear with a fresh drink in his hand. I'm watching Veronica chatting away to one of the other women on the trip and once again, Liam isn't there. As I scan around he's following someone into the steam room and there it is. As his right arm is holding open the door for the vivacious looking woman with a mass of dark curls clipped up on top of her head, he leans forward and steals a kiss on the back of her neck. Unnoticed by the others, the door closes behind them.

I click back to the very beginning and watch the entire video with a fresh pair of eyes. He was careful, but then for a large part of the footage he was safely behind the camera. What gave him away time and time again is the way he seemed to follow that women whenever she appeared in the shot. There was no footage at all of Veronica talking to her and that told me everything I needed to know. Veronica is aware that Liam is having an affair. Either he doesn't realise that and thinks he's gotten away with it, or they have an open marriage.

I let out a slow, depressing sigh. My stomach is already full of butterflies this morning but now it's churning. When I'm not focusing on what I'm doing, Nic drifts into my head and I have to push him away because this is important. What if Veronica walks away from Liam before the article goes live? They seemed to have it all and yet the proof is there in front of me, confirming that what was probably a wonderful love story to begin with is now little more than a sham and I'm gutted. There's no time to find a replacement couple and they so fit the bill. I have no choice but to keep my fingers crossed nothing happens between now and publication day.

It's a stumbling block I hadn't expected, but as the day runs its course I shake off that sense of disappointment. However, a growing sense of dread that I'm ignoring the potential for disaster here niggles away inside my head. Today everything feels like a battle anyway as Nic is there in my head at every turn, no matter what I do. He wasn't just looking at me every time our footsteps brought us closer together last night, he was looking *into* me. He was searching, in exactly the same way that I was doing to him. We were questioning each other's motives.

Is this a case of right man, wrong place and wrong time? How could life be so cruel? After listening to Max's sad story about relationships falling apart because work always came between them, wasn't that a warning?

I skip lunch, preparing myself for the interview with Darren and Paige at three o'clock. It lasts just over an hour and their happiness is infectious; there's a lot of laughter and meaningful eye contact. And playfulness, as they tease each other about their shortcomings. It is all so natural, as if it didn't matter that Darren was untidy and Paige always had to pick his clothes up off the floor. Or that Paige often ran late because she is nowhere near as organised as he is. They both have faults but nothing that bothers either of them. I end the session feeling that what they have is special, very special indeed.

I tidy up, ready to grab a quick sandwich and aim for an early night. I know that although I was irritated by Nic's attitude almost as soon as I jumped into his taxi that first day, I was also intrigued by him. If I was feeling so put out, then why did I book him to take me into town? I could easily have found another number online. I smile to myself, acknowledging that maybe this isn't a surprising turn of events. The attraction was there from the start, I just wasn't sure it was mutual. And now

I know. He kissed my cheek because he wanted to make a statement.

I suck in a breath, wondering what I'm letting myself in for and knowing I can't simply run away, even if I wanted to. Besides, having had my little epiphany the other day, if I want to take control of my future then it's going to be all about change. I just had no idea that would include coping with a heart that misses a beat every time I think about a certain someone.

17

The Deal is Struck

This morning starts with a bang. My phone begins to ping shortly after eight a.m. Clarissa is asking to look at the first draft of interview number one and after a little tidying I'm not unhappy to press send.

Then Hayley calls to say that couple number four are free today and do I want her to rearrange their appointments? Then, Nic texts.

Hey, Tia. How R U doing?

I stare at the words, not sure how to reply.

Good. Busy. You?

Was thinking about Saturday night. Can we talk? I'm not working this afternoon.

I groan. I'm not sure I'm ready to handle this, but that's the old me talking and I quickly pull myself together.

I'm free from mid-afternoon. A walk, maybe?

Perfect. See U later. Don't work too hard.

I don't know whether it's because my mind is suddenly thrown into turmoil by Nic's text, but couple number four, Carol and Steve, don't jump out at me as being particularly romantically inclined. They're in their mid-forties and I feel there's a real effort being made to say what they think I might want to hear. It all feels rather disconnected, but hey, after twenty-five years of marriage and with four kids, it can't be easy.

I wonder if they're going through a bit of a rough patch and are regretting taking part. But if this is a true reflection of a typical, chaotic family life, then even though they seem to have little time for the romance, there are loving gestures. But it's more about giving each other time alone, than organising quality time together. They both admit that with children aged from sixteen down to eight years of age, if they manage an hour together on their own at the end of the day, it's a miracle. And it sounds like they spend a lot of their free time ferrying the kids to and from after-school clubs, dance classes, music lessons and sporting events.

When I raise the subject of Christmas the reaction I get more, or less, reflects the whole tone of the interview. Somehow things get done so it will happen, but as it's seven months away who has the time to start thinking about it now? I sigh, wondering how on earth

I'm going to make this particular story jump off the page, so that readers can engage with it. Underneath it all, though, there's no sense of unhappiness, or resentment, more an underlying feeling of every day being almost impossibly full. They both collapse into bed at night with relief, rather than in pursuit of a romantic interlude.

It seems that sometimes, loving someone is more about putting yourself out to give them time to stop and catch their breath for a moment. Knowing when they are beginning to feel swamped and need a break. The more I reflect upon that thought, the more I can appreciate that this family situation works. The key is that they have good communication skills. Maybe the romance is a little lacking, at the moment, but as the kids grow and they regain some of their quality time together, I have no doubt the flame will still be there.

I'm so deep in thought that I don't hear Olwen until she tiptoes into the kitchen.

'Afternoon, Tia. Sorry I'm late. Rhona twisted her ankle this morning on the way to school. We had to have an emergency dash to the surgery. It's all strapped up now and I've left her at home with Rhys. I'm not sure how he'll cope as she can be a little demanding at times. He spends a lot of time either on the phone, taking bookings, or online. I suspect chocolate and DVDs will be used liberally as bribery in return for a little peace and quiet.' She chortles to herself and I think of couple number four.

'I've just been interviewing a couple who have four children. The feature I'm writing is all about romance, but to be honest they both looked exhausted. I guess things will change as time goes on.'

'Tell me about it. It's non-stop; always someone in need of something.'

'You don't resent it in any way? Running your own business, working a second job and coping with all the family stuff in between?'

She pauses, her forehead crinkling up as she narrows her eyes.

'I've never had time to think about it. You just keep going.'

She sounds very matter-of-fact.

'But you're content with your lot?'

A smile creeps over her face and she stops wiping around the sink to stand back, cloth in hand.

'I wouldn't change a thing. If I had time on my hands I'd end up feeling bored. Everything I do, I do out of love. Everything we have, we've built together as a team. Although it is a struggle at times, it makes for a very strong bond. Besides, we have our moments and it's enough to remind us we still have it.'

'Do you mind if I quote you on that? Anonymously, of course. You've just said more or less what I've spent the last hour trying to paraphrase. Maybe I should throw a few more questions your way when I hit a bit of a stumbling block.'

'Ha! Ha! I'm happy to help.'

I start packing up, conscious of the time. I'm feeling the need to wash my face and maybe apply a little make-up before my company arrives.

'I'll pick you up a few things you're running low on and Rhys can drop them down to you. You're knocking off early. Going for a walk?'

Nic will probably be here before Olwen has finished, so there's no point in being secretive.

'Yes, Nic will be here shortly.'

Olwen purses her lips. 'I've never seen him as animated as he was on Saturday night, twirling you around as if he knew what he was doing. It's nice to see a genuine smile on his face for a change.'

She returns to the job in hand and I quickly head off to the bathroom to make myself presentable. But it's as much to hide the glow I can feel creeping up my neck and into my cheeks, as it is to fuss over how I look.

*

'I thought it would be easier to walk and talk. I know you wanted to get together for this interview thing later this week, but after Saturday night I wanted to... clear the air.'

I will my face not to give anything away. As we begin to climb the hill I forage about in my backpack for sunglasses, as a distraction.

'When I picked you up at the station I know I was a bit short with you. I think I've had a chip on my shoulder for quite a while, about a lot of things. It's a very different life for me here. The constant worry about my financial situation doesn't help, if I'm being honest. So, while I happily banked the cheque, I was harbouring a little touch of resentment there. And I know that makes absolutely no sense at all, but it seemed to remind me of how precarious my situation is at the moment.'

We're walking side by side, sunlight dappling through the trees and turning the wood into what could be a drawing from a children's fairytale book. It looks enchanted. With hardly any breeze, the leaves and twigs underfoot crunch and snap, disturbing the silence until the drone of another car passing on the top road masks the sounds.

'I'd feel the same way – really. I've been overreacting, simply knowing someone else is currently sitting at my desk in London. I don't own the space, I just work there, but it's a territorial thing, isn't it? When people buy a property to rent out, they don't have that same emotional investment with it. It's merely a source of income, whereas to you the cottage is home.'

We hit the part of the woods where the narrow track descends quite steeply and we make our way down to

Caswell Bay in single file. Once on the beach we resume our conversation.

'It was petty of me and unfair. I'm grateful you're here, Tia. Otherwise we'd probably never have met.'

I swallow hard, glad of the foot or so distance between us, as we stroll across the mudflats. Raucous seagulls circle overhead and two dogs run across in front of us, barking excitedly as they take it in turns to chase each other. We begin an upward ascent as we reach the start of the coastal path.

'Sometimes things happen for a reason. But—'

'I know. It's a big "but", isn't it? I mean, it was unexpected, that's for sure.'

'Unexpected? In what way?'

It's hard to talk and climb at the same time and nervousness makes it harder to keep my breathing even. Nic nods in the direction of a bench, set back against an outcrop of rock.

I collapse down onto the seat, gratefully.

'I'm not looking for a relationship, Tia. I can't even sort my own life out at the moment, let alone drag someone else into it. Having another person in your life means getting involved in their lives, too; it adds a whole new level of worry and responsibility. That sounds selfish, but it isn't meant to be. I'm a mess at the moment and my confidence is at a low-ebb. I spend my days driving a taxi, helping out at the farm and writing articles for the local paper about burglaries and lost dogs. If I was ten years younger that might be a way of finding out what I want to do with my life, I suppose. But it's not a very stable work situation. Overnight things could change very quickly and I could find myself struggling to cover the day-to-day bills. There's no long-term future in anything I'm doing at the moment.'

Disappointment sits like a knot in my stomach. He's warning me off.

'Is this some sort of apology for the kiss?'

Nic slumps back against the bench and I shift uneasily in my seat, feeling extremely uncomfortable and hoping he'll change the subject. He doesn't need to explain himself to me at all.

'No. I'm not sorry, only sorry I didn't take it further.'

'Oh, I see. Guess we were on the same page there, then. I wanted to invite you in.'

Well, he's being honest with *me* so I think I owe him the truth. I wanted to invite him in and I didn't, only because I froze. It's been a long time since I took a man home with only one thing on my mind.

He seems to relax a little, stretching out one leg and kicking at a tuft of grass poking up from a mound of sandy grit.

'My situation doesn't alter the way I feel about you. If we'd met five years ago my life wouldn't have been so... messed up. I had a good job with great prospects, a stunning apartment and money in the bank. But that was then and a lot has happened in between. The *now* bears absolutely no resemblance to the *then*.'

A string of walkers pass in front of us in single file and we turn our heads to stare out to sea.

'It's gorgeous when the sun is bouncing off the little waves, like splinters of silver and gold. It seems easy enough to let go of the worries, sitting here without any distractions at all.'

'And that's the problem, isn't it? Are we going to do this, Tia?'

'Yes. There's no point in either of us pretending, Nic. But I think we need to lay down some rules.'

He nods. 'Agreed. You start.'

'No lies,' I say, firmly.

'No pretence. If it's a big mistake, we stop.'

'No guilt.'

'No regrets.' We turn to face each other and shake hands.

'It's a deal.' Nic leans forward and within moments we seal it with a kiss, from which neither of us want to pull away.

18

Night Fires

I'm nervous getting ready for dinner with Nic, tonight, at Langland's Brasserie. That day we called in for a cream tea I went inside to use the bathroom and could see the restaurant was rather smart. The menu looked amazing and tonight I want to show off a little and impress him. So far, he's only seen me either a little sweaty or windswept, and I have the perfect dress to raise the bar without looking over-the-top.

When the taxi pulls up outside I'm surprised to see that Nic isn't driving it. I throw on my coat and walk up to meet the driver.

'Taxi for Langland Brasserie?'

'I guess so, thank you.'

He opens the rear door and I slide inside.

I don't make conversation, puzzling over the fact that Nic hadn't mentioned he was arranging for someone else to pick me up. It's only a short distance in the car anyway, but as soon as we pull up in the car park just behind the restaurant, he's there waiting for us.

The driver does a mock salute to him as we come to a halt. Nic opens my door with a smile, stooping down a little to throw in a "thanks" to the driver, as he helps me to my feet.

'Wow. Just wow.' He looks me up and down as if he's seeing me for the first time.

After such a long break from wearing heels it feels a little strange, but you can't wear a slinky, olive green wrap-around number with flat shoes. I've put my hair up in a fancy clip and with a little make-up, I feel content. It's the old me, the one who attended posh functions on behalf of the magazine and was happy to stand around chatting with a canapé in one hand and a flute of champagne in the other. It's all about working the room, as Clarissa once enlightened me. Make eye contact with the influential, don't just stand around talking with your peers – engage with the people who can do something for you if you have the nerve to grab their attention. That sort of social interaction takes away the fear of being the centre of attention because you get used to selling yourself. The dress isn't wearing me, I'm wearing the dress and I know it.

It's rather strange holding Nic's hand as we walk down towards the rear entrance to the Brasserie. It feels like we're a couple and he keeps turning his head to stare at me.

'Wow.' He says it again and I laugh. If I was hoping for a reaction, then my goal has been achieved, and some.

'You're looking very handsome tonight.' I have to admit that he's certainly made an effort and if I thought he looked good before, I had no idea he could look so... well-groomed. His chin is clean shaven for a change and his hair is styled. He isn't wearing Issey Miyake, tonight, and I don't recognise this one. It's citrusy, with notes of musk and sandalwood. Very masculine and very sexy indeed, as the overall effect is reminiscent of that freshly showered, overtly clean smell.

'Are you getting high on my aftershave?'

I pause mid-inhale and stop trying to sniff the air around him.

'You smell too good, what can I say?'

It raises a smile and he tugs at my hand, drawing my arm against his to give it a squeeze.

You know the moment when an attractive couple enters a restaurant and you see that look on the head waiter's face? He escorts them to the most prominent table in the house, with a flourish. He knows that it sets the tone to attract passers-by and people stepping inside who haven't booked, but are checking it out and then decide to stay. Well, tonight we are that couple.

Nic helps me slip off my coat and as the waiter takes it from him he asks what we would like to drink.

'White?' Nic turns to ask me and I nod.

As we are left to peruse the menu, the tables seem to fill quite quickly. The ambience is a cross between a wine bar brasserie and a glitzy, contemporary bistro that could easily be tucked away in a side street in London. With the raised terrace outside bounded by sheer glass panels, the structure itself looks like a row of very smart, oversized and rather glamorous, beach huts. With jaunty little pitched roofs, it's almost entirely glass-fronted. There is an unobstructed view out over the bay and we have the best table.

'This is amazing,' I whisper and Nic looks up, eyes twinkling.

'It's great at night, isn't it? I've been waiting for an opportunity to bring you here ever since you arrived. I can't remember the last time I took a good-looking woman out on a date. I'd forgotten how obliging waiters can be.'

I chuckle and, as if on cue, the wine waiter appears with a bottle of wine in an ice bucket.

'Madam?' He pours a small amount into my glass and I hold it up to my nose, taking a moment to breathe in the aroma, before taking a small sip.

'Perfect, thank you.'

He pours an inch of wine into each glass and then places the bottle back into the ice bucket. With a polite nod, he takes his leave.

'You do know we are setting the tone here tonight, don't you?' He raises his glass and I do the same, letting them touch very lightly. 'To new beginnings and sweet times.'

As we turn back to the menus I simply can't decide and Nic breaks my concentration.

'The steak is good, but if you like fish then this is the place to eat it.'

'I'm in your hands; I'll have whatever you're having.'

Nic immediately turns his head in the direction of the waiter, who strides over to us.

'The lady and I would like to start with the mussels and then we'll have the seafood scialatielli.'

'Good choice. Thank you, sir and madam.'

I'm impressed; the service is as good as the ambience and I know I'm going to love the food.

'So, while we're waiting it's the perfect opportunity to learn a little bit more about you. All I know so far is that you are a successful feature writer and what was it you said? A bit sensitive at the moment because you're worried some guy back at the office is trying to steal your desk.'

He settles back into his chair, one arm outstretched and his left hand toying with the fork in front of him. He's trying to look relaxed, but his body language is saying something else.

I stare into my wine glass, giving it a little swirl. OK, Nic told me his story but I know it wasn't the whole thing. It isn't easy starting from scratch with someone who knows nothing about you and everyone wants to make a good first impression. But we said *no lies*.

'Well, yes, I've been away from the office for about five weeks now, so by the time I arrive back at my desk it will be the best part of three months. That's a long time and no one is indispensable.' I stop talking, nervously glancing around to avoid direct eye contact.

'Oh, come on, you can't stop there. That tells me nothing.'

I push my head back, raising my eyes to meet his.

'I have an apartment in the up and coming area of Collier's Wood, south west London, with a rather hefty mortgage. No pets, because I don't have time to look after them. My mother died recently and it's been rough, hence the time off work. My brother and I have just begun speaking again after a break of about four years, due to a family row between him and my mum. Aside from that I'm a bit of a loner, really. It's not easy letting people in. Coming here has definitely helped me to get my motivation back and the work is going well.'

'You didn't mention romantic relationships.'

'Well, there's not a lot to say. You meet a guy, you go on a few dates and you split up. Repeat that sentence a few times and there you have it.'

I watch as he slips off his jacket and places it on the back of his chair. When he turns back to face me I can see he's been mulling over my words.

'Being around you, I can't understand why someone hasn't literally swept you off your feet.'

Two waiters carry across the steaming hot mussels and finger bowls. One returns with a basket of artisan bread.

'Mussels with thyme, garlic, white wine and a touch of cream. Enjoy.'

The aroma is amazing and that first bite is heaven.

'Delicious, great choice, Nic.'

He nods, but his eyes are on me and I know he wants me to continue.

'I'm flattered. The truth is that I get bored easily. Well, that's the excuse I use. If I'm being honest, I haven't met anyone who really understands me, yet.'

'That could be because you don't tell them very much about yourself.' He raises an eyebrow, as if it's some sort of reprimand.

'I wish there was something to tell. There was one guy, and he was around for a while but it fizzled out between us. He *sort of* moved into my apartment, uninvited. You know, turning up on a date with a few spare clothes and gradually taking over a bit of space here and a drawer there. The minute we began to spend serious time together he seemed to stop bothering. I mean, it could have been anyone sitting there on the sofa next to me each evening, watching TV and whiling away the hours until bedtime. He blamed his work, but I worked equally as hard and I was trying to make an effort. I don't want to settle for anything, I want the full thing.'

Nic looks wary, so I jump straight in.

'Hey, I'm not the clingy type. We've already agreed the ground rules and that suits me just fine.'

He shakes his head, eating the last of his mussels and wiping his chin with the napkin.

'It isn't that. I have issues.'

The way he says that word sounds ominous.

'Issues?'

I place my fork alongside the dish in front of me, giving my fingers a quick swish in the finger bowl and drying them.

'With women.'

OK, do not panic.

'You're going to have to explain that one, Nic. Pretty quickly.'

It could be a lot worse; we're in a public place and not in the bedroom back at Beach View Cottage.

'As a boy, I idolised my mother, mainly because my father was never around and they led more or less separate lives. Then, as a teenager I began to rebel. When I came to appreciate how controlling she could be I saw that it was either her way, or no way at all. That's how I ended up in a job I didn't enjoy, making lots of money and regretting having given in to an overly-manipulative woman with no heart.'

I don't quite know what to say to that. But I don't have to say anything, as Nic continues.

'I met someone she didn't approve of and my mother turned her back on me. It was liberating for a while, until reality set in and it was obvious the relationship wasn't going to work. Then my father reappeared and the divorce proceedings began. I didn't care much about it when I heard, but it stirred up one unholy mess. I was dragged into it at a time when I was making some big mistakes. I had no real sense of direction going forward, but events finally overtook any indecision I had, anyway. It became irrelevant as I haven't had any dealings with my mother for several years now.'

He stops, a look of shock washing over his face.

'Sorry, Tia, I didn't mean to drop that on you like some rather bizarre confession.'

I reach for his hand across the table, but the waiters arrive with our main course and I only briefly touch his fingertips.

As soon as they are out of earshot I lean into the table and extend my hand once more.

'It's OK, Nic. I'm glad you told me. It means something to me that you've shared what has to be a very painful memory.'

He's toying with his food, even though the linguine-style pasta with a fish sauce is amazing. I take one or two bites, but my appetite is gone.

'I've spoilt our evening and I'm sorry. Well, my parents' sad story has spoilt our evening. How about we ask them to box this up and we take it away?'

I smile, gently taking his hand in mine and giving it a squeeze. Our eye contact confirms this is about more than having our appetites stolen by a few sad memories. The tension between us is building and food is the last thing on our minds.

'Great idea.'

He catches the waiter's eye and explains that we have to leave immediately because of an emergency. I stop myself from bursting out laughing, as the waiter nods seriously and hurries away with our plates.

Nic has his phone to his ear.

'Hey, mate, change of plan. Can you swing by and pick us up, now? Thanks. Appreciated.'

'OK, let me grab your coat. Our car is on the way.'

The waiter is very helpful, returning with a carrier bag containing our cartons of food. He insists on finding a stopper for the wine we've barely touched, so that he can slip the bottle into the bag, too.

Strangely enough, I don't feel at all disappointed. What I feel is a little overwhelmed that Nic, whom Olwen referred to as the man of few words, has really opened up to me. I know that wasn't his intention, but now I know I can trust him. The dilemma for me is that if I can't talk about the overdose, then I'm going to feel that I'm not being honest or fair.

The terms of our non-relationship are crystal clear: no lies, no pretence, no guilt and no regrets.

*

Lying in bed with Nic's arm folded around me, I feel safe. Safe; it's a word that has never really been in my vocabulary. I'm not saying that I felt unsafe in general, but I was often lonely, even when surrounded by people. And then when Mum died I was... cast adrift, as if a thread that was a lifeline had been cut and I'd lost my only constant in life.

'Hey.' Nic lays his cheek against mine. 'Don't dwell on things. Just relax.'

Having told him the full story of the state Will found me in that day, he seemed to understand. He simply said that sometimes we do something and it all goes badly wrong, but the intention was never for that to happen. Without intent, it's simply a mistake and a wake-up call. We need to learn from it, in order to grow.

The remnants of our meal remain on the table downstairs still, untouched. Once our lips brushed there was no way to stop that growing need to lose ourselves in one another. A rapport had been established and it wasn't just about the psychological and physiological effects of that... need to be wanted, to be loved. As the brain releases its pleasure chemical, dopamine, the biological reaction blots out everything else. The all-too-familiar anxiety and pain from life's disappointments simply melt away. It's like a rebirth and nothing matters except each little thrill coursing through your body. Skin on skin: mouths urgently exploring each other and being able to let go, as a sense of total abandonment takes over.

The afterglow is akin to gently coming down from an altered state. The nearness of another person is all the reminder you need that life, when it's good, is a wondrous thing. The fact that Nic understands and recognises, only too well, the turmoil I'm trying to escape is comforting to the soul.

19

The Morning After

I'm in the shower when I hear the doorbell ring, my hair covered in a cascade of soapy bubbles. There's little point in rushing, as Nic is in the kitchen, anyway.

When I do make my way downstairs there's a large box on the worktop and I suck in a deep breath. I totally forgot Olwen told me that Rhys would be popping in some shopping today. Nic is watching and when I look across at him he shrugs his shoulders. He's bare foot, has nothing on his top and is wearing only a nicely cut pair of trousers.

'Sorry, I forgot.' I chew my lip as I berate myself for forgetting. 'Was it awkward?'

Nic screws up his face and clearly, he too feels a sense of unease.

'Rhys will mention it to Olwen. She's discreet, but that's two people who will know that we're... um... acquainted.'

I burst out laughing.

'Well, nice to make your acquaintance. I hope we meet up again at some time in the near future.'

He leans back against the counter top, folding his arms over his chest and those taut abs. I try not to drool as his arms flex and a flashback from last night is catapulted into my mind.

'You can bet on it. Actually, it was quite a bonus being able to dive into a wardrobe and grab some clean clothes. I will take my dirty washing with me, though.' He reaches out and pulls me into him, nestling my head against his neck.

'Cheeky!'

'Anyway, good morning, Tia.' It's a half-whisper and his breath tickles as I sink into him.

We stand, holding onto each other and I can't ever remember feeling this comfortable with anyone, the morning after the first *night before*. Not that there has been a whole string of them, just a few over the years. Most of which I regretted shortly afterwards, because sex is often just about fulfilling a need. But that satisfaction seems to dissipate very quickly when it's over and then things are back to where they were before. The actual act of having sex doesn't touch that little bubble of inner loneliness that won't go away. Like the heat from a fire only briefly warming the skin, when the chill permeates through to the core.

'That's a serious face.' Nic's eyes search mine.

'That was a serious night.'

'No regrets?'

'No lies, no pretence, no guilt and no regrets – I think we covered all bases last night. Now I'm looking forward to the fun bit.'

'You're a bit of a surprise, Tia, that's for sure. I will admit that I'm a little out of practice when it comes to having fun.'

'Well, that will make it even more enjoyable. And now I think we're both running late.'

We glance in tandem at the clock.

'Ooh, I can see that you're a bad influence on me already. I'd better head off as my shift starts at nine and I have the hill to climb. Guess impressing you with a chauffeured car wasn't the brightest idea.'

'On the contrary, it went down well. Although it does rather show that I was a forgone conclusion.'

The look on his face as he stoops to kiss me on the lips is priceless.

'Stop flirting with me, I have to go and you have people to interview.'

'Will you come back after work?'

'Try stopping me.'

*

I force myself to settle down to work as my brain and body are buzzing. A call from Clarissa soon focuses my attention on the job in hand.

'Great first draft, Tia. Couple number one are photogenic, too. Who are you pairing them with for the first part of the feature?'

'Couple number four. I've done the interviews and I'm writing it up now. They're mid-forties, so it's a ten-year age difference and they have four kids. That's obviously higher than the national average for the size of a family in the UK. But it's a perfect example of how everything changes once you make that decision. Keeping the love alive in a relationship with a lot of family pressures to contend with has a rather dramatic impact. It's opened my eyes to a few things.'

What Clarissa doesn't know is how close I came to pulling this couple's story, until I received an email from Carol shortly after I'd spoken to them. She explained that the morning of the interview she'd received a recall for a mammogram she'd had done the week prior. They were both worried sick about it and she admitted their heads were all over the place. Carol went on to say that everything is fine and that she wanted to explain what Christmas meant to them in photos.

When I opened the attachment, I saw that it was a collage. It was a collection of crazy, mad snapshots which summed up the chaos that is a normal Christmas day for their family. But every face had a smile; every eye reflected happiness. In the centre was a photo of Carol and Steve beneath the mistletoe, but I could clearly see the arms of a child wrapped around her waist. Even as their lips touched, Steve seemed to be looking over Carol's shoulder, keeping a watchful eye on what was happening behind them. The same way that on the day of the interview Carol's problem had been in the forefront of Steve's mind and nothing else had mattered to him. I knew then that I had everything I needed to make this article work and that there would be many families who would connect with the chaos, and the love.

'Great stuff, Tia. We want to keep this real, get our readers to engage and see aspects of their own lives reflected in this feature. Then give them practical ideas they can go away and try for themselves. Family life is tough at times and it's comforting to be reminded other people struggle, too. I'll be interested to read the complete thing, once you have it. Will you be able to meet the deadline?'

'It shouldn't be a problem. I'm getting lots of exercise here and sleeping well, so my energy levels are through the roof.'

I'm sure Clarissa can hear the change in my voice and I have to explain it away somehow. I am re-energised and I'm feeling positive again.

'Good to hear. Something interesting has come up and it's sitting on my desk at the moment. I'm not sure if I should push it Finlay's way, but my gut is saying you'd do a better job of it. We've been offered the chance to shadow a Formula One driver. He's a former test driver working his first season on the grid. The working title is *On and Off the Track*. Give it some thought. It would tie you up over the summer and involve a fair bit of travel. I don't know if you'd prefer a period back in the office after your time on the Gower coast.'

Clarissa assigns jobs and you have no choice other than to go with it. In much the same way as she handed me the file for this feature and she wasn't expecting a refusal. It's odd she's asking me what I'd prefer. I mean, I don't think that's a term I've ever heard her use before.

'I'm... um, well I hadn't given it any thought. Of course, it sounds like a great opportunity and I haven't made any plans for after my return.'

Fleetingly, I think that it would be nice to maybe come back to visit Caswell Bay in the height of summer. But after this... little fling, let's call it, with Nic, that might make it rather difficult. When I leave at the beginning of July I have to look back with no regrets.

'I'll pencil you in for that, then. We'll discuss it on your return. In the meantime, keep me posted of any developments. I'm here if you want to talk.'

What? As the line goes dead I find myself staring at the phone in my hand. Something is up and I quickly text Hayley.

Morning Hayley. Interviews now done for couple number 4. Can u let me have an up to date schedule? Is everything OK there?

Seconds later my phone rings and I knew if she was free, she'd call.

'Did Clarissa just offer you the F1 thing? I took some papers into her while you were talking and overheard a bit of the conversation. Finlay will be furious.'

I can imagine the beam on her face. Finlay went through a phase of telling Hayley to fetch his coffee, something she only does for Clarissa, obviously. We all make our own and he knew that. She ignored him every time, of course, but he tried it on for well over a week. In the end, she span around on her heels, glared at him and said, 'Get it yourself, Finlay. I work for the boss, not for you and I doubt you'll ever find yourself in that position.'

It was in the open office and everyone put their heads straight down, but secretly we all wanted to give her a round of applause.

'Well, she's offering it. If I don't have plans for the summer.'

'What?'

'I had the same reaction. What's going on there, Hayley? I was a bit worried about Finlay trying to undermine my position and walking back into an uneasy situation, but Clarissa is acting strangely.'

'Hmm.' Hayley pauses for a second. 'There's no change this end. It's busy, which is good and things are ticking over. To be honest, she's as demanding as ever but when I heard her talking to you I couldn't believe it.

He will feel aggrieved, that's for sure. He's a big fan of F1 and she knows it.'

'Maybe it's a test.'

'Of Finlay, or of you?'

'Who knows?'

That makes two of us without a clue about what's really going on.

'Anyway, what's happening? Any promising little interludes on the horizon?'

My mouth suddenly feels very dry. Hayley knows I'm not going to spend every single waking hour working.

'I went to a barn dance on Saturday night. I danced with the local postman, Tom. I've not met him before as the owner has his post diverted. Tom is a great dancer.'

'Sounds interesting.' I can hear Hayley's mind working overtime.

'He's in his early sixties and has three grandchildren. But he was a good teacher and it was actually a lot of fun. You should try it sometime. How's Jack?'

Nicely diverted, Tia.

'He's wonderful. He wants us to have a weekend away together and I'm so excited about it.'

'That's lovely to hear, Hayley. Has he met your parents, yet?'

'Yes, we've been out for a meal with them. That's partly what the weekend away is about, as his parents live in the Lake District and he's trying to organise a family gathering. Anyway, I'll keep you posted if I hear anything that might be of interest to you. I think there's a plan afoot, so be aware and tread cautiously. And try to have some fun. There has to be at least one handsome, unattached guy hanging around, even if it is a very sedate place.'

'If I see one, I'll grab him. How's that?'

'Well, make sure you do. It's about time you got laid again and reminded yourself what life is all about.'

My coffee mug is halfway to my mouth as she speaks and as my arm wobbles I miss my aim. The result is a fine spray of brown dots down the front of my teeshirt.

'Working on it. Speak to you later.'

Actually, I'm way ahead of target on that front.

*

'Hey, how was your day?'

As Nic steps inside he catches my hand. I step back and with a gentle kick, he pushes the front door closed behind him.

'Good thanks and yours?'

He raises my fingers to his lips, looking over the tops of them into my eyes. He seems genuinely pleased to see me but it's a look of relief, as if he's trying to shrug off something that's weighing him down.

'There was a break-in up at the farm. I can't believe they had the nerve to do it in broad daylight. It's a sprawling place, admittedly, but people are coming and going all the time. It means they've been watching the property for some time and that's a real concern.'

I'm shocked by his words. 'Was much stolen?'

He nods his head. 'They stole yesterday's takings from the office and left a fine mess behind them. They also ransacked one of the bedrooms and stole a jewellery box. Irreplaceable family heirloom stuff by all accounts with some real value to it, but it's the sentimental attachment that has struck home. What's worrying is that there are a lot of bedrooms in that old place and yet they seemed to hone in on the only one worth combing through. Mike's convinced they'd tried before but were disturbed, maybe. Second time around they knew exactly where to head and that's the only way they could have pulled off something as bold and risky as that.'

A slight shiver travels down my spine.

'If you want to head back up there to help out—'

'No, it's fine. I know I said I'd return and I have, but I don't want to crowd you. If it's not convenient, just say and I'll make it a brief visit.'

I wasn't trying to send him away and I pout. He grins back at me.

'Seriously, we are two consenting adults and it won't hurt my feelings if you don't want to spend every waking minute with me.'

We are now standing so close together that he rests his chin on my head, playfully.

'I wonder how different the world is when seen from varying heights.'

He's implying I'm short and I take a step back, tilting my head to peer up at him.

'The taller they are, the harder they fall.'

He still hasn't let go of my hand and it's clear we're both waiting to see what the other person wants to do.

'How about a walk along the beach?'

He nods his head and I wriggle free from his grasp, so I can grab my jacket and slip on my shoes.

As we close the garden gate behind us, and head down to the water's edge, I see that Max is out fishing today. He's too far away to acknowledge as Nic and I stroll hand in hand along the full length of Holly Cove.

'I've been meaning to say, I love the sea views you have hanging on the staircase walls. There are some really great photographs there. I keep forgetting to bring my iPad and take a few snaps of my own.'

'Thanks. It's an outlet for my creative side now I work solely to pay the bills.'

'Oh, I don't think you mentioned what you did for a living before you bought the cottage.'

His jaw tightens a little, but he turns to look directly at me as he answers.

'I was a Marketing Director for a large publishing company in London. Unfortunately, most of my money was tied up in property and house prices dropped at the same time I lost my job. I walked away with just enough equity to buy the cottage and start doing it up. Now I've run out of funds and, as I mentioned, I'm barely getting by financially at the moment. The big problem is next winter, as the roof needs an overhaul and when the boiler was serviced the plumber said they no longer manufacture spare parts for it. And then there's the garden. Then there's the fencing at the front which needs re-painting and at the back I need to take down a few trees to let in more light. It's an endless list, I'm afraid.'

I push back the strands of hair being whipped across my face by the light breeze coming off the water. As I look into his eyes, I can see the uncertainty weighs heavily upon Nic's shoulders.

'You've done a wonderful job of the renovation work, Nic. You have a real sense of design, too. The rooms in the cottage flow beautifully and that's quite an achievement. Everything takes time.'

He looks pleased and I'm glad the opportunity has arisen to tell him that. When you're on your own, there isn't anyone you can share your highs and lows with at the end of the day. That's tough at times. Even now, I catch myself thinking I must call Mum and tell her about something that's happened. Then I remember the cold reality that still doesn't seem quite real.

'Hard work is good for the soul. Bashing down walls with a sledgehammer and carrying out hundreds of buckets of rubble is exhausting. But it was cathartic at the time.'

It must have been a huge adjustment for him. I know that I'm fooling myself if I think that when I'm back in London it isn't going to be a massive step for me, too. I wonder if I'm losing my appetite for the cut and thrust of an industry where your instincts have to be sharp and your conscience flexible.

'It's funny, but life seems to tick over and we rise to each little challenge that comes our way, thinking nothing changes very much. Then suddenly our world is turned upside down and everything changes overnight. It's only with hindsight anyone can appreciate how blinkered we become.'

We're almost at the point where the projecting headland cuts off the beach and we loop around to pass in front of the cabins. There are boards laid out over the softer area in two parallel lines down to the firmer sand. Looking back towards the workshop, the metal fencing is locked and I can see the boat trailer inside.

'That's quite a big boat. It must be hard launching it from here.' I turn towards the sea, raising my hand above my eyes to shield them from the sun. The boat is bobbing around, but it's still too far out to be more than a shape.

'The boards take the weight and stop the trailer wheels from sinking into the sand. Once it's on the firmer stuff a boat like that simply slides off the rollers on the trailer with ease. It's a one-man job. The shore falls away quite rapidly here, so it's a good spot. It's easy enough to winch the loaded trailer back up, afterwards.'

I had wondered about that because I knew there was no way you could drive along the beach.

'It must have been really hard to transport the building materials for the huts to this spot, then.'

I'm thinking as I speak and when I look at Nic, he simply shrugs.

'People don't always do what's sensible. I should have bought a nice tidy little house on one of the little developments off Caswell Road. Instead I chose the difficult option, so who am I to judge someone else's idiosyncratic ideas. Anyway, I'm getting hungry. How do you fancy some hearty pub grub?'

'Great, it's my treat tonight, though. Not quite as special as last night's trip to the Brasserie, for which I forgot to thank you.'

Nic stops, then circles around in front of me.

'You are still OK about this, aren't you? No second thoughts?'

'I am, and I have a suggestion to make, but I'll save that for later. Much later.'

Finally, he seems to relax a little and I can see that aside from the fact that I've made him curious, he's relieved by the implication. Anyway, he's going to have to wait until I've had at least one very large glass of wine before I proposition him.

<u>20</u>

The Talk of the Village

When we arrive back at the cottage I shower and change, leaving Nic in the sitting room leafing through his books.

When I reappear, he looks up from the sofa and his eyes sweep over me appreciatively. I almost wish we weren't going out.

'You look good.'

The words are irrelevant, because his eyes say it all very clearly indeed.

'Come on, we're heading back up to the farm so we can catch a lift to the pub.'

I look at him enquiringly.

'I thought I'd have a pint and I don't drink and drive.'

He stands, walking over to the bookshelves to return the volume he was reading when I came in.

'Great collection, quite diverse.' I decide to dive in and clear up a little question hovering in the back of my mind. 'A few surprises in there. I understand all the books on photography now. But *The Notebook* by Nicholas Sparks? I don't think anyone can read that and have a dry eye.'

The moment I finish talking, I realise I've touched a nerve, but he doesn't look angry, only sad.

'Not all of these books are mine; a few were here originally, when I moved in.'

He looks uncomfortable and I wonder if it belonged to a previous girlfriend. I guess that's a little mystery that will remain unsolved. Besides, it's none of my business, anyway.

'Shall I fetch your coat?'

As Nic heads off to the bathroom I put on my shoes and grab my bag. When he returns he's all smiles and on the way to the farm we pass the time talking about the barn dance. He tells me some funny stories about a few of the people there, the sort that you couldn't miss spotting even in such a large crowd. I'll probably never cross paths again with the vast majority of them during the remainder of my visit, but I am beginning to pick up on how supportive people are in this tight little community. I've not been made to feel like a tourist passing through, but it's as if I've been adopted and given a temporary citizenship.

'Olwen sings your praises. I think she was sad to see Beach View Cottage deteriorating, so in her book you are a hero.'

Nic parks the car up behind the barn where the dance was held. As we head back down to the farmhouse I have a thought.

'Is it far? Could we walk to the pub?'

'It's about a mile-and-a-half, tops, I suppose. Are you up for that?'

'I spend too much time sitting down in front of a computer screen, so any exercise is always welcome.'

'I'll take you the scenic route, rather than along the main road. It isn't muddy, it's a gravel path and well-trodden.'

'I'm really surprised there aren't more signs around to make it clear what is private property and what isn't. I suspect a lot of visitors to the area won't be experienced walkers and it must be annoying to have people wandering around on your land as if they have a right to be there.'

Nic nods in agreement.

'Actually, I wish I didn't own the woods around the cottage. It's a bit of a liability at times. Even woodland needs managing and I have to regularly inspect the trees up near the road, especially after high winds. If something falls on a passing car, or a person is injured, then I suppose I might be held liable if it's down to poor management. But it was part and parcel of the deal.'

Well, the surprises keep on coming. He doesn't just own the cottage, but the woods around it too. As we walk, Nic tells me a little more about the surrounding area. Behind the bay is the Bishop's Wood nature reserve and it's a rare example of a limestone woodland. He goes on to tell me the legend of the local murder mystery case that took forty years to solve. A married couple disappeared without warning shortly before Christmas 1919. In November 1961, a bag of human bones was discovered in a disused local mine; they were proven to be those of the wife. After an extensive manhunt, the husband's body was traced to a cemetery in Bristol, some eighty miles away. He'd died almost three years before the discovery.

'I wonder what really happened. It sounds to me as if they made a few assumptions there. Anyway, thanks for sharing that, Nic.' If I sound a little jaded it's because as the light begins to fade a little, the trees take on an eerie quality. I'm definitely feeling spooked, as the shadows seem to close in around us.

Nic's news about the break-in at the farm has unsettled me and maybe for good reason, following on from what I've read in the local paper. Every night before I go to bed I stare out, combing the trees and second guessing every shadow. I shake off the uneasiness that I can't help feeling but this isn't really helping to allay my fears tonight. Every sound has me scanning around imagining that someone is following us.

'I thought you'd appreciate it, being a journalist. The crime levels here were almost non–existent until this latest little spate. Nowadays, everyone knows everybody's business, aside from their own and there is an upside to that neighbourly nosiness, I suppose.'

Well, Rhys and Olwen know about us now and there's nothing to be done about that but the burglaries are worrying. The farm is nowhere near as isolated as Nic's cottage and whoever broke in must have had to wait for just the right moment.

'We're approaching the Trawlerman's Inn. You can just see the lights ahead of us.' He squeezes my hand reassuringly.

'Look, I didn't mean to spook you and I'm sorry if I did.' Nic sounds genuinely apologetic, realising the setting isn't helping at all.

I'd smile, but in the gloom there's no point, all he would see are my teeth.

Inside the pub there's a fire spitting in the hearth as the wood sizzles and hisses, welcoming us in. It's not cold, but there is a nip in the air tonight even though it's the second of June.

We find a nice little table for two tucked away in a corner and make ourselves comfortable.

'That wasn't the most enchanting walk at this time of the night, but this place is great.'

'I knew you were spooked; wish I hadn't told you that story now.'

'I don't like loose ends, or not knowing all of the details. It's the way my mind works. As you work for the local paper you'll know all about that.'

'Well, let's order and then I'll tell you all about my budding career as a journo.' He gives me a cheesy grin, clearly laughing at himself.

We decide to go for the good old-fashioned fish and chips, with half a pint of local ale. It seems to be what the majority of people around us are ordering and so it must be good.

When Nic comes back from placing our order at the bar, I lean into him as he slides a glass of something he calls *Gower Gold*, in front of me.

'You do know everyone is watching us, don't you?'

He nods, then turns and raises his hand in the air, rather like a royal wave.

'Hey guys, sorry, forgot to say this is Tia. And yes, she's the one renting my cottage.'

Virtually everyone raises their glasses in the air. A chorus of *welcome* has me laughing out loud. I half-stand and raise my glass in the air to return the toast. Then I sink back down onto the bench seat, wishing I could disappear.

'Nic, I can't believe you did that. We're being talked about now.'

'It's my local and everyone knows me. Quite a few will already know you from the barn dance, or seeing you out walking. If people know your face they look out for you and that's a good thing. Besides, my credibility here has just escalated. It's obvious we're on a date and now I'm going to lean forward and kiss you.' And he does just that, then draws slowly away from me with a playful smile on his face.

'The job at the paper is something unexpected that came my way. I'd finished the bulk of the work on the cottage and I'd been taking a few photos that I thought the paper might like to use. The editor, Gareth, asked if I'd be interest in doing a bit of work here and there. Sometimes it's taking photos, particularly in the summer when there are sandcastle competitions down on the beach. Other times it's checking out a lead he might get: missing animals, the occasional burglary, uproar over litter appearing overnight in the car parks. I cover some of the summer events, that sort of thing. It's another source of income and something I enjoy doing.'

The food arrives and it smells amazing. The batter on the fish is golden and the chips are triple cooked.

'British cuisine at its best,' Nic says. He leans in and whispers, 'as long as you aren't calorie counting or worried about your cholesterol. But this is the best you'll find anywhere in the country.'

He's right and I second that. It's a very pleasant evening and when we leave we receive a ripple of *goodbyes* as we head for the door. I try to remain composed and dignified, with a nonchalant smile plastered over my face.

'You fit in well here, Nic. All credit to you as it's a different world to the London scene.'

'Shall I phone for a taxi, or are you prepared to brave the dark? I promise not to move from your side, or to let go of your hand. I'm a black belt in judo so any trouble and you can simply stand back. In mere seconds, I'll have any attacker disabled and on the floor.'

I start laughing as I zip up my jacket. But it is eerie, that I can't deny. Nic stands in front of me, sliding his hands down my arms until he catches both of my hands in his. The contact sends a little tingle up my spine. In the warm glow of the car park lighting his face is animated and there's a spark of life, where before there was a sense of dogged resignation. As if life had punched him once too often and he was only hanging on by a thread.

'Are you? A black belt in judo?'

'Ha, now I know you are gullible, as well.'

'As well as what?'

'Beautiful, warm and intelligent. There has to be a catch somewhere and I'll find it. Now let's start walking.'

We link arms and a little smile hovers around my mouth. I haven't linked arms with anyone since the last time Mum and I were out walking together. We walk, and chat, and stop to kiss, then walk some more and before we know it Beach View Cottage looms up before us. It's bathed in a little pool of light.

'You turned on the outside light; it looks so cosy.'

'I had no intention of fumbling around on the doorstep in the dark again,' he grins.

'I wasn't expecting you to; we aren't teenagers. I was assuming you'd stay.'

'I meant for the key. But maybe you'll need someone around, anyway, in case you have bad dreams about the couple who disappeared.' He makes a ghoulish sound.

I give him a playful shove before putting the key in the lock and opening the door.

'Some reporter you are if you believe everything you read. If he wasn't caught in the act, or he didn't confess – which he couldn't as he was dead – the truth will never be known.'

*

I lie here with my head on Nic's chest, listening to his heartbeat, while his fingers gently stroke my arm.

'Hey, what was that suggestion you were going to make? Did you change your mind?'

'Oh, yes, I... um... I was wondering whether you'd consider moving back in here. I mean, there's a spare room and no one needs to know. The rental agreement would still be valid, but I thought it made sense seeing as poor Sid really doesn't want you walking him. And sometimes it's handy having a man around, in case there's a plumbing emergency, or anything...' My words tail off. It didn't come out sounding quite as casual as I'd hoped; in fact, it sounded rather pathetic and suspect even to my ears.

'That's an interesting proposal. So, you're suggesting I bring my tool kit as well as my suitcase?'

'Just a thought, no strings attached.'

I'm trying hard not to turn this into a big deal but I can see he isn't fooled.

'This is about the burglaries, isn't it? Tia, if you don't feel safe here you need to be straight with me because that's a whole different thing.'

I feel awkward, knowing that it's probably my imagination because I'm not usually easily spooked. But on several occasions over the last week I've looked out of the window after turning out the light late at night and fancied I saw something, or someone, moving between the trees. It's probably only shadows as the wind whips through the canopy above. But it was in the same place at about the same time. Then last night it wasn't there, so now I'm hesitant to voice what is surely only a touch of paranoia.

'I... maybe it's nothing, merely a trick of the light and I'm a little on edge given what's been happening. That's the price you pay for having an over-active imagination.' I try to lighten the mood.

Nic changes his position and I can feel his muscles tense a little. He isn't falling for it and now I wish I hadn't said anything.

'I will admit I'm not totally happy to think of you here all alone at night, but I didn't want to freak you out. Or undermine you in any way.'

'Is there any news up at the farm?'

Nic pulls me closer and I'm more than content to snuggle into him.

Even during the day, I find myself drawn to the window, almost ignoring the vista and checking to see whether anyone is watching the cottage. Which is crazy because they'd be very likely to be spotted as neither Max, or I have a set pattern of comings and goings. Surely even burglars would know a little cottage like this wouldn't hold anything of very great value. The risk wouldn't be worth it. Would it?

'We're hoping the fingerprinting will identify whether it's linked to the other burglaries. Look, if you really don't feel safe at the moment then I'm more than happy to use that spare room until they round up these criminals. Which they will, as everyone is on alert and the paper will continue to give these incidents front page attention so that doesn't ease up.

'You can still throw me out of my own house whenever you want, of course. Well, until the second of July. What it's like to have all that power over a hapless, homeless man, eh?'

I laugh but it comes out like a snort. Nic is trying his best not to make me feel awkward but I do. Maybe this isn't about what I think I'm seeing in the shadows at all, but a sudden desire not to be alone. Nic has somehow wormed his way inside my comfort zone with seeming ease. Maybe what's spooking me is the way in which I'm willing to lower my guard whenever he's around.

'I've figured out what we both have in common; well, two things, actually.' I move back so I can see his face a little more clearly in the moonlit bedroom. The inky black sky seems to make the full moon tonight look translucent and it's quite light considering the lateness of the hour. I want Nic to see that I'm serious.

'I was wondering what was going on inside that head of yours – I knew there was more to this, although I understand your concerns. We're all a little bit on edge at the moment. Anyway, are you going to share your discovery with me?' He sounds intrigued.

I cast around for the right words.

'Neither of us really know what we want, or what we are capable of wanting. We only know that we're going through a transition and that's what draws us together. The other thing is fear. OK, so I'm afraid of the shadow I think I've seen in the woods but I'm also afraid that I'm destined to be that career woman who is successful, but will never find anything else to give me a sense of fulfilment in my life.'

'You can't stop there. What is it that I'm afraid of? Fending off intruders isn't on the list, I might add. I know how to handle myself.' His attempt at injecting some humour falls flat and I realise that he's a tad uncomfortable. 'You're scared that the life you have here in Caswell Bay is the one you are meant to have and that you will end up finding it enough. As if being happy can't be that simple. You've been brought up to be an achiever. If you don't achieve, you will consider yourself to be a failure.'

He lowers his chin, his eyes now in line with mine.

'I think maybe you're right. In the words of Luke, "The sins of the parents are visited upon the children", and maybe he was right in my case. But it's not the same for you, you had loving parents.'

'I know. But that makes it worse, because I've seen how good a marriage and family life can be. I've also seen how easily communication breaks down and the damage that ensues. My brother is starting to come around, but he's been lost to me for a long time. Maybe I can only succeed at pushing people away on a personal level.'

Nic rolls into me so our faces are touching.

'Do you know what I think?'

I sigh, putting my arm around him and hugging him even closer.

'What?'

'I think that you *think* too much, although I'm finding that quality strangely seductive. You certainly haven't succeeded in pushing me away, you are actually reeling me in. I'm like a fish on the end of a line.'

I giggle. 'I have to sleep. My eyelids are closing. You've worn me out.'

'Good, then I've achieved my goal. And Tia, don't worry about the shadows. I have no intention of letting any harm come to you while you are here.'

Within seconds my breathing deepens and I feel myself floating, getting lighter and lighter. For some rather bizarre reason, there appear to be snowflakes all around me. I feel myself letting go, happy to surrender and let my dream take me where it wants to go. Somewhere, quite close, a phrase seems to hang in the air, 'Sweet dreams, lovely Tia' and then the silence takes over.

21

A Little Cloud on the Horizon

When Olwen arrives, I pretend to be busy, giving her a quick 'Hi' and then returning to scan my notes on the papers in front of me.

'It's official, then.' I know she's standing in front of me and hasn't even taken off her coat yet, as I find myself looking down at her feet. They are both firmly planted and pointing in my direction.

I look up at her, anxiety washing over me, tinged with dread.

'What is?'

'The two of you. I know I've been telling him for a while he needs to make an effort and put himself out there, but... is this wise? You're here to ease yourself back into work and when two people fall for each other —'

I drop my pen as my hand flies up to my face, covering my mouth.

'We're not in love, Olwen. We're just... engaging in a little romantic, um... interlude. I'll be gone in four-and-a-half weeks' time. We're both free and single, and lonely. No harm done, just a bit of fun.'

Her expression is more of a scowl.

'I'm not being a prude here, Tia. I've come to know a little more about Nic than he chooses to share with most people. He's a lovely man, but he has his demons. And you're so vulnerable at the moment, but you've been lulled into a false sense of security. For you, this doesn't reflect real life; it's more of a working holiday. You think you can cope with this, and I'm sure Nic feels the same way, but there's a lot that can go wrong. Neither of you is the sort to have sex for the sake of it. There's an attraction steering this, whether you like it, or not. What happens when it's time to leave? What if one of you doesn't want to let go, but the other does? And, after last night, everyone in the village is talking about Nic's new girlfriend. He has a sudden spring in his step and we can all see that.'

I don't want to smile, but I can't help the way my cheeks lift, involuntarily.

'Oh dear. I did tell him off about that. But you shouldn't worry, Olwen. We know what we're doing and we have ground rules. In fact, I also have a confession, even though I know you aren't going to like it. But I've suggested Nic moves back in; purely because of the burglaries, of course.'

226

I might as well get it out of the way and having an excuse helps. Olwen looks shocked.

'You don't feel safe here on your own at night?'

A look of growing concern creeps over her face. It wasn't my intention to alarm her but the uneasiness hasn't left me. If it had just been the once, then I could blame my imagination but it wasn't.

'I think maybe I'm feeling a little unnerved by the latest incident up at the farm and having Nic here will take that away. Please don't worry about it – or our... relationship.'

'Well, it's only natural we're all on alert and that isn't a nice feeling. It's not something we're used to around here and being on your own will make it harder, I'm sure. So, in a way it's a bit of a relief to know Nic will be here until the police catch up with this gang. But as for the two of you, I can't help wondering if all that research you're doing about lovey-dovey stuff is stirring up your hormones. Or maybe it's like one of those holiday romances. Seems like a good idea at the time but afterwards you wonder what on earth you were thinking.' She shakes her head, turns and heads for the bathroom. 'I don't want to see either of you getting hurt. Beach View deserves the sound of happiness echoing between these walls, but an affair that could end in heartache is bad karma. If it goes wrong, then at least I've warned you and I'll be having the same little chat with Nic, the next time I see him.'

When she's out of sight I let out a gasp. An affair? I know Olwen means well, but she's been married for such a long time and I can see how this arrangement might offend her sensibilities a little. This is simply two people having a little fun. When she walks back into the kitchen I clear my throat and look in her direction.

'Um... Olwen, under the circumstances if you want to stop coming here I fully understand. I don't want to put you in a position that makes you feel uncomfortable. I'm not sure if Nic is going to be here every night and at weekends, but he is going to be around. I really didn't expect this to happen, but it has and life is too short not to take a risk occasionally.'

'I'm not saying Nic would hurt you and if you've both talked this through, then that's fine. As I said, I'm not a prude and it's not my place to judge, or advise, you. However, I've never believed that a legal document makes a relationship. If two people are together, for however long, it's a commitment; admittedly, one with a cut-off point for you two. What I'm trying to say is that the idea might sound workable, but when emotions are involved it's not quite so cut and dried. I sincerely hope I don't have to spend time helping one, or the other, of you to get over a broken heart. You are two lost souls at the moment and that brings out the mothering instinct in me. It's in my nature to care about folk and I find myself caring about two people who have been thrown together under an unusual set of circumstances. There, I've said my piece, despite the fact that it's none of my business.'

After that she disappears; we hardly exchange two words before she heads off to the school.

Olwen's words seem to rattle around inside my head for a long time after her departure. Absentmindedly, I find myself chewing the end of my pen, remembering the moment when I first decided I was going to sleep with Nic. As his face fills my head my heart squishes up a little and my stomach starts to flutter. This is that first flush of attraction, the one you think will go on forever. And when it starts to fade that's when it's like a punch in the gut. You know it was only a fleeting attraction and the more you find out about each other, the more it erodes the wonderfully warm feelings that were there at the start. Until you reach the point, sadly, where everything they do is annoying, or bores you to tears. This will run its course. Nic definitely isn't ready for a full-blown relationship and with my track record I know the odds are stacked against me. I don't believe I have the emotional capacity at the moment to give a proper relationship what it requires. Surely Nic is aware of that, though. As I'm equally aware of his situation.

I shift the papers in front of me, around. What was it Paige said? Ah, here it is:

Me: Why do you think your relationship works, Paige?

Paige: Because I'm a better person when I'm around Darren. We work as a team. Without him I'm not the sum of half of that partnership, I'm probably only thirty per cent of it. Does that make any sense? Simply knowing he's mine, and I'm his, alters the way I look at everything in life. Even when he isn't with me I approach life in general with more confidence and a sense of security, I suppose. Knowing someone has your back no matter what happens, is priceless. And I would do anything for him, because my life would be nothing if he walked away. And that's why we work at it because what we have is precious to us both.

I sit back, my eyes filled with tears. She's so young and she's heavily pregnant with her first baby. To me it sounds like a rather scary situation to be in and yet she faces it with a belief that everything will be all right. She's calm, positive and happy. I've never, ever had that feeling and I envy her.

Glancing up at the clock I see it's almost noon and time to begin interviewing couple number five. I quickly square up everything on the desk and put the recorder in place, before clicking on the Skype icon. It takes a few seconds before they accept the call at the other end and the screen opens up in front of me.

Ivor and Mary Chappell are sitting together behind a desk in the corner of what is probably their sitting room. In the background a clock is chiming on the hour and Mary smiles, apologetically, until it finally lapses into silence.

'I'm so sorry about that. It was my father's clock and we love it, but it's such a pain when you're talking to someone. I'm Mary.'

Ivor leans forward, with a little nod of his head. 'I'm Ivor.'

'Lovely to meet you both. I'm Tia Armstrong. Thank you so much for taking part in our feature about how to keep the love alive in a relationship. How long have you guys been married?'

'Forty-eight years—'

'—and counting.'

Mary begins and Ivor finishes off her sentence.

'He's a keeper,' she chimes in. She turns to face Ivor and they smile at each other.

'And she's my angel. Mary keeps me in line and stops me going off the rails.'

'Is it OK if I record our interviews?'

They both nod.

'Great. Then tell me about the beginning and how you both met.'

They are content to casually chatter away, bouncing the conversation back and forth with ease. The joint interview is done in just over forty minutes. Mary then disappears to put the kettle on, while I talk to Ivor. He's a very gentle man but with quite a sense of humour; quite disparaging of himself and very appreciative of Mary's influence throughout their life together.

'I was a rather rash young man, when we first met.' He smiles at the memory the words invoke in him, as his thoughts take him back in time. 'Mary calmed me down and my mother was relieved at the time, as I have a tendency to act first and think later. Mary, of course, had a good head on her. She's very particular, but easy to please.' He chuckles to himself, enjoying some private little joke.

Half an hour later we're done and he goes in search of Mary. When she returns she's carrying a cup of tea.

'I wish you were here, my dear. We could sit over a cup of tea and a slice of cake, which is much more civilised. But what would we do without this new technology. It's wonderful, isn't it? We're able to watch the grandkids growing up, even though two of them are in France and one of them is in the States. It's a big world out there. Where are you based?'

You can't fail to warm to her; we spend a good ten minutes chatting as I tell her about the Gower coast.

Her interview reflects her warm and loving nature. She is a nurturer and it's easy to see that Ivor and Mary were meant for each other. This is enduring love because the flame has never diminished. It's obvious that even after all these years they would still choose each other and that touches my heart in a very profound way.

'I never tell him off,' Mary confides. 'But he needs a little chivvying along at times. Point him in the right direction and he's off and running, quite happily. He tends to procrastinate at times and I've had to learn to be patient with him, rather than giving him a prod and telling him to get on with it. But we're all wired differently and that's what makes life so interesting.'

Neither of them comes across as being judgemental in any way, but what stands out is that deeper understanding and connection they share. They don't dwell over the petty things in life and that graceful acceptance, if you like, of their individual idiosyncrasies is a beautiful thing to witness. When they sit together the body language between them is loving and caring, just little touches of the hand here and there. Lots of proud little smiles pass between them and the way they finish each other's sentences in a seamless and natural way, makes me want to say "aahh" – I have to forcefully stop myself in case it comes across as patronising.

As the article is going to be the one that goes out in January, when Ivor returns, so I can wind up the interview, I ask each of them to give me a list of five New Year's resolutions. We end up in fits of laughter, as Ivor's are surprising and adventurous. He says he is working his way down their bucket list. Mary's are more practical and I realise that contrast is the reason why

Ivor is free to think about the things that would create incredible memories.

'Chalk and cheese, as my mother used to say, but it works.' Ivor's words mirror my own thoughts.

'Tell me about your Christmas traditions. Is every year the same?'

Mary begins. 'Oh no, quite the reverse. We take it in turns visiting the kids. We have one year in France and the next in California. Santa Barbara, actually. Of course, it's such a great contrast to the early years, when it was all about school plays, Christmas carol services and midnight mass.'

Ivor turns to smile at her. 'The nice thing is, we don't have to do the cooking anymore.'

That makes Mary laugh. 'When did you ever cook the Christmas dinner?'

'You wouldn't have eaten it if I had. But I know how to carve and I'm the expert at getting a roaring fire going in the grate. We've had some good times, though, haven't we, my dear?'

This is a great angle for their article. How families come together despite the miles between them.

'Do you have any photos you'd be happy for us to use in the article? Just something that gives a hint of the difference between the Christmas family celebrations in France and Santa Barbara. Some photos of the Christmas table, or the decorations, maybe.'

Ivor nods, enthusiastically. 'Oh, we have lots of photos, all right.'

'This year it's France again and Christmas Eve they hold a party. Everyone in the village is invited. Our son and his wife have a rambling old house which they run as a bed and breakfast business. They never have paying customers over the Christmas holidays. Anyway, when we're all there we fill the entire house.'

'All?'

'Yes, our other son and his family will fly in, too. The following year we will all descend on them. It's the highlight of everyone's year, our Christmas get-together. But we have two Christmases, because when we get back we have a second Christmas celebration with other family members in the UK.'

I guess I can put Ivor and Mary down as being firmly in the *I love Christmas* camp.

'We do love a party,' Ivor adds.

'Ivor, could you sum up what Christmas means to you in one sentence?'

He tips his head back slightly, giving it some thought.

'Being surrounded by the people I love. You can't ask for any more than that.'

'And you, Mary?'

'The new memories we make with every passing year, that our children and grandchildren will remember long after we've gone. In the same way that Ivor and I both have wonderful memories of Christmases with our own parents. I'm a firm believer in counting your blessings and we have been truly blessed.'

They turn to smile at each other and the image of little children running from room to room, playing hide and seek flashes through my mind for some reason.

'We play silly games and take long walks; there's time to reconnect and catch up with what everyone is doing. They all lead busy lives and if they were still in the UK I suspect we'd only get together for one day at Christmas.' Mary has a point and I'm sure that's how it is for a lot of families.

'We always arrive home on a high and it sets us up for the year to come. We speak to the kids every week and as long as they are happy and enjoying their lives, it allows us to pursue our own interests. Isn't that right, love? There's a lot of living still to do.' Ivor looks to Mary, who nods and the eye contact between them speaks volumes.

In that split second a flash of Mum, very pink in the face, as Dad leans in to kiss her beneath the mistletoe hanging in the hallway, springs into my head. The look on Ivor's face is the same look my father had on his face that day. One of pure, adoring love. I gulp, willing myself not to tear-up and clear my throat in an attempt to refocus my attention.

When the interview is finally concluded and I begin to review the notes I've made; my mind starts to go off at a tangent. If I pair their story with Nic's, the angle would be the way in which a new year inspires us all to look forward with optimism and purpose. Even for those whose lives have yet to fall into place. Whether, or not, we formally go through the ritual of making actual resolutions when a new year dawns, we usually have a plan. The one thing that it would demonstrate is that hope is always in our hearts, no matter where we find ourselves on life's journey.

I won't know until I interview Nic if that's true for him, of course. But my gut instinct is that while he isn't quite there yet, the next few months are going to see big changes taking place. If what Olwen has already told me about him is a fair assessment, he's starting to tire of being in a bad place and feeling overwhelmed. It's good to think that maybe my arrival here might have been a bit of a catalyst, triggering a new sense of clarity. He's missed being in the cottage and while it represents a drain on his finances still, the attachment he has to it is meaningful. I hope I've reminded him of the pride he should feel for what he's done here, rather than looking at it and only seeing the list of jobs he still has to tackle. And I know that whatever fee I manage to negotiate for him will be well spent.

My phone pings and it's a text from Hayley.

Just a heads-up. Expect a call from Clarissa, like now. Call me afterwards.

Within seconds my phone starts to vibrate and it's the lady herself. I steel myself, waiting to find out what's going on now.

'Hi, Tia. I need you to pop back to London for a staff meeting in the office on Friday. I've checked with Hayley and she says you don't have any interviews planned for that day.'

I feel myself visibly sagging. It's a command, not a request, but it's a long way to go just for a staff meeting.

'Oh, I was rather hoping to pull together a draft of today's interviews and give you a rough idea of how the January article will go. I still have a candidate to interview for that, but I do need your approval on the slant I'm taking with that one. There's still time to change the focus if you aren't convinced it will work.'

The pause is a surprise, as it's easy enough for me to attend the meeting via Skype, rather than waste a whole day travelling up and back.

'No. I need your presence here on Friday, Tia. Hayley will be in touch with the travel arrangements. See you then.'

Click and she's gone. I dial Hayley.

'What's going on?'

'I don't know. I'm online, making your travel arrangements, now. There's a train leaving Swansea at a minute to eight on Friday morning, gets you into Paddington at eleven. The meeting here is at noon and I was thinking of booking a return at, say, three-fifteen?

That will get you back around twenty-to-seven in the evening. Clarissa said the meeting will take about an hour. I thought we could go for lunch and have a chat before you head back.'

'Great, thanks. That works for me. I can't imagine what's so important that I have to attend in person. Have you heard any rumours about redundancy, or streamlining?'

'No, I would have been straight on the phone if I'd heard anything. Everyone's a bit on edge here after word went out about Friday's meeting. Hand on heart I haven't even seen anything confidential land on her desk. If I knew something that I couldn't divulge, I'd at least warn you that trouble was brewing. It had better not be cutbacks. I'm at the top of my pay scale and I could easily be replaced by someone still climbing the ladder.'

If Hayley hasn't a clue what's going on, then I know this is something that has suddenly blown-up.

'I'm sure that wouldn't happen and Clarissa is well aware how many people came and went before you arrived. You're efficient and you seem to have her sussed, Hayley. The editorial staffing numbers have slowly increased over the past two years and I'm sure that will be the focus if this is a budgetary thing.'

'Well, try not to worry and if I do hear even the teensiest snippet of info I will call you straight away. I've arranged for those train tickets to be sent to you tomorrow. Take care.'

I feel deflated and the thought of heading back to London so soon, even for one day, fills me with dread.

I begin dialling and when I hear Nic's voice it's hard not to launch into a whole rant about my concerns, but I rein myself in.

'Hi, Nic, I need to book a taxi for Friday. My boss called and I have to go back for a staff meeting. I'm catching the eight a.m. train from Swansea and will need picking up at around twenty-to-seven in the evening. Can you do that?'

'This is a surprise. Seems a long way to go for a meeting. I can't do the early one as I'm already booked but I can find someone to cover it. I'll be there to pick you up and bring you home, though.'

He said *home* and it throws me for a moment; then I realise that to him this is home and it's only natural that he would say that.

'Thanks. It's a nuisance and something I could do without, but I can't get out of it.'

'I hope it isn't bad news. It must be quite serious to drag you all that way. They aren't going to change their minds about letting you stay down here to complete the project, are they?'

He sounds a little concerned, but I'm pretty sure they wouldn't be in a position to demand any money back from him, even if I am called back to the office earlier

240

than expected. But I have to admit that had crossed my mind, too.

'It might be a streamlining initiative. That's usually what these staff meetings are for, when someone comes up with a bright idea to increase efficiency. Or maybe a mandatory staff briefing session from the group chairman. What time do you finish?'

'I won't be back until just after six, I'm afraid. I have a meeting with Gareth to look at the events he wants me to cover this summer. That's about as exciting as it gets in my little world.'

He's doing it again, judging himself.

'Well, let's hope that when I arrive in the office on Friday I still have a job. If not, I might have to spend the weekend working on my CV.'

22

Caught in a Trap

I take a calming walk along the beach, finding a dry spot in among the rock pools to sit and ponder. Max appears a few minutes' later and we exchange a cursory nod. It's obvious I have something on my mind that is worrying me and it takes a huge effort to shake it off and appear upbeat.

'Was the fishing good yesterday?'

He nods. 'Enough. And a few to take into the village for one or two folk who aren't very mobile and enjoy a visit, as well as the catch of the day. I'm away for a few days, so I'm glad I've bumped into you. Thought I'd mention it in case you wondered, what with the recent goings on.'

'You're hardly a noisy neighbour. I'm not here on Friday myself, but I'll keep an eye out over the weekend.'

'I wasn't thinking about my place but about you. Just be extra vigilant is all I'm saying.'

I'm half-tempted to tell him about Nic, but I hold back. He looks tired, or maybe he's just preoccupied and he wasn't expecting to find me sitting here. I wonder whether he's noticed anything worrying lately but I'm sure he'd say if that was the case.

'It's unlikely strangers would wander down this far. And everything is locked so no need to concern yourself – things don't mean much to me but people, well, that's something else. I'll leave you to your thinking. The sea is a great calmer of emotions and turmoil. Just let it all go and watch the waves. It's a quick fix, I promise you.'

He nods and turns, my eyes following him all the way up the beach until he disappears inside the cabin.

That's what I like about Max. He doesn't feel the need to delve into your business if you don't offer him information. And he doesn't expect you to be burdened with his anxieties. And yet I know if something went wrong he would probably be the best person to run to, even over Nic. With age comes wisdom, is the saying, and naturally that has an element of truth to it; but life's more traumatic experiences lead to an even greater wisdom. I suspect the learning curve for the latter is a much bigger rollercoaster ride, leaving some ugly scars as a constant reminder.

I head back and when Nic turns up we are both a little unsettled and subdued. We are determined not to let our concerns dampen the enjoyment of our pre-dinner walk and he tells me all about his meeting with Gareth. We head back and work alongside each other to create a very passable spaghetti bolognaise.

It's clear he intends to stay the night and for that I'm grateful, but I don't mention the fact that he didn't bring any clothes with him. Whether that's because he still has a lot of stuff in wardrobes in the second bedroom, or if an element of uncertainty about my future here has made him hold back, I don't know.

When I glance out before drawing the curtains my eyes now instinctively scan the spot among the holly trees but tonight nothing moves in the shadowy darkness. If it had, I realise that I don't know quite how I would handle it. I certainly wouldn't want Nic dashing out and putting himself at risk, that's for sure. Max is right; property can be replaced: people can't.

Thursday passes in much the same way, a day that seems to stretch out forever because I just want it to be over. Like having a rain cloud constantly hanging over me, whatever I'm doing.

A knock on the door, when I find myself staring back at postman Tom's smiling face, is a welcome surprise.

'First time I've been 'ere for a while.' He hands me the envelope containing my train tickets and my stomach turns over.

'Thank you, Tom. I probably won't have any more post while I'm here. And thank you for being so patient with me at the barn dance. It's a lot harder than it looks,' I joke, hoping he didn't think my initial frown was aimed at him.

'I'm not being funny, but you picked it up right quick, there. I'm only saying, like.'

His face is a picture, flushed and a little sheepish. The Welsh lilt of his accent is warming to the ears.

'Is Nic about?' He cranes his neck slightly, as if he's expecting Nic to suddenly loom up behind me.

'No. I'm on my own.'

'Oh, well, I'll drop his post up at the farm as usual, then.' He seems surprised, but heads off with a little salute.

'Hope I see you again before your stay is up, Tia. Maybe I'll catch the two of you in the pub sometime.'

I close the door, leaning back against it with my heart pounding in my chest. Olwen is right and this is getting a little complicated. I shake my head to dispel this chain of thought. Until I find out what is going on at the office it's hard not to let it disturb my concentration, or set my nerves anymore on edge than they are already. I must address that problem first, or I'll be in a real state by the time I jump on that train. Only then can I think about the impact on what's happening here, with Nic, if I end up heading back to London for good on Monday.

*

Nic is up and out very early on Friday morning. He's due to collect a regular fare from Cardiff airport. Apparently, it's a couple who own one of the very large houses off the Caswell Road. He told me that they fly down from Scotland every few weeks for a long weekend. I can see that he's torn and regrets he can't drive me to Swansea. Our parting hug and kiss is poignant. I already fear this is the beginning of the end for us, even though our relationship has hardly begun. I think he feels the same way.

'Just keep a level head,' are his parting words.

'And you drive safely. I'll see you at the station tonight.'

I open the envelope to put the train tickets in my wallet and it's only then that I notice they are first class. I check out the price and it's three times the regular fare. Muttering under my breath, I quickly text Hayley, thinking she's going to be in big trouble for this and only too glad I noticed it before I'd used them.

Just noticed the tickets are 1st class! Really sorry! Can u change asap?

She won't be in the office yet, but she'll be getting ready and I know she'll be scanning her phone. Ten minutes pass and I'm restless. The taxi will be here very shortly and it's stressful swapping between keeping an eye out for the appearance of the car and checking my phone. Ping. At last!

> Not a mistake. Orders from the top. Enjoy!

Not a mistake? Obviously, I had intended to work while I was on the train, but assumed Clarissa wouldn't expect me to have anything ready at the other end to give her right there and then. I thought maybe the meeting had overshadowed that.

> OK. Have a lot of work to do, anyway. Roll on lunchtime aarrgghh!!

I get a smiley face back.

The moment the sound of tyres crunching on gravel hits my ears I'm out of the door, briefcase and handbag in hand. Seconds later we're on the road and as the driver does a cursory check in his rear-view mirror, I wonder what he thinks. This morning, when I looked back at the mirror image of myself in a well-tailored navy jacket and trousers, teamed with a white silk blouse, a sense of terror had hit me full-on. Can I be the person I was before all of this happened? Mum, Nic...

I push down the panic that is making my stomach begin to churn. Slow, deep, breaths. Keep calm, Tia, and remain composed. Whatever happens today you'll come up with a plan for the future. You have no ties and no responsibilities, aside from the mortgage repayments. Your CV demonstrates you are a very capable and professional person, and wouldn't it be refreshing to work for someone who didn't strike fear into your heart?

Anyway, Clarissa isn't the only industry guru and you know you would be headhunted, I appease my troubled thoughts. My reputation precedes me and a wave of satisfaction washes over me. This is a temporary, and understandable, blip requiring some time out. It could happen to anyone. Even so, I'm still on top form and am smashing it. Clarissa was right and this feature needed the attention of someone who could wring out every single drop of emotion. And that's exactly what I'm going to deliver, topped off with a sprinkling of seasonal sparkle.

It does the trick and once I'm on the train I begin polishing the overview of the January article, more than ready to prove my worth. I'm not going down without a fight. I guess that means that I'm back in the game. So, watch out everyone because the gloves are on and I will be reclaiming my seat.

*

Rather worryingly, as I step into the Tube train I can feel the panic begin to rise in me, once more. However, I hope it's more to do with the stifling crush of people around me and the lack of free-flowing air. My breathing becomes shallower and I focus on calming myself. This is *my* home turf and yet my head can't really cope with the contrast between getting up this morning at Beach View Cottage and arriving in London.

I used to hop on the Tube every day without a thought and now I'm almost hyperventilating.

As I take a seat I feel as though I stand out and I've forgotten how to blend in, so people don't notice you. I'm self-conscious, sporting that look infrequent travellers' faces take on as they watch the blackness of the tunnel walls whizzing past. Their struggle to find anything even remotely interesting to focus their gaze on is often painful to watch. It's hard to avoid the awkwardness of staring around at total strangers, so tightly packed together and all going through the same motions. Locals, on the other hand, usually come prepared with something to read to while away the journey.

If I thought that was a trial, as I step through the door of Unicorn Towers I have to focus on moving my feet forward, one at a time. Staff I recognise at the reception desk barely register me, as though I've been forgotten already. The stream of people coming and going purposefully leave me side-stepping to avoid being trampled. That used to be me. Come on, Tia, you've done this so many times before. Why is this such an issue today? Shoulders back, I march towards the lift and head up to the eighth floor.

It's eleven forty-five and I have fifteen minutes to check my hair and refresh my lipstick before I brave the conference room. As the lift doors open, Hayley is hovering. She throws her arms around me in a fierce hug, before stepping back.

'At last! I was getting worried. We need a quick chat.'

I follow her to the cloakroom. While she quickly checks that we're alone, I go through the motions of brushing my hair and re-applying some red lip gloss.

'He's here, Clarissa's boss. He arrived an hour ago and they've been in her office ever since. You should see Finlay, he's practically biting his finger nails off.'

I step away from the mirror, wondering who is this person staring back at me? The deep frown on my face is like some sort of mask and beneath that is fear of the unknown. But as I turn on my heels to look at Hayley, something inside me clicks.

'Calm down, lady. There's no point in worrying until we know what this is all about. Let's go find ourselves a nice seat in the back row.'

Hayley looks at me as if I've gone mad.

'You aren't concerned?'

'My mother used to say that when one door shuts, another door opens. The world doesn't begin and end in Unicorn Towers, although it feels like that sometimes. Shoulders back, head high and deep breaths. Let's stand out from the crowd by exuding an air of quiet confidence. If nothing else, it might annoy Clarissa a little.'

She looks at me and laughs. 'I'd forgotten how formidable you can be. It's nice to see you back on form.' And with that we head into the war zone.

I always sit at the back, usually because you can see so much more. I'm a people-watcher by nature and the general reaction to any news is quite important in a staff meeting. If the troops are in revolt then you must ensure you don't get swept along with general muttering and moaning. I've seen it happen before. Say nothing, digest the information and don't get drawn into something you haven't thought through. You need to evaluate everything you say, so that when you do speak up it really counts if you want to rise above the general ranks in this industry. It's all about singling yourself out by thinking outside the box. If change is coming, then there will also be opportunities and I intend to be front and centre when I know where this is leading.

The room quickly fills up and a few people notice me seated next to Hayley and give a friendly wave in my direction. Finlay clocks me the minute he steps through the door, but all I get is an icy stare. He sits on his own in the front row. Moments later he calls out to one of the guys from the Design department as he enters, to join him. The guy quickly scans the room, before rather reluctantly settling himself down next to Finlay. Finlay doesn't make friends easily and he's upset a lot of people. But he's temporarily sitting at my desk and that gives him a boost up the corporate ladder. At what point does a request become an instruction, looks like the thought that is reflected on the poor guy's face.

When Clarissa arrives, she's in deep conversation with her boss, but I see her steal a glance over his shoulder, her eyes seeking me out. I give a nod, unable to raise a smile in response to her brief stare before she starts addressing the room.

'Welcome everyone and I promise to keep this as short as possible. For those who haven't yet had the pleasure, I'd like to introduce you to Oliver Sinclair. Oliver is Vice President of the Lancing Group and is here today to tour the offices and make an announcement. There are a few things we need to cover and I'm sure there will be some questions, so I'll let Oliver make a start.'

She gives him a dazzling smile and Hayley squirms in her seat.

'Good morning, everyone. The magazine has been in Unicorn Towers now for almost six years and in the last two years Clarissa has been a formidable, and dynamic, force for change. It has seen *Love a Happy Ending* lifestyle magazine grow its market share year-on-year. Now, obviously, to do that she had to have a good team and the first thing I would like to say is that you all deserve a round of applause.'

Everyone is a little stunned, but as he puts his hands together we all follow like sheep. Hayley and I look at each other, our faces showing utter disbelief at this overt attempt to get the staff on his side.

'As I said, very well deserved and it's because of the sterling leadership Clarissa has shown that my presence here hasn't been required. My motto is that if it isn't broken, then don't try to fix it.'

He stops and there's a ripple of laughter. The mood shifts slightly, as people begin to pin their hopes on Oliver's upbeat tone. Maybe this isn't about job losses, after all.

'Now, on to the main reason for today's visit. Lancing are about to announce a new project that will be launching next spring. During the initial setting-up stage I have asked Clarissa to head up the team.'

He pauses and there's a loud collective gasp, as literally everyone in the room does a sharp intake of breath. Heads turn as people look at the general reaction from their peers.

'I understand your concern and I'm here to reassure you all that we are confident Clarissa can continue to *lightly steer* things here, during that phase. I'll hand you back now to the lady herself, to give you a little more information.'

Clarissa is glowing and steps forward as she takes Oliver's outstretched hand. He leans in to kiss her cheek. This is a previously unimaginable demonstration from Clarissa, of her warm relationship with her boss. It's actually rather shocking and I can see I'm not alone in thinking that way.

No one has moved a muscle: it's like watching something unfolding in front of you that you can't believe is happening.

'First of all, I want to apologise for the speed at which things have begun to overtake us. Due to previously unforeseen circumstances, we've been forced to bring forward our plans by one full month. Naturally, this will affect quite a few of you, due to a temporary staffing restructure to accommodate the changes. I'm still working on revised job descriptions for those involved. Over the course of the next week I will be having one-to-one meetings so that everyone is clear about how we are going to proceed if their role has been affected.

'I'm sure you will all see that this bodes well for the future of the magazine, as well as for the overall group. Standing still is never an option and the secret to success is being ahead of the game. I think with Oliver's steer the group is about to take another huge leap forward. Thank you all for listening and now does anyone have any burning questions?'

The usual people put up their hands and there's some back and forth conversation, but it's very clear no further information is going to be given out today. It sounds like the details are still being thrashed-out, but now with a sense of some real urgency. It looks to me like there's been a leak. The panic is on to tell the staff, before the rumours start to circulate. Clarissa thanks everyone and people start to vacate their seats.

Hayley leans in to me to whisper in my ear. 'Well, that said a little about not a lot. They're keeping it all very under wraps. At least it looks like our jobs are safe.'

I nod, noticing that Finlay has risen from his seat and is shaking Oliver's hand. Clarissa is standing next to him, deep in conversation.

I encourage Hayley to hold back, thinking that if we avoid bumping into them then we can sneak out for lunch.

'I need a drink,' she says, as we lean against the wall waiting for the queue of people standing in line to shake Oliver's hand to clear.

We start walking down the aisle, assuming Oliver and Clarissa will be on the move before we are parallel with them. Instead, they both turn and look in our direction.

It's like the proverbial walk of shame, admitting we were hiding ourselves away in the back row.

As we draw level, Clarissa steps forward, immediately introducing Hayley.

'Hayley is the best personal assistant I've ever had. And that's over a period of more years than I care to remember.'

Oliver and Hayley shake hands. The flush on Hayley's face reflects how uncomfortable she's feeling under their scrutiny.

'We need to have a proper conversation about this, Hayley, but you'll be getting an admin person to assist you. We're going to ramp up your role as a part of the general re-organisation. Congratulations on your temporary promotion.'

Hayley turns towards me looking extremely pleased and I smile back at her. I'm rather shocked that Clarissa is happy to talk about this in front of me, although behind us the room is now empty.

It becomes clear Hayley is being dismissed, as both Oliver and Clarissa turn their attention towards me next.

'Perhaps we could take this into my office?' Clarissa suggests and then immediately turns on her heels.

I bring up the rear, spinning back around to give Hayley a brief grimace. She mouths, 'I'll wait.'

*

When Hayley and I arrive at the coffee shop it's packed, so we order sandwiches and coffee to go. There are some benches in a little square a few blocks away from the office. It's tucked away and while there's only one tree and a couple of raised flower beds, we often go there. It's a reasonably quiet and secluded place to sit. I think people assume it is private access only for the impressive Georgian houses that surround it on three sides. It's enclosed by ornate railings and a heavy, metal gate but there are no warning signs. Often, we are the only people sitting there. Our take on it, until someone says something to the contrary, is that it's a space that shouldn't be wasted. It's one of our favourite haunts when the weather is mild.

As soon as we sit down, Hayley half turns, to stare at me.

'What happened? That looked heavy.'

I swallow hard, still coming to terms with it myself.

'The plan is that Finlay takes the F1 assignment because they've earmarked me to be Clarissa's deputy.'

I'm too shocked to eat, so I begin sipping my coffee. Caffeine is probably the last thing I need at this particular moment in time, but it helps calm my jangling nerves.

'That's *huge*, Tia. You've obviously passed the test and I bet she's been a bit worried what with all you've had going on. The Caswell Bay thing now makes sense. And I bet she wants to slide into the new post on a permanent basis when you're ready. Poor Finlay, I can imagine his creepy grin when she gave him the F1 assignment; and how quickly it was wiped off his face, once she mentioned your name.'

'I don't think he knows. I don't think anyone knows, yet. Oliver said I should take a few days to think about it, but Clarissa thinks it's a done deal.'

'Guess we're both in for a pay rise, then. I'll give Jack a call when I get a minute and break the news. Do I sense a little hesitation on your part?'

'No. It was just a surprise.'

I don't know how I feel. Which is a totally crazy reaction because this is the next step for me – the one I've been craving. It's the culmination of everything I've been working towards. I know that short-term Clarissa will keep an eye on me, but I will finally be in charge, in the hot seat and calling the shots. She will have her own workload to consider and all eyes will be on her, so that's where her focus will be directed.

Hayley's mood has visibly lifted, but my mood continues to sink. I look at my watch and make an excuse, saying I'd better get going. I lie, telling her there's something I need to pick up on the way back to the station. Hayley makes a sad face, but I'm not good company at the moment and it's not fair of me to dampen her spirits.

We hug goodbye. 'I've missed you and I will be glad when you are back. Will this shorten your trip?'

'Apparently not. Clarissa said I should make the most of this time to recharge my batteries so I can come back refreshed and ready for the challenge ahead.'

'Well, that's something, at least. Guess I'm going to have two bosses for a while.'

At the moment I can't talk about this, I simply need to think. This was the dream and it's been a long time coming. All the years spent working my way up through the ranks to learn the ropes. Then being groomed by Clarissa, hoping that one day, very soon, I'd be in the right place, at the right time. I should be jumping for joy but I don't think it's sunk in properly yet. I was expecting a fight and it turned out to be a tea party.

Obviously, I'm going to say *yes*, this is finally *it*. Payback.

I promised Nic I'd text him and I guess this is one occasion that calls for a raid on the emoticons. A smiley face would be a bit of an understatement now I'm beginning to savour the sweet taste of success.

23

A Party on the Beach

The train is delayed due to signal power failure and it's almost seven-thirty by the time I make my way out of the station to look for Nic. I eventually spot him, but there is a whole crowd of people between us. It's a two-way stream as it's Friday evening and everyone is eager to head for home.

'Hey, you. A big day, mega congratulations.' By the time I texted Nic I guess I was back on form and full of confidence about grabbing a golden opportunity.

He whisks a beautiful hand-tied bouquet of roses from behind his back, clearly not something he's just picked up in a supermarket.

I feel myself immediately colouring-up, as the gesture is totally unexpected. Not least, because it's so kind of Nic to spend some of his hard-earned cash simply to celebrate my good news.

'Aww, thank you.'

I slip my hand into his and we head off, having to circumnavigate a large queue at the taxi rank and people with luggage blocking the path.

'The car is in the short-stay car park. Are you hungry, because I have a surprise waiting back at the cottage?'

'I'm starving. I've hardly eaten all day. Nervous tension, I think.'

'I'll wait until you've been fed, before I start firing questions at you. You haven't asked about my day.'

'Nic, how was *your* day?'

'I bumped into Olwen.'

I grimace and he laughs. He tells me the whole story on the journey back to the cottage. I wasn't surprised to hear that she gave him a hard time. I know she means well and she has a soft spot for him. If Nic and I had met under different circumstances – when our lives were more settled – who knows what the outcome might have been? That's what Olwen can't grasp, that it's all about timing. Only fate can control that.

When we arrive back at Beach View Cottage it's almost dark. As Nic opens the front door I sniff the air, expecting a waft of something cooking in the oven. I turn to look at him, rather disappointed.

'It's a surprise, remember? Go and slip into something warm for the beach.'

'At this time of night?'

He flips his hand, waving me off in the direction of the stairs, as he walks across to the fridge.

'Give me ten minutes and I'll be back. No peeking.'

I climb the stairs with a little smile hovering on my lips. How different would tonight have been coming back to an empty cottage? The nervous energy that has been coursing around my body for at least half of the day has left me wired and I know that although I'm tired, sleep won't come easily tonight. I'm going to struggle to relax and wind-down after a day full of wide-ranging emotions.

Having Nic here is really helping me not to begin stressing over this unexpected development, but to celebrate it. That isn't easy to do when it's a party of one and, besides, his excitement on my behalf is a reminder that I should pause to mark this momentous occasion because it *is* a cause for celebration. I suppose I've waited for this to happen for such a long time that I never really thought this day would come.

As I pull on some jeans and a thick sweater, I look out onto the beach. One, by one, a semi–circle of lights begins to glow in the darkness. It looks like Nic has raided the cupboards to find as many jars as he can to hold the softly flickering tealights. I see what appears to be a mass of little sparks that suddenly ignite into a flame. Nic is lighting a fire.

How lucky am I, tonight? And how ironic, that it's Clarissa, of all people, that I have to thank for that.

*

Nic throws another log on the fire, stirring up the embers so that flames lick up to engulf it.

'I think I can say those were the best hot dogs I've ever eaten. And the onions were perfectly caramelised.'

'Even the burnt bits?'

'Even the burnt bits, but most importantly it hit the spot. What's for dessert?'

He holds up a finger, indicating I should wait while he digs into the hamper beside his deck chair.

'Ta dah!' He holds a packet of pink and white marshmallows up for inspection and then reaches back inside to pull out two long, wooden-handled skewers.

We sit looking at each other for a moment, as if someone has called time-out. After a few seconds, I find myself breaking the trance.

'It's perfect. This, here… tonight. And how did you know I love marshmallows toasted over a fire?'

I watch as he opens the packet and begins loading three on each skewer.

'You just look like a gooey marshmallow lover. Here you go, toast away to your heart's content.'

I move my chair a little closer to his and we lean forward trying to find a hot spot away from the flames.

In the background that constant roar as the waves roll in and then the swoosh as they ebb away, is like a sound track. Everything beyond the little circle of tealight is consumed by the shadows. The sea and sky would merge seamlessly into one if it wasn't for the moonlight illuminating the rise and fall of the waves, as far as the eye can see. The stars sparkle like little electric light bulbs, a constant reminder that we don't really know what's out there.

We continue toasting marshmallows until they start to melt, searing them in the flames before drawing them away from the heat. They aren't the easiest things to eat and we end up laughing as we stuff our mouths full of the gooey sweetness, or risk dropping them in the sand beneath our feet.

'Here,' Nic leans across and wipes some stickiness from my face. 'So, are you going to tell me a bit more about your exciting day in the big city? I know from my days in London how hard you have to work to make it there and you're acting very cool about it.'

'Well, it's only a temporary promotion for now. But it will look good on my CV. It kind of took my breath away for a minute there. I was actually speechless and then they were quick to reassure me I could take the weekend to think about it.'

'But they are expecting you to go for it and, of course, you will. Why wouldn't you?'

I nod. 'Do you know what the best bit about today has been?'

He looks across at me, his expression blank.

'What?'

'Sharing my news with you and coming back to this.'

His face drops a little and his eyes search mine.

'You missed being able to phone your mum. But she knows what's happening.'

'Do you believe that, Nic? I mean really believe it?'

'I think there's more to life than just this and while I might not subscribe to the heaven and hell theory, I think our souls go somewhere after we die. And if the soul lives on, then love never dies – surely?'

He seems to be able to look inside my head and read my thoughts. The things I can't voice. And the last few hours I've thought of nothing except Mum. She would have been punching the air and oozing excitement, her eyes and heart filled with pride. And that's what loss represents. I've lost being able to hug her and be hugged by her. I've lost being able to share the things that make me happy, or sad. Nic is trying his best to fill that empty void and tonight that means such a lot to me.

'I think what's important is that you proved to yourself today that going back wasn't as bad as you feared it would be. The question you never referred to, but was constantly at the back of your mind niggling away, has been answered. You did it before and you can do it again.'

I sigh, knowing he's right.

'What helps is knowing I have another three weeks here and by then I will be ready to take on the world again. I have to be ready.'

It doesn't come out sounding quite as strong and confident as I'd hoped, as my voice wavers. But I think it's more because of the slight chill in the air.

'Actually, Tia, I do have some news to tell you. Gareth, at the paper, has recommended me to a country park attraction, located about ten miles away. They want to re-brand the business and they need updated photographs for their brochures and future marketing campaigns. I wondered if you fancied a little trip tomorrow to check it out before I commit? The owner has suggested I go along for a brief chat.'

He looks pleased and I'm genuinely thrilled for him, as this could be exactly the boost he needs to bolster his confidence.

'That's fantastic and yes, I'd love that! This could be the start of something that could grow into a nice little business. A lot of photographs will have passed Gareth's desk over the years, no doubt, and for him to recommend you is a big deal.'

Nic hangs his head a little and begins poking the fire to break it down.

'There's one teeny little problem.'

'Which is?'

'I've only ever taken photos of the sea, or mountains, or landscapes. I never photograph people or animals.'

I can't see the problem.

'Does it matter? I mean, it's all about composition, isn't it? So, a good photo is a good photo.'

He shakes his head, sucking in a breath.

'Spoken like an amateur. With nature, you point and shoot. With anything on two, or four legs, you not only have to manoeuvre them into the right pose, but they don't always keep still. Or do what you want them to do.'

Now it's my turn to shake my head at him.

'Well, I think you are looking for excuses. You can do this and if you start doubting yourself just think about the money. That should help focus the mind.'

'Ah.' He looks at me with eyebrows raised. 'Money. The stuff I used to have and the very same stuff that seems to hit my bank account and immediately disappear into thin air.'

I wish I could find a solution to get Nic out of the hole he's in.

'Well, how about we do that interview? A cheque is a cheque, after all. We can use an assumed name for you, if you like. We do that sometimes.'

The embers are beginning to die and Nic continues to spread them out ready to dampen the fire.

'That's an option? You ask me questions and I tell you my story, but I'm not identified in any way?'

'Sure. I have a space in the January article. The slant of the story is going to be about looking forward and what shapes people's New Year resolutions. Not the things you might say you're going to do and give up on within a week, but how you look at the new year as a fresh start and the goals you set yourself. If you take part, the contrast would be with a couple in their sixties, who are very much looking at their bucket list, if you like. You, on the other hand, will be...'

I wait for Nic to fill the gap.

'Oh, that was my prompt. Um... I will be...'

The silence grows.

'OK, it's late and it's getting cold. Let's put out the fire and head back. We can discuss this in the morning when I'm sure things will be much clearer.'

'You think?'

He doesn't look convinced.

'Well, let's just say that I'm not leaving Caswell Bay until you have a firm action plan.'

'When did you join Olwen's team?' he mutters, as we start packing up.

'Since yesterday, when she warned me that our little arrangement could end up in heartache, as it's bad karma. Or something like that. But she was trying to make me feel guilty and she succeeded. So now I'm determined I'm going to leave you on a high and energised, just to prove her wrong.'

He stops what he's doing to look at me, as if I'm joking, but when he sees that I'm not, his head jerks back a little.

'Should I be afraid?'

I start laughing, but say nothing. As we stumble back up the beach every few yards I have to stop to catch my breath, as I now have the giggles.

'First Olwen, and now you. And I always had this little fantasy about two women fighting over me. What is that saying? Be careful what you wish for?'

'It might just come true!'

As we approach the cottage my eyes automatically begin to scan the trees as they loom up in front of us. Nothing jumps out at me and I chide myself for letting myself get spooked. But Nic is here with me now and I'm glad of that, regardless of the reason why.

We collapse into bed, so tired that I'm not sure who falls asleep first. It isn't until the early morning light is streaming in through the window that either of us stir.

'Morning,' Nic whispers into my ear. He rolls into me to snuggle up close. Seconds later his breathing changes and it's clear he's fallen back to sleep. If I move, I'll disturb him and I want him to take advantage of his Saturday morning lie-in.

I'm content to simply lie here, listening to the steady rhythm of his breathing and wondering why things have gone so badly wrong for him in the past. His air of general despondency is clearly starting to shift, as he's much more upbeat now and that can only be a positive step forward.

And as for me, well, the dream is beckoning and on Monday I will be ringing Clarissa to tell her that I can't wait to throw myself into such an exciting opportunity. Wouldn't it have been a horribly impossible situation to handle, if Nic and I had just begun a real relationship?

The timing would have been awful and I'm not sure I could have handled the extra pressure on top of everything else.

Being with someone, but not being swamped by them, is something that's not easy to explain. I know that Olwen doesn't understand, because fate took a hand and she met the right guy at precisely the right time. I can't fathom out anyone who doubts that our destiny is already mapped out for us. The alternative is to believe that life is full of random coincidences, rather than a series of steps that lead each of us in a particular direction for a reason. Now that, to my mind, *is* ridiculous. And yes, I'm envious of anyone who has found their soul mate – of course I am. Who doesn't want to feel that special moment when you know beyond any shadow of a doubt that the search is over? I like to think that when you find *the one*, then everything slots neatly into place. Hopefully, there's absolutely no room for error. If it's meant to be then there's no way you can mess up or get it wrong.

Whenever I began dating someone new, I always made an effort to be different; as if just being myself wouldn't be enough to keep his interest. I tried to become a better version of myself. Once we moved on from the trips to the movies and the intimate little restaurant meals for two, we were into the awkward stage. An evening back at my apartment, or his place, was supposed to be fun and allow us to get to know each other in a more relaxed environment. Instead, for me that's when the relationship always stalled and shortly afterwards fizzled out. It hasn't been like that with Nic because of our ground rules and that works so well. I'm happy to have Nic lying next to me, knowing there is no pressure, or expectation. The weekend is here and whatever time we spend together, we are going to enjoy.

It's simple, really. When you need something, you look for a solution that fits. At this point in my life I need to feel desired; it's a little reminder that I'm not a totally lost cause and can still keep that little spark of hope alive for the future. Nic is my temporary solution and I'm his – without the need to make demands upon each other, we are having fun and boosting each other's morale. I really think I can help him if I can succeed in getting him to talk about the past. The bit he doesn't want to share. It could be the real start of letting go of his negativity.

OK, so he's good looking and very, very sexy in an understated way, but a part of the attraction for me is his vulnerability. Maybe the old Nic was someone who thought material success was important, but if that was the case he's not like that now; his self-esteem is at an all-time low. Ironically, once he picks himself back up we might find we don't have anything at all in common. When I'm in London work-mode maybe I am a watered-down version of Clarissa and that's why guys give up trying once they get to know me. Maybe my standards are impossibly high. Who knows why the head-over-heels thing hasn't happened for me? I want someone who is confident, competent at what they do and won't feel threatened by the fact that my work has to come first.

'I can almost hear your brain ticking over. It's annoying,' Nic whispers, pulling me on top of him.

'I was thinking about how refreshing it is to be with someone with no pressure whatsoever.'

He moves his lips to the top of my arm and starts to work his way across my shoulder with purposeful, yet tantalising, little kisses. That first day we met when he was driving the taxi I thought he was the rudest guy on earth. But since then I've discovered that beneath that tough shell is a man who is hurting and now I'm a woman on a mission to turn that around.

<u>24</u>

Getting to the Heart of the Matter

Nic's nerves begin to kick in as we head for the offices of the Natureland Experience Park and he's silent for most of the journey. Thankfully, while having an informal chat with the owner, John Llywelyn, Nic really perks up.

'The house and grounds have been in the family for generations, but it was my father who realised he would have to be creative, if he wanted to keep up with the maintenance of it as a whole. Obviously, farming has always been a big part of our history here and he was very passionate about local wildlife, too. It was quite small-scale in the beginning, with the mini-farm, aimed at attracting young families. My father retired eighteen months ago and having taken over the reins it's time to update our marketing materials.'

As he takes us on a tour around some of the most popular visitor areas, we can see that the park isn't quite as commercial as we were expecting. It feels very much like a family-run business.

'Next year is the tenth anniversary of the opening of the park,' he explains. 'The problem is that our overheads are very high and my father only ever dabbled with local advertising. Our cash flow problems could end up shutting us down if we don't begin taking marketing much more seriously. However, I have to make it all happen on a very tight budget.'

John's honest appraisal of the situation is what really seems to trigger the change in Nic. With only a modest budget, John's options are very limited, but judging by the new logo he's working on, he has a clear vision of the new branding for the business.

'There's a lot I can do myself, as I have a little marketing experience, but what I desperately need are some really professional shots of the park. As you can see from these,' he hands Nic a brochure, 'they are way out of date. We're stuck in the past and it doesn't reflect the facilities we have here today.'

'As Gareth no doubt explained, I'm not a professional. I'm simply trying to take something I'm very passionate about, to the next level. I'd be more than happy to take a few shots today and get something over to you. If my work is of interest, then maybe we can talk in more detail. How does that sound?' Nic appears to be both positive and excited about this potential opportunity.

John holds out his hand and they shake, as if the deal is already done. To my mind this is a great opportunity for both parties and I know Nic can deliver. His photographs of the sea are hauntingly beautiful. Now it's time to boost his confidence and encourage him to begin snapping away.

'Appreciated.' John seems delighted with Nic's reaction and I have a good feeling about this.

'Great. I'll be in touch in a couple of days' time.'

The sun is already overhead and it's the hottest day we've had since I arrived on the Gower coast. I wonder how that will bode for some action shots of the animals that Nic is hoping to get. I only hope they aren't all lying down, resting. As we begin the walk along the Farm Trail, my question is answered when we reach the first field. While several goats are mooching around inside a large wooden shelter and munching on a part-bale of hay, two younger goats are playfully fighting only a couple of feet away from the fence. Nic starts snapping away and then asks if I can pull out one of the other lenses in the bag I'm carrying. He swaps them over and I feel like a real photographer's assistant, replacing lens caps and standing back to watch.

We move on to the sheep next and it's wonderful to see him so absorbed in what he's doing. He might be an amateur photographer, but he sure looks like a pro to me.

'Tia, can you drop the bags and stand over there? Lean against the fence and look out across the field. Side-on is what I'm looking for.'

I can't help a little grin creeping over my face as, with my back to Nic, I walk towards the fence, as instructed. I wonder how many photographers' assistants end up being in the final shots?

'Lovely. It helps to give the photo a sense of scale. After this, perhaps we could focus on the visitors' centre and then head back? I'm anxious to see how these look up close.'

It takes about an hour. As soon as we arrive back at the cottage Nic gives me a hug and a lingering kiss of thanks, before heading up to his office in the small bedroom. He has a buzz to him and it's almost like being with a different person. Enthused, energetic and involved, which is in stark contrast to the slightly negative vibe that previously surrounded him.

I don't disturb him and wait until he comes to find me, sitting in the kitchen typing up one of the interviews.

'I guessed you'd be working and wouldn't miss me too much. I've downloaded all the photos now and had a quick skim through. I should have enough decent shots to give John a feel for what I can produce. I'd love to be involved, to be honest, even if it isn't going to be a big pay cheque.'

Nic slides into the seat opposite me.

'It could open up a whole new direction for you, Nic, and that's exciting. It isn't always about the money, is it?'

He nods, smiling. 'No. It's about gaining experience and having something solid to put on my CV.'

'Who knows? This time next year you might be well on your way to having your own photographic business.'

Nic's reaction tells me that has crossed his mind, too.

'Talking about money, how about I make us a sandwich and as we sit here I do that interview we keep talking about? I can turn on the recorder and just throw out a question, or two. What do you think?'

'OK, the money can go into the boiler fund. And you don't have to use my name?'

'I'll refer to you as David, how's that?'

'OK, let's give it a go.'

He seems genuinely upbeat, so I set up the recorder in the middle of the table.

'Right, in your own words explain to me what being in a romantic relationship means to you.'

As I quickly assemble two sandwiches, I purposely turn my back on Nic, letting him talk without feeling he's being scrutinised.

'Hmm... well, I suppose it's when you meet someone and there's a spark which begins to develop. You find yourself wanting to spend more time with them, hoping that it's a mutual thing.'

I don't say anything, but continue with the job in hand.

'It's not that easy to put into words the way you feel about someone and it's always a risk, because there are no guarantees they will feel the same way. That first flush of excitement when you are getting to know more about a person you feel attracted to, is heady stuff. But often it's a fleeting thing that's more about the physical side, than anything else. And then, one day, along comes a person with whom it all feels very different.'

I carry the plates over to the table, casually slipping into my seat and glancing across at Nic.

'What was her name?'

Nic takes a huge bite out of his sandwich, nods in appreciation and chews in silence for a moment or two.

'Katie. We met at work, although I always said I'd never date a colleague. It's unprofessional and a potential nightmare situation when things start to go wrong.'

'But there were others, before her?'

'Well, aside from the usual casual dates, up until then my longest-running relationship had lasted for almost six months. Nice girl, though, and I can't say anything went wrong exactly, but you can tell when it starts to cool off. We stopped dating but we're still friends. Now with Katie it was a very different story and it all went badly wrong.'

He comes to an abrupt halt and I'm not sure if it's because he's hungry, and it's a good sandwich, or whether he's struggling to find the right words. Either way, I don't interrupt, but go on eating.

'There's a whole part of this sorry little story that is nothing at all to do with romantic relationships, or Katie. Let's call it *family interference*. The result was a rather unfortunate row at work, which didn't involve her in any way, but...'

He stops once more. My eyes stray towards the light on the voice recorder, checking it's still green. I don't want to lose a word of this, but it would stop Nic's flow if I begin making notes.

'We broke up shortly afterwards. I wasn't sacked, *per se*, but I would have been if I hadn't walked out. It's the reason I had to leave London about a year later, as it ended up killing my career. I still can't think about it without getting so angry I want to punch a wall. But, at the time, it never occurred to me that I wouldn't simply find another position, or that Katie would show another side of herself that I hadn't seen before. I still find it painful to admit that she saw me as a way of furthering her career and introducing her to influential people. She was very intelligent, astute and had an outgoing personality, but eventually I came to see that she was also a skilled manipulator of people and situations. She had her own agenda and I think it was there from day one. They do say that guys often fall for women who remind them of their mothers. A manipulative personality is unfortunately something I had to contend with from early childhood. A more-or-less absent father and an overbearing mother makes for a rather dysfunctional upbringing. In fact, it was my mother who introduced me to my last boss. Maybe I knew all along what Katie was doing, but alarm bells didn't sound because it was normal practice around me. What I failed to appreciate was that my mother's agenda had an element of wanting what *she* wanted for *me*. In a rather bizarre way I guess there might have been a crumb of good intention buried in there, somewhere. But even that requires quite a stretch of anyone's imagination. Katie's agenda was entirely self-serving. When my world came crashing down she tore into me before she walked away for good. She asked me if I realised what I'd just thrown away? Suddenly I was of no benefit to her and she couldn't get away fast enough, as it turned out.'

I can't even swallow, so I push my plate away. Nic's face looks pained.

'Is this the sort of thing you expected? Am I the poster guy for people who are easily conned, because they are so emotionally screwed they have no idea what love is? It sounds tragic, doesn't it? You also mentioned something about new year, new starts?'

'Don't worry about the emphasis of the article, just finish telling me your story and then I'll ask you a specific question looking ahead. And Nic, remember that there's nothing you can say that I haven't heard before.'

His body language is open and he's not being at all defensive. In fact, he's sitting back in his chair, one arm on the table and the other on his knee.

'There's not a lot more to tell. I never saw Katie again and as my social life more or less revolved around work and colleagues, it was tough. I was in a bad place, obviously, and I turned my back on everyone. I had invested heavily in property and with no income at all, and high monthly outgoings, I had to quickly raise some cash. The property market had just taken a nose-dive and the equity I thought I had just wasn't there. Everything had been wiped out overnight and the wise move was to sit and wait for the market to pick back up. But time was a luxury I didn't have. I went from having a very lucrative job and a portfolio of properties, to getting out with just a couple of hundred thousand pounds. Enough to buy this and do most of the renovation work. In a way, Beach View Cottage saved me but it's all I have, literally.'

He stares at me from behind partially-closed eyes, as if he's trying to gauge my reaction. There's a little more to this than he's willing to share with me but I can't imagine what, exactly. Why head away from London and his business connections? I sit here, feeling his pain, my face probably reflecting nothing but sadness.

'Oh, I forgot the best bit. My medical records now show that I officially had a nervous breakdown. I'll spare you the gory details but it wasn't a pretty sight.

That's why Olwen is so protective of me. When I first arrived here I was still in a mess and she took me under her wing. She's one of life's nurturers, is Olwen, and for that I'll always be grateful.'

The way he tossed that in as an afterthought demonstrates it's not something that scarred him. It's simply a fact. So, what is it that he still can't face up to? I may never discover the unknown in all of this that really broke him because it sure as hell wasn't his parents, or losing everything he had. It was something bigger: much bigger and that thought scares me. Sometimes there are no words you can offer someone. I walk around the table and as I approach Nic, he rises up out of his chair. I fling not just my arms, but my whole body around him, wanting to hug away the hurt and the trauma of what still haunts him.

'That's enough for today. I saw some steaks in the fridge. Olwen must have called in this morning after we left. So how about you go down to the beach and light the barbecue, while I sort out the food?'

Nic nestles his face into my hair, drawing in a big breath.

'It feels good to get that out of my system, Tia. For the first time in so long I'm feeling hopeful again. A part of that is down to your influence, but I think you already know that.'

'Everything in life has a risk attached to it, but don't let the risks you don't take be the regrets of the future.

It's time to start believing in yourself again.'

25

Hope is Like a Bright Light on the Horizon

It's Monday morning and several hours since I waved Nic goodbye. As he headed off to pick up his first fare of the day there was a little skip to his walk that I couldn't help noticing. After wrapping up the interview with him yesterday, it made me remember how cathartic it can be to share one's pain. Owning it is the start of moving on and in tandem with this new opportunity that has come his way, I think his self-esteem is definitely on the rise. I do have this lingering doubt over whether there's still one piece to this puzzle that hasn't been revealed. But as he begins to put the past firmly where it belongs, he really is sounding a lot less like the guy with a big chip on his shoulder. I'm getting a peek at the real Nic; the person he tries so desperately hard not to reveal.

Our barbecue on Saturday night was relaxed and full of laughter. Actually, that was probably helped along rather nicely by the bottle of wine we shared. After we'd eaten, we lazed back on a blanket spread out on the sand. We laid there, enjoying the sounds of the sea, which was soothing. I ended up going back to the cottage to collect my recorder, after Nic suggested we finish off the interview. I thought it might spoil our relaxation, but then I could see that it was helping him. Emotional healing is a unique experience; it can take a long time to start the process, but then suddenly it begins to speed up, positivity making each improvement a huge boost up to the next level.

As soon as I switched on the machine, Nic looked to me for guidance.

'You need to set the scene so I know where to start.'

Wine glass in hand, he leant on one elbow and seemed to be completely relaxed about it all. I settled myself back down, lying parallel to him and mirrored his position.

'Life is now a blank page. I know it's only June, but let's pretend it's New Year's Eve and you are looking forward. You feel secure in the knowledge that the past is dead to you and what happens now is in your own hands. There will be other people out there reading your story and facing similar situations. Starting over again can be daunting, but it can also be a challenge that throws up previously unimaginable opportunities. What would you say to someone if they were asking for your advice?'

In the fading light and with only the glow of the fire, hissing and popping from the fresh twigs Nic carried down from the woods earlier, there was a cosiness as we talked. It was like a cocoon and easy to forget the world out there for a while, as if it was only about the two of us.

'My forward plan would be to reflect upon a few of the more recent lessons I've come to learn. The first one is that I can't commit to anyone until I'm in a good place. Having almost hated myself for a long while, I've now stopped wanting what I used to have. Maybe that never was going to be the source of my happiness, anyway. Perhaps it was more about looking successful and the obscure satisfaction of knowing other people envy what you have. I had what many people were fighting every single working minute to achieve. Losing my pride in such a public way was devastating, but now I realise that I'm actually free. I've faced what I feared the most and I'm still here. So, face the demons and move on.'

I remember that he had looked up at the sky and smiled, some transient thought making him sigh, but it had been one of acceptance and not dismay. I was pleased for him as the anger he'd been storing up was beginning to ebb away.

'I suppose, the next action point is to think about what you want and make a plan. I need to concentrate on building myself a new career and this time around it's not about pleasing anyone else. Yes, I need to pay the bills, but it has to be something that fires me up.

Freedom is empowering, but it's also a huge responsibility. I'm lucky that I don't have a wife, or kids, to mix into the equation. I have plenty of time to sort myself out before I begin to think about a relationship, again. Next time around, and my final item on the list, is to listen to my gut instincts more often. If it looks too good to be true, then it generally is and I was guilty of seeing what I wanted to see, instead of the truth. We all fear rejection; getting hurt dents our confidence and, often, our hearts. It will change the way we look at things, but after the disillusionment phase comes an awakening of sorts. When I give my heart to someone I will be very sure it's forever, but I'll also understand that forever means one day at a time, with each new day being a renewal of that commitment. Forever is a destination that stretches out ahead of you.'

I'd had to brush away a stray tear, then, as Nic's words had gone straight to my heart. Yes, it was going to be perfect for the article, but more importantly he was firmly back in control.

'Hello.' Olwen's voice breaks my thoughts and I compose myself as she walks through into the kitchen.

'Sorry, I've disturbed you.'

'No, it's fine. I was just going over some of my interview stuff. All walks of life, all age groups and all situations. A lot of joy, but some sadness, too.'

There's no point in trying to hide the fact that I feel a little emotional this morning.

'Well, as long as it's work and there's nothing wrong between you and Nic. I thought I'd give the bathroom a clean and generally whip the vacuum around. Is that all right with you?'

'Fine, but sit and have a coffee first. I know Mondays are really hectic, so take ten minutes to rest those legs.'

I pop the kettle on, noticing that Olwen seems more than happy to ease herself into the chair for a break.

'Thank you, Tia, that's very kind of you. I've been on the go since five this morning and I haven't had time to grab a drink, yet. I should be stick thin, really, as I rarely stop for long.'

I open a packet of biscuits and place them in front of her, swiftly followed by a mug of strong coffee.

'You're an angel. Biscuits keep me going and will be the first thing I cut out on my next diet. I will miss you when you go back to London. Your presence brings a bit of life and optimism back to Holly Cove.'

'And, if I'm being totally honest with you, it's hard for me to walk away. But Nic's batteries are recharging and I think you are going to see a lot of changes in him over the coming weeks. Max has been away for a few days, but even he might notice when he returns.'

Olwen sits, cradling her mug.

'Oil and water need to be kept apart if you don't want a disaster. Did Max say where he was going?'

I can feel myself frowning as I'm not sure what she means and why there should be any trouble. Max is a

288

little withdrawn at times, but he's harmless enough.

'No, I don't think he did mention it. He's a kind man, though, and you were right; he did invite me in for a quick look inside one of his cabins.'

'He doesn't take to many folk, but I knew he'd make time for you.'

'Why?'

'You're good for Nic and that fact won't have been missed. Oh my – look at the time! Thanks for the little chat. I was a bit worried Friday's meeting would upset things, but clearly you seem fine. And now I really must get on.'

As Olwen grabs her cleaning materials and heads off upstairs, my phone pings.

> Finlay isn't flaunting his F1 jaunt, surprise, surprise. Your name is the buzzword today and he's seething. Make sure you call Clarissa this morning as she's out of the office from noon. Hope you found someone to celebrate with at the weekend! Surfer guys can be fun company, I hear.

I can't believe I'd totally forgotten about making the call!

> I'm grateful for the heads-up. I'll phone Clarissa shortly. I celebrated in style and you would approve, but my lips are sealed.

> Well, that's no fun!

> Oh, but it was, I can assure you.

I laugh out loud as I can imagine her reaction and sheer frustration at not knowing what's going on at this end. It is important she thinks I'm living it up a little. If Clarissa throws out one of her *straight to the point* questions that Hayley can't sidestep, hopefully she will say I'm working hard but also having a good time. Actually, that's the truth, anyway. Admittedly, thoughts of Mum are never very far away, but when I start to feel angry that she was taken from me, I flick a switch inside my head. It's too early to be able to let the memories flow, as it doesn't help at the moment. I can't enjoy trawling through the archives of my mind without stirring up some very raw emotions.

Thoughts of Will pop into my head and I know that Mum wouldn't harbour a grudge for what happened. Maybe he never really managed to let go after we lost Dad and that's why he couldn't accept it when Mum and Ed grew close. It was a purely selfish perspective, because loneliness is an awful thing and I wouldn't wish that on anyone. I wonder if Will is sorry now for the way he reacted and for the years he didn't have with her. A wave of nostalgia rolls over me and I find myself dialling his number. He won't be at home, I know that, but Sally is easier to talk to, anyway. It rings several times before she picks up.

'Hi, Sally, it's Tia. How are you all?'

'Oh, Tia, I think Will meant to give you a call over the weekend, but it ended up being rather hectic here. Bella had a sleepover Saturday night and I don't think any of us had more than an hour's sleep. I've just collected her from school a little early as she has a dental appointment.'

I try to imagine what Bella looks like now and know that if we passed in the street she wouldn't recognise me, or I, her. That hurts and it's something I need to change once I'm back home.

'Sounds like she had fun then, and I hope that appointment goes well. I thought I'd check with you how Will is doing. The sadness can be a little overwhelming at times and it must be difficult for him … given the circumstances. But Mum never stopped loving him, or thinking about you and Bella. I hope he knows that.'

There's a brief pause. 'He has so many regrets, Tia. I know how much he's hurting and how angry he is with himself. It has changed the way he looks at everything now and he actually talked to Bella about you the other day. He said you were going to come and visit us. Is that true?'

'Last time we spoke we talked about that and he admitted Mum wouldn't want us to be distant.'

'Well, that's a real breakthrough and I'm so happy to hear it. He needs you, Tia, and as a family we should be supporting each other through this sad time. Bella doesn't really understand what happened as she was too young when Will cut the ties. When are you coming back to London?'

'My last day here is the second of July. It's going to be frenetic when I get back. I'm stepping into my boss's shoes for a while, but I will make that visit happen sooner, rather than later.'

'Don't mistake Will's silence for lack of concern, Tia. It's an uphill climb for him and he has to learn to forgive himself for the decisions he made and the things he said. He's a proud man and a good one, but everyone makes mistakes.'

I know that, but it's great to hear that Sally understands it too.

'Maybe it's best not to mention the fact that I called. He'll call me again when he wants to talk.'

'I don't think you'll have to wait too long, Tia. And I'm glad to hear you have so much going on, because you have to get through this phase as best you can. You deserve your success and I know how hard this will have been for you. Your mum was a wonderful person. All any mum wants for their children is to see them using their potential to the full and leading a happy life.'

Knowing that Sally is there for Will every step of the way means a lot and I know she'll look after him, as he looks after her and Bella. Some of life's lessons are harsher than others, that's for sure.

'Thank you for understanding and being so supportive. Will is a very lucky man to have you by his side, Sally. It's all a bit of a mess still, but we'll work through it. I don't suppose I could have a quick chat with Bella?'

'Of course you can! She'll be delighted.'

The muffled sounds of walking confirm that Sally is now seeking out her daughter and after a few moments I hear her speaking.

'It's Aunty Tia on the phone and she'd like to speak to you, Bella.'

I hear an excited little squeal.

'Hi, Aunty Tia. How are you?'

Ah, she sounds so grown-up now and so polite. Her sweet little voice puts an instant smile on my face.

'I'm good, thank you, Bella. You've grown quite a bit since I last saw you I suspect. How is school going?'

A slightly muffled response soon clears as she moves the phone from one hand to another.

'Good. My teacher gave me three house points this week for volunteering to be a tidy-up helper. And now the reds are in the lead!'

Just to hear her enthusiasm tweaks my heart as I consider how much I've missed since Will cut me off.

'Wow – that sounds like an important job and well done the reds.'

'Oh, it is important, Aunty Tia. You have to check everyone's desks and make sure nothing is left out because it's not fair on the cleaners. They don't have time to be moving things around because we don't tidy away properly.'

She sounds so serious that I find myself suppressing a chuckle.

'I'm very proud of you, Bella, I hope you know that. And it's good to hear that your teacher appreciates your help as that's quite a responsibility. Do you still love to draw?'

'Oh, yes. But I'm also learning to play the piano and the recorder. There's an after-school music club and I go there with my best friend, Alice. We have sleepovers, too.'

Sally said Will had mentioned me recently, but she must talk about me too, from time to time, because Bella doesn't sound distant at all, just pleased to catch me up with her news.

'Well, I hope I can see you really soon.'

'I'd love that, Aunty Tia. I wish you didn't live so far away.'

Her little voice wavers a little and suddenly Sally jumps back in, taking over the phone but speaking directly at Bella.

'Don't worry, Bella, we'll sort something out. I promise. Now, off you go to get your coat as we mustn't be late for the dentist.'

I reassure Sally that I will make that visit happen as soon as I possibly can.

The natural order of things revolves around the cycle of birth and death, but as with the seasons, there is a fundamental reason for everything that happens. It simply strikes me as so very, very sad that it took Mum's death to begin the process of healing old wounds.

26

Highs and Lows

It's a long and busy week. Not least because of an unexpected email from Veronica breaking the news that she's leaving Liam. She assured me that they had discussed the article and were in agreement that it should go ahead, especially as they didn't intend sharing their "news" with friends and family until the New Year. She sounded prosaic about it, saying he was in love with someone else and while she was gutted, you can't make someone love you back just because you love them. It was such a poignant, heart-felt email and I felt awful having to contact Liam direct to get his authority not to pull the article. But from a data protection point of view that was necessary. He came back with a one-liner 'Fine by me to go ahead' and that was it. I guess it would have been too embarrassing to have to explain to people why the article wasn't appearing. My conscience prickled a little but when the article comes out they will still officially be together and so I looked at it pragmatically.

Nic is still helping out at the farm once his shift finishes and then he heads back to the cottage. He works away upstairs in his office, while I work downstairs and we settle into a nice little routine.

The police have confirmed that two separate sets of fingerprints found up at the farm could be linked to a growing string of other break-ins. However, the official statement that appeared in the local paper confirmed the investigations were ongoing. Which means they still have no clues at all about who is behind it all so for the time being everyone stays on alert.

When I spoke to Clarissa at the start of the week she said she never doubted for one moment that I was the right person to take her place while she's away. It did send a little thrill coursing through my veins at the thought and what it represented. You spend years working towards that final goal and suddenly it's in sight.

I asked her to put me through to Hayley, who said the mood in the office had completely turned around, now people knew their jobs were safe. And I was right, Clarissa did quiz her about how things were going down in Caswell Bay. She's well aware we are friends, aside from work colleagues. Hayley admitted she was a little shocked, saying that Clarissa wanted to be kept up to date with any developments.

'Does Clarissa know something about that seemingly sleepy little village that you aren't choosing to share? You aren't going to come back engaged, or anything, are you?'

She sounded hopeful and I soon dispelled that thought, although I was a little annoyed to think Clarissa was spying on me. When we talked she was so positive, but obviously I have to keep delivering in order to allay any fears she might have that I'm not ready, mentally. I then sent Nic's bank details to accounts and asked if they could speed through his payment. It usually takes at least a month to go through the system, but I pulled a few strings and they promised to have it sent out within the next seven days. After all, a few more weeks and people will be jumping to my commands and not Clarissa's. OK, so I'm more of a people-person and have a gentler approach, but I still know exactly what to do to make things happen.

With an interview scheduled for this morning, there's plenty to do, but I've been a little worried about Max. His few days away have stretched out into a week. Well, today it will be eight days. Every time I take a break from the laptop I wander across to the window, looking out in the hope that I'll see his boat anchored in the bay.

Just after lunch, as I'm about to turn away from the window and return to work, I'm relieved to see Max trudging past the cottage with a carrier bag of groceries in each hand. I decide to finish up what I'm doing and then saunter down to the beach for a walk. I could do with some fresh air anyway and if he wants to have a chat I'm sure he'll appear.

Today the weather has changed and it's overcast again, but mild. There's a light breeze coming off the sea which is refreshing, rather than invigorating. I stroll down to the water's edge, picking up the odd pebble and trying to skim it across the water. It's something I remember Will doing whenever we took a trip to the seaside and he made it look so easy. But that seems like another lifetime.

'Clearing your head?'

I hadn't even realised Max was on the beach, I was so caught up in my thoughts.

'Hey, Max. You were right, it does help. There's something so therapeutic about watching the waves cresting and the tide coming in and out. When you stand still and listen to the sound it's so calming: it seems to blot out everything else.'

We stand, side by side, looking out at the heaving grey mass that, today, looks cold and uninviting.

'Do you miss it on the days you aren't out there fishing?'

He nods, turning to look at me and there's a sadness behind those gentle, greyish-blue eyes, which makes my stomach do a somersault. Whatever it is that has happened has ignited some inner conflict.

'It's the only time I feel at peace. It's not just about the fishing, it's about being out there surrounded by nothing but the sea. Once my feet step off dry land and I'm looking back towards the shoreline, I feel like I've stepped away from the world for a while.'

I let a few minutes pass before I comment.

'Everyone needs a sanctuary. Either some place they can go, or something they enjoy doing to take a break away from it all. I like that analogy, about stepping away from the world for a while. When I first came here it was more about wanting to run away; to run away and hide. In some ways, I wish I could slow down time to prolong my visit here, but on the other hand I'm keen to get back to the life I know.'

'Hiding isn't a solution, is it, Tia? Even here, life catches up with us all, eventually.'

I watch as Max scuffs at the sand with the toe of his boot. Making little ripples on the, otherwise smooth, surface.

'Is it something you can share?' There, I've said the words and that's all I can do.

Max stops mid-scuff and looks straight ahead.

'Some things can't be fixed, Tia, and it's hard to accept that. I'm worn-down with the worry of it all and the guilt.'

I wonder what has gone so badly wrong that Max has chosen to give up on it. Whatever it is has hit him hard. I wonder if it's to do with his family and why they disowned him. Maybe they can't understand that after a life spent mostly at sea, this is the only place he feels at home. Ideally, people head into retirement knowing they can enjoy a new-found freedom from a lifetime of constraints. Suddenly there is time to do all those things you've always longed to do. I vaguely remember him saying that he was an embarrassment to his ex-wife and son, because of the lifestyle he had chosen. Was he looking for reconciliation and now his hopes have been dashed? Or was it the other way around and his refusal to conform to their rules has severed that connection once and for all?

'I'm sorry for your troubles, Max. Is there really no way to patch it up, or start afresh?'

He lets out a noise that's rather like a low groan and I freeze, horrified to think I've said the wrong thing. But I can see he isn't angry.

'No. It's much too late for that. But thank you for caring, Tia. Most people don't have time to notice a stranger's troubles. But you aren't like that and I appreciate it.'

He turns and begins walking away.

'Is there's anything I can do, anything at all?'

He turns his head slightly, not to look at me, but to talk over his shoulder.

'Life is full of surprises, it seems. Help my son to see that this is where his future lies. Knowing he has someone positive around him at the moment is worth more to me than I can convey. Nic's a stubborn man, but then the apple never falls far from the tree.'

My jaw drops and I'm left gasping as I watch Max trudge slowly back across the sand. After he disappears inside one of the cabins it takes me a little while to re-engage my brain. Is this the last piece of Nic's puzzle? But why hide this from me? It doesn't make any sense. I make my way back up the beach to the cottage in search of my phone.

'Olwen, it's Tia.'

'Hi, Tia. Did I forget something?'

'No, no. Um… is there any chance you could pop in for five minutes sometime this afternoon? I know how busy you are but I wanted to ask you something. Nic won't be back until five o'clock at the earliest and I would prefer it if he wasn't here.'

'Oh, OK, then. Give me an hour.' I can hear the concern in her voice but this isn't something I want to talk about over the phone.

I have a quick tidy of the kitchen table, then I go and wash my face, hoping the cold water will revive me. It was such a shock and I didn't see it coming. Why didn't Nic tell me? I keep going over the little I can remember from a few references he made to his family, to check whether it was something I missed. Has he been lying to me by omission? One of our ground rules was *no pretence*. Even if he thinks it's none of my business, it's obvious I'm going to bump into Max. Whether Nic is aware that Max and I chat, is another thing entirely, but I now feel really awkward. Do I tell Nic that Max mentioned him to me? Or do I carry on letting him think that I'm still in the dark, as then I'd be the one who was lying to him. What I'm feeling now is bordering on confusion as I'd assumed I had a real grasp on Nic's situation.

When Olwen arrives she has a small, boxed cake in her hands.

'I thought you sounded like you might need a sugar boost. Is there a problem?'

We sit opposite each other at the table and I don't try to hide my confusion.

'It's about Nic and Max.'

Olwen lets out a sharp breath and slumps back in her chair.

'Feeling a bit caught in the middle? I didn't realise Max was back.'

I nod, reluctantly, and cast around for some words that won't make me sound angry and a little upset.

'Nic never mentioned Max, not even once. I had no idea they were even related, let alone father and son. Why would he hide that?'

Olwen's lips are pursed together in disapproval and I wonder if she's going to tell me straight that it's none of my business.

'I didn't know for sure whether you knew or not, and it wasn't my place to share that fact. Like I said, oil and water.'

Absentmindedly, I run a hand through my hair, scooping it back from my face.

'When Max mentioned Nic's name, I was grateful it was a parting comment. How hurtful would it have been if I'd had to admit I didn't know? At the very least, you would expect Nic to have enlightened me to avoid any potential awkwardness, even from a tenant's point of view. But now we're... friends and Max is aware of that, he'd be hurt to think Nic doesn't acknowledge his presence at all. I hate to ask, but you're right and I really am caught in the middle. Max asked me to do something for him, which means I need to understand what's going on between them, first.'

Olwen doesn't seem at all surprised by my reaction. Shaking her head sadly, she gives me a look tinged with what I can only describe as exasperation.

'Even I don't know the whole story. The open animosity between them has died down a lot in the last year, or so. At least it's quieter now they choose to ignore each other, but it's sad to see father and son so caught up in a bitter feud.'

I'm still trying to recall any clues Nic might have given me. 'Nic said something about an overbearing mother and a father who was never around, but he never mentioned a name. I suppose Max was away at sea for long periods of time, but while it's not an ideal situation, it's not uncommon. He also said something about family interference just before he left his job in London. But that's all I can remember.'

'All I know is that Nic bought the cottage from Max, who had already moved into the cabins at that time. What I can't understand is why Nic was so angry, as if he didn't want the cottage at all and was resentful in some way. I think I told you, no one even knew Max was thinking of selling it. Let's just say it wouldn't have been on the market for very long, that's for sure.'

'So, Max was coming down and staying here in the cottage at weekends before building work began down on the beach?'

'Yes.'

'Who owned it before Max, then?'

'No one is sure about that. One of the older people in the village recall a family coming down here years ago for the odd holiday. I only remember a stream of people from the time it was rented out. Whether Max bought it at that point, isn't clear. Rhys was always a bit annoyed they used a firm from London to handle the rentals, but then they didn't seem to have any real links down here. So, Max might have bought it as an investment, I suppose. I'm sorry, that doesn't help you very much, does it?'

'Well, it's better than nothing. Max asked me to help Nic to see that his future is here, in Caswell Bay. That's rather an odd request, because Nic hasn't said anything about going back to London.'

I think Olwen can see the dilemma. 'Perhaps you are better off waiting to see what happens. At least you are aware of Max's concern and you think Nic should stay here, don't you? There's no reason he'd suddenly up and leave?'

It's clear why she's asking that question and it's to do with the growing friendship between Nic and myself. I know she's protective of him and I hope she can see that I like Nic enough to want what's best for him, too.

'His future is here, Olwen, I have no doubt of that. And thanks for listening and for the advice. I guess I'll wait and see what happens, rather than raking it all up. Sometimes things have a way of sorting themselves out over time.'

We both know this isn't going to go away, but there's little point in either of us stepping into the situation in case that actually makes it worse. Olwen probably came to that conclusion a long time ago. But if the opportunity arises to mention the bridges I'm building with my own brother, it might start Nic talking. However, the timing will have to be perfect, because it's such a sensitive issue. I don't want anything to mar our last three weeks together. What Nic doesn't need right now, is an argument that might threaten to undermine his newfound positivity.

It's not long after Olwen leaves that Nic walks in through the door on a high.

'Thank goodness it's Friday and the weekend beckons. *And* we've been invited to a drinks party tomorrow night.'

'We?'

He lifts me off the floor and spins me around. Any stray, little angry vibes that I felt are dispelled. His happiness is infectious.

'Yes, and I took the liberty of accepting on behalf of us both. I didn't think you'd mind. Gareth is having a small celebration to mark his fifteenth year as editor of the paper. It won't be a large gathering and it's informal. A couple of glasses of wine and a few canapés, but John Llywelyn from Natureland Experience will be there.'

He looks down at me, then plants a quick kiss on my forehead.

'Oh, so I'm there to circulate while you chat to John?'

He at least has the decency to look guilty as charged.

'There will be some interesting people there and as a journalist yourself, I know that nothing is ever wasted. All material is stored up here.' He taps the side of my head. 'You never know when something is going to come in useful.'

In the same way that being told Max is your father might have been just a tad helpful to me? I shake the thought off, wanting to raise my own spirits rather than dampen them.

'Being a people-watcher is a part of the job and I hold my hands up to that.'

He takes half a pace backwards, letting his hands slide down my arms to catch my fingertips in his hands. It is now becoming an endearing habit, which sends little tingles rippling through me every time. I'd forgotten how wonderful and special it makes you feel to be desired. Hayley was right, I do need this.

'So you should. I can't believe you had me pouring out my entire story.'

Not the entire story, Nic, and you know that.

'Well, when the cheque arrives I hope I'm still here, because you can take me out to dinner.'

'Sorry, it's going to have to be a barbecue on the beach as the boiler is going to suck up every single penny. I can't risk another winter knowing it could break down at any moment.'

'That reminds me, Max is back.'

Nic glances at me, his face blank and showing no emotion whatsoever.

'Well, we'll just have to keep the noise down a little, then.'

27

Life is Seldom Predictable

I decide to dress up a little for the celebration tonight, now I'm going as Nic's significant other. Well, we know our situation is only temporary, but I'm sure there will be people there who might not feel so comfortable with that thought. In fairness, it doesn't really change anything about the way we act when we are together, so what harm can it do? I have no reason to hide the fact that I enjoy being with him.

Gareth is very personable and we have a little chat after Nic introduces us, then shoots off the moment John arrives. I congratulate him on his achievement. Fifteen years is a long run as editor. He's the one who has shaped its future and ensured it continued to thrive.

'It's the hub of our little community,' he admits. 'Nic has been a great addition to the team. He tells me you will be returning to London in a few weeks' time? I expect you are missing the buzz. I still miss it after all these years, but life is gentler down here.'

'I didn't realise. Which publication did you work for?'

'*Sea, Sand and Surf Monthly*. Those were the days. But I'm content here and I'm able to indulge my hobby of deep sea fishing. Besides, my wife is happy, which is the main thing.'

He lifts his eyebrows and I stifle a laugh.

'You and Max will have a lot in common, then; although he seems to stay quite close to the shore when he's fishing.' I'm really only making polite conversation, especially as Nic is nowhere to be seen.

'We go back quite a way. Fishermen tend to gravitate towards each other. Not a lot of people understand the fascination of it, but it's the thrill of the chase and the skill in landing the fish. Of course, most of our stories are about the ones that got away.'

He has a throaty, belly-laugh that carries and eyes turn in our direction.

'Beach View Cottage will have seen a lot of people come and go, but I don't expect too many of them were fisher folk.'

Gareth nods in agreement.

'It's seen it all, has that old cottage. Happy and sad times, that's for sure. The tragic death of Max's daughter, Georgina, almost destroyed him.' He looks down into his drink, his expression one of deep sadness.

Max lost his daughter?

'That must have been an awful time.' The blood is rushing around my veins like it's on fire. Trying to stay calm and hide any sense of being thrown by yet another totally unexpected revelation, is very difficult.

'I do believe Max's wife never visited the cottage again after that.'

'I didn't realise you'd known Max for such a long time.'

Gareth scans the room, catching sight of Nic and John sitting at a table in the corner and chatting away, oblivious to the mingling going on around them. When his gaze returns to me I can see he's slightly hesitant to answer my question.

'Look, I'm aware that none of the locals seem to know anything much about the history of Holly Cove and its visitors, but my intentions are good, I can assure you of that and I can be trusted.'

I can see from his expression that his friendship means a lot to him.

'I gathered as much. But this has to be just between the two of us, Tia. Old wounds and all that but sometimes the past hampers the future and there's still a lot of pain that hasn't gone away.' I nod my head in agreement and he can see that I'm not taking my pledge lightly.

'Max didn't always come down when the family were able to make it for the odd weekend and short break. I first met him in the local pub when he was home on leave and had come down for a few days on his own to fish. That was probably fifteen years ago and since then we've fished together countless times.

'I didn't have occasion to meet his wife or Nic during that time and I've only known Nic since he moved here three years ago. What I know is what I heard directly from Max on his fishing trips. Towards the end of Georgina's illness, she spent a lot of time here with Nic as her carer and few knew that at the time. It was in two thousand and eight. Max was rarely around as he was often at sea still in his capacity as a trainer. No one really knows what happened in Holly Cove but over a pint Max admitted there was some sort of dispute going on. His wife wanted to move Georgina into a hospice in London, I believe, but she refused to go. In the end Nic brought in a private nurse as Georgina needed twenty-four-hour care and he was struggling. No one can simply step out of their life for an unknown period like that but Nic did, until it was over. That's why he came back to rescue the cottage because to him it's the only place where he can still feel close to her.'

It's hard to hide my confusion. I can understand Max not mentioning this, as he hardly knows me, but I really thought Nic was making a concerted effort to confront the demons in his past. He said he came from a dysfunctional family, but surely the loss of a sister is way outside of that and a major life event that will have affected everything.

Knowing that Nic would be horrified by this conversation, I decide to change the subject as quickly as I can.

'It helps to understand a little more about what went on, Gareth, and I'm more grateful than you can ever know. I won't say a word to anyone, I promise. And what about your future? Is there any intention to take things a little easier?'

'There's no one in the wings to take over, so I guess they're stuck with me. Nic's destined for much bigger things, of course, but his contributions will always be much appreciated.'

'He'd be very pleased to hear that. I'd better let you mingle I suppose and I ought to say a brief hello to John. It's been lovely talking to you, Gareth. Thank you.' I labour my parting words, my head still trying to process the unexpected information. This is the missing piece of the puzzle that is Nic's past.

By the time I walk across the room John has already left and Nic is talking to someone else. He indicates for me to take the seat next to him and we pass a very pleasant couple of hours, as our little group grows in size. There's a lot of banter and talk about the coming summer season and the events everyone hopes will bring a record number of visitors to the area.

When the taxi drops us back at the cottage, Nic doesn't want to end the evening with a walk along the beach, despite my encouragement.

'Let's cosy up together on the sofa and listen to some music,' he whispers in my ear. I continue unlocking the front door, as he plants little kisses on my cheek.

'Don't you miss not having a decent size TV, even if it's just to watch a film, now and again? It's not quite the same on a laptop, or iPad.'

His face visibly falls, but almost instantly he regains his composure. What did I say that he could have possibly taken the wrong way? Or does this hark back to the precious time he spent here with Georgina? He stepped away from his career at probably quite an important time in his life to honour his sister's wishes. That can't have been easy and I wonder who paid for the private nurse? The questions whirl around inside my head; questions I know I can't ask.

'It's over-rated and I'd rather read a book, or go for a walk on the beach.' He tries to shrug it off and walks out into the kitchen to put the kettle on. I'm still puzzling over the boxes in the cupboard under the stairs, which seem to be full of DVDs. It's frustrating because I wish he'd just open up to me but that's a decision Nic has to make and not something I can force.

It was only a moment ago he turned down my suggestion for an evening stroll, which would have been a lovely way to end a relaxing Saturday together. I hope he isn't stressing after his long chat with John. Obviously, the project is going ahead. He's already warned me he'll be heading to the park tomorrow and will be gone most of the day, even though it's Sunday. It's difficult working two jobs Monday to Friday, so he has no choice in the matter. I fully understand he's eager to begin working, but on the other hand it's kind of sad as I only have two full weekends left at Beach View Cottage.

He returns, leaning back against the doorway with a meaningful grin on his face.

'Besides, I have other plans for the rest of the night. The sofa was just the prelude.'

His mood has lifted again and whatever little cloud had suddenly appeared on the horizon has now passed over. But it shows he's still getting his moments of... anxiety, flashbacks, or guilt for what he's still holding back, who knows? I guess I'll never know for sure if he chooses not to share those thoughts with me. I can't pretend I'm not upset to think he doesn't trust me enough to bare all, but he made his intentions clear from the start and he hasn't lied, as such. He said a few things about the loss of my mum that really connected with me. After hearing about the death of his sister, I can now appreciate why – because it came from the heart. I should have known that it wasn't sympathy, but empathy, and that's something only someone who has experienced a similar loss can offer.

*

Nic is gone by ten a.m. and for the first time since I arrived I feel at a loose end. I have a leisurely brunch, as Nic said he would grab something at the park's cafe. I don't feel like working and there's only so much walking you can do when you are on your own. It's infinitely more enjoyable when you have company.

The sun is back and the sea is sparkling, so I decide to play the good tenant and do a little weeding in the front garden. The difference three weeks has made to how the garden has come alive, is incredible. There's colour everywhere you turn and it lifts the spirits. It also encourages the dandelions, which have a sort of charm to them, admittedly, but one turns into fifty if you don't keep on top of them. Before I know it, I have half a black sack full of garden debris.

'Looking tidy, Tia. I didn't know you were a gardener.'

Max looks on, approvingly.

'I'm not. I can't face working today and Nic's not around until later. I fancied some fresh air.'

'I'm heading up to the car to grab some new fishing lines ready for tomorrow. I was going to put the boat away, but how do you fancy a trip along the coast and back? It's a great way to spend an hour, or two, and the views are magnificent.'

'I'd love that, thank you Max.'

'Grab a jacket and maybe something for your hair, as it will be a bit breezy out there. I'll be back in about ten minutes.'

I head in to change into some jeans, a teeshirt and a long-sleeved top. Layers might be good and I pull out some old, comfy trainers and go in search of a waterproof jacket. By the time I've found my sunglasses and have everything ready, Max is walking back down the hill. I lock up, having left a note for Nic, in case he returns earlier than expected.

Max and I trudge along in silence, but it's a comfortable silence that's more about taking in what's going on around us. The seagulls are wheeling overhead, their raucous cries seem to echo from one end of the beach to the other. The cliffs give Holly Cove the distinctive shape of an amphitheatre, lending a similar sort of acoustic to the sounds created within it.

I've never seen Max's boat up close before. It stands on a trailer, which is sitting at the water's edge. Max unclips the heavy cable attached to the trailer and makes his way back up to his workshop. The sounds of a winch grinding away, temporarily drowns out the noise of the birds overhead and it takes a few minutes to wind it in. Max walks back down and pushes against the end of the trailer until the rear half of the boat is submerged. Then with one hand he pushes the boat with apparent ease, off the trailer and into the water. There's a small black line attached to the boat and I move closer, fascinated by the rollers on the trailer that are doing all the work.

'I'll lift you on board and then I need to turn her around.'

I notice the boat's name is *Lazin'* as I stop short of the incoming waves. Max lifts me with ease and then strides out into the water, ignoring the waves lapping at the bottom of his cut-off jeans.

'Grab hold and over you go.'

The boat rocks wildly from side to side and I collapse in a heap on the deck. With two seats up front and what looks like a large storage compartment taking up nearly half of the open area behind them, I ease myself into the available space as the boat continues to bob up and down, rather alarmingly.

'Don't worry, once we're further out it will calm down.'

Although we are only a few feet away from the edge of the beach, it's already much deeper than I thought it was going to be. That day when I scrambled out over the rocks, Max wasn't joking when he said the ground falls away rather sharply.

Max turns the boat by hand and hops over the side. He looks at my face as I'm still in a heap, holding on as if the boat is going to tip over. The engine kicks into life.

'Stay there for a moment; another minute and we'll be out of the shallows. I'll sort you out a life jacket and then you can hop over into the passenger seat.'

True to his word, it's not long before the boat has stopped bobbing around and aside from a gentle movement as the sea swells, I feel much happier. Max opens the storage box and helps me slip the life jacket harness over my head.

'Here, take my hand and step into the cockpit.'

The sides of the boat are actually much higher than they look. Once I'm settled into the poly-plastic seat, thankfully, I feel quite secure. The solid windscreen provides good cover to stop the spray from soaking the front seats and above our heads is a large canopied arch to keep off the sun.

'This is quite some boat,' I acknowledge. Not that I know anything at all about them. It is very stylish and new; not at all what I was expecting.

'Hold on, I'm going to open the throttle and take us out a bit further.'

'Is this a speed boat?' I shout over the sound of the engine and the slapping of the waves.

Max eases back and lets it idle.

'There you go. Now that's the view every visitor needs to see.'

Looking back at the craggy cliffs it's easy to identify Langland Bay, then trace the headland back along to Caswell Bay. I can't see Holly Cove any longer, but I know it's tucked behind the headland, on the far side.

'This is amazing, Max. No wonder you spend quite a bit of time out here.'

'She's a Stabicraft 1650 Fisher; one of the most versatile boats on the market. I wanted something solid and compact enough to fit into my workshop. She's easy to launch from this type of beach and designed for offshore coastal fishing. The sea is a changeable beast and you need to know what you have is seaworthy. *Lazin'* is certainly that, all right.'

He opens the throttle once more and we head on past Langland Bay.

'That's the golf course.' Max points inland. 'Ahead of us is Mumbles. There's a pier there.'

I nod, the noise of the engine and the slapping of the water against the boat makes it hard to hear. My hair is whipping around my face, so I grab a band from my pocket to pull it back into a ponytail.

'Not very hair-friendly, is it? This isn't too fast for you?' Max inclines his head towards me.

I give him a thumbs-up and settle back for the ride.

A short while later he kills the throttle and the engine idles. Max points out a few of the more prominent features along the coastline. Things you would never see from a car, or on foot. After Langland Bay the sheer cliffs rise up out of the sea, majestically. Max opens the throttle once more and does a three-hundred-and-sixty degree turn, to start heading back.

I don't think you can say you've seen the Gower coast until you've seen it from a boat. With the sun in our eyes and the sparkling glint reflecting back from the mirror-like surface of the water, we could be in some very exotic place on the other side of the world. I fleetingly wonder if Max has ever taken Nic out on the boat, but think it's unlikely. And that's a real shame, because I know he'd love this.

By the time Max heads the boat back into Holly Cove and I stand watching as he winches the trailer back up to the workshop, there's a chilly edge to the breeze. I help Max lift the boards that are placed over the deeper, dry sand in front of the workshop doors and he rewards me with a smile.

'It was lovely to have your company today, Tia. This will probably be my last year on the beach, so every trip out is special.'

I raise my head, to look at him.

'The last year? You've leaving?'

'I have a lady friend, someone I've known for a long time. She worries about me and my lifestyle choices. As time passes I'm coming around to the idea of being with someone, permanently, again. But she wants us to move away from the area so we can start afresh and she's a Yorkshire lass. I don't want to leave here until I'm sure Nic is settled. I want to spend one more Christmas at Caswell Bay. Some people like the summer, but I love the winter and the elements that remind me of a lifetime at sea.'

I feel humbled that Max has shared this with me and now I understand a little more about his life. Having lost his daughter, he must feel his son is also lost to him, but even so he can't walk away until he can see Nic is strong enough.

'He's doing well, Max. He's found something that inspires him and he's looking forward with a real sense of purpose. It's time to think about your own future, now.'

He nods, placing his hand on my shoulder and giving it a squeeze.

'I hoped you'd stay, Tia; make this your *home*, but I understand. I know the circumstances that brought you here are devastating. I hope it's been a time of healing for you, too. We must have another trip out before you leave.'

'I'd like that. Thank you, Max, for one of the most amazing afternoons I've had in a long while.' I lean in and kiss his cheek. He looks back at me a little sheepishly, but his eyes are smiling.

28

An Impossible Situation

Over dinner, Nic enthuses about his day. I listen as he tells me all about the staff he met and the composition of some of the shots he feels will be keepers.

'This is turning out to be an amazing opportunity, Tia. There's also a huge herd of fallow deer we didn't see when I took you there, but John had someone drive me out to a good spot to catch a few shots. It's the first time I've really been that close to a deer and the colours of their coats are amazing. I spotted, red, brown and black, and even a few pure white deer. They have a black line that runs along the back down to the tail and they are really majestic, powerful looking animals. The antlers on the males were impressive.'

He pauses long enough to shovel in some pasta bolognaise and chew much faster than is probably good for his digestion.

'This isn't just going to give me photos for John's project, but this will start off a collection. Photos I can sell to wildlife magazines, newspapers, journals. I'm thinking prints, even.'

I've stopped eating to sit back and watch him. I can almost see his mind ticking over.

'There is one little problem. I need a lens with a much longer focal length than the ones I have at the moment. They don't come cheap.'

I know nothing about photography and was surprised that day, when I saw he had several different lenses.

'Is it worth the investment? How often will you be photographing animals again?'

'It's not just for wildlife shots, but anything that moves. It captures images with a narrower angle of view than a human eye. Distant subjects appear larger in the frame and it allows you to draw closer to the action. Panning can also be used to capture a range of moving subjects, such as cars at a racetrack. The combination of a sharp object in focus and a blurred background, gives a real sense of speed to the picture. It tracks the subject as it moves closer, or further away, and as it travels around the frame. We're talking real pro stuff here and the best part of a grand. But it's a game-changer and if I'm going to take this further, then I have to find the cash somehow.'

I don't know his past, only that at the peak of his career he was a Marketing Director for a big company. What led up to that could have been a grounding in media studies, for all I know, which I think covers film and photography.

'Sorry, it's all technical stuff and rather boring. The point is that this is a direction that I didn't even consider as an option going forward. And now this could be a chance to pull together a portfolio that has some impact. Getting on board with John's little project could be the start of a very lucrative business. He's happy for me to take as many photos as I like without having a claim on them. Anyway, sorry, as you can tell I'm on a bit of a high at the moment. The thought of not having to drive the cab, or lug hay bales around anymore, is enough to raise my spirits.'

'It's wonderful to see you so inspired and happy. The cheque from the magazine is due to arrive any day now. It should cover the cost of that new lens and a small amount to kick off the boiler fund. Hopefully it will be well worth the investment.'

'Really? That's awesome, Tia. It would mean a lot. Anyway, enough about me. How was your day? Did you work through?'

Oh, this is awkward.

'You mean to say you didn't notice your weed-free front garden?'

As he swallows another mouthful of pasta I lean across the table and wipe the side of his mouth with a napkin. He smiles back at me with that cute grin of his.

'Sorry. This is delicious and I'm starving. Thanks for doing the weeding, but now I feel guilty for leaving you all alone.'

'I wasn't alone all day. I did have some company for a few hours.'

Nic's head jolts upwards. I think he knows what I'm going to say.

'I spent most of the afternoon on Max's boat.'

His face hardens, not quite a scowl but not far off.

'I can't tell you what to do with your time, or who to socialise with, but be aware he might have another motive. The man is a meddler and usually it doesn't end well.'

I've upset him and I didn't mean to do that. But you can't live your life ignoring what's going on around you.

'He's your father, Nic, and he cares about you. Besides, the trip was very enjoyable and it was kind of him to offer.'

Nic pushes his half-empty plate back away from him.

'So he told you. And now he's getting you to meddle, too.'

Our eyes lock across the table. His face is stern.

'As a friend and a bystander, I see two men who carry a very deep hurt that is gnawing away inside of them both. But I've come to know a little about each of you and he's no monster, Nic. And neither are you. So, while I'm not trying to underestimate the damage that has been done, all I'm saying is that he doesn't wish you ill in any way whatsoever. It might be worth mulling that over.'

He stands, shakes his head and turns to walk towards the stairs, grabbing his camera bag.

'I'll be in the study downloading the photos. Thanks for dinner, Tia.'

And with that, he's gone.

I clear the table, nursing a heavy heart. It's so hard knowing both men and seeing how alike they are in many ways. Private, stubborn, a little lost in some respects; both desperately trying to manoeuvre themselves into a good place. But they must forgive themselves, before they can forgive each other.

At shortly after nine o'clock I go up to bed. Entering the darkened room, I walk across to the window to peer out before drawing the curtains. All is as it should be and I smile to myself, wondering why I ever thought anyone would venture down here at night. For someone to wander around in the dark would be little short of madness, given the steep, rough terrain and the lack of lighting. Settling down to read my Kindle there's no sign of movement from the other room. Even after I turn out the lights and snuggled down to sleep, I can still see a stream of light coming through the crack in the study door. I'm gutted that Nic is shutting me out and maybe I've been kidding myself that this thing between us is creating some sort of a bond. The bed feels so empty without him next to me but I have to remind myself that this will end soon. Then I will have to get used to being on my own once more.

*

When I wake up I'm alone; a quick check confirms that Nic slept on the sofa bed in the study last night. I was a fool to think that I could start the healing process in a relationship I don't really understand. Good intentions mean nothing if it makes a situation even worse and I fear that's what I've done. I hope Nic calms down enough to call in for a chat today, because I feel really horrible this morning. My head is aching and my stomach is churning with the upset. So much so, that I can't wait for Olwen to arrive; anything to save me from sitting here at the table surveying my work and finding myself unable to function. When I hear the click of the front door shutting, it's a relief. But Nic's face as he stands before me now is angry and he is waving an opened envelope in the air.

'What's this? Have you been spying on me?'

I rise up out of my chair, but he strides across and throws some paperwork down onto the table in front of me. I pick it up and see the magazine's letterhead. It's the standard letter with a printed cheque attached to it. I look up at him, confused.

'You can buy that lens now.'

'You think I'm going to take it? That's my mother's name printed on the bottom of this letter. She sent you here to spy on me and now she's dealing a really low blow. She said if I walked away I'd end up with nothing and this is her way of demonstrating how low I've sunk in her eyes. What was the next step, Tia? You make me fall in love with you and then the unstoppable Clarissa Cooper gets her son back as part of the deal?'

I'm rooted to the spot, totally horrified by Nic's tirade and struggling to comprehend what he's saying.

'Clever, but I'm not a fool. You've certainly earned your promotion and you're a great little actor. You can go back to her and make it very clear that I don't need her interference, or her help. If you use that interview I will sue the magazine. It will give me great pleasure to do so and be very vocal about her controlling behaviour and under-handed tactics. Now I want you out of my house by the end of the day. Tell her that I'm not so desperate for money I will take it under false pretences.'

'But—'

I watch as Nic turns, striding away from me with his face hard-set in anger.

Tears start to trickle down my face. Now that I realise Clarissa has been using me I'm angry, but to what end, I have no idea. The thought of what I've lost is totally crushing. I'm well aware that I had already ripped up the rules Nic and I had agreed. The tiny fragments are now scattered, like discarded confetti, to which no one lays claim. I'd tried so hard not to fall in love with Nic, because he was clear about not wanting a permanent relationship. Too clear, and now I can see that wasn't true, it was only ever about protecting himself. And I had been doing exactly the same thing.

But this? I pick up the piece of paper he threw on the table and glance over the proforma invoice letter above the cheque. It's standard stuff but he's right, her name is at the bottom beneath the printed signature.

Clarissa is his mother and Max's wife? I've been manipulated and used in a way that's not only calculated, but under the circumstances, is cold-hearted. Why would she inflict this on either of us?

Eventually I sit back down, eyes puffy but more in control and begin searching online for a few answers. It seems Clarissa has always used her maiden name in a professional capacity and there's no way I could have made the link. Heck, I didn't even know Nic's surname until Max told me he was his father. What breaks my heart is that Nic really believes I was party to this deception. Obviously, Hayley had no idea, or she would have warned me about it.

Olwen walks into the kitchen and takes one look at my face, before coming to an abrupt halt. She can see something really bad has happened.

'My poor dear, what's wrong?'

She walks around the table and I stand, while she gives me a gentle hug. The tears keep on coming and it takes a few minutes to compose myself.

'I feared this would happen. When love seeks you out you aren't always ready for it and Nic finds it hard to trust anyone, still. He isn't ready, Tia, but that doesn't mean—'

'I don't think that's the problem at all, Olwen. He believes he's been set up. My boss is Clarissa Cooper.'

Olwen frowns and looks at me intently as I wipe my eyes.

'Clarissa Cooper? Is that a name I should recognise?'

'Max's ex-wife. Nic's mother.'

Her hand flies to her mouth and she looks like she's in shock.

'His mother rented out his cottage? Oh, Tia. Nic will think that—'

I finish her sentence.

'That Clarissa sent me here to talk him into going back to London. He thinks I've been spying on him and passing information back to her. That isn't true, Olwen. I had no idea there was a link – why would I? What a horrible, horrible mess. I've hurt him when I all I wanted to do was love him.'

Olwen's eyes fill with tears as we both know this is one hurt too far.

'He wants me out by the end of the day.'

'Oh, my poor, dear, girl. You don't deserve to have been used in this way. Is there anything I can do?'

'I have no option other than to leave. I need to talk to Max before I go and tell him what has happened. He'll be as horrified as I am and I need to explain that I had no part in this deception. Can you drag out my suitcases and start packing my things? The sooner I get out of here, the better. I've unwittingly hurt Nic more than enough, already. It breaks my heart to know that.'

Olwen steps forward to wrap her arms around me and she understands that it's at times like this I'm going to miss my mother the most.

<u>29</u>

Going in Search of the Truth

I shower and dress; making myself look as presentable as possible before I head out to talk to Max. Olwen makes a phone call to arrange for a friend to cover her playground duty. She says she'll have everything packed and ready when I return. We look at each other, hardly able to take in what is happening.

'Thank you, Olwen, and I'm sorry about the mess I'm going to leave behind me. I will get to the bottom of this, though, even if Nic won't listen to my explanation once I know the whole story.'

'You're doing the right thing. Max needs to know what's happened as it affects him, too.'

'Could you call me a taxi? I won't be long.'

As I make my way across the sand, shuffling my feet as I try to hold it all together, I feel hurt that Nic wouldn't even let me talk before he walked out in disgust. I know how it looks but if, as he seemed to indicate, he feels anything at all for me, then wouldn't he have given me a chance, or at least wanted to hear my side of things?

As I approach Max, he's leaning up against the steps to the second cabin and is sanding a piece of wood.

'You're deep in thought.'

When our eyes meet he immediately stops what he's doing.

'You look like the sky has just fallen down.' He continues to study my face and I can see his intuition is telling him this isn't going to be good news.

'I'm going back to London, today.'

He straightens, his shoulders going back and his pose rigid. His eyes flick over my face before he turns, lowering himself onto one of the wooden steps.

'You tried to fix him and you couldn't. You did your best, Tia.'

'No, you don't understand, Max. I've hurt Nic without even knowing it. My boss is Clarissa Cooper.'

Max looks stunned. Anger flashes over his face and even when he composes himself, his eyes are steely. Gone is the characteristic gentleness of those pale blue eyes that I usually see reflected back at me.

'You were a pawn in her little game and I'm gutted for you, Tia, because I know you wouldn't have been a party to this. You've fallen in love with my son and I'll admit, I'm not a man who prays that much these days, but I've said a few since you arrived. She wants to meddle in his life again and she'll use any ploy to make that happen.'

Knowing Max, at least, believes without a shadow of a doubt that I would never have hurt Nic in this way, means so much to me at this moment.

'So it seems, Max. So it seems.'

He stands and we hug, sharing a goodbye that's full of sadness and a sense of loss. Both rendered speechless, I reluctantly turn. Head down, I walk away. As I approach the cottage my taxi is waiting and the driver has already loaded my luggage.

I can't even bring myself to go inside for one last look around.

'Keep in touch, Tia,' Olwen says through her tears. 'I'll look after Nic, don't you worry. I hope you have someone who can be there for you, my dear. But I'm only a phone call away and I'm a good listener.'

Words fail me and I give Olwen one final hug, as we stand just inside the little gate. Shutting it for the last time I turn to gaze out over the water. This view will be imprinted on my mind forever. Today my wonderment is accompanied by a feeling of abject misery. My heart feels leaden inside my chest, as if it no longer belongs within my body.

*

> Hayley, I'm on my way back to London. Is Clarissa in the office?

She texts back almost immediately.

> Problems? She's here all day but only free from two o'clock onwards.

I think the train journey back is going to be plenty long enough for me to prepare what I want to say to her.

> I'll be there at 3. Block out an hour on her calendar and tell her I'm coming. She'll know what it's about.

> Oh, OK. Consider it done.

*

I've never been one for melodramatics, it's not my style. However, Hayley is thrown into confusion when she sees the look on my face. I throw my luggage on the floor in the corner of her office and her jaw drops. I'm not sure if she is about to say something, but I'm already back out the door and walking down the corridor. I'm vaguely aware of her jumping up out of her seat and she's now standing in the doorway, watching me. As I walk into Clarissa's office she looks up and what I see on her face isn't quite what I was expecting, either. She indicates for me to take a seat and eases the glasses away from her eyes.

'I know you are angry. The fact that you're standing here in front of me means that I made a big mistake. Please, don't say a word; just listen to what I have to say. And then you can tell me exactly what you think of me. I doubt there is anything you can say, that I don't deserve.'

I force myself back in the chair, my body language reflecting the animosity I feel for her, as I stare through squinted eyes. My lips are so tightly pressed together I doubt I could utter even one word, because my jaw feels rigid and my teeth are clamped together. Rage isn't something I'm used to handling and I'm struggling to hold it in. Clarissa knows that and there's a hint of fear in her eyes, as she stands and begins to pace back and forth.

'You probably won't believe this, but I love my son. I simply want him to be happy. I thought that maybe... two people re-building their lives, thrown together... stupid, I was stupid and I see that now.'

She stops pacing for a moment. Her back is to me and she's deep in thought. This isn't easy to hear but my body is still shaking a little from the anger and I'm a captive audience.

'My children meant everything to me, but as a wife whose husband was in the services, once they were at school it was a rather lonely existence. Work was my salvation and I did well for myself. Each promotion spurred me on. But when Max was home on leave it became increasingly obvious that we had nothing in common; nothing at all – except Nic, and our daughter, Georgina. Oh, it's a long story. So much hurt and pain… she died. Cancer. Our holiday cottage on the beach became her home during the last months of her life. Max couldn't cope with it and besides, he was away still, at sea, for long periods of time. Nic was struggling to come to terms with it but they both refused to let me bring her here, to a hospice in London. I thought if my daughter was close by that maybe I could be there for her but it was already too late. The only person George wanted around her was Nic. Max and I were with her at the very end, but Nic was angry for the way our lives had turned out. We were all high achievers, but at what cost?'

She's still pacing and I've never seen her lose her composure like this, ever before.

'When I saw how deeply the death of your mother had affected you, I was reminded of George and how hard it had been to let her go. Nic has never fully recovered from that loss and what followed afterwards made things even worse. You remind me of her, you know. George had a big heart and people always came first. I envy that quality because I have a practical head and I'm simply not wired that way. Emotion has never ruled me, well, except in regard to my children, but I wasn't good at expressing what I felt.'

She stops suddenly and spins around to face me.

'If anyone could understand what Nic was still going through, I knew it would be you. Somehow the mistakes Max and I had made hadn't tarnished Nic, but he'd stopped believing in himself and he wouldn't allow anyone to draw close to him.'

I take a huge breath and expel it slowly.

'You thought six weeks was enough to heal the wounds; two broken people with seemingly no connection and therefore no reason not to trust each other? No hidden agenda?' I laugh and the undertone is one of total amazement. How could such an intelligent woman be so naïve, for one thing. Or manipulative.

'Well, your master plan worked a little too well. I fell in love with Nic and I think if I'd stayed a little longer he would have been brave enough to face up to his feelings for me, too. But now I'm the last person on earth he'd ever talk to. He believes I was a part of your plan to drag him back to London, in return for a promotion. He assumed I was spying on him and passing you information. The fact that I'd interviewed him to replace the couple who pulled out, convinced him of that. I know that was unfortunate, but understandable under the circumstances. I hate that I've had a role in destroying his ability to trust someone, all over again. Can you even begin to imagine how I feel about that?'

Clarissa sinks down into her chair, totally drained and it's shocking to see how devastated she truly is about what's happened. I believe every single word of what she has told me, I just think that it's unfortunate she can only ever see things from her, rather emotionless, point of view. The fact that she gave this so much thought astounds me, but when people's hearts and minds are involved there is no winning formula. And that's what Clarissa can't understand, or the fact that relationships will flounder if people aren't honest with each other.

'Is he safe? I mean... he's alone. If what you say is true —'

'Max is there, not that the two of them speak at all, but he keeps an eye without interfering. Olwen, well she'd taken him under her wing long before I arrived. He's a part of the community and Olwen knows his boss on the local paper, as well as everyone he sees on a daily basis. If his normal routine changes in any way at all she'll be there, checking on him and you can count on that. It doesn't mean it's going to be an easy time, but I saw such a remarkable change in him over the few weeks I was there. What I think he needs now is to be left alone to prove to himself that he doesn't need anyone's help to become the man he wants to be.'

'I trust your judgement, Tia. I know sorry doesn't cut it. Are you staying?'

That's the full extent of Clarissa's apology and yet it is an acknowledgement of the way she misjudged the situation.

'There's one condition. You let me run things without interference. I'll report to you – daily if you want. But our management styles are very different. Besides, I have ideas of my own that I will run past you first, but I'm not interested in simply carrying out your orders.'

She pauses; even after the way she's used me, her work head kicks in to evaluate the pros and cons.

'Agreed. But anything that is a departure from the norm has to receive my stamp of approval.'

I nod. The only way I'm going to get Nic out of my head is to bury myself in my work. Losing Mum broke my heart and now losing Nic feels as if I have nothing left inside of me. Being productive is the only way I have a chance of keeping myself sane.

'I'll be back at my desk first thing tomorrow.'

30

Success is All About Perception

'Hayley, can you see if we can push the meeting with Oliver and Clarissa back an hour, please? Tell them I'm about to take a call from the manager of Mean Machine; that exclusive back-stage coverage on the London leg of their tour. Can you also ask Finlay if he's finished that report I asked for? We'll need three copies ASAP as the sales analysis is the first item on the agenda.'

'Yes, boss. No problem.' Hayley winks at me and I raise a disapproving eyebrow.

She knows I hate to be called *boss* and that I took the call over an hour ago. If she wasn't my confidante, I'd sack her. Who am I kidding? Turns out I'm no little clone of Clarissa but I can still do the business. My time sitting in this chair has flown by and I can hardly believe November is almost upon us.

Now it's time for my weekly chat with Olwen. She parks up in her car between jobs and gives me a little update on Nic. Even hearing her mention his name, sends a flutter through me every single time. But it's always accompanied by a dull little ache inside my chest and it takes a long time to subside, afterwards.

I sit down and spin my chair around to face the window. It's a beautiful day in mid-August and with the air conditioning pumping out it is slightly chilly inside, while the other side of the glass it's meltingly-hot. The hands on the clock move around until the big hand is on the twelve and my phone springs into life.

'It's only me. It's not a bad time, is it?' We take it in turns to ring each other every Friday morning at ten.

'Hi, Olwen. No, of course not. I miss everyone and I'm envious just thinking about how beautiful the beach will be with all of this glorious sunshine. And I bet Max is out fishing every single day. Anyway, how are you? Rhys and the kids doing OK?'

'They're fine. Rhona has turned out to be a great little helper this holiday. She's a hard worker and I think I would be struggling if she hadn't wanted to earn herself a little extra pocket money. In fact, she's going to have quite a sum to put in the bank by the time she's back at school. Rhys is pulling his hair out wishing he had more properties on his books. Anyway, this week I have some *real* news and you are the first to know. Well, aside from Nic, myself and Rhys.'

I find myself holding my breath. I'm sure if it was bad news in regard to Nic, she would have mentioned it first.

'Nic has asked Rhys to rent out the cottage for him over the lucrative Christmas/New Year period. Two weeks, from the twenty-first of December through to the third of January.'

She sounds excited.

'That's a good decision. It will be a nice little boost to his income. Is he going away?'

Olwen tuts.

'Silly! You're missing the point, here. What are *you* doing this Christmas?'

Oh, right. Really?

'Coming back to Caswell Bay wasn't something I'd thought about doing. Besides, he's hardly likely to let Rhys rent it out to me.'

'Nic isn't going anywhere. In fact, he's going to be designing a website, he tells me; for his new photographic business. He'll be staying up at the farm. He's going to be helping out at some of the functions they're running and, in between, working on the computer getting it all sorted. It's so exciting.'

I enjoy Olwen's updates, but as time goes on it's getting harder and harder to hear about what Nic is doing. There will be a point at which his name has to drop out of the conversation. We've had no contact at all and it sounds like he's doing well. He never did cash that cheque, but Olwen said he did double shifts in the taxi for a while in order to buy his new lens.

'So shall I tell Rhys it's taken?'

The sigh that escapes my lips is tinged with longing.

'If only it were that simple. He won't agree to it.'

Olwen groans, so loudly my hand instinctively jerks the phone away from my ear.

'If you want a man you have to fight for him. I don't mean fending off other women, but fight for the right to convince him he's a fool for not letting you explain. When love comes knocking you have to open the door, or you'll never know if it was *the* chance to grab that happy ending.'

I start laughing and my spirits lift a little.

'What's your secretary's name?'

'For goodness' sake never call her that, she's my PA. It's Hayley O'Connor, why?'

'What a coincidence. That's the lady who has reserved Beach View Cottage.'

I sigh once again, but this time it's one of acceptance.

'OK, you win. Tell Rhys to set it up. I can only hope that your intuition is correct and this is the right thing to do. It feels manipulative and you know that's a red flag for Nic.'

'I know. But there's a big difference between forcing your ideas onto someone and grabbing an opportunity to ask for a second chance.'

Olwen says a hurried, 'Must go, running late.' The line disconnects and the deed is done. She did that on purpose, of course.

I can't dwell on this now as it's time to prepare for this important update meeting, but I buzz through to Hayley on the intercom.

'Hayley, can you tell HR I'll be away on holiday from the twenty-first of December through to the third of January, please? I'll be back at my desk on the Wednesday. And can you let me know when Clarissa and Oliver arrive and escort them straight to the meeting room, please? I'll be along shortly.'

'Will do.'

I know she'll quiz me later when we go for a drink tonight, but this is one little secret I'm not about to share with anyone. Well, scrap that – maybe just three people to begin with, as Christmas is all about family, isn't it? And that means Will, Sally and Bella.

31

Confession Time

'It seems to have been a remarkably seamless transition.' Oliver shifts his gaze from last quarter's sales report, to bring them to rest upon Clarissa. They exchange a brief glance, then both sets of eyes turn in my direction.

'Very well done, indeed.' His voice is congratulatory.

Clarissa's facial expression hardly changes at the best of times, so I have no clue as to whether that was the reaction she was hoping to achieve. Or, will it grate on her just that teensiest bit, knowing how little involvement she's had since I returned? But I am her protégé, so she no doubt regards it as a win-win situation, anyway.

My deeply ingrained sense of loyalty doesn't allow me to take full credit.

'Thank you, Oliver. Of course, the real test will be the year-on-year comparison for the last quarter of this year, as it will very much reflect the period during which I will have been flying solo. I've had the best mentor possible, of course, and I like to think that I won't let Clarissa down.'

Oliver's gaze travels around the table once more, to alight upon the woman herself. There is some disconcerting eye contact going on here between the two of them. I notice that Clarissa is tapping her pen, rather absentmindedly, on the notepad in front of her.

'I'm expecting to see an overall increase, Oliver, so you have no concerns there. Tia's project, which we've entitled *Love is, Actually, All Around*, will headline the next three issues. In fact, article one is featured in the edition which is currently out on the newsstands. Sales are brisk.'

Oliver nods his head, returning his gaze to me. It's like this is all happening in slow motion. I feel that there's something more going on here, other than a review meeting that was scheduled several weeks' ago.

'We've rather thrown you in at the deep end, haven't we, Tia?'

I swallow hard, determined to remain cool and composed. This is not the time to show any sign of nerves whatsoever. It isn't only my reputation at stake here, but my pride.

'I believe this particular feature has gone way beyond the original remit. Aside from reaching out to the widest audience ever, in terms of age-range, social and marital status, it's more akin to the magazine equivalent of reality TV. Not the trashy, ill–conceived version that people either love, or love to hate, but real people leading normal lives.

'It's not an exposé, it's a sharing of love and lifestyle stories; our audience will read about problems they can connect with and how those were overcome. It also capitalises on the Christmas feelgood factor and the hope that the dawning of a New Year can inspire. We've taken it to the next level by analysing and extracting positive aspects across the full spectrum. In the past, the traditional way of handing out advice was either in the form of an advice column, or a love quiz. The latter has always been gimmicky and is now, I think, outdated.

'Clarissa has allowed me to take this project and really push the boundaries. Whether married, cohabiting, or single – there really is something to engage everyone. And giving them practical tips, based upon what has worked for our interviewees, doesn't come across in any way at all as condescending. We aren't talking *at* people, simply sharing best practice, if you like.'

Oliver's gaze shifts once more.

'I've read all three articles, Oliver, and they come across as investigative journalism with heart. It's going to be our biggest ever Christmas and New Year draw; of that I'm very sure.'

Clarissa's endorsement almost has me doing a double-take.

'My fear,' she continues, 'was that it would lack impact, or real depth. I'm sure there are feature writers

349

who wouldn't have delved as deeply as Tia has done. She has connected on an emotional level and that is what will bring it alive for our readers.'

'Sterling work, Tia. I'm very impressed. I think this is an appropriate moment to mention that there will be several opportunities coming up in the first half of next year, that I'm hoping will be of interest to you. Whilst this must not go beyond these four walls, I can confirm that Clarissa is currently considering a permanent position elsewhere in the organisation. But that's something to discuss at another time. Right, if we are done, then I'd like to do a quick walk around to thank the staff.'

Oliver and I rise from the table, but Clarissa remains seated.

'Hayley is waiting outside to conduct the tour, Oliver. I need to touch base with Tia about a few things, but I'll join you shortly.'

'Of course. Thank you, Tia, excellent meeting.'

I was hovering, but now I sink back down into my seat. Clarissa doesn't begin speaking until Oliver is outside in the corridor and the door is firmly closed.

We sit, looking at each other and I'd forgotten how piercing those steely-grey eyes, can be. Am I in trouble?

'There aren't any problems, Tia, so you can relax. I meant every word I said. Thank you for your, typically thoughtful, support but from here on in you really do have to be shouting your own praises. I represent your past now, not your future.'

So she isn't coming back.

'It really is the point of no return, for you? This magazine is your baby, Clarissa, and you've grown it exponentially in the two years you've been at the helm.'

The look in her eyes is indeterminable. Has she ever felt a real and honest connection to anything in her life?

'I've been offered a place on the board of directors and I'm going to take it. Oliver and I will be announcing our engagement at Christmas and as soon as the new initiative has been launched in the spring, we will both be taking a little time off to formalise our arrangement.'

Formalise their arrangement? Does she mean *get married*?

'Oh, then congratulations are in order, Clarissa. I'm very happy for you.'

She looks at me with a blank expression, as if my words are slightly inappropriate, but makes no comment.

'Oliver has several different options he feels might be appropriate for you to consider, once things have settled down. Of course, you may feel that you would prefer to stick with what you know. But I, too, think you have much more to offer. Still, all will be made clear to you once we have evaluated the results of the launch of our newest project. If it continues to be as successful in the coming weeks, then Oliver will be keen to divert our very best resources into that endeavour. This could be an amazing opportunity, Tia – either way you decide to jump.'

My hands grab onto the arms of the chair as if I'm about to fall off.

'There is one other thing I would like to discuss.' She looks hesitant, a trait Clarissa seldom displays as it's akin to weakness in her rule book. 'When I read the final article, which included the interview with an unnamed, single woman, I wondered who exactly she was?'

She's sharp, that's for sure. I've done nothing dishonest and I certainly didn't take any money, but I also didn't come clean about it.

'Look, Clarissa, this isn't easy to say. When I talked Nic into being interviewed I had no idea who he was and no reason to believe he wouldn't be the perfect candidate.'

The muscles around her mouth tense slightly. I wonder if she's offended that I've raised the rather unfortunate issue for the first time since that day in her office.

'I conducted the interview, two in fact, and it would have been an honest story that many could attest to from their own experiences. It was appropriate to the aims of the feature. I had every intention of using the content in good faith, because it was extremely relevant. Suddenly, that was no longer an option and time was running out.'

She pulls a copy of my draft January article from the file in front of her and slides it across to me.

I glance down at it, probably able to recite it almost word for word, so I push it back towards the centre of the table.

'From a purely professional point of view the essence of what I had gleaned from the time I spent talking to him, wasn't so very far removed from my own story. After all, the focus was on why relationships hadn't worked out and how to move forward. I was the perfect candidate to slot into his place.'

That's the honest truth and I thought long and hard about it before I made the final decision to go ahead using my own story.

She extends her fingertips and withdraws the paper, tilting her glasses to read aloud a portion of the copy.

'Some of the baggage we carry around can shape us in a very positive way, if we choose to use it as a reminder of how badly things can go wrong. Often, it's through no apparent fault of our own, but through circumstances outside of our control. How can we change that? The truth is that we can't, we can only deal with the consequences.'

She lowers her head, staring across at me from over the top of her reading glasses.

'Are you dealing with the consequences?'

'Running the magazine is a very demanding role, as you well know, Clarissa. I think I've more than proved that any baggage I carried is no longer a burden and certainly will not affect my performance.'

The gaze doesn't falter.

'That day we talked you said you were in love with my son; and yet the article talks about moving on as if the failed relationship you left behind was simply another of life's lessons.'

Why is she grilling me? Well, I'm not playing this game. If she has her doubts then she has Oliver's ear and there's nothing I can do about that. I sit in silence.

'Tia, are you telling me you didn't love Nic, after all?'

She drops the paper down onto the desk with disdain, then places both hands palm down on the table, leaning forward.

'That, Clarissa, is none of your business. If you want to know the answer to that then you need to speak directly to your son. I gather it's been several years since you last had contact. At the very least he deserves to hear your latest news first-hand and if you really do care about him at all, then maybe it's time to let him know that. Now if we're done here, I need to get back to work.'

I gather my papers, turning my back on her as I make my way to the door.

'If there's any hope at all that it could work out between you, please consider any offer Oliver makes you very carefully indeed. Once you cross that line there is no turning back. I thought you and I were from different moulds, Tia, but I guess I was wrong and that's rather disappointing.'

*

'Will, it's Tia. I'm sorry it's rather late. You weren't in bed, I hope?'

'No. Is anything wrong?'

There's a hint of anxiety in his voice and I realise that maybe I'm not the only one who misses the closeness we used to have. We've been almost like strangers now for too long.

'I'm fine and sorry, I should have waited until tomorrow but my mind is churning and I wanted to hear your voice.'

There's a pause at both ends and in that momentary silence I know we've both thinking about Mum.

'This is what happens to other families, isn't it? But I never thought for one moment it would ever happen to us.' He sounds sad, not angry and his tone isn't accusatory so it isn't levelled at me personally.

'I have so many regrets—'

'And I have a lot to thank you for, Tia. I let my stubbornness take over because I couldn't deal with my emotions. It was easier for me to shut things out than face them and Sally kept saying that to me, hoping I'd come round. So if anyone has regrets, it's me.'

In the gloomy darkness as I stare out of the window, I shake my head sadly.

'I know you were adamant she shouldn't stay in the house alone, because you were worried she wasn't well. But she wasn't rejecting you, just the offer to move in with you all. I know you thought that Bella would help raise her spirits after Ed died. She didn't want any of us with her through the anger and tears as she picked up the threads of her life for a second time.'

He sighs.

'I was little more than a bully but I feared she'd go downhill. I was angry when you sided against me because I felt pushed out. You were the one she turned to when Dad died, but we were only kids then. I never accepted Ed and I felt guilty about that; I needed her to lean on me and, in the process, possibly forgive me for that. I wanted to be her rock, Tia, that's all.'

I brush away a tear forming in the corner of my left eye and take a deep breath. I never thought we'd ever talk like this – openly and honestly about what happened.

'I simply gave her the space she needed and when she wanted company she lifted the phone. I know you think we spent a lot of time together but we didn't really. Mum had no intention of commanding all of my spare time, as she put it. Even though it wouldn't have mattered to me if she had. When she grew close to Ed they were simply supporting each other as the years advanced. When she found herself alone once more, I know you wanted to take care of her but Mum wanted to retain her independence because she wasn't ready to sit back and have things done for her.'

He sniffs and I wonder if he, too, is shedding a tear. After a second or two his softly spoken words echo down the line like a hug.

'I was wrong to jump to conclusions about her friendship with Ed, I see that now. It felt like the final straw at the time, as if she was willing to turn to anyone for comfort, except her own son. I thought as the years advanced she'd eventually turn to me. I didn't stop to see it from her viewpoint and that was a big mistake. I've missed you, Sis. In more ways than you can know. Thank you for giving me a second chance because I'm not even sure I deserve it.'

Now my tears are falling haplessly down over my cheeks, plopping onto my fleece as if it's raining indoors. I suck in a deep breath so I can force the words I want to say past the huge knot of emotion which seems to be stuck in my throat.

'I need you in my life, Will, and I miss Sally and Bella so much it hurts like a physical pain. I might not be here talking to you now if it wasn't for your actions that day. It means so much to me that it was you who found me and Mum will rest in peace knowing that. If she taught us one thing, it's that family is everything. Let's make this Christmas a family one.'

He tries to laugh through his tears but his voice breaks up a little. 'You bet.'

As we bid each other goodnight a sense of well-being begins to wash over me. The dread I was feeling about the forthcoming festivities has been replaced with a sense of optimism and excitement. The healing has begun.

Wednesday, 21st of December...

32

The Breeze Through My Hair

The taxi driver is not only very polite, but also extremely helpful. His smile doesn't waver for one second, despite the amount of luggage I have brought with me. When I give him a ten-pound note as a tip he seems a little embarrassed.

'Are you sure, Miss? That's very generous, indeed, thank you.'

'No, thank *you* and Merry Christmas.'

I make my way up the path towards Beach View Cottage and it feels like coming home: familiar, comforting. Even before I have time to raise my hand to the bell, Olwen swings the door open and I almost fall inside.

'Let's get you and that pile of luggage into the warm, quickly. That's a bitterly cold wind today.'

As soon as the door shuts she spins around to gaze at me.

'You look good, Tia. I thought you might arrive in need of a rest, but you are glowing.'

I glance back at her, rather sheepishly. We both know there's only one reason for that glow and it might all be a rather pointless exercise, anyway.

'And you've lost weight. We need to Skype as I had no idea. Are you pleased?'

'Over the moon. No more biscuits or doughnuts and I have so much more energy. A part of that is down to Nic.'

My expression is one of surprise.

'Well, at first it was an excuse to pop in. He does his own cleaning and there's only so many times I can say I'm passing. It's not exactly a drive through road, is it?' She laughs and I nod. 'So, I asked him if he knew anything about healthy eating, in conversation, as you do. Bless, he knows I don't have much spare time what with two jobs and the family. And I'm not good on the computer. He admitted he, too, tended to live on ready meals. Anyway, Nic did some research and printed off a few recipes for me. He tried them out for himself and now there are five of us who share new recipes we come across. Nic has recently started up a fortnightly foodie column in the paper. Not focusing on losing weight as such, but about using some of the good quality farm produce available locally and recipes that are quick and simple to do.'

'He's happy, then?'

She shrugs.

'I think he's thrown himself into his work and that in turn has given him back a sense of purpose. Gareth has kept an eye on him, too, encouraging Nic to become involved in the Safe Communities scheme. It's a voluntary thing, but he liaises with the police and the locals to raise awareness in general. Crime rates are generally low here, but there are always a few opportunist thefts in summer and every couple of years there is a spate of winter crimes, mainly targeting second homes that are locked up for long periods of time. This year, as you know, there's been quite a bit of activity and we've all had to be extra vigilante. It means Nic's circle of contacts is widening and the boost it has given him is lovely to see. He's a valued member of the community and he's helping to make a difference.'

It's good to hear and not quite what I expected. My eyes flit around the room.

'A lot has changed since I was last here, then, in many ways.'

Olwen thinks I mean the Christmas decorations.

'Nic thought the family renting the cottage would expect there to be Christmas trimmings; well, that's the excuse he gave but he enjoyed doing it. He has great taste, doesn't he?'

He certainly does. There's no Christmas tree, but instead he's recycled one of the fallen trees from the woods. It reaches almost to the ceiling and Nic has stripped most of the smaller branches away, leaving five main branches that angle upwards like a tulip. He's sprayed it white and attached some very pretty metal reindeer heads. A garland hangs on the long wall behind the sofa, made up of small pieces of driftwood, interspersed with stars made out of twigs.

'It's beautiful.'

Olwen can see I'm a little overcome to be here again and she gives me a gentle hug.

In my head I'm transported back to the last Christmas that Mum, Dad, Will and I were together. As dutiful offspring we were making the pilgrimage home without realising it would prove to be a landmark occasion. Nothing would ever be the same again and yet it seemed normal at the time, as in the *new* normal given that we no longer lived at home.

Traditionally, every year Mum used a different theme when decorating the tree and that particular year was her nod to the Victorians. Strewn with handmade popcorn garlands, small bags of homemade fudge and sparkling chains of silver beads, she'd even managed to find small white candles in tiny silver holders. They graced the ends of each branch, although they remained unlit.

It had served to remind both Will and myself of the years gone by and the fun it had been getting hands on with making decorations for the tree. Making biscuits to decorate and hang from ribbons and the year of the white paper lanterns; Mum had shown us how to fold the paper and with a few deft cuts create latticework. And the year of the handmade crackers that drove us all crazy as it's a lot harder than you might imagine. But it was all a big part of our family Christmas preparations as children and suddenly we realised how lucky we'd been. It was a Christmas for being grateful for the time and effort Mum and Dad had always put into making it more than simply about the presents waiting to be unwrapped. I realise that it was being surrounded by the people I loved the most that made it special and this Christmas I intend to make sure that my loved ones know how special they are to me.

'When do your brother and his family arrive?'

I shake off the wave of sadness that clutches at my heart for the briefest of moments as the loss of Mum and Dad weighs heavily upon me. Gone but never forgotten. This year, Mum, it's going to be different – I promise.

'Tomorrow, late afternoon. We'll have a leisurely meal and they can settle in. I thought I would take them into Mumbles on Friday for some shopping and general sightseeing. Then, Christmas Eve morning it will be all go preparing for the party.'

'Ah, before I forget. Someone from the farm,' she stops to raise her eyebrows and give me a knowing look, 'will drop the turkey down later today. I said after four. I've loaded up the fridge and freezer as instructed. The last-minute stuff you ordered will also arrive sometime today. When you pop out to see Max just leave a note on the door and they'll either come back, or leave it on the doorstep. I wish I could stay and help you unpack but I have non-stop bookings right through until six tonight. Good luck, you know, for later.'

'You are a star, Olwen and I can't thank you enough. And no one knows it's me, right, except for those you've given party invites to – Rhys, Gareth and his wife, and Tom? And they will keep it quiet?'

She swipes her hand across her mouth as if zipping it up.

'It's our little secret. You do need to tell Max you're here, before anyone else breaks the news.'

After she's gone the cottage feels empty. I begin ferrying my things upstairs and end up having to gulp back down the lump that rises in my throat. I didn't think the memories would be so vivid.

'Pull yourself together, Tia.' My voice echoes back at me as I climb the stairs.

Tomorrow Will, Sally and little Bella arrive. A day and a half is plenty of time to relax, in between introducing them to the area. Then on Saturday, it will be fun preparing for the Christmas Eve party. Hopefully, it will pull us all much closer together and we'll forget this is a first, because there will be so much going on around us. The cottage isn't huge, so although I've only invited a handful of guests, it should be enough to make it a lively gathering. I'm hoping that Max and Nic will accept the invite I'll be extending to them both, too. Whether they will turn up, well, that's entirely up to them, but this Christmas if I can't be with Mum, then at least I'm not going to be maudlin. Life is what you make it and if you choose to wallow instead of grabbing as much happiness as you can, then that's a personal choice. I choose happiness and even if Nic snubs me, I'll have to accept there's nothing I can do about that. What's important is that I will, at least, have tried.

*

Max opens the door and a waft of heat blasts out at me, rather like a furnace.

'Well, this is an unexpected, but very welcome, surprise.' He looks really pleased to see me.

'Come in, Tia, don't stand out there in the cold. It's so good to see you.'

As I step over the threshold Max scoops me up in a hug that lifts me off the floor a good inch.

'I can't stay. I only wanted to let you know I'm here for the holidays.'

He looks rather disappointed, as clearly he'd like me to sit for a while, but then his face breaks into a smile.

'You need to settle in. I did wonder who had rented the cottage. Guess there's going to be a little Christmas cheer in Holly Cove this year, after all.'

'I need you to do something for me. I know you are a very private man and I understand that, but I'm going to ask you to step outside your comfort zone to help me out. I'll explain later. Can you come up to the cottage around three-thirty this afternoon? We can chat while I do some food prep as I have guests arriving tomorrow.'

His eyes narrow slightly, but the impact of my arrival is enough for him to shrug it off.

'Thank you, Max. I have missed our talks, you know, even if they were always rather short.'

'Well, people chatter on about a lot of nothing, if you ask me. But you didn't. I'll see you later, then.'

As I trudge back across the beach, I pull the collar of my coat up around my ears. It's freezing cold and the wind is literally stinging my face. The sea looks choppy and is a dirty grey, reflecting the dark clouds above. But I realise what I've missed the most is the feeling of freedom. No one can tame nature, it is what it is and what I feel is a sense of life being about more than—

The sound of a van door slamming interrupts my thoughts. I hurry along the path to unlock the front door to the cottage. The delivery of fruit and vegetables has arrived. Now I have a couple of hours to unpack and make everything ready. It's wintry outside and cosy within, but that could all change when the next van pulls up alongside the cottage. What I could be dealing with is not just a frozen turkey, but frozen looks and cold, angry words.

33

A Storm is Brewing

Max settles himself down at the kitchen table with an air of reluctance. I pour him a large mug of coffee and set it down on the table, with a smile.

'There's more than coffee brewing in this kitchen. I'm not a fool.'

I glance at the clock as I take up my position in front of the chopping board, where I was slicing cooking apples for a pie. I'm sideways on to Max and I can feel his eyes on me.

'No, you aren't, but you are stubborn. Do you trust me, Max?'

'At this moment I want to say *no*, but that isn't the truth.'

I'm not going to give him a warning about what I have planned, because I know he would get up and leave.

'Tomorrow my brother Will, his wife Sally and my little niece, Bella, are coming down here for a few days to stay with me. On Christmas Eve I'm going to be holding a small party here – now don't panic.'

He squirms in his chair.

'This is a tough Christmas for me as it's the first without Mum. It's hard, too, for Will and his family because they had lost contact with her and hadn't seen her for several years. I don't know many people here, so it will be Olwen, Rhys and Rhona, Gareth and his wife, and Tom. Now that's not such an ordeal, is it? It would mean so much to me for you to be here.'

'Why?'

Oh, I wasn't expecting that.

'Because there aren't many people whose kindness touches my heart, but you are one of them, Max.'

He looks away, then sits quietly drinking his coffee.

'Have you decided what's going to happen to the cabins when you leave?'

Changing the topic of conversation works and Max explains that he's decided not to sell up, although he's only likely to make it back here a couple of times a year.

'Have you told Nic?'

He grunts.

'No. We haven't spoken.'

There's a knock on the door and I rinse my hands, dry them quickly and walk past Max's chair.

'Now might be the appropriate time then,' I half-whisper. I know it won't soften the blow but it gives him a few seconds to compose himself.

When I open the front door Nic is standing there, carrying a very large frozen turkey in his arms.

'*Tia.*' The colour begins to drain from his face as he stares at me. He blinks and I wonder if he, too, is having a flashback to happier times.

'Hello, Nic. Merry Christmas. Can't celebrate the day without a turkey, can you? Sorry, I'm in your way. Come in, you know where the kitchen is—'

My heart is jumping around inside of my chest like it's trying to escape. As I follow Nic he suddenly stops in his tracks and I almost run into the back of him.

'Um… I've just made coffee, I'll fetch you a cup.'

Nic and Max are staring at each other and the sudden chill in the air makes me shiver. I quickly fill two mugs, one for Nic and one for myself, and carry them across to the table. Then I walk around to Nic, lift the turkey out of his arms and sit it in a large roasting tray to begin defrosting.

'Take a seat. As you're both here, there's a little matter I'd like to clear up, but first I was telling Max about a small gathering I'm having on Christmas Eve. My brother and his family are arriving tomorrow and as it's our first Christmas without Mum, I thought it would help everyone if we did something a little different. I don't know many people here, so it will only be a small gathering, but Max has already agreed to make an effort on my behalf and join us. I was rather hoping you would, too.'

370

Nic has taken the seat opposite Max, but is still in shock; Max is extremely ill-at-ease but says nothing.

'Christmas is a family time and I'm trying my hardest to make it special for the people I care about. As for the other matter, well, when I left here it was under a cloud. I know how it looked, but there was no way I could possibly have linked my boss, Clarissa Cooper, to either of you as she has never, as far as I can tell, used the surname Hartington. The day Max, out of concern for you, told me the two of you were related I was shocked. It was hard for me to take it in.'

Nic clears his throat, shifting uneasily in his seat.

'Look, Tia, there's too much you don't understand. OK, I was a little out of line as I realised afterwards you wouldn't knowingly have put yourself in that situation. You were manipulated. Good intentions don't always turn out well and getting Max and me around the same table means nothing at all.'

It's a start and at least no one is shouting – yet. Max shakes his head, then stares down into his coffee mug as if there's something of interest at the bottom of it.

'Manipulated is a strong word, Nic, with a nasty undertone. I admit, Clarissa is an expert at it and it's because she usually has her own agenda. It goes with the job and you have to be tough to survive and even tougher to rise to the top of the heap. I believe that her explanation, that she was actually worried about *you*, was the real truth. It was never about me passing information back to her, because I didn't know she knew you. Clarissa saw the two of us as damaged people, through no fault of our own, and thought we would recognise that in each other. Maybe bolster each other's confidence a little and then part the better for it.'

'But that wasn't quite what happened, was it Tia?' Max looks up at me and then turns his gaze towards Nic.

'I think you should stay out of this, Max.' Nic's tone is abrupt.

'So, what exactly are you blaming me for, Nic? Not being there because I was at sea? Divorcing your mother? I seem to have spent a lot of my adult life feeling guilty but not quite sure what I did wrong. I never meant to hurt anyone, least of all you. You were there for Georgina when I couldn't be... when she didn't want me to be.'

Max turns his head away from us both and I want to reach out to him, but I know I can't interfere.

Nic lets out a sound like a low growl.

'Where should I begin? My mother needed a man who could stand up to her, not one who turned a blind eye and pretended everything was fine. I needed you to fight for my rights. And your right to instil in me the qualities you thought were important for your son to value. You trained so many men in the Navy and yet you left me under the total control of a woman who pushed and pushed and pushed, until her values became mine. With success comes power, was her favourite saying. I never heard her mention the word happiness, ever.'

Max is now sitting with his head slumped forward, chin almost touching his chest. He rolls his shoulders back, straightening and sits upright, facing Nic square on and with his hands on the table.

'It's hard for a man to hear his son say something like that. To my mind, I was simply working to support my family. I know it's tough on the families of anyone who is in the services, but it was also hard for me every time I returned home. In the early days, Clarissa didn't have a high-flying career. She looked after both you and Georgina until you went to school and then she went back to work, part-time. She was different then, but you were probably too young to remember. As time went on it was clear that the only emotional connection between Clarissa and myself was the love we shared for our two children. She came to resent my visits home because it disrupted everyone's routine. I no longer had a functioning place in your lives.'

I swallow hard, pulling my gaze away from Max to look at Nic. He turns his head slightly and he can see the sadness on my face.

'It's a plausible excuse, but you as good as got me fired. I lost virtually everything because of that day. You see, Tia, there are two sides to every story. I'm only sorry you were pulled into this one.'

Max lets out a mumbled expletive.

'When I returned to London to confront Clarissa about why she was still refusing to think about a divorce, despite her longstanding affair, she was livid. Yes, Oliver Sinclair was a thorn in my side for a long time, but when she told me you were working for him I was horrified. It was like my worst nightmare had come true.'

'Your. Worst. Nightmare?' Nic's staccato rhythm makes each word sound like an accusation. 'So you walked into his office and when he called security and a brawl broke out you didn't think that I'd jump to your defence and end up hitting him? Everything I'd worked for was gone in one split second because of your jealous rage.'

My eyes go from one to the other, seeing their pain and feeling helpless.

'I wasn't there to reclaim my wife, or exact revenge. I'm a man who is used to living in a disciplined way; keeping oneself under control under extreme duress is a part of my training and it's now a part of me.'

Nic gasps, floundering for words.

'You meant to cause trouble and get me sacked?'

'It seemed to be the only way to rescue you. I knew the dream you were chasing wasn't yours; neither Georgina, nor you, had inherited Clarissa's obsessive need for more. More money, more power – it's a vicious circle. She'll never be satisfied with what she has and that's why Oliver is such a perfect partner for her; they understand each other. Whether there's any real love there, who knows? But if that's what she wants, then good luck to her.'

Max looks at Nic, but he doesn't answer for several minutes. He sits with a deep frown on his forehead, staring down at the table. Suddenly his head tips back and he looks at Max, but this time it isn't a stare.

'And selling me the cottage when this wasn't where I wanted to be. What was that about?'

'I didn't want anything from the divorce settlement except the cottage and Holly Cove. It was never about money. I had succeeded in getting you away from London, Clarissa and the mess you were making of your life just to please her. But you were vulnerable and without focus. I knew what this place meant to you and to us as a family. Those months you spent here with Georgina, a few years beforehand, were happy times for her despite the pain. When I told you that it was my intention to sell Beach View Cottage, I instinctively knew you couldn't let me do that. With every penny you had tied up here, it was obvious that you wouldn't be able to pay someone to do the renovation work.

'I figured that by the time it was finished you'd be fitter both mentally and physically. And in doing that your sister would be very much in your heart. Love heals, my son. It's important that you don't let the past define who you are, Nic. Follow your own destiny because going forward there's no one to blame but yourself. As harsh as that sounds, it's true.'

With that, Max pulls himself up out of the chair and heads out of the kitchen. I jump up and throw my arms around him, kissing his cheek.

'Thank you, Max,' I whisper. He steps out to brave the bracingly-cold wind, without so much as a glance my way.

When I return to Nic he's slumped forward, his head in his hands. He looks up and I don't try to hide the tears in my eyes.

'I thought he was walking away from any form of commitment with his threat to sell. That he couldn't handle the memories here, because it only served to remind him that he was never around when we needed him. I blamed him for turning me into a failure.'

'He was only trying to save you, Nic, to do what he thought was best for you. And you were right in what you said earlier on. I set this up tonight with the best of intentions because I care about you and Max. That's why I came back. But my own family is struggling, too and somehow this seemed like the right thing to do. I'm sorry if I was wrong.'

Nic stands and walks towards me. Taking a deep breath, he raises his hand to touch my cheek for the briefest of moments.

'I have to go. I'm helping Mike put the orders together for the morning's collections. The shop opens at seven and closes at noon. It won't re-open until after New Year, so it will be chaos.'

There's nothing left to say and at the door he simply smiles and gives a curt nod as he walks past me.

Closing the door my body sags back against it. My heart aches for their pain and sorrow; two different versions but one truth and now, at least, they both know what really happened. I've done what I can and I can't heal the rift for them, or make Nic love me in the way I need him to do.

It's in your hands now, Nic, because tomorrow I must focus on my own family as this is all about honouring Mum's memory.

Things I want to say to my mother start whizzing around inside my head. I can't be with you making new memories, Mum and it hurts. This Christmas Eve I'd hoped we'd be somewhere amazing, like Paris, staring up at the Eiffel Tower and waiting with bated breath for those snowflakes to fall. Maybe that was only ever destined to be the magic of New York and Paris would have been special in another way. Instead, I'm doing the next best thing and that's making memories with Will, Sally and Bella. I know you'll be smiling and that your heart will be overjoyed.

34

In the Dark of Night

Lying in bed, staring out of the window at a beautiful star-lit sky, it dawns on me that I'm not used to looking upwards. In London, everything is about people or buildings, so it's eye-level, or a little tilt of the head.

I wander across to open the window a few inches, to fill my lungs with that bracing night air. The sound of the waves pounding on the shore indicate that the tide is in although it's too dark to tell how far up the beach it has come. I think Max is safe enough and well above the high tide line. But when the sea is in a frenzy, there must be times when he looks out and the swell is violent enough to remind him of how harsh an environment it can be. I can't even begin to imagine a life spent mostly at sea. I find that thought rather frightening, as the risk of being dragged down into a seemingly bottomless pit would be one of my worst fears.

As I'm staring out into the darkness, I suddenly see what appears to be a shape moving slowly along the beach from right to left, almost indistinguishable in the pitch-black shadows. Straining my eyes, I'm not even sure it is a shape, or just the blurred vision of tired eyes. But as I adjust to the darkness, suddenly there seem to be two shapes and as I watch they merge into one. I wonder if it's the smoke from one of the cabin's flues, forced low on the beach, trapped beneath a current of air. I'm spooked enough to go downstairs and check the doors and windows.

When I return to bed, Max is on my mind. What if it was someone up to no good? I leap out of bed, feeling around in the darkness for my jeans and sweatshirt. Within minutes I'm letting myself out of the house, locking the door behind me as quietly as I can. The torch in my hand is as much for protection, as it's quite a hefty one, as it is for light. I stop to pull the drawstring around the hood of my padded jacket as tightly as I can, in order to keep out the icy chill. I manage to stagger down to the beach as the strong winds try to push me back, then decide that it's probably better to turn the torch off before I'm out in the open.

The crashing of the waves is enough to mask any noise, but stumbling along in the deep, soft sand is difficult. There's no warning of large stones, or rocks that have fallen from the cliff. Once or twice my feet almost give out beneath me, when I encounter a sharp object in my path.

Keeping as close to the cliff wall as I can, using it as a source of support, enables me to move a little faster. I'm probably half-way to the cabins now; it's obvious I wasn't imagining it and the two shapes I saw are very real. I stop in my tracks, trying to control my breathing as I seem to be gulping in way too much air. Slow it down, Tia, slow it down; if you panic now you are in big trouble and so is Max. Think about what you are doing.

There's little point in going any closer. One aluminium torch isn't a weapon that will fend off two people.

I sink down low on the ground, making myself as small as possible. Pulling my mobile out of my pocket I turn around, slipping down the zip on my jacket a little and cradling it inside to hide the light, as I dial Nic's number. He takes forever to answer, or so it seems, but it's probably mere seconds. His voice is sleepy and he sounds a little disorientated, no doubt woken abruptly from a very deep sleep.

'Who is it?'

'Nic, it's Tia. I'm on the beach. I think two men are trying to steal Max's boat and I don't know what to do.'

'Get off the phone, I'm on my way. Don't do anything.'

My fingers are so cold I have trouble slipping it back into my pocket. I struggle to pull the zipper back up, as my hands are now trembling. Fear is adding to the effects of my falling body temperature and beginning to restrict my actions. I ease myself back around and even above the sound of the surf I can hear a noise. The intermittent dull thud of metal on metal carries on the wind in little bursts like a musical accompaniment. I'm downwind though and the sound is travelling away from the far cabin where Max sleeps. I can't see any light at all coming from either cabin. It would have to be very loud indeed to be easily heard above the constant pounding of the waves and stir him from a deep sleep.

I stay curled up, straining my eyes to monitor the movement. They seem to be struggling with the padlocked steel gate across the front of the workshop. Then one of them turns and starts trudging towards me. My heart nearly stops. I lie prostrate on the sand, as close to the base of the cliff as I can get. Everything I'm wearing is dark, so if I hide my face and hands I might fade into the night.

I know I can't make any movement at all and as I can't risk looking up, I start counting. Fear takes my slight tremble to another level again and my teeth begin to chatter. I wonder how long it will take Nic to find me. Ten minutes by the time he dresses and parks the car, before he's on the beach? How long has passed since I spoke to him? Two minutes perhaps, or is it longer? A horrible chill settles in the pit of my stomach which has nothing to do with the biting cold of the winter night. Nic has no idea someone will be walking towards him and there's no way I can warn him without alerting the thieves. If Max awakens now, there's someone standing only feet away from him with a heavy metal object in his hands.

My heartbeat is now almost as loud as the waves and I start counting the seconds, my ears straining for any sounds that might warn me someone is approaching. One hundred and twenty-three, one hundred and twenty-four.

How long does it take to cross the cove? It's slow going in the dry sand, but the person who passed me walked down the beach a little, probably to where the sand is firmer and walking is quicker and easier.

When I get to three minutes, I move my head slightly. The person is still on the beach but now heading back up onto the softer sand. Think, Tia, think. It's going to take Nic probably another seven or eight minutes at least to drive down here from the farm on the top road, so I doubt he's here yet. He might even have woken Mike to accompany him. There's nothing unusual I can hear above the roar of the incoming water and the *swoosh* as it's sucked away. Max is safe as long as he stays sleeping, so my focus has to be on warning Nic. I turn around and begin to crawl on all fours. It's actually easier than walking, as the wind keeps buffeting my body. My hands quickly identify any stony obstacles in the way, but they are sharp. Even with almost totally numb fingers I can still feel the sting from the cuts. My teeth are chattering a little, even though the effort of moving along brings a little warmth back into my limbs. I think it's more from nerves and adrenalin than the dropping temperature.

I pick up the pace a little and it probably takes no more than a couple of minutes to retrace my steps. I guesstimate it's been about six minutes by now since my call for help. As I reach the end of the sand I half-stand, crouching low as I enter the approach to the lane, alongside the cottage. I didn't leave any lights on when I left, but that wasn't a conscious decision. I'm not sure, though, if that makes it worse in a way. A glimmer of light might have been a deterrent. Anyway, there's no one to be seen. It dawns on me that Nic will probably park at the top, adding at least another five minutes to his arrival time. I assume that's where the other person has gone, back to their vehicle to find something to cut, or prise off the padlock.

I walk as fast as I can now, conscious that I have to maintain a steady pace and can't risk getting too out of breath. Any sound at all seems to echo, trapped by the tall trees on either side of the lane. I try to control my breathing so I don't let out any gasps, which is more difficult to do than it sounds. There's also a chance that at any moment I might have to start running if the guy reappears in front of me. A cold sweat begins to chill my skin as I increase the pace yet again. I'm pretty sure the top road is just around the next bend, when suddenly

I'm grabbed from behind and a cold, hard, hand presses against my mouth. I'm too shocked to struggle but the mouth next to my ear whispers 'It's Nic. The police are on their way.'

I sag against him for a few seconds, then straighten. He has some sort of stick in one hand as it touches against my leg, but he grabs my arm with his other hand. Giving a little tug, he leads me back down the hill. I have to half-run to keep up with him. I can hardly make him out in the darkness and it looks like he's wearing a ski mask, or balaclava, which obscures his face and hair. Just before we round the corner at the bottom of the lane he leans in close.

'When we reach the first cabin, I want you to make a noise and run down towards the water's edge. Hopefully that will distract this guy for the few seconds I need to step out of the shadows and get close enough to tackle him to the floor. The other guy has gone up to their van, which is in a lay-by up near the farm. The police will catch him. We need to move as quickly as we can, so I can jump this guy before Max wakes up as he'll be an easy target, unaware he's in real danger.'

I have to brush away the image of Max opening the door and being struck down before he can even assimilate what's happening. Desperate people do desperate things and I steel myself, realising that Nic will be putting himself in real danger, too. The adrenalin begins to pump around my body and I move forward with determination.

When we hit the sand, we crawl along the base of the cliff, much in the same way that I had done a few minutes ago. The person outside the workshop seems to be using a crowbar, trying to lever one of the side hinges to the gate on the right.

We are totally hidden by the first cabin and Nic places his hand firmly on my shoulder, giving me a little shake. Our eyes meet and he nods his head. I start screaming and then I run, as fast as my legs will carry me. Churning up the sand in my wake, I head towards the sound of the waves.

I have no idea what is going on behind me and with my heart pounding in my ears I can't hear a thing. When I stop and turn, I see that the door to the second cabin is open and there is a little shaft of light, but it isn't very bright.

Someone is lying on the sand and another person is leaning over them. Already I'm running back up the beach, my eyes trying to make sense of what's happening. A third shape looms up in front of me and I see a flash out of the corner of my eye as I turn to run. I hear the roar of Max's shout as he appears to leap through the air, launching himself at my attacker. But in that split second something cracks down on the side of my head. As I collapse in a heap on the sand I'm vaguely aware of the struggle going on next to me. Then there is a flicker of lights bobbing around, which seem to be edging closer and closer. The pain is overwhelming me and I can't fight anymore to keep my eyes open, so I lie here trying to make sense of what's happening. Where's Nic? Is Max OK?

The darkness isn't just around me, it's inside of me, too. The pounding in my head and chest increases and I find myself struggling to breathe. This isn't merely panic, but something else. An overwhelming sense of light-headedness takes hold and I feel myself sinking down and down, before total darkness overwhelms me.

A sudden warmth seems to envelop my body and I stir, but can't quite rouse myself. I'm in someone's arms and I can feel the weight of something being placed over me.

'Tia, stay awake my darling. Please, try to stay with me, it's important. It's Nic and you're safe; the ambulance is coming. Just stay with me, baby, I'll keep you warm and I won't leave your side, I promise.'

Mumbled voices and sounds that don't mean anything at all seem to wash over me like waves and I wonder if I'm drowning.

35

I'm Not Alone

Out of the black nothingness comes a loud buzzing sound which seems to echo around inside my head. Is it a bee? As it grows louder I start to panic, wondering whether it has crawled inside my ear and is now manically trying to escape. I want to raise my hand and see if I can reach it, but nothing happens and fear takes a hold of me. *Buzz, buzz, buzz—*

'Shh, shh. Keep still, Tia. I'm here, so you have nothing to fear. I'm holding your hand and I haven't left your side for a moment.'

Who is holding my hand? I can't feel anything and I want to let them know that I need help, but the blackness drags me back into its lair and I seem unable to fight it.

*

My eyes lids are so heavy it's a struggle to open them, even a little. A glint of brightness sears across my left eye and I wince, then give up trying. I can hear the rasp of my laboured breathing and gradually sounds from within the room begin to come at me from all angles. There's a rustling noise, the low murmur of voices and a bleeping sound. I focus on that and let it guide me back to consciousness. But as it does, stabs of pain seem to attack me from my head to my toes. I can now open both eyes a tiny fraction but the light is too strong and I focus instead on what hurts and where. My head is throbbing, a dull pain that is like a constant drumming making me feel slightly nauseous. My hands are very sore, as are my knees. My left elbow, too, feels bruised and a gnawing ache adds to my overall discomfort.

'Tia, can you hear me?' A shape looms over me, coming close and I try to concentrate, squinting to bring it into focus, while still shielding my eyes from the glare of light.

'Where am I?' My throat is so dry, it burns as I force out the words.

'You're in hospital. You arrived here late last night after an incident on the beach.'

'Beach?'

'Your boyfriend and your brother are here. I've asked them to wait outside as Dr Evans is on his way to see you. While we're waiting, I wonder if you can sip a little water for me? Here, I'll guide the straw into your mouth.'

The liquid is cool and very welcome, but after a few sips I can't seem to swallow anymore and I pull my head away.

'Thank you.' It comes out as a hoarse whisper.

'I'm going to very gently wipe some moist cotton wool across your eyes and then perhaps you can try to open them fully for me.'

I nod, the effort of speaking seems to make the pain much worse and all I want to do is rest. But as the soft wetness sweeps across my closed eyelids it feels surprisingly refreshing. It still takes a lot of effort to force them open, as a wave of tiredness seems to accompany any movement at all.

'Good evening, Tia. My name is Doctor Robert Evans. Jane, can we raise the head of the bed a little, please?'

There's a clicking sound and very slowly I'm brought up into a semi-sitting position. Both of my hands have been bandaged and there's a drip attached to a needle in the crook of my arm.

'I've spoken to your brother and your boyfriend about the results of the CT scan. What is the last thing you can remember?'

My eyes are so blurry that it's like having double vision. Any movement anywhere in the room makes me automatically turn towards it. Each time I find myself wincing with the pain radiating out from the side of my head.

'I remember lying on the beach. There was shouting. I heard a loud buzzing sound at some point, but that's all.'

'How about what happened before that?'

My brain feels foggy and it hurts to think, so it takes me a few moments to kick it into gear. The men... and Max.

'People, men I think, trying to break into Max's workshop. Nic arrived, he isn't hurt, is he? Can I see him? Is Max, here, too?' Suddenly the words gush out of me like a torrent.

'Take it easy. You lost consciousness for a significant period following a nasty blow to the head. We then had to sedate you in order to carry out a CT scan as you were disorientated and rather distressed. The good news is that your skull isn't fractured and there's no sign of swelling or internal bleeding. We've stitched up the wound but it will be quite sore for the next few days. You will feel a little drowsy still from the meds, but the effects should completely disappear over the next hour or so. Rest is very important at the moment. Try not to get agitated or expect too much progress too soon. We're keeping you under close observation at the moment, but it's all looking good.'

'What day is it? What time is it?' My mind starts to process what has happened and yet it's like clutching at fragments and trying to pull them together to form a complete picture.

'It's the twenty-second of December, just after five in the evening.'

'My brother is here?'

The nurse nods and steps forward. 'Yes, he arrived a couple of hours' ago. Your boyfriend is here, too, and he only briefly left your side when you had your scan. I sent them off to grab a cup of coffee; shall I see if they're back?'

I nod, it's too difficult to explain about Nic. Dr Evans adjusts my drip and I wince as his hand brushes against my elbow.

'The skin isn't broken but you seem to have hit your elbow on something sharp when you fell to the ground. It will be painful but it's only bruising. The bandages on your hands can come off tomorrow morning. You have a lot of cuts and a few broken nails, which should heal quite quickly. We removed a few tiny pieces of flint and then cleaned them up to avoid infection; there's nothing to worry about there.'

'But I want to go home.' I feel tearful, although my eyes remain dry.

'When someone with a head injury loses consciousness for a significant period, our protocol is to keep the patient under observation for up to forty-eight hours. That's for your own safety. We're not expecting any complications but sometimes your hearing, vision or memory can be affected and we need to monitor that. But if you continue to improve we might be able to send you home early Christmas Eve morning.'

'That would be wonderful. It's my first Christmas celebrating with my little niece and that's very special to me.'

The nurse returns and already it's easier for my eyes to focus when I move them quickly from one object to another. Everything's still slightly fuzzy and a little unreal to me; but I don't feel so disconnected to what's going on around me, now.

'I think we can take this drip down, nurse. I'll be back to see you in the morning, Tia. I've prescribed something for the pain but I don't want to give you anything to help you sleep. You shouldn't need it anyway, as you will tire easily, but if you develop any new symptoms, Jane here will be checking you throughout the night.'

'Thank you, Dr Evans.'

Even before he has had time to walk out of the door, Jane is already easing back the plaster on my arm. The door opens once more and this time I look up to see Will and Nic walking towards the bed. Will's forehead is knotted up in a frown and Nic looks as pale as a ghost.

'I won't be a moment, guys. I'll disconnect the drip and take out the needle, then I'll settle Tia into the armchair. The sooner we have her moving around, the better.'

I feel like a child with my parents anxiously fussing over me after a fall. Moving between the bed and the chair isn't easy, but it's a relief to be doing something normal. Lying in bed I felt like an invalid.

Will carries two chairs over, placing one each side of me.

'Here, Nic. Sit down before you fall down, my friend.'

My eyes follow every movement. My brain is slowly ticking over.

'What time did you arrive?' I look up at Will as he lowers himself into his seat.

'Three hours ago, and I came straight here. Olwen is back at the cottage with Sally and Bella. Don't concern yourself about anything at the moment, other than getting some rest.'

Gingerly he places his hand very gently on my forearm, giving it a tiny squeeze of reassurance. It's about the only place on my body that doesn't hurt.

I turn my heard towards Nic and it's horrible to see him looking so exhausted and pale. He shifts in his chair and lets out an involuntary groan.

'You're hurt? And Max, they didn't—?'

Nic raises his hand, putting one finger to his lips to gently hush me.

'There's nothing to be anxious about, Tia, please trust me. I have a couple of bruised ribs that will heal. Max sprained his wrist but they put it in a splint and we packed him off back to the cottage in a taxi an hour ago.'

'Don't worry, Sis. He has Olwen and Sally fussing over him.'

For the first time since I woke up, tears begin to well-up in my eyes.

'Hey,' Nic leans forward with obvious difficulty, to place a hand gently on top of my heavily-bandaged one. 'It's over. The two thieves are in police custody. You were really brave, Tia, but you put your own life at risk. Max is very aware that the noise would have disturbed him at some point and if he'd blindly rushed out he would have been defenceless. This could have had a really tragic ending if it wasn't for your very prompt action.'

I hang my head as images from last night flash across my mind like blinding shards of light. *Flick, flick, flick* – still images coming together to play out a sequence of events.

'Try not to dwell on it, Tia. Let your mind rest and save that for another day. It will all come back to you, but now is not the time to dwell on it.'

I smile at him and he gives me a weak smile in return. Will shifts in his chair. I turn my head to look at him, shaking it slightly.

'I'm so sorry, Will; such a horrible thing to happen when I so desperately wanted this to be a joyful family occasion. Poor Sally and Bella. What sort of a start to

Christmas is this? Please, go back to them and try to salvage what you can. I don't want this to spoil Bella's Christmas. Send them all my love and tell them I'll be home soon, I promise.'

'Hey, this isn't your fault. I'm sure Olwen and Sally have everything under control. Christmas will happen and the festivities will begin at soon as you are safely back at the cottage. Look after her, Nic, won't you? Love you, Sis.'

He stoops to kiss me lightly on the temple before offering his hand to Nic. They shake, exchanging a meaningful glance before he leaves.

36

Sometimes Just Being There is Enough

Jane returns shortly afterwards with two cups of tea and some biscuits on a tray.

'How are those ribs?' she asks Nic.

'Sore, but us men have a high pain threshold.'

Jane and I start laughing. It lifts the mood a little and I'm grateful to him.

'Well, it will be front page news when the *Gazette* is out,' she says, pursing her lips.

'I know,' Nic retorts. 'That's one of my jobs and I'm already writing up the copy in my head.'

She raises her eyebrows in surprise. 'Better watch what I say, then. You know what reporters are like. I'll be back in an hour to check Tia's blood pressure and temperature. Enjoy the tea.' She smiles as she turns to walk away.

We sit in silence for a short while and then Nic lifts his cup to sip his tea.

'It's drinkable, Tia. Let me hold it up for you.'

I look at my hands as if they don't belong to me. Trying to bend my fingers sends little stabbing pains radiating out over my knuckles and down to the tips. I wince, despite my best attempt to hide it.

'Here, take a sip.'

I'm not a tea lover but tea has never tasted so good before. Warm and comforting it hits my empty stomach and seems to lift the nausea a little.

'Thank you, Nic. For everything. They keep referring to you as my boyfriend, sorry about that.'

'I didn't say anything, as I didn't think they'd let me stay if they knew.'

His eyes stray past mine, as he stares over my shoulder for a few seconds and then he brings them back to focus on me.

'Can you stand? You need to see this.'

I nod and he moves the tray over onto the bed. I half-stand and he gently pulls me on to my feet, letting me lean against him. My knees are bruised and battered from the crawl along the stony ledge at the foot of the cliffs and it wasn't just the razor-sharp flint but the dried holly leaves which also pierced my skin. It's just my luck, I muse, enjoying the effects of the medication which seem to blur the edges of everything. We both groan out loud in tandem, which makes me giggle. It's only half a dozen steps to the window, but it's a painful walk.

It's well worth the effort, though, because the sunset is amazing. The deep red glow fills the entire panorama. It permeates out, turning the dark night into a floodlit arena. We stand, half–hugging and half–supporting each other, staring out over the roof tops of the suburban area surrounding the hospital. Although it's only four miles away from Caswell Bay we could be in any little town. We watch the fiery rays as they sink down behind the roof tops. It's as if someone is slowly extinguishing the burning embers of a fire. It's a reminder that life is full of wondrous moments and you can't let the negative things detract from that.

Nic leans in, grimacing at his own pain as he gently, so gently touches his lips to mine.

'I'm so glad you came back for Christmas, Tia.'

'This wasn't quite what I had planned and I'm sorry for what happened. But thank you, Nic, for coming to my rescue and for staying with me.'

'When I held you in my arms, waiting for the ambulance to arrive, I found myself praying for the first time in years. I'd lost you once through my own stupidity and I didn't want to lose you again. Suddenly, I saw clearly all the idiotic anger and resentment that had taken over my life, and it made me feel ashamed for what I'd become. I don't want to be that person anymore.'

'It puts everything else into perspective, doesn't it?'

All I can think of is that one split second could have destroyed the rest of our lives.

'I can't think of anywhere I'd rather be, than here with you, now.'

As we hobble back to our seats, we both chuckle in between sharp intakes of breath and low, mumbling groans.

'Except at the farm in front of a roaring fire, or in the pub enjoying a pint or–'

'OK. So I owe you one. I'll make it up to you, I promise.' And I will.

*

Early evening, feigning tiredness, I eventually persuade Nic to return to the farm. I manage to convince him that after a good night's sleep we will both feel a lot better. There is a little more colour in his face now, but the bags under his eyes are a clear sign of his underlying exhaustion. I know sleep will take a long time to silence the thoughts whirling around inside my own head, but I also have a lot of thinking to do.

Nic returns the next morning looking a little more like his usual self. We are both feeling achy, battered and bruised, but surprisingly upbeat. There is no way of knowing what might have happened that night, all we know is that luck was on our side. So, even in the aftermath when the shock begins to kick in and it makes you feel slightly disorientated, as if things aren't quite *real*, we simply keep talking. Not about anything important, but it's enough to help while away the time. Nic tells me all about his plans for the new website and I talk about the way Will and I have finally begun to heal our rift.

Will, Sally and Bella come for a visit, but I wave them off after an hour, not wanting them to waste the day I had planned for sight-seeing. Olwen, bless, has given them a map of the area and highlighted some of the things I would have shown them.

What touched my heart was when Bella suddenly ran back to me as they were literally giving a last wave before heading out of the door. She stood on tiptoe to whisper in my ear, her face quite solemn.

'Aunty Tia, will Santa know that we're staying with you for Christmas?' As she pulled away I caught her hands up in mine and she winced slightly as she glimpsed down at them. 'Your poor sorely hands, I hope they feel better soon.'

Love and affection for my gorgeous little niece sent a wonderful sensation of happiness rushing through me, safe in the knowledge that from here on in we were going to have a wonderful relationship.

I turn my head to whisper my reply. 'Of course! It was the first thing I did as soon as I knew you were coming. The cottage doesn't have a chimney, so I sent Santa a key in the post and we mustn't forget to put out a glass of milk, a plate of biscuits and some carrots for the reindeers.'

She tentatively gave me a hug. 'Sorry, I don't want to hurt you,' she whispered, 'but you are just the best Aunty ever and I love you so very much. You've made my daddy very happy and that means Mummy and I are very happy, too.'

With that she ran off, leaving me to wipe away a few stray tears.

What also surprised me was how easy Will and Nic seem around each other. I know they spent several hours alone together yesterday, watching me as I slept, but I hadn't realised they'd talked. Not simply making polite conversation, it would seem. Before he left, Will kissed my cheek and then placed his hand on Nic's shoulder. It was a gesture that took me by surprise.

'Look after her, Nic. Make sure she gets plenty of rest.'

A look had passed between them that implied solidarity and trust. That can only exist where there is some form of common ground. It made me smile to myself.

We spend the remainder of the day playing either card games, or chess. I had no idea how competitive Nic is; he certainly has no intention of letting me get away with anything.

'Can't you let me win just one game?' I chide him.

He looks at me quite seriously. 'Why?'

'Because that's the polite thing to do.' I can see from his expression that this has gone completely over his head. 'I'm tired of playing games.'

As Nic packs away the chess pieces I catch the strains of *Oh Come All Ye Faithful* coming from one of the other rooms.

'I can't believe Christmas is almost here, considering I've spent a large part of this year thinking about nothing else, I'm rather sick of it before it even starts. What were your Christmases like?'

It's a question I haven't liked to ask him before now. He glances at me with a small shrug, as if it doesn't hold any real meaning for him.

'Christmases in front of the fire with Georgina, I suppose. And the nanny. We toasted bread, marshmallows and chestnuts. Clarissa was always at some drinks party or other and Max, well, he rarely made it home before Christmas Eve – and there were many years when we didn't see him at all.'

He can't keep the sadness out of his voice, even though I know he'd be mortified to realise I'd picked up on that.

'That's sad to hear, Nic. I swear if I ever have children then they will always come first, no matter what else is going on in my life.'

He turns to look at me, his face grave.

'Ironically it served to bring us closer together, as siblings. We didn't really know what we were missing out on, I suppose.'

'So, what would be your perfect Christmas experience?'

I can see from his side profile that a hint of a smile is beginning to creep across his face.

'Nothing too special, actually. Simply being around people who mean something to me, so I guess that's friends and neighbours, really. Good food, a little wine. A few of the Christmas oldies playing in the background.'

He doesn't ask for much. 'That's it?'

'I wish George was here, of course. But that's life. I've learnt that it's better to lower one's expectations, or face a future full of disappointment.' My heart constricts in my chest, leaving a dull ache. It reminds me of my situation. Expect nothing, Tia, or face a future full of disappointment because Mum isn't coming back.

I think that what we've been through recently has changed us both. We end up laughing a lot and sharing obscure, childhood memories; deciding to put our sadness to one side. Laughter doesn't only soothe the soul, it also helps to raise the spirits. Once again, he is reluctant to leave, but I send him home with a list of things for Olwen to throw in a bag, in anticipation of being released early tomorrow morning. I'm counting the hours, as it simply has to be a day all about family and friends because that's what Christmas means to me.

Drifting in and out of sleep I'm scared to let my dreams take over tonight. Maybe it's the medication I'm on, but whenever I close my eyes I see a world full of shadows and each time I'm back on the beach. Fear runs like a chill through my veins and I have to keep pushing those thoughts away.

I refuse to be haunted by negative thoughts and trawl through my memory bank for a happy moment, something to cling on to which will get me through tonight. Lying here, meandering through the thought garden of my childhood begins to dispel that chill. Summer mornings eating breakfast sitting on the step by the back door. Planting sunflowers and using the battered old watering can believing that my seeds would grow higher than Will's. My mother's face appears and she's standing in front of the sitting room window; behind her, the snow begins to fall. She's watching me and I realise I'm opening a present and it's Christmas morning.

The box in front of me has a big, green velvet bow and it's covered in gold paper, not simply wrapped but permanently glued on. Ah, it's my special gift and as I lift off the detachable lid and look inside my heart skips a beat. Then the memory comes flooding back in full force, triggering the overwhelming sense of pure delight I'd no doubt experienced as a young child. The gift that year was a Cinderella doll and I think it was the year before I started school. Doll's clothes were expensive I should imagine but my letter to Santa was clear – I wanted a doll with a wardrobe of dresses.

That box Mum had so lovingly covered with shiny paper continued to be my doll's wardrobe for several years until I outgrew that phase and it was passed on. The dresses inside were all lovingly sewn by Mum; it reflected hours of work cutting up old frocks to create ball gowns worthy of a princess. How I wish I'd kept just one as a memento I could hold, knowing it had been in her hands and she had toiled away, fuelled by the love in her heart. As I slip into a dreamless sleep I hold onto the feeling of warmth that has consumed me, as if Mum is wrapping her arms around me once more. When you are loved that much you will never, ever be alone because not even death can break something that strong.

*

It's just after eleven a.m. Christmas Eve morning, as helping arms are reaching in to ease me out of Will's car. Nic surprises me with his agility, although most of his moves are still accompanied by stifled groans. I made him pull up his jumper earlier this morning to inspect the damage for myself. His entire right side is already black and blue with bruises so livid, they don't actually look real. I could have cried on the spot. How on earth he didn't end up with broken ribs, well, it's little short of a miracle.

Walking back into Beach View Cottage is like coming home. The sound of a Christmas tune filtering out into the garden as we walk up the path, lifts my spirits. It's a little warmer today and there's hardly a breeze.

I lean heavily on Nic as he escorts me inside, where Olwen, Max, Sally and Bella stand to welcome me back.

Olwen's hands fly up to her face as she watches my every step, until Nic lowers me down onto the sofa. The wound that extends from the top of my right cheek up into my hairline is still covered with a dressing, but the shock on her face is clear to see. Sally and Bella, at least, knew what to expect. I know the scar will be a permanent reminder and all I can do is accept that I'm lucky to be alive.

'It's good to be back.' I breathe a big sigh of relief, trying hard not to acknowledge my legs are still a little bit wobbly.

I look up and find myself staring into Max's familiar, greyish-blue eyes. When I walked through the door one of the first things I noticed was the livid purple bruise on one side of his jaw. His wrist is in a sling, but he looks relaxed and surprisingly comfortable to be here with everyone.

'How are you doing, Max?'

He kneels down next to me beside the sofa.

'I'm good, lovely lady. I'm alive and it's thanks to you and Nic. Burglaries sometimes go badly wrong and things spiral out of control. I heard that the two thieves were also in A&E that night.'

My eyes widen as I look across at him in surprise.

'I think they got a little more than they bargained for and, hopefully, a little spell at Her Majesty's pleasure in the not too-distant future. I would gladly have let them have the boat to save you and Nic what you've been through, Tia.'

His eyes flick over the dressing on my face and the rawness of the wounds on my bare hands. He shakes his head, muttering to himself.

I reach across and pat his good arm, gently.

'I remember some of it quite clearly now. You launched yourself at my attacker, Max. I saw a shape out of the corner of my eye as someone lunged towards me. If you hadn't stepped in at that precise moment—'

'Someone was watching over us that night, of that I'm sure.'

He eases himself up into a standing position and gives me a brief nod. 'I'd best give Olwen a hand; my good one.' He gives a low, throaty laugh and walks off in the direction of the kitchen, where Olwen is busy organising hot drinks and sandwiches.

I sit here, surveying the scene and smile up at Bella as she presents me with a Christmas cookie. Nic is rather cautiously lowering himself down onto the sofa next to me.

'Thank you, Bella, that's lovely. I promise to try it in a moment.'

'OK, Aunty Tia. Mum says we have to build you up, now. I'm not sure what she means, but if you don't eat something I think she's going to be a bit cross.'

Bella gives me a knowing look and I nod enthusiastically. 'Of course. You can count on me.'

Nic's mouth twitches as he watches Bella head back to the kitchen.

'She's cute,' he says, turning towards me.

'I know; and it's lovely to be a part of their lives again. It's my Christmas present to Mum. I'm relieved that what has happened hasn't totally spoilt tonight's little party and now we can get on with the holiday festivities.'

I can see a flicker of something in Nic's eyes.

'This cottage has seen its share of sadness and now it's time to put that firmly in the past with everything else.'

My heart starts to beat quickly.

'*The Notebook*, it was your sister Georgina's, wasn't it?'

Nic angles his head to one side, so he can look directly at me.

'Yes. I bought it for her when she came back here for that last few months. It was her favourite book of all time. The well–loved copy Georgina owned was falling apart. I found this one in a little bookshop in Swansea. She was a true romantic, ruled by her heart. I gave the

TV away shortly after she died. We'd spent hours together watching films, laughing and crying. It was a reminder of her that I didn't need. But she would have loved seeing the cottage come to life like this. It was made for a family.'

I think of the inscription on the last page ... *I know you are crying, you always do. I'm here to hold your hand and wipe away your tears. Always.*

'When you are up to it, there are a stack of cards and presents for you on the dresser in the kitchen, from some of the people in the village. And you have three bouquets of flowers. You seem to be very popular; no one bought me or Max flowers.' His look is full of warmth and happiness.

'I thought I could smell lilies, as soon as I walked through the door.'

Olwen approaches with two steaming mugs on a tray.

'And we don't have to worry about the party food tonight. Several people are spending the afternoon in the big kitchen up at the farm and it will be delivered to the door.'

'Oh, Olwen, that's so very kind.'

'Folk are appalled by what has happened. Everyone is sending you their best regards, Tia. You didn't stop to think of yourself and it takes one brave lady to do that. Poor Max, it could have been a whole different story. And as for you,' she nods her head at Nic. 'A wooden stick is no match for a heavy crow bar. But you did well and your dad is so proud of you.'

I can't even chance a look in Nic's direction, until after Olwen walks away. Those words will have meant something to him.

He shifts position and he winces, a painful groan reminding him he still needs to take it easy.

'Are you really up to this party tonight, Tia?'

'Of course. I'm not going to let two low-life thieves spoil my Christmas plans. Bring it on!'

<u>37</u>

Let's Make it Happen, Guys

The entire afternoon is a flurry of activity with Olwen assigning everyone tasks. Will and Max return with two large sacks of holly, mistletoe and ivy after a forage in the woods. Olwen indicates for them to place the sacks at Nic's side. He's still sitting next to me on the sofa, nursing those bruised ribs. She disappears for a moment and returns with two trays, some pruning shears and a reel of twine.

'Right guys, I have an important task for you. Nic, if you can trim some of the greenery into manageable pieces so that Tia can tie them into little bunches, that would be great. I'm not very artistic, so I'll leave the two of you to work it out. We need a few pieces for the buffet and drinks tables, then something clever for in here.'

We're left trying to puzzle out how we're going to make this happen.

'Do you have any wire, Nic? I have an idea but it won't work with twine.'

He nods, edging himself forward and groaning a little as he stands. I watch him as he disappears out of view. With everyone busy doing something or other, and the strains of Mariah Carey's *All I Want for Christmas is You* filling my ears, it's almost surreal. To see my family and some very special friends, who have quickly earned a place in my heart, pulling together to make this party happen, is touching. In my line of vision through to the kitchen I can see Bella and Max working together to slide a white tablecloth in place. Her eyes are shining as she looks at him and fusses to make sure the overhang on the table is equal on all sides. He's watching her now, a bemused look on his face. She gives him a thumbs-up as her seal of approval and they head off out of view.

'Will this do? It isn't florist's wire, but it's strong and flexible.' Nic hands me a large reel.

I nod. 'Perfect, thank you.'

He eases himself back down onto the seat next to me and begins to pull out a handful of cuttings from one of the sacks on the floor next to him.

'OK. Tell me what you need me to do.'

'Keep any long lengths of ivy and we'll wire them together to make a garland from which to hang smaller bunches of greenery. To begin with, anything smaller I'll need you to trim into lengths of about nine inches, I think. Keep them coming and don't forget to watch out for the holly.'

It's too late and he winces, immediately pulling back his hand. But within a minute or two he's beginning to fill my tray with cuttings and I can start gathering handfuls to neatly tie together with the twine.

'That looks rather good.' He sounds impressed.

'Nature doesn't need anything to enhance it. But it's the smell; isn't it lovely?'

Nic produces a small cutting from a fir tree. 'I won't chop this up as I think you'll be able to do something different with it. Maybe for the centre of the table?'

The background music has changed and the strains of *Santa Claus is Coming to Town* filter out into the sitting room. Bella walks towards us singing and to my surprise, Nic joins in. It's a lovely moment and I watch them both, enthralled.

When the last chord is struck, Bella disappears and comes back with a large plastic tub. She begins layering in the small bunches of greenery that are now threatening to topple from my tray. The three of us continue to work as a team and in between we singalong with songs old and new.

Max suddenly appears in the doorway.

'Anyone for eggnog if I make some?'

I'm transported back a year and think of Mum, sitting in Starbucks and sipping her Eggnog Latte. She would have loved being here today; I hope you are watching

Mum, because it doesn't get much better than this, does it?

I catch sight of Will and Sally stealing a quick kiss as they pass each other in the kitchen. Will is ferrying in bottles of wine and beer after a trip to the local off licence. Sally is opening packs of paper plates, having folded a mountain of napkins.

In the background, Olwen is like a mother hen, fussing around and making sure everyone has what they need for their allotted tasks. Then she turns her attention to assist Max in the serious business of making the eggnog.

I truly believe that the spirit of Christmas is embodied in this room, today. It's not about the gifts, or the amount of money you have to lavish on the occasion. It's about the desire to make it special for other people and in doing so, it makes it special for you, too.

38

It's People Who Make the Magic Happen

Will coughs and all heads turn in his direction. There are nineteen of us packed into the two rooms and it's... cosy. But it's touching to see Mike and some of the people from the farm who helped with the buffet. I'm sure they already had plans of their own, so this means a lot to me.

'Normally it's the host who proposes a toast, but I think Tia will forgive me, on this occasion, for butting in to do the honours. Tonight, I'd like to ask you all to join me in raising your glasses to wish my lovely sister, Tia, Nic and Max, a speedy recovery. Sometimes it takes a near-tragedy to make us all remember to count our blessings.'

Will pauses for a moment to gather his thoughts and heads nod, vigorously.

'Merry Christmas everyone and a huge thank you on behalf of Tia, my wife Sally, my daughter Bella and myself, for the way everyone has rallied around us during the last couple of days. We have all been touched by your kindness and generosity. And Olwen, well, you haven't stopped since we arrived and you've looked after us all as if we were family. Here's to friends and family, old and new.'

The room erupts and I'm the one who is feeling blessed tonight. As the general hub–hub dies down, Will begins speaking once more.

'Bella has a little surprise for Aunty Tia. Bella, would you like to take centre stage?'

She's not yet seven and tonight she looks like a little princess in a soft cream–coloured sweater dress, with hand–beaded pearly–white snowflakes cascading over one shoulder. I can see she's nervous as she looks first at Sally and then at Will, before turning to face me. And then she begins to sing.

Silent night
Holy night
All is calm, all is bright ...

Everyone is transfixed as Bella's beautifully clear, sweet little voice fills the room. Nic rests his hand gently on mine as we stare in amazement at the little angel standing in front of us. I look around and I can't see one single eye that isn't glistening.

Everything happens for a reason. As my emotions threaten to overwhelm me, I realise that Mum's passing is the reason why Will, Sally and Bella are here with me, tonight. As horrible as it feels to acknowledge that, I know it's a fact. I had every intention of whisking her away to some exciting destination in an attempt to fill our Christmas void. But the underlying sadness would still have been there because family is everything.

Will and Sally are standing there watching Bella with obvious pride in their eyes, but they are also genuinely overjoyed to be here. I'm sure Sally's parents will be missing them this Christmas, but they gave up what was their normal Christmas tradition, in order to keep me company. My brother and his family put me first and that says more than words can express.

To know that Bella is singing this song for me because she hopes it will make me feel better, is the only gift I want this Christmas. It means that we are a real family again. We all make mistakes and sometimes, in the process, hearts can be broken. I've learnt to forgive Will because I've seen how bitterly he regrets what happened. And, in turn, he has forgiven me for my harsh judgement of him. He simply couldn't let go of our father's memory and wasn't able to acknowledge the fact that life has to go on, no matter how much it hurts.

The smiling faces around me give me hope and make me feel like a woman who has been blessed. Even when bad things happen, if you have friends and family around you then you can overcome anything.

*

With the benefit of a little hot food and some wonderful company I can feel myself perking up. The liveliness inside the cottage is a tonic and as I'm chatting to Tom, laughing about the night of the barn dance, Nic suddenly appears. He's holding my coat in his hands.

'Sorry to butt in on you, Tom, but I know you'll forgive me. There's something I want Tia to see. We'll be back in a few moments.'

Tom offers me his arm so I can stand and Nic helps me on with my coat. In the background Olwen's daughter, Rhona, and Bella, are dancing to the strains of Slade's *Merry Christmas Everybody*.

I look at Nic and he leans towards me so our foreheads are touching. 'Come on, let's grab a little fresh air.'

Opening the door, he pauses to zip up his own coat and I step ahead of him, over the threshold. As I survey the crisp white scene before me, my breath is literally taken away. Well over an inch of snow has already fallen and the sky is heavy with thick, white flakes, that almost don't look real. Pulling the door closed, he sidles up next to me.

'I know, it's unbelievable, right? Christmas Eve at Holly Cove and it's snowing. How often does that happen? Guess there is a little magic in the air, after all.'

He takes my arm in his and we walk steadily towards the front gate.

'I've never seen snow on sand before,' I comment, thinking how surreal it looks.

Snowflakes descend upon us in increasing numbers, but we hardly notice as we make our way down the beach. Although it's late, the eerie grey light from the sky makes it feel much earlier.

Nic gives my arm a gentle squeeze.

'We both tried so hard not to fall in love, Tia, didn't we? What has become very clear to me is that love isn't something you can control, is it? It grabs you by the heart and fills your head with impossible dreams. Yes, it's scary and it takes a brave person to make that leap of faith. But life is about taking risks, if you want to live it to the full.'

'Olwen said, "When love comes knocking you have to open the door, or you'll never know if it was *the* chance to grab that happy ending" and she was right, Nic. There are no guarantees but if we don't try, we'll never know.'

His eyes quiz mine and I can see a vein pulsing on the side of his temple. His heart is racing and it's for all the right reasons.

'But how is this ever going to work, as our worlds are so far apart? The thought of going back to London after what happened… it's not a good place for me, Tia. And yet, I can't hold you back – I love you too much to do that to you. However, I've seen how long-distance relationships fall apart when two people are forced to have separate lives, outside of the one they share together.'

'Loving someone means making sacrifices and believing in your heart that it's worth it, Nic.' My eyes seek out his and I can see his dilemma is over.

'I'm not going to be the same man going back, so why should I fear that I'm going to succumb to old ways rather than embracing my new direction? I know you'll support me in everything I do, Tia, and that's the difference. I want to prove to you I can do this. The future is going to be what we make it. I'm still reeling over the fact that my mother is the one who brought us together. Does that mean she really does have a heart beneath that cool exterior of hers?'

I smile and I can see by the look in his eyes that it has touched him.

'Will you talk to her about it?'

He eases his head back, stretching his neck and looking up at the sky while he considers my question.

'She saw in you the very thing that I needed to make me feel complete. That takes a lot of soul searching for a woman who is ruled by her head and not her heart. I doubt she will ever change but she's given me the one thing I need to make my life meaningful again and that's you. I intend to let her know that and then it's up to her what happens next.'

My eyes begin to mist over, although I refuse to give in to the tears.

'I'm glad, as this must have been a journey into the unknown for her with no guarantees it would work out as she had planned. It was certainly unexpected and now here we are!

'But you are an idiot at times, Nic. This is where we are meant to be and I wouldn't dream of dragging you away. Not least because Georgina's memories are here and that grounds you. I've had the satisfaction of knowing I'm good enough to do the job, but you never asked me whether it was what I wanted. Maybe a few weeks ago, given our misunderstanding, I would have answered *yes* to that question. Now I know that I would have been fooling myself. What I want more than anything is to be with *you*. Just because I work from an office in a little cottage on the beach, doesn't mean my journalistic skills won't be in demand. Besides, in between doing my research, and writing, I think you're going to be in need of an assistant. I did a pretty good job of holding your camera bags and handling those precious lenses. I'm a woman of many talents.'

He raises one eyebrow.

'I guess that includes teaching this stubborn guy a lesson, or two. You had my heart from the moment I first caught sight of you, Tia, but it was scary. Will was right, it takes a near-tragedy to put things into perspective. I'm here for you always and nothing, and no one, is going to hurt you again.'

We kiss as the snow continues to tickle our faces and settle upon us, like a soft downy blanket melting in seconds and then being replaced with yet another layer. I'm not cold. I feel wrapped in the love of a man I know is my Mr Right. I fleetingly wonder if the snow this year was a very special gift, reassuring me that Mum is watching over us and that she approves of my choice.

I look up into Nic's loving gaze, content in the knowledge that this is what my life is all about now. Home is where the heart is and mine is here.

'And I love you too, Nic. We'll take this one day at a time and when eventually we look back I know that this will be the start of our forever.'

Acknowledgements

So many kind & generous people...

Writing is a solitary pursuit, but getting a book published is a mega team effort, which includes *you*!

First up - team Aria you rock. To my awesome editor, Lucy Gilmour, it's a pure delight working with you. Thanks go to copy editor Claire Rushbrook, for tightening everything up. And to Sue Lamprell, for being the final set of eyes to make sure everything sparkled! And a shout out to Melanie Price, social media guru, for the behind the scenes work she does supporting everyone.

My lovely agent, Sara Keane, and Aria's Sarah Ritherdon get a special mention as they were instrumental in turning me into an Aria author – for which I'm very, very grateful!

There are some wonderful reviewers and readers who have been there for me every step of the way since I began writing. Forgive me if I miss anyone out (I'll catch you next time, promise and in no particular order as I love you all:

Shona, Noemie, Debbie, Anniek, Suze, Nikki, Nicky, Charlotte, Jo, Susan, AJ, Kate Verrier, Shaz, Tracey, Kaisha, Michele, Katie, Beverley, Rachel, Jane, Ali, Cathy, Grace.

I'm also sending a virtual hug to everyone who has read, reviewed, Tweeted and generally helped spread the word about my debut Aria Fiction novel, *The French Adventure*. For those who have taken the time to contact me via my website to share their reading experience, I feel both humbled and loved at the same time.

And last, but not least, there is *YOU*, dear reader. *YOU* keep me writing and because of that I'm living my dream each day that I write.

With much love and thanks,

Lucy x

HELLO FROM ARIA

We hope you enjoyed this book! Let us know, we'd love to hear from you.

We are Aria, a dynamic digital-first fiction imprint from award-winning independent publishers Head of Zeus. At heart, we're avid readers committed to publishing exactly the kind of books we love to read — from romance and sagas to crime, thrillers and historical adventures. Visit us online and discover a community of like-minded fiction fans!

We're also on the look out for tomorrow's superstar authors. So, if you're a budding writer looking for a publisher, we'd love to hear from you. You can submit your book online at ariafiction.com/we-want-read-your-book

You can find us at:
Email: aria@headofzeus.com
Website: www.ariafiction.com
Submissions: www.ariafiction.com/we-want-read-your-book
Facebook: @ariafiction
Twitter: @Aria_Fiction
Instagram: @ariafiction

Printed in Great Britain
by Amazon

48894396R00236